Lightning Source UK Ltd.
Milton Keynes UK
12 January 2011

165559UK00003B/72/P

The History of British Women's Writing
General Editors: **Jennie Batchelor** and **Cora Kaplan**

The History of British Women's Writing is an innovative and ambitious monograph series that seeks both to synthesise the work of several generations of feminist scholars, and to advance new directions for the study of women's writing. Volume editors and contributors are leading scholars whose work collectively reflects the global excellence in this expanding field of study. It is envisaged that this series will be a key resource for specialist and non-specialist scholars and students alike.

Titles include:

Liz Herbert McAvoy and Diane Watt *(editors)*
THE HISTORY OF BRITISH WOMEN'S WRITING, 700–1500
Volume One

Caroline Bicks and Jennifer Summit *(editors)*
THE HISTORY OF BRITISH WOMEN'S WRITING, 1500–1610
Volume Two

Mihoko Suzuki *(editor)*
THE HISTORY OF BRITISH WOMEN'S WRITING, 1610–1690
Volume Three

Ros Ballaster *(editor)*
THE HISTORY OF BRITISH WOMEN'S WRITING, 1690–1750
Volume Four

Jacqueline M. Labbe *(editor)*
THE HISTORY OF BRITISH WOMEN'S WRITING, 1750–1830
Volume Five

Mary Joannou *(editor)*
THE HISTORY OF BRITISH WOMEN'S WRITING, 1920–1945
Volume Eight

The History of British Women's Writing
Series Standing Order ISBN 978–0–230–20079–1 hardback
(outside North America only)

You can receive future titles in this series as they are published by placing a standing order. Please contact your bookseller or, in case of difficulty, write to us at the address below with your name and address, the title of the series and the ISBN quoted above.

Customer Services Department, Macmillan Distribution Ltd, Houndmills, Basingstoke, Hampshire RG21 6XS, England

---

Also by Mary Eagleton

ATTITUDES TO CLASS IN THE ENGLISH NOVEL (with David Pierce)

A CONCISE COMPANION TO FEMINIST THEORY (*ed.*)

FEMINIST LITERARY CRITICISM (*ed.*)

FEMINIST LITERARY THEORY: A Reader (*ed.*)

FIGURING THE WOMAN AUTHOR IN CONTEMPORARY FICTION

RICHARD HOGGART: Culture and Critique (*ed.*) (with Michael Bailey)

WORKING WITH FEMINIST CRITICISM

Also by Emma Parker

CONTEMPORARY BRITISH WOMEN WRITERS (*ed.*)

KATE ATKINSON'S *BEHIND THE SCENES AT THE MUSEUM*: A Reader's Guide

The History of British Women's Writing, 1970–Present

Volume Ten

Edited by

Mary Eagleton

and

Emma Parker

palgrave
macmillan

First published 2015 by
PALGRAVE MACMILLAN

Palgrave Macmillan in the UK is an imprint of Macmillan Publishers Limited, registered in England, company number 785998, of Houndmills, Basingstoke, Hampshire RG21 6XS.

Palgrave Macmillan in the US is a division of St Martin's Press LLC, 175 Fifth Avenue, New York, NY 10010.

Palgrave Macmillan is the global academic imprint of the above companies and has companies and representatives throughout the world.

Palgrave® and Macmillan® are registered trademarks in the United States, the United Kingdom, Europe and other countries.

ISBN 978–1–137–29480–7

This book is printed on paper suitable for recycling and made from fully managed and sustained forest sources. Logging, pulping and manufacturing processes are expected to conform to the environmental regulations of the country of origin.

A catalogue record for this book is available from the British Library.

A catalog record for this book is available from the Library of Congress.

Typeset by MPS Limited, Chennai, India.

Contents

Series Editors' Preface

One of the most significant developments in literary studies in the last quarter of a century has been the remarkable growth of scholarship on women's writing. This was inspired by, and in turn provided inspiration for, a postwar women's movement, which saw women's cultural expression as key to their emancipation. The retrieval, republication and reappraisal of women's writing, beginning in the mid-1960s, have radically affected the literary curriculum in schools and universities. A revised canon now includes many more women writers. Literature courses that focus on what women thought and wrote from antiquity onwards have become popular undergraduate and postgraduate options. These new initiatives have meant that gender – in language, authors, texts, audience and in the history of print culture more generally – are central questions for literary criticism and literary history. A mass of fascinating research and analysis extending over several decades now stands as testimony to a lively and diverse set of debates, in an area of work that is still expanding.

Indeed so rapid has this expansion been, that it has become increasingly difficult for students and academics to have a comprehensive view of the wider field of women's writing outside their own period or specialism. As the research on women has moved from the margins to the confident centre of literary studies it has become rich in essays and monographs dealing with smaller groups of authors, with particular genres and with defined periods of literary production, reflecting the divisions of intellectual labour and development of expertise that are typical of the discipline of literary studies. Collections of essays that provide overviews within particular periods and genres do exist, but no published series has taken on the mapping of the field even within one language group or national culture.

The History of British Women's Writing is intended as just such a cartographic standard work. Its ambition is to provide, in ten volumes edited by leading experts in the field, and comprised of newly commissioned essays by specialist scholars, a clear and integrated picture of women's contribution to the world of letters within Great Britain from medieval times to the present. In taking on such a wide-ranging project we were inspired by the founding, in 2003, of Chawton House Library, a UK registered charity with a unique collection of books focusing on women's writing in English from 1600 to 1830, set in the home and working estate of Jane Austen's brother.

Jennie Batchelor
University of Kent
Cora Kaplan
Queen Mary, University of London

Acknowledgements

We would like to acknowledge the helpfulness of the General Editors of this series, Jennie Batchelor and Cora Kaplan, who have carefully guided and supported us throughout the production of the volume. The astute advice of anonymous external readers significantly improved the material and the whole enterprise has been most efficiently enabled by the professionalism of Paula Kennedy, Ben Doyle, Peter Cary, Tomas René, and Monica Kendall at Palgrave Macmillan. We are deeply grateful to Sarah Kirby whose wonderful print, 'Room to Write', was specially commissioned for the cover of this collection. Her image captures so much about the present moment and the future promise of women's writing. We are also grateful to the National Portrait Gallery, London, for kind permission to reprint Sarah Raphael's painting *Women's Page Contributors to the Guardian* in Chapter 4. Our major debt is to our contributors who have brought not only knowledge and insight to the collection but a positive and upbeat response throughout what was, inevitably, a lengthy process. We hope we sustained them as much as they have sustained us. Mary Eagleton would like to thank David Pierce for his daily advice and encouragement, and Emma Parker for being the best of co-editors – a wise head, sharp eyes, and unfailing enthusiasm. Emma Parker would like to thank Sarah Graham for good council and technical support, and Mary Eagleton for the invaluable expertise and abiding good cheer that has made her an exemplary collaborator.

Notes on Contributors

Linda Anderson is Professor of Modern English and American Literature at Newcastle University, UK, and Director of the Newcastle Centre for the Literary Arts. She has written widely on autobiography including *Women and Autobiography in the Twentieth Century* (1997) and *Autobiography* (2nd edition, 2011). She has recently published a monograph on the American poet Elizabeth Bishop, *Elizabeth Bishop: Lines of Connection* (2013).

Claire Chambers is Lecturer in Global Literature at the University of York, UK, where she teaches twentieth- and twenty-first-century writing in English from South Asia, the Arab world, and their diasporas. She is the author of *British Muslim Fictions: Interviews with Contemporary Writers* (2011) and *Britain Through Muslim Eyes: Literary Representations, 1780–1988* (2015). Claire has also published widely in such journals as *Postcolonial Text* and *Contemporary Women's Writing*, and is co-editor (with Susan Watkins) of the *Journal of Commonwealth Literature.*

Deborah Chambers is Professor of Media and Cultural Studies at Newcastle University, UK. Her publications include *Social Media and Personal Relationships: Online Intimacies and Networked Friendship* (2013); *A Sociology of Family Life: Change and Diversity in Intimate Relations* (2012); *New Social Ties: Contemporary Connections in a Fragmented Society* (2006); with Richard Johnson, Parvati Raghuram, and Estella Tincknell, *The Practice of Cultural Studies* (2004); with Linda Steiner and Carole Fleming, *Women and Journalism* (2004); and *Representing the Family* (2001).

Hywel Dix is Senior Lecturer in English and Communication at Bournemouth University, UK. Between 2003 and 2006 he was Raymond Williams Research Fellow at the University of Glamorgan, leading to the publication of *After Raymond Williams: Cultural Materialism and the Break-Up of Britain* (2nd edition, 2013). He has published extensively on the relationship between literature, culture, and political change in contemporary Britain, most notably in the monograph *Postmodern Fiction and the Break-Up of Britain* (2010). His wider research interests include modern and contemporary literature, postmodernism, critical cultural theory, and British writing about Republicanism.

Jane Dowson is Reader in Twentieth-Century Literature at De Montfort University, UK. Her publications include (ed.) *The Cambridge Companion to Twentieth-Century British and Irish Women's Poetry* (2011); with Alice Entwistle, *A Cambridge History of Twentieth-Century Women's Poetry* (2005);

(ed.) *Women's Writing, 1945–1960: After the Deluge* (2004); and *Women, Modernism and British Poetry, 1910–1939: Resisting Femininity* (2002). She is currently working on a monograph on Carol Ann Duffy for Palgrave Macmillan (2015).

Mary Eagleton was, formerly, Professor of Contemporary Women's Writing at Leeds Beckett University, UK. She has published widely on twentieth- and twenty-first-century women's writing, feminist literary theory, and feminist literary history. Titles include (ed.) *Feminist Literary Theory: A Reader* (3rd edition, 2011); *Figuring the Woman Author in Contemporary Fiction* (2005); and (ed.) *A Concise Companion to Feminist Theory* (2003). She is the founding Chair of the Contemporary Women's Writing Association and the founding co-editor of the journal *Contemporary Women's Writing*.

Gabriele Griffin is Professor of Women's Studies at the University of York, UK. She has written extensively on women's theatre, including *Contemporary Black and Asian Women Playwrights in Britain* (2003). Further publications include (co-ed.) *The Emotional Politics of Research Collaboration* (2013); *Doing Women's Studies: Employment Opportunities, Personal Impacts and Social Consequences* (2005); and *Research Methods for English Studies* (2005). She is editor of the Research Methods for Arts and Humanities series (Edinburgh University Press).

Clare Hanson is Professor of Twentieth Century Literature at the University of Southampton, UK. She is the author and editor of several books, most recently *A Cultural History of Pregnancy: Pregnancy, Medicine and Culture, 1750–2000* (2004), *Uses of Austen: Jane's Afterlives* (co-edited with Gillian Dow, 2012), and *Eugenics, Literature and Culture in Post-war Britain* (2012). She has published widely on twentieth- and twenty-first-century women writers, including Angela Carter, Doris Lessing, and Rachel Cusk. She has a special interest in the interactions between literature and science and in 2012 led an AHRC-funded Science in Culture project 'Beyond the Gene'. She is currently working on literary engagements with neo-Darwinism and 'soft inheritance' in the postwar period.

Elizabeth Wanning Harries is Helen and Laura Shedd Professor Emerita of Modern Languages at Smith College, US. Her work on literary fairy tales includes *Twice upon a Time: Women Writers and the History of the Fairy Tale* (2001), and recent essays on women writers from Marie-Catherine d'Aulnoy to A.S. Byatt, redemptive violence in French fairy tales, Nobel Prize winners' versions of 'Sleeping Beauty', and the story of Melusine in Dvořák's *Rusalka*. She also writes frequently about eighteenth-century fiction, literary fragments, and fictional framing.

Maroula Joannou is Professor Emerita of Literary History and Women's Writing at Anglia Ruskin University, UK. Recent publications are (co-ed.)

The Women Aesthetes: British Women Writers, 1870–1900 (2013); *Women's Writing, Englishness, and National and Cultural Identity: The Mobile Woman and the Migrant Voice, 1938–1962* (2012); and *Contemporary Women's Writing: From* The Golden Notebook *to* The Color Purple (2000). She is the editor of *The History of British Women's Writing, 1920–1945* (2012).

Jeannette King is Professor Emerita of English at the University of Aberdeen, UK. Having taught part-time for many years for the Open University while bringing up her children, she moved into Further Education before becoming a Lecturer in Women's Studies in the Department of English at Aberdeen in 1995, where she taught until her retirement. Publications include *Discourses of Ageing in Fiction and Feminism: The Invisible Woman* (2012); *The Victorian Woman Question in Contemporary Feminist Fiction* (2005); *Women and the Word: Contemporary Women Novelists and the Bible* (2000); and *Doris Lessing* (1989).

Gail Low is Senior Lecturer in English at the University of Dundee, UK. She has published widely on the history of publishing and on Black British writers including *Publishing the Postcolonial: Anglophone West African and Caribbean Writing in the UK, 1950–1967* (2011) and *White Skins/Black Masks: Representation and Colonialism* (1996). With Marion Wynne Davies, she is the co-editor of *A Black British Canon?* (2006).

Rebecca Munford is Reader in English Literature at Cardiff University, UK. She is the author of *Decadent Daughters and Monstrous Mothers: Angela Carter and European Gothic* (2013), and co-author, with Melanie Waters, of *Feminism and Popular Culture: Investigating the Postfeminist Mystique* (2013). She is also the editor of *Re-visiting Angela Carter: Texts, Contexts, Intertexts* (2006), and co-editor of *Third Wave Feminism: A Critical Exploration* (2007).

Emma Parker is Reader in Post-War and Contemporary Literature at the University of Leicester, UK. She is a founder member of the Contemporary Women's Writing Association and has published widely on feminist fiction, including essays on Angela Carter, Rose Tremain, Michèle Roberts, and Sarah Waters. She is author of *Kate Atkinson's* Behind the Scenes at the Museum: *A Reader's Guide* (2002); editor of *Contemporary British Women Writers* (2004); and co-editor of the journal *Contemporary Women's Writing*.

Ruvani Ranasinha is Senior Lecturer in Postcolonial Literature in the Department of English, King's College London, UK. She is the author of *South Asian Writers in Twentieth-Century Britain: Culture in Translation* (2007) and *Hanif Kureishi: Writers and their Works Series* (2002), and the lead editor of *South Asians Shaping the Nation, 1870–1950: A Sourcebook* (2012). She is currently writing a monograph provisionally titled *Contemporary South Asian Women's Fiction* for Palgrave Macmillan.

Suzanne Scafe is Reader in Caribbean and Postcolonial Literatures at London South Bank University, UK. She has published on Black British writing and culture, including Black British women's autobiographical writing, and Caribbean women's fiction and poetry. She is co-editor of *I Am Black/White/Yellow: The Black Body in Europe* (2007), which includes her chapter on the drama of Roy Williams. She has written articles and book chapters on Diana Evans and the Caribbean short story during the pre-independence period.

Susan Watkins is Reader in Twentieth-Century Women's Fiction in the School of Cultural Studies and Humanities, Leeds Beckett University, UK. She is the author of *Doris Lessing* (2010) and *Twentieth-Century Women Novelists: Feminist Theory into Practice* (2001). She is also co-editor of *Doris Lessing: Border Crossings* (2009); *Scandalous Fictions: The Twentieth-Century Novel in the Public Sphere* (2006); and *Studying Literature: A Practical Introduction* (1995). She was a founding Associate Editor of *Contemporary Women's Writing* and is currently co-editor (with Claire Chambers) of the *Journal of Commonwealth Literature*.

Imelda Whelehan is Research Professor and Pro Vice-Chancellor (Research Training) at the University of Tasmania. She has written widely on feminism, women's writing, popular culture, and adaptation studies. Her publications include *The Feminist Bestseller: From* Sex and the Single Girl *to* Sex and the City (2005); *Helen Fielding's* Bridget Jones's Diary*: A Reader's Guide* (2002); *Overloaded: Popular Culture and the Future of Feminism* (2000); and *Modern Feminist Thought: From the Second Wave to 'Post-Feminism'* (1995). She has co-authored, with Deborah Cartmell, *Screen Adaptation: Impure Cinema* (2010) and, with Jane Pilcher, *Fifty Key Concepts in Gender Studies* (2004). She is co-editor of the journal *Adaptation* and Associate Editor of *Contemporary Women's Writing*.

Sue Zlosnik is Professor Emerita of Gothic Literature at Manchester Metropolitan University, UK. With Avril Horner, she has published five books, including *Gothic and the Comic Turn* (2005) and *Daphne du Maurier: Writing, Identity and the Gothic Imagination* (1998). Alone, she has published on a range of fiction, including a monograph, *Patrick McGrath* (2011). She is co-editor (with Agnes Andeweg) of *Gothic Kinship* (2013).

Chronology

Major events

1967 Passing of the Abortion Act; homosexuality decriminalized in England and Wales (for men over 21 not in the armed forces)

1968 Reintroduction of International Women's Day; Theatres Act abolishes censorship in the theatre

1969 Passing of the Divorce Reform Act abolishing the concept of matrimonial offence; British troops sent into Northern Ireland; first issue of *Shrew* magazine (ceases publication in 1974)

1970 Passing of the Equal Pay Act; voting age reduced from 21 to 18; passing of the Matrimonial Proceedings and Property Act; Family Planning Associations obliged to make contraception available to unmarried women; National Council for the Unmarried Mother and Her Child, set up in 1918, renamed the National Council for One-Parent Families; the first National Women's Liberation Movement conference held at Ruskin College, Oxford; publication of Eva Figes's *Patriarchal Attitudes*; publication of Germaine Greer's *The Female Eunuch*

1971 Immigration Act; introduction of internment without trial in Northern Ireland; Women's Street Theatre Group founded

1972 Bloody Sunday/the Bogside Massacre in County Derry, Northern Ireland; Northern Ireland placed under Direct Rule from Westminster; Cambridge colleges Churchill, Clare, and King's admit women students; first issue of *Spare Rib* (ceases publication in 1993)

1973 Britain joins the European Community; Virago Press founded; establishment of the Women's Theatre Group (later becomes Sphinx Theatre Company); first Women's Theatre Festival, London; establishment of *Red Rag: A Magazine of Women's Liberation* (ceases publication 1980)

1974 Contraception made free to all women; passing of the Employment Protection Act, giving women paid maternity leave and protection during pregnancy; founding of the Women's Aid Federation, to support women and children experiencing domestic violence; Oxford colleges Brasenose, Jesus, Wadham, and Hertford admit women students

1975 Passing of the Sex Discrimination Act, Matrimonial Causes Act, Disability Discrimination Act; end of internment without trial in Northern Ireland; establishment of the Monstrous Regiment Theatre Company (disbands in 1993); establishment of Gay Sweatshop (disbands in 1981)

1976 Passing of the Race Relations Act and Sexual Offences (Amendment) Act; Grunwick Film Processing Laboratories strike begins; Equal Opportunities Commission founded; passing of the Domestic Violence Act; the Small and Specialist Publishers' Exhibition is renamed the London Book Fair

1977 Feminist theatre group Cunning Stunts founded

1978 Southall Black Sisters established; The Women's Press founded; Julia Pascal appointed the first female director at the National Theatre; feminist theatre group Beryl and the Perils established (disbands in 1986)

1979 Margaret Thatcher becomes the first female Prime Minister of the United Kingdom; urban uprising in Southall; feminist theatre company Mrs Worthington's Daughters founded (disbands in 1982); publication of the first issue of *Feminist Review*

1980 Urban uprising in Bristol; homosexuality decriminalized in Scotland; Sheba Feminist Publishers founded

1981 Greenham Common Women's Peace Camp established; British Nationality Act; urban uprising in Toxteth and Brixton; Pandora Press founded

1982 The Falklands War between Great Britain and Argentina; the Fawcett Society Book Prize established; Bernardine Evaristo, Patricia Hilaire, and Paulette Randall start the Theatre of Black Women (disbands in 1988)

1983 Passing of the Equal Pay Amendment Regulations; Black Woman Talk Press founded; Edinburgh Book Festival established

1984 Miners' Strike begins; the first International Feminist Book Fair is held in London; Asian Women Writers Workshop (later Collective) established; Betty Trask Award established

1985 Jenny Killick appointed first female Artistic Director of the Traverse Theatre, Edinburgh; Talawa Theatre Company founded by Yvonne Brewster; publication of the first issue of *Women's Review* (folds in 1987)

1986 Further Sex Discrimination Act passed; Honno Press founded in Wales

1987 Commonwealth Writers' Prize established

1988 Enactment of Section 28, commonly known as 'Clause 28', of the Local Government Act, banning the 'promotion' of homosexuality in schools as a 'normal family relationship'; the Commission for Racial Equality recommends that people of South Asian origin should no longer be classified as 'black'; first Hay Festival of Literature

1989 Fatwa issued against Salman Rushdie following publication of *The Satanic Verses*

1990 Margaret Thatcher leaves office; Women Against Fundamentalism established; founding of Justice for Women, an organization campaigning against violence against women; World Wide Web established; Feminist and Women's Studies Association established; publication of the first issue of *Women: A Cultural Review*; British Book Awards (or 'Nibbies') established, later the Galaxy and then Specsavers National Book Awards; the Encore Award, for the best second novel, established (ends 2011)

1991 Gulf War; Britain opts out of European single currency; rape in marriage made illegal

1992 The Church of England authorizes the ordination of women priests; Wales Book of the Year established

1993 David Cohen Prize for Literature established

1995 Passing of the Disability Discrimination Act; Asham Award established, a short story prize for women of any nationality resident in the UK

1996 Launch of the Orange Broadband Prize for Fiction

1997 Tony Blair becomes Prime Minister; Net Book Agreement collapses, enabling books to be sold at a discount (which leads to the demise of many independent bookshops)

1998 Passing of the Human Rights Act; signing of the Good Friday Agreement (or Belfast Agreement), a major step in the Northern Ireland peace process; Northern Ireland Assembly opens; Natasha Walter publishes *The New Feminism*, heralding the advent of 'postfeminism'

1999 Scottish Parliament opens; National Assembly of Wales opens; introduction of parental leave for men; publication of the first issue of *Mslexia*, a magazine for women writers; Samuel Johnson Prize for Non-Fiction founded; the *Guardian* launches its First Book Award

2000 Repeal of Section 28 of the Local Government Act in Scotland and, in 2003, in the rest of Great Britain; age of consent equalized for homosexual and heterosexual men and women; Greenham Common Peace Camp disbanded; publication of the first issue of *Feminist Theory*; Dundee International Book Prize established; Bollinger Everyman Wodehouse Prize established

2001 Terrorist attacks on the US on 11 September; webzine *The F Word* started by Catherine Redfern

2003 Invasion of Iraq by US and British forces

2004 Passing of the Civil Partnership Act; passing of the Gender Recognition Act; accession to the EU of eight Central and Eastern European countries: the Czech Republic, Estonia, Hungary, Latvia, Lithuania, Poland, Slovakia, Slovenia; Maggie Gee appointed first female Chair of the Royal Society of Literature since its foundation in 1820

2005 London is bombed by terrorists on 7 July; Citizenship Test established for immigrants who wish to become British; Twitter launched; Gwyneth Lewis becomes National Poet of Wales; Jude Kelly appointed Artistic Director of the Southbank Centre, Europe's largest centre for the arts; Contemporary Women's Writing Network (later Association) founded

2006 Vicky Featherstone appointed the founding Artistic Director of the National Theatre of Scotland

2007 Accession to the EU of Bulgaria and Romania; National Council for One-Parent Families renamed Gingerbread; Linen Press Books founded; publication of the first issue of the journal *Contemporary Women's Writing*

2008 UK banking crisis; Orange Broadband Prize for Fiction becomes the Orange Prize for Fiction; Gillian Clarke becomes National Poet of Wales

2009 Carol Ann Duffy appointed Poet Laureate

2010 Establishment of a UK coalition government between the Conservatives and the Liberal Democrats, the first full coalition government since 1945; passing of the Equality Act, replacing previous anti-discrimination laws with a single Act; UK Feminista established; Natasha Walter publishes *Living Dolls: The Return of Sexism*; Walter Scott Prize for historical fiction established; Northern Ireland Book Award established; People's Book Prize established (founding patron Beryl Bainbridge)

2011 British troops leave Iraq after eight years; Caitlin Moran publishes *How to be a Woman*, a bestseller credited with reigniting popular interest in feminism; Liz Lochhead named as the Scots Makar

2012 Laura Bates launches the Everyday Sexism Project; Vagenda website launched; the Tricycle Theatre, London, appoints Indhu Rubasingham as its artistic director; Josie Rourke becomes Artistic Director of the Donmar Warehouse, London; SI Leeds Literary Prize for unpublished fiction by Black and Asian women established

2013 Charlotte Raven launches *Feminist Times*; Vicky Featherstone becomes the first female artistic director at the Royal Court Theatre, London; the Orange Prize for Fiction loses its sponsorship and becomes the Women's Prize for Fiction

2014 Gay marriage legalized in the UK; end of UK combat operations in Afghanistan; Scottish referendum on independence from the UK resulted in a 55.3 per cent vote against; first woman bishop appointed by the Church of England; *Feminist Times* collapses; the Women's Prize for Fiction regains sponsorship and becomes the Baileys Women's Prize for Fiction

Recipients of major British literary prizes and honours

1970 Bernice Rubens wins the Booker Prize for *The Elected Member*; Jane Gaskill wins the Somerset Maugham Award for *A Sweet, Sweet Summer*; Lily Powell wins the James Tait Black Memorial Prize for *Birds of Paradise*

1971 Susan Hill wins the Somerset Maugham Award for *I'm the King of the Castle*

1972 Susan Hill wins the John Llewellyn Rhys Prize for *The Albatross*; Gillian Tindall wins the Somerset Maugham Award for *Fly Away Home*; Kathleen Raine wins the W.H. Smith Literary Award for *The Lost Country*

1973 Iris Murdoch wins the James Tait Black Memorial Prize for *The Black Prince*

1974 Ruth Pitter named Companion of Literature by the Royal Society of Literature; Beryl Bainbridge's *The Bottle Factory Outing* wins the Guardian Fiction Prize

1975 Ruth Prawer Jhabvala wins the Booker Prize for *Heat and Dust* (was a British citizen at the time but later became a US citizen); Sylvia Clayton's *Friends and Romans* wins the Guardian Fiction Prize

1978 Iris Murdoch wins the Booker Prize for *The Sea, The Sea*

1979 Penelope Fitzgerald wins the Booker Prize for *Offshore*; Sara Maitland wins the Somerset Maugham Award for *Daughter of Jerusalem*

1981 Isabel Colgate wins the W.H. Smith Literary Award for *The Shooting Party*

1983 *Granta*'s first Best of Young British Novelists list includes Pat Barker, Ursula Bentley, Buchi Emecheta, Maggie Gee, Lisa St Aubin de Terán, Rose Tremain; Lisa St Aubin de Terán wins the John Llewellyn Rhys Prize for *The Slow Train to Milan* and the Somerset Maugham Award for *Keepers of the House*

1984 Anita Brookner wins the Booker Prize for *Hotel du Lac*; Angela Carter wins the James Tait Black Memorial Prize for *Nights at the Circus*

1985 Jane Rogers wins the Somerset Maugham Award for *Her Living Image*

1986 Patricia Ferguson wins the Somerset Maugham Award for *Family Myths and Legends*; Jenny Joseph wins the James Tait Black Memorial Prize for *Persephone*; Doris Lessing wins the W.H. Smith Literary Award for *The Good Terrorist*

1987 Penelope Lively wins the Booker Prize for *Moon Tiger*; Jeanette Winterson wins the John Llewellyn Rhys Prize for *The Passion*; Janni Howker wins the Somerset Maugham Award for *Isaac Companion*; Elizabeth Jennings wins the W.H. Smith Literary Award for *Collected Poems: 1953–1985*; Rosamond Lehmann and Iris Murdoch both named Companion of Literature by the Royal Society of Literature

1988 Carol Ann Duffy wins the Somerset Maugham Award for *Selling Manhattan*; Lucy Ellmann's *Sweet Desserts* wins the Guardian Fiction Prize

1989 Claire Harman wins the John Llewellyn Rhys Prize for her biography, *Sylvia Townsend Warner*

1990 A.S. Byatt wins the Booker Prize for *Possession: A Romance*; Pauline Melville's *Shape-shifter* wins the Guardian Fiction Prize

1991 Timberlake Wertenbaker wins the Critics' Circle Theatre Award (Best New Play) for *Three Birds Alighting on a Field*; Clare Tomalin wins the Hawthornden Prize for *The Invisible Woman*; A.L. Kennedy wins the John Llewellyn Rhys Prize for *Night Geometry and the Garscadden Trains*; Lesley Glaister's *Honour Thy Father* and Helen Simpson's *Four Bare Legs in a Bed* both win the Somerset Maugham Award; Muriel Spark named Companion of Literature by the Royal Society of Literature

1992 Kathleen Raine wins the Queen's Gold Medal for Poetry; Rose Tremain wins the James Tait Black Memorial Prize for *Sacred Country*; Jackie Kay wins the Forward Prize for Best Single Poem for 'Black Bottom'

1993 Michèle Roberts wins the W.H. Smith Literary Award for *Daughters of the House*; *Granta*'s second Best of Young British Novelists list includes Anne Billson, Esther Freud, A.L. Kennedy, Candia McWilliam, Helen Simpson, Jeanette Winterson; Carol Ann Duffy wins the Forward Prize for Poetry (Best Collection) for *Mean Time*; Vicki Feaver wins the Forward Prize for Best Single Poem for 'Judith'; Pat Barker's *The Eye in the Door* wins the Guardian Fiction Prize

1994 Jackie Kay's *Other Lovers* and A.L. Kennedy's *Looking for the Possible Dance* both win the Somerset Maugham Award; Sybille Bedford named Companion of Literature by the Royal Society of Literature; Candia McWilliam's *Debatable Land* wins the Guardian Fiction Prize

1995 Pat Barker wins the Booker Prize for *The Ghost Road*; Melanie McGrath wins the John Llewellyn Rhys Prize for *Motel Nirvana*; Kathleen Jaimie's *The Queen of Sheba* wins the Somerset Maugham Award; Kate Atkinson wins the Whitbread Book of the Year Award for *Behind the Scenes at the Museum*; Jenny Joseph wins the Forward Prize for Best Single Poem for 'In Honour of Love'

1996 Helen Dunmore wins the Orange Broadband Prize for Fiction for *A Spell of Winter*; Hilary Mantel wins the Hawthornden Prize for *An Experiment in Love*; Nicola Barker wins the John Llewellyn Rhys Prize for *Heading Inland*; Katherine Pierpoint wins the Somerset Maugham Award for *Truffle Beds*; Alice Thompson wins the James Tait Black Memorial Prize for *Justine*; Kathleen Jamie wins the Forward Prize for Best Single Poem for 'The Graduates'

1997 Kate Clanchy wins the Somerset Maugham Award for *Slattern*; Siân James wins the Wales Book of the Year Award for *Not Singing Exactly*; Lavinia Greenlaw wins the Forward Prize for Best Single Poem for 'A World Where News Travelled Slowly'

1998 Rachel Cusk's novel *The Country Life* and Kate Summerscale's biography *The Queen of Whale Quay* both win the Somerset Maugham Award; Jackie Kay's *Trumpet* wins the Guardian Fiction Prize; Beryl Bainbridge wins the James Tait Black Memorial Prize for *Master Georgie*; Sheenagh Pugh wins the Forward Prize for Best Single Poem for 'Envying Owen Beattie'

1999 Jo Shapcott wins the Forward Prize for Poetry (Best Collection) for *My Life Asleep*; Andrea Ashworth wins the Somerset Maugham Award for *Once in a House on Fire*; Beryl Bainbridge wins the W.H. Smith Literary Award for *Master Georgie*

2000 Linda Grant wins the Orange Broadband Prize for Fiction for *When I Lived in Modern Times*; Sarah Waters's *Affinity* and Bella Bathurst's *The Lighthouse Stevensons* both win the Somerset Maugham Award; Zadie Smith wins the James Tait Black Memorial Prize and the Guardian First Book Award for *White Teeth*; Sheenagh Pugh wins Wales Book of the Year Award for *Stonelight*; Tessa Biddington wins the Forward Prize for Best Single Poem for 'The Death of Descartes'; Michèle Roberts appointed Chevalier de l'Ordre des Arts et des Lettres

2001 Charlotte Jones wins the Critics' Circle Theatre Award (Best New Play) for *Humble Boy*; Helen Simpson wins the Hawthornden Prize for *Hey Yeah Right Get a Life*; Susanna Jones wins the John Llewellyn

Rhys Prize for *The Earthquake Bird*; Doris Lessing named Companion of Literature by the Royal Society of Literature

2002 Ali Smith wins the Scottish Arts Council Book of the Year Award for *Hotel World*; Stevie Davies wins Wales Book of the Year Award for *The Element of Water*; Claire Tomalin wins the Whitbread Book of the Year Award for *Samuel Pepys: The Unequalled Self*; Alice Oswald wins the T.S. Eliot Prize for Poetry for *Dart*; Medbh McGuckian wins the Forward Prize for Best Single Poem for 'She is in the Past, She has this Grace'

2003 *Granta*'s third Best of Young British Novelists list includes Sarah Waters, Monica Ali, Rachel Seiffert, Rachel Cusk, Nicola Barker, Susan Elderkin, A.L. Kennedy, Zadie Smith; U.A. Fanthorpe wins the Queen's Gold Medal for Poetry; Charlotte Mendelson wins the John Llewellyn Rhys Prize for *Daughters of Jerusalem*; Charlotte Williams wins the Wales Book of the Year Award for *Sugar and Slate*

2004 Andrea Levy wins the Orange Broadband Prize for Fiction and the Whitbread Book of the Year Award for *Small Island*; Kathleen Jamie wins the Forward Prize for Poetry (Best Collection) and the Scottish Arts Council Book of the Year Award for *The Tree House*; Charlotte Mendelson wins the Somerset Maugham Award for *Daughters of Jerusalem*; Maureen Duffy awarded the Benson Medal by the Royal Society of Literature

2005 Hilary Spurling wins the Whitbread Book of the Year Award for *Matisse: The Master*; Carol Ann Duffy wins the T.S. Eliot Prize for Poetry for *Rapture*; Maggie O'Farrell wins the Somerset Maugham Award for *The Distance Between Us*

2006 Zadie Smith wins the Orange Broadband Prize for Fiction and the Somerset Maugham Award for *On Beauty*; Rachel Trezise wins the Dylan Thomas Prize for *Fresh Apples*; Stef Penney wins the Costa Book of the Year Award for *The Tenderness of Wolves*; Sarah Hall wins the 2006/7 John Llewellyn Rhys Prize for *The Carhullan Army*

2007 Doris Lessing awarded the Nobel Prize in Literature; A.L. Kennedy wins the Costa Book of the Year Award and the Saltire Society Book of the Year Award for *Day*; M.J. Hyland wins the Hawthornden Prize for *Carry Me Down*; Rosalind Belben wins the James Tait Black Memorial Prize for *Our Horses in Egypt*; Alice Oswald wins the Forward Prize for Best Single Poem for 'Dunt'

2008 Rose Tremain wins the Orange Prize for Fiction for *The Road Home*; Ali Smith wins the Scottish Arts Council Book of the Year Award for *Girl Meets Boy*; Jen Hadfield wins the T.S. Eliot Prize for Poetry for *Nigh-No-Place*; Nicola Barker wins the Hawthornden Prize for

Darkmans; Gwendoline Riley wins the Somerset Maugham Award for *Joshua Spassky*; Clare Wigfall wins the National Short Story Award for 'The Numbers'

2009 Hilary Mantel wins the Man Booker Prize for *Wolf Hall*; Deborah Kay Davies wins the Wales Book of the Year Award for *Grace, Tamar and Laszio the Beautiful*; Janice Galloway wins the Scottish Arts Council Book of the Year Award for *This is Not About Me*; Evie Wyld wins the John Llewellyn Rhys Prize for *After the Fire, A Still Small Voice*; Helen Walsh wins the Somerset Maugham Award for *Once Upon a Time in England*; A.S. Byatt wins the James Tait Black Memorial Prize for *The Children's Book*; Kate Clanchy wins the National Short Story Award for 'The Not-Dead and the Saved'

2010 Jo Shapcott wins the Costa Book of the Year Award for *Of Mutability*; Gillian Clarke wins the Queen's Gold Medal for Poetry; Alice Oswald wins the Hawthornden Prize for *A Sleepwalk on the Severn*; Amy Sackville wins the John Llewellyn Rhys Prize for *The Still Point*; Helen Oyeyemi wins the Somerset Maugham Award for *White is for Witching*; Julia Copus wins the Forward Prize for Best Single Poem for 'An Easy Passage'

2011 Lucy Caldwell wins the Dylan Thomas Prize for *The Meeting Point*; Leila Aboulela wins the Scottish Arts Council Book of the Year Award (fiction) for *Lyrics Alley*; Jackie Kay wins the Scottish Arts Council Book of the Year Award (non-fiction) for *Red Dust Road*; Jo Shapcott wins the Queen's Gold Medal for Poetry; Candia McWilliam wins the Hawthornden Prize for *What to Look for in Winter*; Miriam Gamble wins the Somerset Maugham Award for *The Squirrels are Dead*; Diana Athill awarded the Benson Medal by the Royal Society of Literature

2012 Hilary Mantel wins the Man Booker Prize for the second time, and the Costa Book of the Year Award, for *Bring up the Bodies*; Lucy Prebble wins the Critics' Circle Theatre Award (Best New Play) for *The Effect*; Ali Smith wins the Hawthornden Prize for *There But For The*; Jenny Uglow awarded the Benson Medal by the Royal Society of Literature; Angela Carter's *Nights at the Circus* wins Best of the James Tait Black Awards; Denise Riley wins the Forward Prize for Best Single Poem for 'A Part Song'; Avril Joy wins the Costa Short Story Award for 'Millie and Bird'

2013 *Granta*'s fourth Best of Young British Novelists list includes Naomi Alderman, Tahmina Anam, Jenni Fagan, Xiaolu Guo, Sarah Hall, Joanna Kavenna, Nadifa Mohamed, Helen Oyeyemi, Taiye Selasi, Kamila Shamsie, Zadie Smith, Evie Wyld; Rhian Edwards wins the Wales Book of the Year Award for *Clueless Dogs*; Sarah Hall wins the

National Short Story Award for 'Mrs Fox'; Angela Readman wins the Costa Short Story Award for 'The Keeper of the Jackalopes'

2014 Sinéad Morrissey wins the T.S. Eliot Prize for Poetry for *Parallax*; Emily Berry wins the Hawthornden Prize for *Dear Boy*; Nadifa Mohamed's *The Orchard of Lost Souls*, Daisy Hildyard's *Hunters in the Snow*, and Amy Sackville's *Orkney* all win the Somerset Maugham Award; Imtiaz Dharker wins the Queen's Gold Medal for Poetry

Introduction

Mary Eagleton and Emma Parker

In *A Room of One's Own* (1929), Virginia Woolf (1882–1941) laments the empty bookshelves which, she believes, should be full of women's literary works and histories of their lives. She thinks about the absence of material support for the woman writer – no quiet space away from family duties and no economic independence – and she thinks of what she calls the 'immaterial' difficulties – anything from a lack of encouragement to open hostility and derision. So often, '[h]er mind must have been strained and her vitality lowered by the need of opposing this, of disproving that'.[1] Woolf suggests a series of possible research projects for the women of Girton and Newnham Colleges, Cambridge, her audience for the lectures on women and writing that became *A Room of One's Own*: they could explore parish records and account books to discover the daily lives of Elizabethan women; they could explain the consequences of being undervalued; they might even account for men's opposition to the emancipation of women.

As Sarah Kirby's specially commissioned cover image for this collection shows, the shelves are now filling rapidly. Indeed, one of the issues we faced in putting together this volume was finding a route through an abundance of material since it covers the most vibrant and active period in the history of women's writing. Kirby calls her print 'Room to Write', a play on Woolf's title. This room might be a study of one's own or a corner of the bedroom, but the history of women's writing, since 1970, has also been about finding room within the literary field more generally, and women's writing is now published, bought, discussed, and evaluated to a greater extent than ever before. The gaps and marginalization that confronted Woolf have, in considerable measure, been addressed. Women have found not only rooms of their own, but publishing houses, prizes, reading groups, and online literary forums.

Kirby's image also suggests the time-span of this volume. The woman writer of 1970 would be writing on a typewriter or with a pen in a notebook. Today, she may use a pen but she will most likely be working on a computer;

the social, literary, and technological changes that occur in the period are reflected in a shift from the paper notebook to the electronic notebook. These technological changes have implications for the production, publication, and reception of writing. The author usually remains solitary, and there is only one chair in this image, but the new technologies indicate other options. A book can be the product of a collective endeavour, exist only in the virtual world, be read online either alone or in reading groups, and be reviewed in literary blogs and on websites. Performances of drama and poetry are watched on YouTube. Doubtless, the woman author will be checking her 'Amazon Bestseller Rank'. Whatever the mode, the writer who will sit at the desk in Kirby's image has a wealth of choices before her.

'History', 'British', 'women's writing'

It is impossible to survey comprehensively this explosion of women's literary activity since 1970 and we are very aware of the many excellent writers not mentioned in this collection. Instead, we focus on the keywords of the series' title – 'history', 'British', 'women's writing'. The contributors convey a sense of the continuity and change within women's writing from 1970 to the present; they explore the contested understanding of 'Britishness'; they are highly conscious of the discourses surrounding 'women' and 'women as authors'; and they are responsive to the generic and formal variety of the writing. Though periodization is always invidious, 1970 is the appropriate date for the start of this collection. It was the year that the Equal Pay Act received Royal Assent, that Family Planning Associations were obliged to make contraception available to unmarried women, and the first National Women's Liberation Movement conference in the UK was held at Ruskin College, Oxford. It was the year too that saw the publication of *Patriarchal Attitudes* by Eva Figes (1932–2012) and *The Female Eunuch* by Germaine Greer, studies which had a popular impact and began to give an interpretative shape to the burgeoning feminist movement. Landmark academic studies soon followed: Juliet Mitchell's *Woman's Estate* (1971); Sheila Rowbotham's *Women, Resistance and Revolution* (1972); and Rowbotham's *Woman's Consciousness, Man's World* (1973).

This collection is sensitive throughout to the historical conditions that change the literary field and produce the writing. However, in certain chapters, a sense of history is to the fore. In Chapters 1–3, we have an overview of the major literary genres from 1970 to the present, while Chapters 6–8 offer an understanding of women's writing within the context of a political history. Moreover, certain genres – for instance, historical fiction, and auto/biography and memoir – particularly lend themselves to a questioning of history. These chapters illustrate changing politics, identities, and modes of writing but they are equally alert to continuities and to that interplay in any culture between what Raymond Williams calls 'dominant', 'residual', and 'emergent' forms.[2] Patricia Waugh, similarly, writes about 'phases' in women's writing, 'each drawing on aesthetic strategies and thematic preoccupations which predate and outlast that particular historical moment'.[3]

Thus, we reject narratives of loss, implicit in the view that women's writing has moved from a commendable, politicized 1970s to an individualized new millennium. Equally, we reject narratives of progressive development, for example that domestic realism has been 'superseded' by the playful and knowing. What we find in the messiness of history are interesting lineages, reversals, and overlaps. Many of the *grandes dames* of contemporary writing, whose careers began before 1970, have been impressively productive throughout most of the period of this volume; the remarkable publishing career of Doris Lessing (1919–2013) ran from 1950 to 2008 and covered a range of genres, forms, and styles. Many of the questions of third-wave feminism about the body, sexuality, and femininity were similarly of concern to earlier generations. In addition, any attempt to produce a neat sequencing of literary movements from realism, through modernism, postmodernism, and metamodernism is always questioned by the actual practice of the writing. One encounters unexpected conflations such as A.S. Byatt's 'self-conscious realism', or Zadie Smith's discussion of the novel as on the two paths of 'lyrical Realism' and 'constructive deconstruction'.[4]

Though we are defining as 'British' writers who were born in the United Kingdom and/or have made it their writing home, we are aware of the slipperiness of the term. Geographically, politically, and historically there are significant differences between 'Britain', 'Great Britain', 'the British Isles', and 'the British Islands'. In recent years, the constituent parts of that 'Britain' have become increasingly uncertain. A movement towards devolution has gathered pace with the establishment of the Scottish Parliament and the Assemblies of Wales and Northern Ireland, and, despite the 'no' vote in the Scottish referendum of 2014, many continue to pursue greater independence. Furthermore, since the economic crisis of 2008, discussions of 'Britishness' in the media have, intermittently, been formulated as a return of the 'condition-of-England' problem. Both the Conservative and Labour parties have invoked Benjamin Disraeli's appeal to 'one nation', lest it would divide, as he feared in the 1840s, into 'two nations', the rich and the poor.[5] National unity is equally threatened by an understanding of 'Britain' and, specifically, 'England' that has taken on a growing isolationist and racist formation – from the establishment of the British National Party (BNP) in 1982, to the formation of the United Kingdom Independence Party (UKIP) in 1993, and the English Defence League (EDL) in 2009.

Questions about 'Britishness' are given added urgency when nationalism confronts immigration or transnationalism, or when a rooted sense of belonging confronts the insecurities of diaspora. 'Home', 'origins', 'relation', 'place', and 'community' become deeply unresolved and emotionally freighted concepts. As several contributors demonstrate, writers are interested in the cultural richness of an ethnically diverse Britain while the political history of this period has, more often, focused on the 'problem' or management of immigration: from Margaret Thatcher's perception of immigration as a 'threat to our national identity', to the debates around 'multiculturalism', as discussed in Chapter 16, to the promotion of 'cool Britannia' during Tony Blair's premiership, to the increasingly fraught arguments, since the establishment in 2010 of the Conservative/Liberal Democrat coalition government, about quotas and immigration flows, particularly from Eastern Europe.[6] Suzanne Scafe (Chapter 14) and Ruvani Ranasinha (Chapter 15) show the difficulty of defining terms of origin. They consider the meanings of and connections between 'black', 'Black', 'Asian', and 'British', with Scafe referring to 'black British' as a 'leaky and imprecise' category (p. 214).[7] Where once the nation of origin might be set against the nation of destination, increasingly, as Scafe indicates, one has to think of 'multiple positioning' (p. 215) and, as Ranasinha suggests, 'new ways of being British' (p. 239) through refusing categorization, or deconstructing colonial history, or 're-territorializing' identity.

This collection explores the striking range of women's writing, thematically, formally, and stylistically. Whatever the category 'women's writing' is, it is not homogeneous. Nor is 'women's writing' a synonym for 'feminist writing'. Though many women authors are interested in feminism's literary history and supportive of feminism as a politics, others are resistant, critical, or qualifying. Andrea Levy, for example, speaks warmly of books published by Virago and The Women's Press: '[T]hose were my books; they were my people. That's where I started on the journey.'[8] Others are reluctant to identify with feminism and attracted to writing as a space that can 'escape' the determinations of gender. Yet even when an author has no declared interest in feminism and no particular preoccupation with women characters, the writing is inevitably influenced by feminism; one cannot be writing in the post-1970 period without that being the case. Hence, a writer such as Lessing can, at the same time, have a long history of making barbed comments about feminism *and* a body of work readily open to feminist analysis.

Unsurprisingly, the contributors to this volume recognize the importance of feminist approaches to literature but they are not constrained by those approaches. They accept the need for a practice of intersectionality so as to understand multiple identities and shifting structural positions and power relations.[9] In this they are helped by a responsiveness to literary and social history and to other critical theories, particularly since 1970, to poststructuralist, postcolonial, and queer studies. Thus, the essays in this volume draw and build on a pioneering tradition of feminist analysis of women's writing.

Critical review

One defining feature of the literary history of the period is the emergence of feminist criticism, which has had a fundamental impact on attitudes and approaches to writing by women. Feminist criticism connected literature to politics in provocative and exciting new ways. It exposed a deep patriarchal bias in literary studies, debunked the myth of objectivity that presented a masculine perspective as neutral and normal, questioned androcentric conceptions of literary value, and undertook a radical reassessment of the overwhelmingly male-dominated canon. However, while feminist perspectives revolutionized the study of literature by linking sexual and textual politics, it is striking how little attention was initially paid to contemporary and British women writers. Inspired by the ground-breaking American analysis of gender in books like *The Feminine Mystique* (1963) by Betty Friedan (1921–2006), *The Dialectic of Sex* (1970) by Shulamith Firestone (1945–2012), and *Silences* (1978) by Tillie Olsen (1912–2007), and in Britain by Greer's *The Female Eunuch* (1970), feminist critics on both sides of the Atlantic began to reassess representations of women in canonical texts by men. Studies such as *Thinking About Women* (1968) by Mary Ellmann (1921–89), Kate Millett's *Sexual Politics* (1969), Figes's *Patriarchal Attitudes* (1971), and Lisa Appignanesi's *Femininity and the Creative Imagination* (1973) unveiled the politics of representation by showing how stereotypical images of women reflect and endorse the patriarchal status quo. When British and American feminist scholars did turn to women writers, they cast their gaze backwards in an attempt to recuperate forgotten or neglected authors, and to recover or (re)construct a female literary tradition – as in *Reader, I Married Him* (1974) by Patricia Beer (1919–99), Patricia Meyer Spacks's *The Female Imagination* (1975), Ellen Moers's *Literary Women* (1976), and Sandra Gilbert and Susan Gubar's *The Madwoman in the Attic: The Woman Writer and the Nineteenth-Century Literary Imagination* (1979). Seeking to counter the prevailing masculinist literary bias in what Ellmann calls 'phallic criticism', such books endeavoured to develop new, woman-centred theories and interpretive strategies that Elaine Showalter, in *A Literature of Their Own* (1977), dubs 'gynocriticism'.[10]

Showalter's survey of British fiction 'from Brontë to Lessing' was exceptional in its inclusion of a chapter on contemporary writers but, towards the end of the seventies, critics started to look beyond the 'famous five': Jane Austen, George Eliot, Charlotte and Emily Brontë, and Woolf.[11] Anthologies such as Lilian Mohin's *One Foot on the Mountain: An Anthology of British Feminist Poetry, 1969–79* (1979) and Alison Fell's *Hard Feelings: Fiction and Poetry from Spare Rib* (1979) featured critical introductions. At the same time, interest in the literature emerging from second-wave feminism – much of it published by The Women's Press, reviewed in magazines like *Spare Rib*, taught in Higher and Further Education on new Women's Studies courses, and discussed in academic journals such as *Feminist Review* – produced studies of *contemporary* women's writing through the 1980s and 1990s.[12] As Imelda Whelehan notes in Chapter 7, feminist publishing and feminist criticism benefited from 'intellectual cross-fertilization' (p. 120). However, such books tended to discuss British writers – principally, Fay Weldon, Lessing, Angela Carter (1940–92) – alongside American and Canadian authors, on the understanding that Western women shared specific experiences and aims – principally, oppression under patriarchy and the desire to imagine an alternative world.[13] Recognition that recurrent themes and motifs stem from a position of social marginality rather than biology enabled feminist critics to identify points of commonality whilst subverting essentialist ideas about 'the female condition' or 'the female imagination' based on sexual difference.

Amongst studies of the relationship between 'Women's Lib.' and 'women's lit.', Patricia Duncker's *Sisters and Strangers* (1992) is distinguished by its almost exclusive focus on British literature. Duncker explains this choice as determined by the fact that 'the women's liberation movement in Britain has been significantly different from the women's movement in America'.[14] The attention accorded to *British* women's writing develops across the period. *British Women Writing Fiction* (2000), edited by Abby H.P. Werlock, and *Contemporary British Women Writers* (2004), edited by Emma Parker, aim to raise awareness of authors not widely known in the States, such as Elaine Feinstein, Susan Hill, P.D. James (1920–2014), Michèle Roberts, and Emma Tennant. Likewise, in *A History of Twentieth-Century British Women's Poetry* (2005), Jane Dowson and Alice Entwistle choose to 'spotlight' writers like Carol Ann Duffy, Denise Riley, and Carol Rumens, who tend to be overshadowed by their American peers.[15]

Testimony to the impact of feminist criticism, the number of academic journals devoted entirely or significantly to women's writing grows since 1970: *Tulsa Studies in Women's Literature* is founded in 1982; *Women: A Cultural Review* in 1990; *Contemporary Women's Writing* in 2007. In books and journals, gender separatism is justified on the grounds of what Mary Jacobus, drawing on Woolf, calls the 'difference of view'.[16] As Regina Barreca notes, 'women have different stories to tell from their male counterparts and contemporaries'.[17] Susan Watkins proposes that women's writing is frequently different in form as well as theme. Disputing the view that women are imitators rather than innovators, Watkins contends that marginality has propelled experimentalism: 'it is women writers who have made real innovations in the genre of the novel'.[18] Likewise, in *Feminist Views on the English Stage: Women Playwrights 1990–2000* (2003), Elaine Aston notes that energetic new departures undertaken by women dramatists towards the end of the last century break with theatrical tradition whilst maintaining a distance from the 'in-yer-face' theatre of the day, which she aligns with 'new laddism'.[19] Similarly, Dowson and Entwistle claim that women poets write against the social and literary grain to construct a separate female tradition, in line with Woolf's view that it is better to be locked out than locked in. An irreverent and rebellious attitude to a poetic mainstream epitomized by Wordsworth is underlined by the title of Vicki Bertram's edited essay collection, *Kicking Daffodils* (1997).

Where early feminist criticism tended to privilege connections between quite disparate women writers on the grounds of gender, difference is stressed increasingly. In Duncker's terms, any suggestion that women constitute a unified or coherent group is rendered untenable by their contradictory status as 'sisters' and 'strangers'. Mirroring the diversification of feminist discourse in the 1980s and the new emphasis on intersectionality, Watkins's *Twentieth-Century Women Novelists* (2001) reads texts through a series of different critical lenses: liberal, Marxist, psychoanalytic, poststructuralist, postmodern, lesbian and queer, black and postcolonial. Chapters on class, race, and sexuality reflect the prevalence of identity politics in literary studies. Britain's racial and ethnic diversity is celebrated in Gabriele Griffin's *Contemporary Black and Asian Women Playwrights in Britain* (2003), Claire M. Tylee's *In the Open: Jewish Women Writers and British Culture* (2006), and Lynette Goddard's *Staging Black Feminisms: Identity, Politics and Performance* (2007). Although black British women writers in the 1970s and 1980s like Buchi Emecheta and Joan Riley never enjoyed the success of their African American counterparts Toni Morrison and Alice Walker, black women's writing has flourished in Britain since the 1990s. Deirdre Osborne highlights a new generation of black British writers including Zadie Smith, Jackie Kay, Andrea Levy, debbie tucker green, Patience Agbabi, SuAndi, and Helen Oyeyemi in a guest-edited special issue of the journal *Women: A Cultural Review* devoted to 'Contemporary Black British Women's Writing' (2009). The Black British Women's Writing Network, founded in 2014, promises to develop research in this field. As Linden Peach's *Irish and Welsh Women's Fiction* (2007) attests, different experiences of gender are shaped by region as well as race. Like black and Asian women's writing, texts by Scottish, Welsh, and Northern Irish authors not only expand the field of women's writing but also 'rethink traditional notions of national identity'.[20]

Patricia Waugh's *Feminine Fictions: Revisiting the Postmodern* (1989) considers the growing resistance to realism in the period. Despite apparent affinities between feminism and postmodernism (which both question authority, disrupt boundaries, and subvert hierarchies), Waugh proposes that women writers are just as sceptical of the postmodern dissolution of the self as the universal subject of the liberal humanist tradition. Women's 'ambivalent' relationship to postmodernism means that their work often does not fit established cultural and aesthetic categories.[21] Tracing a line from the realist novel of self-discovery by writers like Margaret Drabble and Anita Brookner to postmodern writers such as Muriel Spark (1918–2006), Lessing, Weldon,

Carter, and Jeanette Winterson, Waugh argues that female authors tend to 'challenge dominant social and aesthetic constructions of identity and gender' (p. 32) in ways that embrace neither 'a complacent liberalism nor an anarchic postmodernism' (p. 217). In this respect, women writers – even those who are not explicitly feminist – typically assert a non-essentialist gendered perspective.

Waugh's observation that postmodernism plays with popular genres is reflected in an expanding critical interest in the use that literary fiction by women makes of Gothic, fantasy, and fairy tale. Paulina Palmer's *Lesbian Gothic: Transgressive Fictions* (1999), Lucie Armitt's *Contemporary Women's Fiction and the Fantastic* (2000), and Susan Sellers's *Myth and Fairy Tale in Contemporary Women's Fiction* (2001) demonstrate how female authors appropriate and transform disparaged 'feminine' genres in order to challenge social and sexual convention. Armitt's contention that 'women's fantasies remain imprinted by what must always be that "other-space" of the maternal' indicates how gendered subjectivity shapes this engagement with genre.[22] Monica Germanà's *Scottish Women's Gothic and Fantastic Writing: Fiction Since 1978* (2010) illustrates how Gothic and fantasy give voice to a national as well as a gendered sense of otherness. According to Germanà, writers such as Fell, Tennant, Ellen Galford, A.L. Kennedy, and Ali Smith intervene in a tradition of non-realism through the deployment of feminist and postmodern narrative strategies in ways that bring questions of nation to the fore.

The explosion in historical fiction towards the end of the twentieth century demonstrates that this, too, is a significant genre for women. In *The Woman's Historical Novel: British Women Writers 1900–2000* (2005), Diana Wallace challenges the established view that historical fiction is escapist, nostalgic, and reactionary. Instead, it is 'a political tool' that enables women to critique the present through the past.[23] Part of the appeal of the genre to women writers, Wallace argues, lies in the ability of costume to expose femininity as a historically contingent 'masquerade' (p. 23). Similarly, in *The Victorian Woman Question in Contemporary Feminist Fiction* (2005), Jeannette King avers that the rise of neo-Victorian fiction since the 1980s can be attributed not only to a resurgence of cultural interest in the nineteenth century but also to a desire to revisit the period that gave rise to debates about gender that remain unresolved in contemporary culture.[24] According to both Wallace and King, women rewrite the past from a female perspective, constructing an alternative 'herstory' to challenge androcentric accounts of history. However, by inventing or reimagining previously unrecorded lives, writers such as Byatt, Pat Barker, Carter, Sarah Waters, Roberts, and Victoria Glendinning do more than simply add women and other dispossessed subjects to existing versions of the past. By presenting history as selective and incomplete, they also challenge the authority of historical discourse and question the validity of historical 'truth'.

In *The Feminist Bestseller* (2005), Imelda Whelehan offers a survey of women's popular fiction. Although often overlooked by feminist literary critics, Whelehan argues that writers who incorporate feminism into fiction that attracts a mass readership succeed 'in communicating core feminist ideas simply and effectively'.[25] Comparing how popular novels by women respond to second- and third-wave feminism, Whelehan situates chick lit in the context of postfeminism. Stephanie Genz and Benjamin A. Brabon's *Postfeminism: Cultural Texts and Contexts* (2009) and Stephanie Harzewski's *Chick Lit and Postfeminism* (2011) further explore how modern romantic fiction reflects debates within feminism and confronts the problems and paradoxes of twenty-first-century womanhood.

Recent monographs and essay collections devoted to prize-winning, best-selling new, or newly recognized, authors such as Zadie Smith, Ali Smith, Levy, and Waters, have tended to include such figures within the category 'contemporary' rather than separate them as 'women writers'.[26] This development reflects a divide between women's writing and feminist criticism, identified by Cora Kaplan as early as 1989, and a move 'beyond' a preoccupation with feminist aesthetics and gender.[27] As Rita Felski argues, 'art is shaped but not fully determined by femaleness'.[28] At the same time, multiple or devolved identities displace a focus on gender as the sole determinant of subjectivity. The reclassification of women's writing also reflects Nicci Gerrard's point that, since the 1980s, greater engagement with 'grand issues and world events' has moved it from the margins into the mainstream.[29] Certainly, as Claire Chambers and Susan Watkins show in Chapter 16, contemporary women writers embrace the dominant social and political concerns of the day from ageing and environmental disaster to terrorism.

In a putative 'postfeminist' era, a book about women's writing may seem anachronistic. However, the presence of some women at the centre of literary culture does not herald a straightforward move from ghetto to glory. Like all histories, women's literary history simultaneously provokes progressive and regressive responses. Hence, success is accompanied by areas of under-representation and the persistence of literary sexism in some quarters. Dowson and Entwistle's warning that illusions of literary equality create a 'false democracy' is rendered compelling by the notable lack of women writers in books devoted to 'contemporary literature' (p. 169).[30] Statistics published by VIDA demonstrate that women writers are also seriously under-represented in the literary press.[31]

Literary sexism has been voiced by several prominent figures in recent years. Launching the National Short Story Prize in 2005, *Prospect* magazine deputy editor Alex Linklater implicitly echoed Robert Southey's declaration to Charlotte Brontë that '[l]iterature cannot be the business of a woman's life, and ought not to be', when he asserted: 'The novel is a capacious old whore; everyone has a go at her, but she rarely emits so much as a groan for their efforts. The short story, on the other hand, is a nimble goddess: she selects her suitors fastidiously and sings like a dove when they succeed.'[32] Linklater's gendered metaphor implies that writers are heterosexual men, ignoring the contribution made to the short story by numerous women, including Helen Simpson, who has devoted herself entirely to this form. In spite of the major awards and honours bestowed on women throughout the noughties, in 2011 V.S. Naipaul disparaged literature by women as 'narrow', 'sentimental', 'feminine tosh'.[33] Such remarks are later discredited by Hilary Mantel's status as the first woman to win two Booker Prizes – for *Wolf Hall* (2009) and *Bring up the Bodies* (2012) – and by the inclusion of more women than men on the fourth *Granta* Best of Young British Novelists list (2013), for the first time in its history.

Despite attempts by women writers to destabilize the boundaries of genre and subvert literary hierarchies, the commercial success of J.K. Rowling's bestselling *Harry Potter* series (1997–2007) and E.L. James's *Fifty Shades of Grey* (2011) – the fastest and bestselling book in Britain since records began – brings the danger that women writers continue to be associated primarily with children's literature and romance.[34] As Naomi Alderman notes, 'Novels by women are less likely to be called "important", women writers are less likely to be thought of as essential voices.'[35] Likewise, Maggie Gee contends: 'When people think of really good writers in the culture, they tend to think of the men first – still.'[36]

History has shown that without serious and sustained critical attention even the best-known or respected writers can disappear. (The now obscure Felicia Hemans was once more popular than her peer Charles Dickens.) As Kate Clanchy, quoted by Jane Dowson at the end of Chapter 2, suggests: 'It's the critical response that determines how we are historicised and how we are anthologised and how we are remembered: how we're put into literary history' (p. 48). Thus, the number of authors mentioned in these chapters who have, to date, received scant critical attention illustrates that, far from being redundant, the study of post-1970 British women's writing still has a long way to go. Despite the problems and complexities of definition, by celebrating the distinctiveness and diversity of the field the essays in this volume confirm that the critical analysis of writing by women in Britain remains a valuable enterprise.

Aesthetics, politics, commerce

This volume is divided into four main sections. 'Women and Literary Culture' introduces the major literary genres of fiction, poetry, and drama (Chapters 1–3), discusses women's place in newspaper and literary journalism, and in the digital media (Chapter 4), and the part women have played in publishing and literary prizes (Chapter 5). 'Feminism and Fiction: Evolution and Dissent', the second section, concentrates on three groupings: firstly, the *grandes dames*, those writers with long and distinguished careers who continued writing into our period (Chapter 6); secondly, 'the monstrous regiment' and the writing produced with a consciousness of second-wave feminism (Chapter 7), and, thirdly, the writing of the third wave and postfeminism (Chapter 8). The next section, 'Gender and Genre', focuses on four of the most popular genres of the contemporary period in which women writers have been significant players: the Gothic (Chapter 9), fairy tale and myth (Chapter 10), historical fiction (Chapter 11), and life-writing (Chapter 12). In the fourth section, 'Writing the Nation: Difference, Diaspora, Devolution' (Chapters 13–15), an understanding of space, both national and global, the movements between countries, and what this means for identity and literary production is central. A final short section, 'Writing Now', takes us into the present and the future.

Running throughout the collection is a rich seam of debate about the relation between aesthetics, politics, and commerce. In Part I, Clare Hanson (Chapter 1) makes a strong claim for aesthetic diversity, stressing that 'a self-conscious approach to narrative form' (p. 23) is the notable feature of contemporary women's fiction. She shows how writers, sometimes seen in dismissive ways as 'realist', or 'humanist', or 'domestic', are in fact innovative, and very aware of formal devices. Hanson traces the movement of fiction through realism, postmodernism, and the neodomestic but she indicates that these are not progressive stages. The domestic realism of Byatt, Drabble, and Brookner is not an abandoned form but reconstructed in the neodomestic fiction of Rachel Cusk, Tessa Hadley, Kate Atkinson, and Ali Smith. There is some irony in Hanson's claiming Smith's work as 'neodomestic' given Smith's disparaging comments on the 'disappointingly domestic' writing of her contemporaries.[37]

Dowson (Chapter 2) and Griffin (Chapter 3) extend Hanson's perception about the range of women's writing into the genres of poetry and drama. Dowson discusses the deployment of different forms of poetry – the lyric, the dramatic monologue, performance poetry – and the varied effects of the polylingual, defamilarization, the multivocal, the embodied. Griffin shows how debates around gender roles in women's theatre led to a questioning of representation itself and changes in theatrical conventions, in both language and performance styles. New forms of dramatic practice such as workshopping and all-female casts became more common. These aesthetic practices are not separate from the political. Dowson notes, for instance, the particular use made by Scottish and Welsh poets of the dramatic monologue while Griffin links 'in-yer-face' theatre to a period of gang culture in the UK and genocidal wars in Europe, notably the former Yugoslavia. Here, in contrast to Aston, Griffin suggests that women writers appropriate a masculine genre in order to critique male violence. Nor are the aesthetic practices separate from the commercial. Griffin indicates something of the cultural consequences of the post-2008 economic crisis as arts funding ebbed and flowed but, importantly, did not totally inhibit new initiatives.

Following Woolf's lead in attempting to find a place within literary history has been a struggle. At different moments the woman author is integrated, ghettoized, happily separatist, critiqued for being too political and self-serving, or over-hyped. Deborah Chambers (Chapter 4) discerns a similar problem for women journalists when confined to 'women's issues' or 'human interest stories'. Over time, they gradually extend and reform their prescribed role whether by becoming hard-hitting columnists or feminist and social campaigners. In so doing, they bridge the division between the personal and the political, and diversify styles of writing. But, of course, nothing is ever resolved. As Chambers concludes, 'Women's journalistic status is distinguished and constrained in both new and recurring ways' (p. 77); the role of literary journalism, for instance, remains ambiguous in the hierarchy of genres.

It is the 'tension between politics and commerce' (p. 81) that, Gail Low (Chapter 5) suggests, is important in understanding the history of women's publishing. That tension has expressed itself in battles about editorial and financial control, methods of working, and modes of production. Yet, it has resulted in important benefits. As Low shows, Virago's strategic use of the term 'classics' to describe its major list, its positioning of itself as an international publisher, and the commitment of The Women's Press to the work of black and Third World women all had commercial advantages but were also aesthetically and politically productive. A similar tension surrounds literary prizes. On the one hand, women's presence is to be welcomed but prize-winning raises uncomfortable questions about the relation between 'quality' and commerce, while the history of the Orange/Baileys Prize for Fiction replays all the old debates about the advantage, or not, of separatism.

In Part II, we concentrate on political history on both the national and international stage. The texts discussed move from postwar readjustments, through the social movements of the late 1960s, to the postfeminism of the 1990s. Maroula Joannou (Chapter 6) perceives in writers such as Byatt and Drabble the influence of a postwar optimism. But equally telling, in Lessing, Spark, and Iris Murdoch (1919–99), are the legacies of the Holocaust, the fear of a nuclear future, and the moral and philosophical dilemmas of the age. In the novel sequences of Byatt and Drabble and the family sagas of Margaret Forster, national and more local histories are told. But, as indicated by the title of Part II, 'Feminism and Fiction: Evolution and Dissent', we are concerned also with a history within feminism itself and these three chapters trace ongoing debates about how women's writing relates to feminism. Joannou's authors, for instance, might not all be 'talking feminism' and some are explicitly antipathetic, but in their intertextual interest in other women writers, their explorations of feminine sensibilities, their preoccupation with matrilineal narratives are responses which others would characterize as 'feminist'.

For Whelehan's authors (Chapter 7), feminist politics and feminist literary theory play an active and prominent role in their writing. That the personal is political was a contentious enough claim for 1970s feminists to make but, as Whelehan suggests, there is another concern when the *aesthetic* is seen as political or tied to the commercial. The three areas relate in ways that are, in Whelehan's words, 'both mutually strengthening and deeply problematic' (p. 114). Whelehan shows one strategy for negotiating the difficulties as feminist writers deliberately embrace their 'monstrous' political image. Writing becomes not a space for escaping gender but for confronting it. By the 1990s, though, as Rebecca Munford explains (Chapter 8), the very category 'woman' was in dispute while feminism as a political movement had come to be regarded as unspeakable and offensive: the 'f-word'. In Munford's discussion, the problematic mother–daughter relationship – a repeated concern throughout this collection – takes on a new political incarnation across the generations. The figure of 'the girl' need not signify simply immaturity and frivolity. In experimental fiction, she takes on a darker resonance, just as the 'singleton' of chick lit can offer a useful *entrée* into issues facing women in contemporary culture.

Throughout the three chapters, we again see the range of generic interest – not only the novel sequences of Byatt and Drabble and the family sagas of Forster but the futuristic fiction of Lessing, the macabre mode of Beryl Bainbridge (1932–2010) and Spark (Chapter 6); utopian and dystopian fiction, the *bildungsroman* (Chapter 7); chick lit, experimental fiction, the historical fiction of Barker and Waters (Chapter 8). Moreover, the contemporary is the first period in history when women writers have, in significant numbers, had access to Higher Education and when many are quite clearly both knowledgeable of and interested in critical theory. Some have pursued their studies to doctoral level and/or taught in universities.[38] This has had its own writerly consequences. Whelehan, for example, explores the close links in the 1970s and 1980s between women's writing and an academic feminism which contextualized, interpreted, even generated new writing. Munford remarks on the impact of queer theory on a fiction already preoccupied with the uncertainty and ambiguity of sex and gender, and on the interest in problems of temporality.

The generic diversity of contemporary women's writing is explored further in Part III. In Chapter 9, Sue Zlosnik illustrates the adaptability of the Gothic mode. Not confined to eighteenth-century horror, it is just as likely to occur in twentieth- and twenty-first-century literary fiction, popular romance, folk tales, crime fiction, even mordant comedy. As Hanson shows in Chapter 1, the ghost can haunt the smart homes of the upwardly mobile. Zlosnik also illustrates how effectively the Gothic mediates in that interplay between the creative and the theoretical that Whelehan and Munford discuss. The anxieties and discontents of the Gothic heroine can approximate those of the second-wave feminist; psychoanalytic feminism is well placed to understand the closeness in the Gothic between 'the normal' and 'the abnormal'; Julia Kristeva's concept of the abject could be applied to the Gothic's respectable bodies and their monstrous doubles; the refashioned body of the Gothic relates to arguments about gender performativity; the ghostly might signify Queer Gothic; and conflicts of cultural identity find expression in the Postcolonial Gothic.

A preoccupation with the historical is also strongly present throughout Part III. In Chapter 10, Elizabeth Wanning Harries returns to the old stories from sacred texts, myth, and folk tale. It is striking how a genre so far removed from the verifiable can nevertheless be concerned with history and 'truth'. Whether the contemporary writer is 'twisting' the tale or putting the tale 'straight', she is challenging history and received versions and, as Carter suggests, revealing 'the latent content' (p. 159). As we see in Chapter 7, the 'monstrous' woman claims her place. Here, the figure of the hag, the crone, or the Corbie bears witness to the past and, Cassandra-like, might predict a catastrophic future.

A critique of the past is, of course, central to historical fiction. Jeannette King (Chapter 11) discusses writing that can 'supplement' or 'challenge' the historical record. As in Chapter 10, there is a political potential in rewriting narratives, whether literary or historical. Women are put back into history, become agents in their own stories, and their own revisionary historians. For example, in both Booker-winning novels by Mantel and fiction judged by some as 'bodice-rippers', there is a questioning of gender and sexuality. Barker returns to the history of class relations, Levy to that of colonialism while, in Waters's novels, there is a disruptive 'queering' of norms. Across the genre, King finds approaches that are realist and focused on historical evidence, others more preoccupied with what Linda Hutcheon calls 'historiographic metafiction' (p. 179), and yet others, such as in the work of Winterson and Helen Dunmore, that take an unexpected Gothic turn.

In life-writing there is often a conflation of personal and social history. As Linda Anderson reveals (Chapter 12), auto/biography too can be an account of historical change and, once more, this is frequently generational as the daughter tells both her own and her mother's life stories. Interpreted through the lens of feminist theory, the form is full of contradictions: the self is revelatory but should not be too assertive, unique but also representative, non-essentialized but capable of agency. Does one prioritize the life (*bio*) or the writing (*graphe*)? And is that writing telling a truth, or a fiction, or producing what Anderson, drawing on Adriana Cavarero, terms a 'narratable self' (p. 190)? In life-writing, historical fiction and in the rewriting of fairy tale and myth, there is a 'doubleness' as the present confronts the past, occasionally with nostalgia or pathos but more often with critique. The contemporary writer produces, as American poet Adrienne Rich (1929–2012) would say, a 're-vision' or, as Winterson remarks of her own rewritings, 'Cover Versions'.[39] In these subtle readings, old questions about aesthetic value and genre fiction – when is historical fiction 'literature'; is the Gothic 'middlebrow'; is popular fiction 'trash' – suddenly seem irrelevant.

Part IV focuses on space and place. The context for Hywel Dix (Chapter 13) is, specifically, the rise of a heightened sense of national identity and national histories, and the complex ways in which a national identity might, or might not, relate to gender and ethnic identities. Dix mentions Katie Gramich's phrase, 'duality of allegiance' (p. 198). In fact, as his chapter shows, that allegiance might be triple or quadruple. With increasing cultural confidence, women writers have begun to question their allotted place in national histories and Dix surveys some of the major responses: 'writing back' to that literary and national history; the use of historical fiction to represent what cannot be easily said in the present; the interest in intertextuality to reinterpret the past; the rejection of a disabling discourse of 'fate' or 'chance'. An even wider sense of space is considered in Chapters 14 and 15 as Scafe and Ranasinha discuss the work of black British and British Asian women writers within the context of Britain's post-imperial legacy. Scafe explains how the black British author might 'speak for' others, highlighting the hidden lives and injustices. Yet awareness of the complex cultural and national identities of these writers makes it impossible to ascribe to them a position as, simply, 'representative'. Their position is intrinsically uncertain and questioning. While the earlier generation who would 'speak for' others was likely to employ realist forms, Scafe finds in later writers the use of parody, the reworking of myth, and the merging of autobiography and fiction – once again, forms of self-conscious experimentation.

For Ranasinha, too, the political and the commercial can interrelate positively with the aesthetic. She remarks on the importance for South Asian writing of the kind of material support of which Woolf spoke, notably the establishment of university courses in Commonwealth Literature and the financial aid of the Greater London Council throughout the 1980s and 1990s. Moreover, as we see elsewhere in the volume, Ranasinha alerts us to how various forms of critical theory raise issues about writing that are, at once, aesthetic and political. She comments on the role of postcolonial feminist scholarship from the 1980s, subcontinental feminisms, the importance of countering Eurocentric Western feminism, and the rise of Men's Studies in the 1990s – all of which find their way into the writing.

Going forward

The final chapter points to what is pressing and current in women's writing, but it also allows reflections on the continuities and changes in the period. Throughout the collection, 'British' is the most disputed term. Never adopted unconditionally by either authors or critics, it is, rather, refocused, questioned, often resisted. Joannou points out in Chapter 6 how writers such as Lessing (Rhodesian), Spark (Scottish), and Murdoch (Irish) always felt estranged from 'Britishness'. For others, the search for a national identity, as Dix discusses in Chapter 13, exists alongside the search for 'post-national' identities, as Scafe and Ranasinha explore in Chapters 14 and 15. In Chapter 16, Chambers and Watkins consider what that much-disputed entity, 'multicultural Britain', signifies and the difficulty of achieving 'a genuine (if multifarious) sense of citizenship' (p. 252). Both this chapter and Chapter 3, for instance, discuss the furore around Gurpreet Kaur Bhatti's play, *Behzti* (2004). Any unified notion of 'British' is constantly undermined by the recurring figure of the migrant, the asylum seeker, the trafficked, the illegal alien. But this 'British' person can also be the highly mobile daughter of the middle class, born in one country with parents from elsewhere, educated internationally, working for a multinational company, with a global social network.[40]

Chambers and Watkins return the collection to issues of generation and temporality. With an ageing population the focus now in women's writing is not only the daughter's story but the mother's and even the grandmother's, and the older woman can be both the subject and the object of the narrative. Adapting Edward Said's concept of 'late style', they consider the stylistic and formal innovations in the representation of the ageing woman, but, equally, the 'lateness' of history itself as explored in apocalyptic fiction. As we see also in Chapters 6 and 7, the anxieties of the moment and aspirations for a changed world find their way into different modes of futuristic fiction. Often at the centre are issues of embodiment – controlling the female body, the maternal body, the trans-gendered or post-human body.

New technologies can radically destabilize national boundaries and fixed subject positions. Chambers and Watkins look for a creative synergy between 'new narrative forms, new technologies, and new approaches to nation' (p. 260). Nevertheless, all the contributors considering new technologies are aware of both the assets and the debits. Hence, Deborah Chambers (Chapter 4) sees the potential in an online presence and digital self-publishing for women's and feminist issues to be heard and for the development of supportive online communities, a new sisterhood. But, then, there is also the impact of online harassment. Similarly, Griffin (Chapter 3) recognizes how new media, particularly YouTube, has widened access for women's theatre and aided conservation through online documentation. Yet the mobility of the medium, positive in many ways, raises its own questions about 'the aesthetics, ethics, and politics of contemporary drama' (p. 62), not least that it becomes removed from the context of its production.

If the term 'British' comes under stress across the period then, as Chambers and Watkins explore, so too does 'writing'. Literature itself is being increasingly redefined by technology. New genres like 'flash fiction' (stories of no more than one thousand words) lend themselves to digital formats, and genres such as 'twiction' (fiction written and read via Twitter) have grown directly out of the wired world. At the same time, graphic fiction resists the dematerialization of the book engendered by digitization, and a new generation of graphic authors such as Hannah Berry, Nicola Streeten, Karrie Fransman, Isabel Greenberg, and Simone Lia are now joining Posy Simmonds – originally known as a cartoonist – in transforming a genre traditionally dominated by men.

Clearly, today's literary landscape is significantly different to that inhabited by women in 1970. Just as writing has changed across the period, so has the symbolic significance of the writer. Feminist critics who challenged Roland Barthes's pronouncement about the 'death' of the author in 1967 may equally question a return, encouraged by the growth of bookshop signings, television programmes, literary festivals, and authors' websites and Twitter accounts.[41] In a context in which contracts and sales can depend as much on the marketability of the woman herself as of her work, there is an understandable wariness of the cult of literary celebrity and the socially acceptable forms of femininity it demands. Winterson, for instance, is an intriguing example of an author who has, at different moments, resisted literary celebrity, been a victim of it, and deliberately exploited it.[42] Updating, in *A Jury of Her Peers* (2009), the three historical phases of women's writing identified in *A Literature of Their Own* ('feminine', 'feminist', 'female'), Showalter reflects on the position of the female author at the millennium and adds a fourth: 'free'.[43] If not completely liberated from critical prejudice, the twenty-first-century woman writer is free to write about any topic, in any form, creating an unprecedented sense of possibility. As this book's cover image suggests, she has her room, the screen is blank and waiting, and the window is open.

Notes

1. Virginia Woolf, *A Room of One's Own* and *Three Guineas* (Harmondsworth: Penguin, 1993), p. 50.
2. Raymond Williams, *Marxism and Literature* (Oxford University Press, 1977), pp. 121–7.
3. Patricia Waugh, 'The Woman Writer and the Continuities of Feminism', *A Concise Companion to Contemporary British Fiction*, ed. James F. English (Oxford: Blackwell, 2006), p. 191.
4. A.S. Byatt, *Passions of the Mind: Selected Writings* (London: Vintage, 1991), p. 4; Zadie Smith, 'Two Paths for the Novel', *The New York Review of Books*, 20 November, 2008, pp. 89–94, subsequently included in *Changing My Mind: Occasional Essays* (New York: Penguin, 2009).
5. See Benjamin Disraeli, *Sybil or The Two Nations* (1845).
6. See Margaret Thatcher's speech to the First International Conservative Congress, 28 September 1997, www.margaretthatcher.org/document/108374, accessed 28 November 2014. 'Cool Britannia' is a pun on 'Rule Britannia'. In the 1990s, it became associated with New Labour and a melding of national pride and cultural innovation.
7. Throughout the collection, we have deliberately sought not to regularize the use of 'black' and 'Black' but to retain the usage as given by individual contributors. On the definition of terms, see also note 14 in Chapter 5 and note 2 in Chapter 15.

8. Andrea Levy, 'Andrea Levy in Conversation with Susan Alice Fischer', *Andrea Levy: Contemporary Critical Perspectives*, ed. Jeannette Baxter and David James (London: Bloomsbury Academic, 2014), p. 122.
9. 'Intersectionality' is a term developed by women of colour to explain the interrelation between race and gender. Kimberlé Crenshaw (1989) was an early explicator of the term with relation to the law. It now refers to the complex mapping of multiple forms of oppression and has been applied across the disciplines: see *Intersectionality: A Foundations and Frontiers Reader*, ed. Patrick R. Grzanka (Boulder: Westview Press, 2014).
10. See Elaine Showalter, 'Toward a Feminist Poetics', *The New Feminist Criticism: Essays on Women, Literature and Theory*, ed. Elaine Showalter (1985; London: Virago, 1986), pp. 125–43. Maud Ellmann, *Thinking About Women* (San Diego: Harcourt Brace Jovanovich, 1968), p. 27. Further examples of gynocriticism include Figes's *Sex and Subterfuge: Women Novelists to 1850* (1982), Janet Todd's *Dictionary of British and American Women Writers 1660–1800* (1984), and Dale Spender's *Mothers of the Novel* (1986). For a discussion of many of these books see Helen Carr, 'A History of Women's Writing', *A History of Feminist Literary Criticism*, ed. Gill Plain and Susan Sellers (Cambridge University Press, 2007), pp. 120–37. For further detail, see Mary Eagleton, 'Literature', *Feminist Theory*, ed. Mary Eagleton (Oxford: Blackwell, 2003), pp. 153–72.
11. Mary Eagleton, 'Literary Representations of Women', in Plain and Sellers, p. 109.
12. For example, in an article published in the second issue of *Feminist Review*, Rebecca O'Rourke and Phil Goodall discuss work by Fell, Andrea Newman, Zoë Fairbairns, Michelene Wandor, and Roberts. See 'Summer Reading', *Feminist Review*, 1 (1979), pp. 1–17.
13. Examples include Helene Keyssar's *Feminist Theatre* (1984), Molly Hite's *The Other Side of the Story: Structures and Strategies of Contemporary Feminist Narratives* (1989), Paulina Palmer's *Contemporary Women's Fiction: Narrative Practice and Feminist Theory* (1989), Linda Anderson's *Plotting Change: Contemporary Women's Fiction* (1990), Gayle Greene's *Changing the Story: Feminist Fiction and the Tradition* (1991), Lorna Sage's *Women in the House of Fiction: Post-War Women Novelists* (1992), Palmer's *Contemporary Lesbian Writing: Dreams, Desire, Difference* (1993), and Maroula Joannou's *Contemporary Women's Writing: From* The Golden Notebook *to* The Color Purple (2000).
14. Patricia Duncker, *Sisters and Strangers: An Introduction to Contemporary Feminist Fiction* (Oxford: Blackwell, 1992), p. ix.
15. Jane Dowson and Alice Entwistle, *A History of Twentieth-Century British Women's Poetry* (Cambridge University Press, 2005), p. 4.
16. Mary Jacobus, 'The Difference of View', *Women Writing and Writing about Women*, ed. Mary Jacobus (1979; London: Routledge, 2012), pp. 10–21.
17. Regina Barreca, 'Foreword', *British Women Writing Fiction*, ed. Abby H.P. Werlock (Tuscaloosa: University of Alabama Press, 2000), p. x.
18. Susan Watkins, *Twentieth-Century Women Novelists: Feminist Theory into Practice* (Basingstoke: Palgrave Macmillan, 2001), p. 3.
19. Elaine Aston, *Feminist Views on the English Stage: Women Playwrights 1990–2000* (Cambridge University Press, 2003), pp. 1–2.
20. Linden Peach, *Irish and Welsh Women's Fiction: Gender, Desire and Power* (Cardiff: University of Wales Press, 2007), p. xii.
21. Patricia Waugh, *Feminine Fictions: Revisiting the Postmodern* (London: Routledge, 1989), p. 30.

22. Lucie Armitt, *Contemporary Women's Fiction and the Fantastic* (Basingstoke: Palgrave Macmillan, 2000), p. 220.
23. Diana Wallace,*The Woman's Historical Novel: British Women Writers 1900–2000* (Basingstoke: Palgrave Macmillan, 2005), p. 2.
24. Jeannette King, *The Victorian Woman Question in Contemporary Feminist Fiction* (Basingstoke: Palgrave Macmillan, 2005), p. 6.
25. Imelda Whelehan, *The Feminist Bestseller: From* Sex and the Single Girl *to* Sex and the City (Basingstoke: Palgrave Macmillan, 2005), p. 3.
26. For example, Continuum's 'Contemporary Critical Perspectives' and 'New British Fiction' series, and Manchester University Press's 'Contemporary British Novelists' series feature books on women writers.
27. Cora Kaplan, 'Feminist Criticism Twenty Years On', *From My Guy to Sci-Fi: Genre and Women's Writing in the Postmodern World*, ed. Helen Carr (London: Pandora, 1989), pp. 21–3. See Rita Felski, *Beyond Feminist Aesthetics: Feminist Literature and Social Change* (London: Hutchinson Radius, 1989) and Chapter 1, '"Beyond" Gender: The New Geography of Identity and the Future of Feminist Criticism' in Susan Stanford Friedman, *Mappings: Feminism and the Cultural Geographies of Encounter* (Princeton University Press, 1998), pp. 17–35.
28. Rita Felski, *Literature After Feminism* (University of Chicago Press, 2003), p. 93.
29. Nicci Gerrard, *Into the Mainstream: How Feminism Changed Women's Writing* (London: Pandora, 1989), p. 162.
30. For example, in Vanessa Guignery's *Novelists in the New Millennium: Conversations with Writers* (2012), only one of the eight featured authors is a woman. Moreover, the one woman that Guignery interviews is Indian (Arundhati Roy), which means that the book features no British women writers alongside seven British men.
31. VIDA is an American organization for women in the literary arts that conducts an annual survey of the number of reviews written by and about women in publications such as the *London Review of Books* and *Times Literary Supplement*. See www.vidaweb.org, accessed 15 March 2014.
32. Michelle Pauli, 'Short Story Score with New Prize and Amazon Project', *Guardian*, 23 August 2005, www.theguardian.com/books/2005/aug/23/news.michellepauli, accessed 15 March 2014.
33. See Chronology for details of honours and prizes. Amy Fallon, 'VS Naipaul Finds No Woman Writer his Literary Match – Not Even Jane Austen', *Guardian*, 2 June 2011, www.theguardian.com/books/2011/jun/02/vs-naipaul-jane-austen-women-writers, accessed 25 March 2014.
34. Kirsten Acuna, 'By the Numbers: The "Fifty Shades of Grey" Phenomenon', *Business Insider*, 4 September 2013, accessed 30 December 2014.
35. Naomi Alderman, 'Wild West Video', *Fifty Shades of Feminism*, ed. Lisa Appignanesi, Rachel Holmes, and Susie Orbach (London: Virago, 2013), p. 14.
36. Maggie Gee, 'Writing Novels is a Ghastly Profession', *Guardian*, 15 June 2014, www.theguardian.com/books/2014/jun/15/maggie-gee-interview-writing-novels-ghastly-profession-virginia-woolf, accessed 29 June 2014.
37. See Toby Litt and Ali Smith, eds, *New Writing 13* (London: Picador, 2005), p. x.
38. For example, Waters, Maggie Gee, Duncker, and Hadley hold doctorates; Byatt, Drabble, Marina Warner, and Duncker move between literary or cultural criticism and creative writing; particularly since the establishment of creative writing programmes, numerous contemporary women writers hold appointments in universities.

39. See Adrienne Rich, 'When We Dead Awaken: Writing as Re-Vision', *On Lies, Secrets, and Silence: Selected Prose 1966–1978* (New York: W.W. Norton, 1979) and Winterson, *Weight* (Edinburgh: Canongate, 2005), p. xviii.
40. As an illustration of this, see recent discussions on the term 'Afropolitan' in, for example, Taiye Selasi, 'Bye-Bye Barbar', http://thelip.robertsharp.co.uk/?p=76, accessed 14 December 2013, and Emma Dabiri, 'Why I'm Not an Afropolitan', http://africasacountry.com/why-im-not-an-afropolitan/, accessed 1 March 2014.
41. See Mary Eagleton, *Figuring the Woman Author in Contemporary Fiction* (Basingstoke: Palgrave Macmillan, 2005).
42. See, for example, 'Jeanette Winterson: "You Shouldn't Grow up in Public, it's a Really Bad Idea"', *Independent*, 6 November 2009, www.independent.co.uk/arts-entertainment/books/features/jeanette-winterson-you-shouldnt-grow-up-in-public-its-a-really-bad-idea-1815328.html, accessed 11 April 2014.
43. Elaine Showalter, *A Jury of Her Peers: American Women Writers from Anne Bradstreet to Annie Proulx* (London: Virago, 2010), p. xx.

Part I
Women and Literary Culture

1

Fiction: From Realism to Postmodernism and Beyond

Clare Hanson

Over the last four decades, fiction written by women has moved from the margins to the centre of British culture. In 2012, for example, Hilary Mantel dominated the literary landscape, winning the Man Booker prize for the second time with *Bring up the Bodies*, which also won the Costa Novel and Costa Book of the Year awards. Congratulating Mantel, the chair of the Man Booker panel described her as 'the greatest modern English prose writer', an accolade that was widely endorsed.[1] What is striking about Mantel's success is that it came out of her return to the historical novel, a genre which has often been dismissed as popular and escapist.[2] Mantel rereads and reinvents the genre, exploiting its ambivalent position between fact and fiction in order to probe the permeable boundaries between the past and the present, the living and the dead. Taking Mantel's achievement as its cue, this chapter argues that a self-conscious approach to narrative form is the most salient feature of fiction written by women in this period. The existing conventions of realism came under pressure as such writers probed the limits of representation, aiming to put 'new wine into old bottles', as Angela Carter (1940–92) so memorably expressed it.[3] Realism is an umbrella term, referring to a disposition rather than a form. As Andrzej Gasiorek has suggested, it signals 'not so much a set of textual characteristics as a general cognitive stance *vis-a-vis* the world, which finds different expression at different historical moments'.[4] Realist texts are connected, however, by a commitment to referentiality which is interrogated and often radically reconfigured in the fiction discussed below.

Varieties of realism

The 1970s saw a renewed focus on the domestic sphere in literary fiction, at a time when second-wave feminism was identifying the family as the major site of women's oppression. Many writers knew little of the emerging feminist movement but a generation of women who had benefited from the postwar education system were struggling to reconcile professional ambition with the continuing demands of domesticity, and novelists such as Margaret Drabble, A.S. Byatt, and Anita Brookner turned to the genre of domestic realism to address this conflict and the challenge to gender roles that went with it.[5] Their fiction is self-reflexive and richly allusive, located within the tradition it seeks to subvert. In Drabble's early work, for example, the protagonists are named after the heroines of nineteenth-century novels, who are frequently invoked and mocked as outdated figures only for the narrative to register significant continuities in terms of constraints on women's lives. In *The Waterfall* (1969), Jane Grey smugly contrasts her liberated life with that of Austen's Emma, reflecting that 'Emma got what she deserved, in marrying Mr Knightley. What can it have been like, in bed with Mr Knightley?'[6] Yet Jane's adulterous affair leads indirectly to a thrombosis caused by the pill, which the narrator represents in terms which signal women's limited progress towards sexual autonomy, commenting that the blood clot is 'the price that modern woman must pay for love ... in old novels, the price of love was death' (p. 239).

From this point on, Drabble's fiction moves outwards to map the connections between the domestic sphere and social and political forces. In the late 1980s, for example, she published a state-of-the-nation trilogy probing the radical shift in values associated with Margaret Thatcher's government.[7] This was a time of reaction against the welfare state and an aggressive emphasis on competitive individualism, which Drabble critiques from the perspective of protagonists such as the social worker Alix in *The Radiant Way* (1987). Responding to the cuts and job losses of the 1970s, Alix feels 'a kind of terrible grinding disaffection' which leads her to abandon her efforts 'to serve the community'.[8] However, as the trilogy progresses, her moral sense finds an outlet in the acceptance of extended family commitments, reflecting the privatization of social responsibility associated with neoliberal values. Here again Drabble highlights continuity and change in women's lives via literary allusion, comparing the status of Jane Austen and George Eliot's protagonists with the less-privileged circumstances of her female characters. The form of these novels is also opened up to scrutiny through self-reflexive endings which draw attention to their own artifice, though Drabble retains her commitment to realism as a form which enables the writer 'to use your eyes and tell the truth'.[9]

Byatt's fiction engages explicitly with the challenge posed to realism by poststructuralism. This is an issue she has explored in a number of her essays, where she argues against what she sees as the poststructuralists' overemphasis on the disjunction between word and world. In her view, it is possible for a text to be 'supremely mimetic ... but at the same time to think about form, its own form, its own formation, about perceiving and inventing the world'.[10] She argues that the novel can both invoke and reflect on materiality, a potential which she exploits in order to explore the relationship between language and being. This is a central theme of her fiction and a recurring concern for all her main protagonists. Frederica Potter, for example, the main character in the so-called Frederica Quartet (1978–2002), reflects on D.H. Lawrence's claim that the novel is 'the one bright book of Life' and concludes that in such a book 'you have to have it all, the Word made flesh, the rainbow, the stars, the One'.[11] As these comments suggest, the discourse of religion offers another key resource for Byatt's thinking about the relationships between word and flesh, mind and matter, fiction and reality. These oppositions overlap and fold into one another through the analogical structure of her fiction which suggests parallels between, for example, the pleasures of sex and those of reading. However, such connections are always heavily qualified, for Byatt is suspicious of facile pattern-making. For her, patterns of thought are both seductive and dangerous, a point of view expressed by the character Roland in *Possession* (1990) when he says 'everything connects and connects – all the time ... these connections seem both endlessly exciting and then in some sense dangerously powerful – as though we held a clue to the true nature of things'.[12] Roland argues that the textual play associated with poststructuralism and postmodernism is inadequate to the truth of experience because it is ultimately solipsistic, leading us to a point where 'we're imprisoned in ourselves – we can't see *things*' (p. 254). Byatt is committed to the representation of the inner life *and* the external universe and to the belief that words refer to each other but also, necessarily, to things, insisting in a 1989 essay that 'I do believe language has denotative as well as connotative powers'.[13] So although her fiction is sometimes seen as postmodern because of its self-reflexive qualities, it would be more accurate to say that it incorporates postmodern insights in order to shape a more flexible and expansive kind of realism.

Byatt's fiction is firmly located in Leavis's 'great tradition' of the English novel and is in dialogue with the work of George Eliot, Hardy, and Lawrence. Brookner's work is similarly allusive but freighted with references to the European literature which formed the backdrop to her career as an art historian.[14] The intertexts of her early novels include Balzac's *Eugenie Grandet* (1833) and Benjamin Constant's *Adolphe* (1816), both of which invoke a Romantic ideal of love with which she has expressed sympathy. In an interview she suggests that her novels can be aligned with a Romantic tradition which she distinguishes from popular romance on the grounds that 'in the genuine Romantic novel there is confrontation with truth and in the "romance" novel a similar confrontation with a surrogate, plastic version of the truth. Romantic writers are characterized by absolute longing – perhaps for something that is not there and cannot be there.'[15] This distinction is both dramatized and called into question in her Booker Prize-winning novel *Hotel du Lac* (1984), in which the protagonist Edith Hope is a writer of formulaic romances with titles like *Beneath the Visiting Moon*. Brookner's novel, in contrast, 'confronts the truth' of the likely fate of a woman such as Edith, who rejects a marriage of convenience in order to remain true to her idea(l) of love. This ideal is ambiguous: it can be dismissed as a fantasy just like the romances Edith writes but, on the other hand, her commitment represents fidelity to the truth of her feelings, to 'absolute longing'. The apparently clear-cut distinction between the ideals of Romanticism and the emotions associated with popular romance is thus undercut in Brookner's text, which in this sense offers a challenge to rigid genre boundaries and gendered cultural hierarchies. However, Edith's fidelity involves renunciation and self-abnegation, recurring themes in Brookner's work which have attracted a good deal of hostile criticism. Reviewing *Hotel du Lac,* Adam Mars-Jones, for example, comments on Brookner's 'masochism' and her 'passive-aggressive heroines'.[16] Yet her novels offer far more than this critique suggests in their subtle exploration of the ways in which character is formed by the pressures of early life: one of the novels even has the Freudian title *A Family Romance* (1993). Brookner is particularly interested in parents who subordinate their children's needs to their own, and in this respect her comment in the interview quoted above that 'I was brought up to look after my parents' is telling, suggesting that in her own family the roles of parent and child were reversed.

The domestic realism of Drabble, Byatt, and Brookner focuses on women like themselves, highly educated and employed in the media or as writers and critics. In sharp contrast, the social realism of Pat Barker and Maggie Gee explores the lives of working-class women in the context of the postwar shift from an industrial to a post-industrial economy. The title of Barker's novel *Union Street* (1982) is profoundly ironic, calling up the image of a close-knit working-class community only to undercut it by exposing the fractured society of the north-east of England in a period of economic decline. Setting up an implicit contrast with the working-class fiction of John Braine and Alan Sillitoe, Barker switches the focus from male to female experience and highlights an intensification of violence against women at a time of unemployment and industrial unrest. Her writing maps women's vulnerability to sexual exploitation and abuse in circumstances of poverty and dispossession, where men have been rendered impotent by the loss of a masculine identity bound up with their role as miners or steel-workers. Barker's women experience rape, abortion, teenage pregnancy, and domestic violence as a matter of routine and in *Blow Your House Down* (1984), which reworks the case of the serial killer Peter Sutcliffe (dubbed the Yorkshire Ripper), sex workers confront the possibility of murder on a daily basis. Barker is particularly interested in the pathologies of violence and of victimhood, and has said that the major theme of her fiction is 'recovery'.[17] As this implies, her fiction is marked by an empathetic humanism rather than a postmodern scepticism, but it is formally extremely innovative. Barker's frequent switching between first- and third-person narration reflects the split and decentred subjectivity of her protagonists, while her use of second-person narration works to align the reader closely with their consciousness.

Gee's early fiction similarly combines social realism with the use of experimental narrative techniques. In *The Burning Book* (1983) she melds the forms of family saga and dystopian fiction to map the shifting parameters of twentieth-century domestic life, which is located within the wider context of global politics. Concerned with three generations of an English working-class family, the novel explores the effect of two world wars with a particular focus on the impact of conflict on family life. For example, a father deserts his family after one of his sons is killed in the First World War: mourning one 'ineradicable loss' he creates another which reverberates down the generations, affecting his grandson and grandchildren.[18] Gee also highlights the cumulative effects of the low-grade poverty which depresses the expectations of her protagonists and leads to unfocused aggression and domestic violence. An implicit parallel is suggested between the wider political violence of the twentieth century and the breakdown of the family unit, and the fragmentation of the domestic sphere is in turn reflected in the form of Gee's novel. The narrative is frequently disrupted by short sections of text which read like fragments of a nightmare, as voices from the atom-bombed Japan of the Second World War merge with cries from a future nuclear disaster. The very form of domestic realism implodes at the point when a bomb is dropped and the text stutters to a halt, leaving only blank sheets of paper. Exploiting Henry James's metaphor of the house of fiction, Gee suggests that the 'bricks and mortar' density of Western domestic realism has given way to more transient paper houses of fiction (p. 52). Her subsequent work is less formally experimental but continues to express strong political commitment and an increasing concern for the global future. *Grace* (1989) returns to the threat of nuclear war, implicating the forces of the British state in the real-life murder of an anti-nuclear activist; *Where Are the Snows* (1991) and *The Ice People* (1998) are dystopian fictions which explore the potential effects of global warming and a new ice age respectively. *The White Family* (2002) addresses the fraught issue of racism in white, working-class Britain. In its energetic engagement with the changing geo-political landscape, Gee's work can be read in terms of Satya Mohanty's influential concept of 'post-positivist realism', that is, as a form of contemporary fiction which maps the connections between diverse cultures in order to identify points of ethical and political convergence.[19] Andrea Levy's novels (particularly her early autobiographical fiction) come into a similar category, tracking overlapping histories and mapping cross-cultural affinities.

Postmodern fictions

Postmodernism encompasses a range of cultural theories and practices linked by scepticism about the foundational narratives of Western culture. Indeed, the philosopher Jean-François Lyotard defined 'the postmodern condition' in terms of 'incredulity towards metanarratives' and a suspicion of principles grounded in Enlightenment claims to universal knowledge.[20] In place of such claims, postmodernism embraced philosophical relativism and the idea of identity as relational and in flux. The concept of identity as fluid and contingent resonated with feminist arguments about the constructed nature of gender and to this extent postmodernism was a powerful tool for many women writers. Yet the undermining of a belief in absolute values raised the obvious question of how a society could reconcile the competing claims of its diverse citizens: the resulting tension between philosophical relativism and ethical commitment is at the centre of the work of Muriel Spark (1918–2006), Carter, and Jeanette Winterson. Spark has been described by David Lodge as 'a postmodernist before the term was known to literary criticism' and her elegant, crystalline fiction engages with postmodernism in two key ways.[21] In its self-conscious textuality, its use of prolepsis and emphasis on the autonomous power of the author, her writing can be understood as a response to the crisis of realism and a means of exploring the heuristic value of post-realist fiction. At the same time, by invoking religious and metaphysical perspectives Spark's fiction calls into question the Enlightenment narrative of progress critiqued by Lyotard, for whom Auschwitz signifies the end-point of the project of modernity, exposing the inadequacy of the progressive Hegelian philosophy which underpinned it. The Holocaust is also a central point of reference in Spark's fiction, the dark subtext which underlies many of her scintillating comedies. In *Territorial Rights* (1979), for example, which is set in present-day Venice, the plot turns on adultery, murder, blackmail, and terrorism, and in the detective-style plot these crimes are traced back to the chaos of Europe immediately after the war and the collaboration of several key protagonists with the Nazis. The novel juxtaposes without comment the violence of the past and the corruption of the present, underscoring the continuities between the horrors of Nazi Germany and the mundane (or in Hannah Arendt's term 'banal') evils of the present.[22] Meanwhile, a metaphysical perspective is drawn into this text through allusions to the abandoned churches which now function primarily as a picturesque backdrop for the Venetian tourist trade. In this text and in others, like *Loitering with Intent* (1981) and *A Far Cry from Kensington* (1988), Spark does not adjudicate between rationalism and religion; rather, she invites the reader to reflect on their intertwined legacies in the context of postwar Europe.

Carter's fiction is also centrally concerned with the Enlightenment and its legacy, though she approaches it from a different perspective. A rationalist through and through, Carter has written of her 'absolute and committed materialism' and her belief that '*this* world is all that there is' (1983, p. 70). In this respect she is located firmly within the progressive Enlightenment tradition, yet she is also acutely aware of the limits of a world-view which has, historically, occluded the subjectivity of those outside the circle of white Western privilege. Her work opens up a space for excluded voices but avoids the trap of 'writing back' to dominant culture and thereby replacing one kind of privilege with another. Carter is, as she famously put it, 'in the demythologising business', and the characteristic note of her writing is one of sceptical critique (1983, p. 73). She has also noted that she 'started very early on to regard the whole of Western European culture as a kind of folklore' and it can be argued that the overarching aim of her work is to create something like a Foucauldian genealogy of culture.[23] Her fiction operates on multiple levels, incorporating philosophy and myth, film and fairy tale, resisting the dichotomy between high and low culture on the grounds that, as she told John Haffenden, 'the imaginative life is conducted in response to all manner of stimuli – including the movies, advertising, all the magical things that the surrealists would see in any city street' (p. 92).

In her best-known novel, *Nights at the Circus* (1984), 'high' and 'low' forms of cultural production are inextricably intertwined; the narrative is picaresque in form and encompasses a bewildering array of characters, from the circus owner Colonel Kearney (an allusion to Colonel Sanders, founder of an American fast-food chain) to the Marxist ex-sex worker Lizzie, from the great clown Buffo to the mute manservant Toussaint (an allusion to Toussaint L'Ouverture). The novel embodies the Bakhtinian concept of heteroglossia, much of its energy deriving from the varied, contradictory voices co-existing within it, and it also draws on Bakhtin's insights into the carnivalesque, enacting ludic reversals of existing hierarchies. One particularly telling example involves 'Monsieur Lamarck's Educated Apes' (the name being an allusion to the evolutionary biologist Jean Baptiste de Lamarck), a circus act in which the intention is to present the apes to the human audience as freaks and curiosities. However, in Carter's circus not only has M. Lamarck's role as keeper been taken over by one of the chimps, known as the Professor, but in an exact mirror of human attitudes the chimps are shown as eager to study their captors. When the journalist Walser realizes that 'his speech was of surpassing interest to them' he begins to recite from *Hamlet*, specifically the speech beginning 'What a piece of work is man!', and the question of man's status and relationship with other species is radically called in question as the Professor looks into Walser's eyes and 'produc[es] afresh in Walser that dizzying uncertainty about what was human and what was not'.[24]

Winterson's fiction resembles that of Carter in many ways, most notably in its use of a freewheeling narrative form in which stories proliferate and are nested within one another. Ranging boldly across historical periods from the classical to the present, her writing exemplifies Linda Hutcheon's concept of 'historiographic metafiction' which is grounded in the view that the world it creates is 'resolutely fictive and yet undeniably historical'.[25] As Hutcheon points out, what history and fiction have in common is their constitution as discourse, a perception Winterson endorses when she argues that 'people have an enormous need to separate history, which is fact, from storytelling, which is not fact ... and the whole push of my work has been to say, you cannot know which is which'.[26] Stressing the importance of narrative in the making of the 'official' historical record, Winterson creates alternative histories which map the subjectivities of those who lie outside the norms of tradition and convention. *Sexing the Cherry* (1989) is set during and immediately after the Civil War and is narrated by the Dog Woman and her son Jordan, a foundling. What is often overlooked about this novel is that it is set amongst the very poor and gives a voice to a woman who is triply marginalized by her poverty, her sexuality, and her exaggeratedly grotesque body. As she asks, rhetorically, 'How hideous am I? My nose is flat, my eyebrows are heavy. I have only a few teeth and those are a poor show, being black and broken. I had smallpox when I was a girl and the caves in my face are home enough for fleas.'[27] Vast and dirty, the Dog Woman nonetheless embodies the principle of what she herself calls 'maternalism', fiercely protecting Jordan and at the same time setting him free to embark on his boyhood adventures and subsequent voyages of discovery. In the figure of this powerful, sexually ambiguous woman, Winterson thus reconfigures maternity, setting it outside the parameters of sex/gender norms. These norms are called into question throughout her work, which explores the multiplicity and fluidity of sex/gender identities in ways which resonate strongly with the perspectives of queer theory. Her fiction seems to exemplify Eve Kosofsky Sedgwick's contention that 'sexuality extends along so many dimensions that aren't well described in terms of the gender of object-choice'.[28] *Gut Symmetries* (1997), for example, maps the shifting relationships between three people in an adulterous triangle where the mistress falls in love with the husband but has her first real experience of desire with the wife; the three are caught up in a complex relay of emotion and desire which holds the possibility of identifications that cut across sex/gender categories.

Nicola Barker shares Winterson's interest in marginal experiences, although her fiction is more sharply focused on the present moment, mapping lives lived on the borders of respectability in contemporary Britain. She has said in an interview that 'if something's rejected that makes me like it more' and her fiction repeatedly explores damaged individuals and various kinds of failure.[29] *Wide Open* (1998), set on the desolate Isle of Sheppey, explores the effects of their father's paedophilia on two brothers, one of whom becomes his father's accomplice. The novel engages with a range of extreme experiences, including breakdown and suicide, but is shot through with intimations of other ways of being. *Darkmans* (2007), which was shortlisted for the Man Booker Prize, is set in Ashford, a drab suburban town in the Thames Gateway area which has been opened up by the construction of the Channel Tunnel and which has recently been identified for further commercial development. Focusing on the relationship between Daniel Beede and his prescription-drug dealer son, the novel explores the interplay between the weight of the past and the brutality of modernity in shaping and constraining the lives of Ashford's inhabitants. Barker can be aligned with Carter in her stylistic exuberance and in the eclectic range of her cultural references, but her fiction is distinctive in its ethical dimension and commitment to exploring lives usually considered beyond the pale of literary fiction.

Neodomestic fiction

Over the last decade a number of women writers including Rachel Cusk, Tessa Hadley, Kate Atkinson, and Ali Smith have opened up new perspectives on the meaning and significance of the domestic. Their fiction offers a powerful understanding of the home as a relational space which is shaped as much by what lies 'outside' it as what lies within. In many respects this fiction epitomizes Kristin J. Jacobson's concept of 'neodomestic fiction', which she defines in terms of three notable characteristics: its interest in relational (as opposed to oppositional) domestic space, its emphasis on domestic mobility, that is the idea that home, both as an ideology and as physical space, can occupy multiple locations, and its interest in reconfiguring (or 'renovating') the traditional home.[30] These themes are threaded through Cusk's fiction, which critiques the oppositional shaping of domestic space that is still too often associated with the experience of motherhood. *Arlington Park* (2006) explores the tenuous friendships between a group of middle-class mothers who bitterly resent their confinement in the home; they feel trapped and rootless, geographically removed from their own families, distanced from them by the experience of upward social mobility. In the chapter devoted to Amanda, the tropes of renovation and haunting intersect to create a vertiginous sense of the friability of family ties. Amanda and her husband have improved their home to signal their increased social status, but when she hears of her grandmother's death Amanda recognizes that the changes have created 'not space but emptiness', an insight which is reinforced by the news that her grandmother, on her deathbed, has condemned Amanda as 'cold ... no love in her heart' (p. 68).[31] She tries to repress awareness of this judgement but it returns in the form of her grandmother's ghost, who appears not to her but to her young son, prompting his first intimation of mortality and signalling the way in which alienation is transmitted across the generations. Atkinson's fiction is similarly preoccupied with intergenerational hauntings, depicting families which have been broken apart by accident or violent trauma. The perpetrator of the violence is often a family member, as in *Case Histories* (2004), in which a young girl who has been systematically abused by her father murders her younger sister. This is the first in the series of novels featuring the private investigator Jackson Brodie, and Atkinson exploits the detective format to explore the pain and aggression that are frequently hidden behind the closed doors of the home. In Atkinson's work the idea(l) of the happy family is a dangerous illusion and home is always uncanny, marked by absence, loss, and trauma.

Hadley's fiction is more optimistic in its mapping of the ways in which in the twenty-first-century 'home' is becoming increasingly fluid in form, as a result of changing patterns of employment and the social trend towards 'blended' families.[32] In *The London Train* (2011) these themes are principally focused through the narrative of Paul, who lives with his second wife and young daughters in a cottage in Wales where he has tried to put down 'roots'. When he discovers that the daughter from his first marriage is living in a grimy London flat he moves in to create an 'improvised family' with his daughter and her Polish boyfriend.[33] This interlude gives him time to recover from his mother's death and reconfigure his life: the displacement enables an acceptance of the multiple forms that 'home' and 'family' can take. This theme is further developed in *Clever Girl* (2013), in which the main protagonist decisively rejects the hermetically sealed structure of conventional family life. Pregnant at 17, Stella leaves her suburban home and lives in a succession of shared houses. These open spaces enable fluid family relationships and the text concludes with a powerful endorsement of the modern blended family. When her sons have grown up, Stella marries a man who has two daughters and they adopt another: reflecting on Max's love for this new daughter, Stella concludes that 'the biology ... only means as much as you choose it to. You either confer that power, emotionally, on the genetic connection, or you don't.'[34]

Ali Smith's fiction also highlights the oppressiveness of normative family structures and promotes a politics of openness and change in relation to the configuration of domestic space. Strikingly, in two of her novels a stranger insinuates themself into a family home to reveal the intricate connections between what is inside the home and what is ostensibly excluded from it. In *The Accidental* (2006), the intruder is Amber, who claims that she has killed a child in a car accident and after this has decided that she can never again 'live in a place that could be called home'.[35] Whether or not this story is true, Amber takes on the role of trickster who exposes the dramas that lie beneath the surface of domestic life; when she moves into the Smart family's holiday cottage she draws a number of secrets into the open. The adolescent Magnus confesses that he has had a part in cyber-bullying which has led to a girl's death, while his stepfather's multiple infidelities are exposed and he loses his university job. Meanwhile the family home in London is burgled, to liberating effect from the perspective of Magnus's sister, who comments that 'getting home and walking in through the front door and it all being bare was like hearing yourself breathe for the first time' (p. 217). In the image of this empty space, free of the emblems of middle-class stability (or stasis), Smith points to the possibility of a freer and more open way of life. A similar effect is achieved in *There But For The* (2011), in which a dinner guest, Miles, locks himself inside the bedroom of his hosts' house and stays there for several months. As one of the hosts, Genevieve Lee, exclaims, 'It makes you strangely self-aware, strange to yourself' and, as this implies, Miles's action turns the house inside out, exposing the fragility of family ties.[36] In the weeks that follow, the Lees' marriage breaks up and a number of revelations queer the space of this apparently ordinary home, showing the ways in which it has both relied on and subverted gender norms. It turns out that Hugo, one of the married guests at the original dinner party, has been having a homosexual affair with another guest; in a further plot twist, he moves in with Genevieve when her husband leaves her. Smith's plotting highlights the fluidity of desire and of sex/gender identifications, as does the characterization of the central figure Miles, who is at first taken to be gay (although he says he is straight) and who veers towards the performance of femininity or masculinity according to the needs and desires of others.

While domestic fiction is structured around a tension between an ethics of stability and an ethics of progress, the neodomestic fiction of Hadley and Smith, and to a lesser extent Cusk, is oriented towards multiplicity and change, promoting what Jacobson calls 'a politics of instability and heterogeneity' in relation to the shaping of domestic space (p. 4). In this respect it offers a striking contrast to Zygmunt Bauman's influential critique of 'liquid modernity'. Bauman laments what he sees as the 'social disorder' arising from the dissolution of patterns of behaviour which were previously legitimated by nation-states, among them the patterns of dependency and interaction which structured family relationships. These, he argues, 'are now malleable to an extent unexperienced by, and unimaginable for, past generations; but like all fluids they do not keep their shape for long ... Keeping fluids in shape requires a lot of attention, constant vigilance and perpetual effort.'[37] Whereas Bauman views such malleability in predominantly negative terms, neodomestic fiction, which has emerged in the context of second- and third-wave feminism, embraces the ideological and geographical reconfigurations associated with the blended and/or post-familial home.

Notes

1. Peter Stothard, quoted in Tim Masters, 'Man Booker Prize Won by Hilary Mantel's *Bring up the Bodies*', BBC News, 16 October 2012, www.bbc.co.uk/news/entertainment-arts-19965004, accessed 3 June 2013.
2. Mantel's first novel was the historical fiction *A Place of Greater Safety* (1992), which explores the French Revolution. A number of other writers, notably Sarah Waters, Rose Tremain, and A.S. Byatt, have re-energized the form, using it in a sophisticated, self-referential way to critique dominant historical and cultural narratives.
3. Angela Carter, 'Notes from the Front Line', *On Gender and Writing*, ed. Michelene Wandor (London: Pandora, 1983), p. 76.
4. Andrzej Gąsiorek, *Post-War British Fiction: Realism and After* (London: Edward Arnold, 1995), p. 14.

5. Margaret Drabble, for example, discussing *The Waterfall* in an interview, comments, 'It was written in 1967 or so, before the first of the feminist critical books, and so I was not in a way conscious of any feminist reaction. I don't suppose I would have cared if I had been.' See Janet Todd, ed., *Women Writers Talking* (London and New York: Holmes and Meier Publishers, 1983), p. 166.
6. Margaret Drabble, *The Waterfall* (Harmondsworth: Penguin, 1971), p. 58.
7. The novels in the trilogy are *The Radiant Way* (1987), *A Natural Curiosity* (1989), and *The Gates of Ivory* (1991).
8. Margaret Drabble, *The Radiant Way* (Harmondsworth: Penguin, 1988), p. 342.
9. Drabble comments that 'an important role for a writer is simply to use your eyes and tell the truth' in a discussion of the moral basis of her work. See Olga Kenyon, *Women Writers Talk: Interviews with Ten Women Writers* (Oxford: Lennard Publishing, 1989), pp. 33–4.
10. A.S. Byatt, *Passions of the Mind: Selected Writings* (London: Vintage, 1993), p. 23.
11. A.S. Byatt, *Babel Tower* (London: Chatto & Windus, 1996), p. 311. The Frederica Quartet consists of *The Virgin in the Garden* (1978), *Still Life* (1985), *Babel Tower* (1997), and *A Whistling Woman* (2002).
12. A.S. Byatt, *Possession: A Romance* (London: Vintage, 1991), p. 253.
13. A.S. Byatt, '"Sugar"/"Le Sucre"', *Passions of the Mind*, p. 24.
14. See F.R. Leavis, *The Great Tradition* (London: Chatto & Windus, 1948). Brookner was Reader at the Courtauld Institute of Art and is the author of *The Genius of the Future: French Art Criticism* (1971) and *Jacques-Louis David* (1980).
15. Anita Brookner, 'The Art of Fiction', p. 98, Interview with Shusha Guppy, *Paris Review*, 104 (Fall 1987), www.theparisreview.org/interviews/2630/the-art-of-fiction-no-98-anita-brookner, accessed 10 April 2013.
16. Adam Mars-Jones, 'Women Beware Women', *New York Review of Books*, 31 January 1985, p. 17.
17. Rob Nixon, 'An Interview with Pat Barker', *Contemporary Literature*, 45:1 (Spring 2004), p. 3.
18. Maggie Gee, *The Burning Book* (London: Faber and Faber, 1983), p. 127.
19. See Satya P. Mohanty, *Literary Theory and the Claims of History* (Ithaca: Cornell University Press, 1997) for a discussion of this.
20. Jean-François Lyotard, *The Postmodern Condition: A Report on Knowledge*, trans. Geoff Bennington and Brian Masumi (Manchester University Press, 1984), p. xxiv.
21. David Lodge, 'The Prime of Muriel Spark', *New York Review of Books*, 19 August 2010, www.nybooks.com/articles/archives/2010/aug/19/prime-muriel-spark/?pagination=false, accessed 29 April 2013.
22. The full title of Hannah Arendt's book on the Eichmann trial (which Spark also attended) is *Eichmann in Jerusalem: A Report on the Banality of Evil* (1963).
23. Angela Carter in John Haffenden, *Novelists in Interview* (London: Methuen, 1985), p. 85.
24. Angela Carter, *Nights at the Circus* (London: Chatto & Windus, 1984), p. 110.
25. Linda Hutcheon, *The Politics of Postmodernism* (New York and London: Routledge, 1989), p. 142.
26. Jeanette Winterson, BBC 4 interview, Autumn 1990, quoted in Sonya Andermahr, *Jeanette Winterson* (London: Palgrave Macmillan, 2009), p. 20.
27. Jeanette Winterson, *Sexing the Cherry* (London: Vintage, 1990), p. 24.
28. Eve Kosofsky Sedgwick, *Epistemology of the Closet* (Berkeley: University of California Press, 2008), p. 35.

29. Susanna Rustin, 'A Life in Writing: Nicola Barker', *Guardian*, 1 May 2010, www.theguardian.com/books/2010/may/01/nicola-barker-life-in-writing, accessed 30 July 2013.
30. Kristin J. Jacobson, *Neodomestic American Fiction* (Athens: Ohio University Press, 2010). Jane Gardam's fiction (both her novels and short stories) can also be considered neodomestic in the light of her sceptical, often darkly comic rendering of familial and domestic relationships.
31. Rachel Cusk, *Arlington Park* (London: Faber and Faber, 2007), p. 68.
32. A blended family is one where the parents have children from previous relationships but the members come together in a single unit.
33. Tessa Hadley, *The London Train* (London: Vintage, 2012), p. 120.
34. Tessa Hadley, *Clever Girl* (London: Jonathan Cape, 2013), p. 287.
35. Ali Smith, *The Accidental* (London: Penguin, 2006), p. 101.
36. Ali Smith, *There But For The* (London: Penguin, 2012), p. 106.
37. Zygmunt Bauman, *Liquid Modernity* (Cambridge: Polity Press, 2000), p. 8.

2

Poetry on Page and Stage

Jane Dowson

Reflecting the zeitgeist of second-wave feminist separatism, scholars established a genealogy of women's poetry through collections, conferences, and critical works. Anthologies of the previous centuries and movements, such as *Salt and Bitter and Good: Three Centuries of English and American Women Poets* (1975), compiled by Cora Kaplan, or *Scars Upon My Heart: Women's Poetry and Verse of the First World War* (1981), selected by Catherine Reilly, recuperated names that had been excised from literary histories to illuminate the extensive genealogy of women poets. The conference *Rethinking Women's Poetry 1770–1930* (1995) and the three *Kicking Daffodils* conferences (1994, 1997, 2006) – that looked forward as well as back – brought together poets and academics to generate conversations about critical and creative interactions. In common, they loosened long-standing conceptual oppositions between woman and poet, feminism and literature.

Anthologies of contemporary poets both documented and fed into contingent discussions about the desirability, viability, and aesthetic of an identifiable 'women's poetry'. Overtly feminist poetry, often originating in writers' collectives and first published in feminist magazines, was produced by feminist presses in several notable anthologies: *Without Adam: The Femina Anthology of Poetry* (1968) by Joan Murray Simpson; *Cutlasses and Earrings* (1977), edited by Michelene Wandor and Michèle Roberts; *Licking the Bed Clean: Five Feminist Poets* (1978) by Alison Fell, Stef Pixner, Tina Reid, Roberts, and Ann Oosthuizen, who also produced *Smile, Smile, Smile, Smile* (1980); and *One Foot on the Mountain: An Anthology of British Feminist Poetry, 1969–79* (1979), edited by Lilian Mohin. In emphatic reaction and asserting her literary credentials, Carol Rumens published *Making for the Open: The Chatto Book of Post-Feminist Poetry* (1985), stating: 'the greater part of explicitly feminist poetry has foundered on its own political imperatives: it is self-centred, uninterested in language and form, stereotyped in imagery. Anthologies laden with this kind of anti-writing do no service to women poets' (p. xv). In the same year, Jeni Couzyn's *The Bloodaxe Book of Contemporary Women Poets: Eleven British Writers* (1985) brought together lyric voices that demonstrated a non-feminist women's poetry. They did, however, centre a female subject, as in Jenny Joseph's popular anti-ageist 'Warning' – 'when I am an old woman I shall wear purple' (p. 174), 'For a Child Born Dead' by Elizabeth Jennings (1926–2001), or Anne Stevenson's 'The Mother'. Couzyn also included Kathleen Raine (1908–2003), Denise Levertov (1923–97), Fleur Adcock, Elaine Feinstein, and Ruth Fainlight along with their respected predecessors Stevie Smith (1902–71) and Sylvia Plath (1932–63). *The Faber Book of C20th Women's Poetry,* edited by Adcock (1987), arranged authors by date of birth to endorse an evolving female canon. Like Rumens, Adcock dissociated herself from overt feminist outlooks and emphasized wit against '"primal scream" writing: slabs of raw experience untransformed' (p. 13). However, Diana Scott's *Bread and Roses: Women's Poetry of the 19th and 20th Centuries* (1992) had a lengthy final section, 'The Renaming: Poetry Coming from the Women's Liberation Movement 1970–80', that connected consciousness-raising poets with both their suffragette and literary predecessors. This connection was rare in a climate where most editor-poets were reluctant to claim feminist poetry as literature.

In step with third-wave feminist diversification, several anthologies in the late 1980s, the 1990s, and beyond were framed by race, nation, or sexuality.[1] They avoided essentialist assumptions about gender and asserted the individuality of each poet. Linda France, editor of *Sixty Women Poets* (1993), was motivated by the politics of inclusion and celebrated women's experience across generations, races, and stylistic trends: 'the guiding force behind this anthology: women being positive, creative and in control of their lives'.[2] Even so, she articulated the same ambivalence about distinctly female creativity and the labelling that recurs through this period: 'Ghettoising and separatism are not options I willingly court' (p. 14). Into the twenty-first century, Eva Salzman introduced *Women's Work: Modern Women Poets Writing in English* (2008) with the same reservations: 'Given the space – and a more perfect world – these poets should appear alongside their male counterparts.'[3] These reservations register a defensive stance against male critics' persistent tendency to sideline women by emphasizing their difference.

In the poetry industries too, there were both advances in and obstructions to women's participation on equal terms. Women became more visible while their detractors put their achievements down to marketing rather than talent. In 1990, Rebecca O'Rourke's statistical overview pointed out how women had been barred from 'the hushed and reverential house of poetry'.[4] However, key initiatives to broaden poetry's readership and audience increasingly involved women: in the New Generation promotion of 1994, 8 of the 20 poets were women while in 2004 the 20 Next Generation included 11 women.[5] No longer confined to women's presses, their volumes were published by Bloodaxe Books and Carcanet Press, and their poems were printed and reviewed in the major organs of national poetry: *PN Review, Poetry Review*, and *The Poetry Book Society Bulletin*. The special 'woman poet' numbers of *Poetry Wales* (1987), *Aquarius* (1987), *Women: A Cultural Review* (1990), *Poetry Review* (1996/97), and *Feminist Review* (1999) marked women's output but also endangered their integration into literary mainstreams. Nevertheless, by the end of the century and into the next one, women had infiltrated new sanctuaries by winning prizes, becoming judges, reviewers, and writers-in-residence. Mimi Khalvati, Jane Duran, and Pascale Petit founded London's Poetry School in 1997 (Khalvati served as coordinator from 1997 to 2004); SuAndi is Director of the North West Arts Board, serves on the board of Akwaaba Pan European Network, and has been awarded an OBE. Sarah Maguire is founder and director of The Poetry Translation Centre (2004–) and Ruth Padel wrote a weekly column on contemporary poems for *The Independent on Sunday* (1998–2001), was Chair of the Poetry Society (2004–6), and in 2009 became the first woman to be elected Professor of Poetry at Oxford University.

At the same time, scepticism about the merit of women's poetry was still pervasive. In *Poetry Review*'s special edition on women poets, the (male) editor asked, 'Must it be said that, for all the trumpeting about women poets, the empress has no clothes?'[6] As a result, some poets distanced themselves from segregated treatment: Sheenagh Pugh followed Ruth Bidgood in opposing women-only anthologies; Rumens complained of too many women publishing; and, in 1995, Elizabeth Lowry slated *Sixty Women Poets* with a review headlined 'Down with women's anthologies' on the front cover of poetry journal *Thumbscrew*.[7] Carol Ann Duffy was passed over for Poet Laureate in 1999 but her subsequent appointment to that post in 2009 registered a newly diverse mainstream British culture so that her sex, lesbian identity, and Scottish roots were no longer barriers to being a national representative. The corresponding appointments of Gillian Clarke and Liz Lochhead to National Poet of Wales and Scotland respectively suggest similar advances in establishing women as public poets. However, such status is still fragile: Padel's Chair in Oxford was surrounded by controversy that resulted in her resignation and Duffy's success at democratizing poetry was smeared by Padel's successor, Geoffrey Hill.[8]

Reclaiming and reframing the lyric voice

In a context where critics both proclaimed and denounced its distinctiveness, the cohering aesthetic of women's poetry is the creative representation of women's experience and perspective; this crosses a spectrum between gender-denying and assertively female ways with language and poetic forms. In her influential essay 'When We Dead Awaken: Writing as Re-Vision' (1971), American poet Adrienne Rich (1929–2009) recounts her progress from 'want[ing] women poets to be the equals of men' to 'be[ing] able to write, for the first time, directly about experiencing myself as a woman'.[9] Rich influenced a generation of writers and readers but the pattern of conforming to received literary straightjackets, finding them ill-fitting and then feeling comfortable in her own poetic skin, recurs through the decades. In 1999, Scottish poet Kathleen Jamie reflected: 'As women we still find ourselves in a tangle of briars. We are told what to write, and then told that real art can't be made from those experiences anyway. We have to spend energy clearing space.'[10] Duffy's account of her creative journey in her poem 'Little Redcap' (1999) uses the same symbolism of a thicket: the wolf (male poet) 'I knew, would lead me deep into the woods, / away from home, to a dark tangled thorny place'. On killing him, Duffy discovered her literary predecessors – 'the glistening virgin white of my grandmother's bones' – and found her own voice.[11]

As Clair Wills observes, the lyric is particularly thorny ground for women:

> Arguably, the representation of an inner life in lyric poetry, through personal address or solitary meditation and reflection, has always also been a mirror of social and cultural forces. But, given the nature of the poetic tradition and the history of poetic practice, this mirroring has also been gendered. This has led some contemporary women poets to seek to 'reclaim' the lyric.[12]

In 'Pulse', Jane Holland asserts a distinctly female lyric that is formed around this conundrum: 'I'm not a woman poet. / I am a woman and a poet. / The difference is in the eyes.'[13] Her playful pun on 'eye' / 'I' reclaims a subjectivity that is owned rather than imposed. Like Holland, the best poets carve out a creative territory that both exploits and tampers with lyric conventions to depict their own states of mind and feeling. They use and mix such enlivening strategies as: anti-feminine language and regenerating metaphors; 'ex/centricity' – empowering parody and satire that deflate gender stereotypes; disruptive forms and syntax; dramatic monologues that mask and dialogues that fracture a fixed lyrical 'I'; and exuberant performative strategies from the theatrical to the purely vocal or digital.

There is some correlation between linguistic radicalism and its social moment, but not uniformly so. The 1970s embraced both consciousness-raising expressiveness and innovative anti-poetics. Fell, Judith Kazantzis, Pixner, Roberts, and Valerie Sinason were among the foremost British consciousness-raisers. Their bold first-person pronouns switched between the singular and plural, collapsing the distinction between individual and communal identities. 'A Day in the Life' by Pixner brings the mundane into literature and may be consciously counter-discursive to W.H. Auden's politically idealist 'Spain' (1937) that was structured around the incantations of 'Yesterday', 'Tomorrow', and 'To-day'. 'Today' at the start of Pixner's lines introduces a list of women's roles and duties to enact and question their choices about sexuality and lifestyle: 'Today I felt nauseous with grey anxiety as we drove to / buy a reconditioned vacuum cleaner, Dougie and I';

'Today I fucked Dave but I didn't want to kiss him'; 'I gave Lisa a massage and liked the feel of her back'.[14] As here, these poets' frank biological or psychological details about women that included abortion and abuse, along with an adversarial thrust, defied literary and social convention to engender political sisterhood.

In the following decades, women's lyrics continued to express and explore exclusively female experiences, such as breast cancer and mastectomy, sexuality and infidelity, childhood or domestic abuse, and a complex relationship with food. Intimate lyrics and elegies to loved ones by Deryn Rees-Jones, Penelope Shuttle, and Pauline Stainer do not have an obvious political edge but register women's freedom with unashamed self-expression that challenges any charges of sentimentality. Maguire argues that the lyric's emphasis on personal experience is always socially significant: 'It's precisely because the poem can render the most intimate and elusive of subjective experiences in language that it's able to bear witness to what's excluded from dominant discourses.'[15] French/Welsh Petit exemplifies the politics of personal witness in reworking the abuse then abandonment by her father along with her mother's mental illness in *The Zoo Father* (2001) and *The Huntress* (2005) respectively. Her private anguish was unlocked by watching animals that operate as symbols in the poems: 'To visit you Father, I wear a mask of fire ants. / When I sit waiting for you to explain' ... 'I can't remember what you did to me, but the ants know.'[16] This interface between revelation and concealment through symbolism distinguishes the best from the weakest confessional lyricism.

With 12 volumes stretching between 1974 and 2012, Duffy excels in exploiting, scrutinizing, and extending poetry's expressive function. Her acclaim was jeopardized by the feminist politics of *The World's Wife* (1999) and explicit female-centricity of *Feminine Gospels* (2002), but *Rapture* (2005) was welcomed for 'mark[ing] a return to the interiority and personal lyrics of *The Other Country* and *Mean Time*'.[17] It revived her waning reputation and won her the coveted T.S. Eliot Prize. *Rapture*'s lyrics transcend specific contexts and the pronouns are gender neutral. Arguably, the intimacy and interconnectedness are female features, but Duffy asserted the universality of her lyrics: 'I hope that these poems deal with matters common to us all and that they transcend the particulars of any individual life.'[18] Here, she corresponds to Irish poet Eavan Boland, who spelled out her own specifically female negotiation with poetic traditions in *Object Lessons: The Life of the Woman and the Poet in Our Time* (1995), evoking an ideal that opposes 'humanising femininity' in favour of a more radical feminizing of humanity.[19]

Paradoxically, since *Rapture* retells an actual relationship between female lovers, it raises the questions asked by Liz Yorke in 1999 about whether 'British lesbian poets now feel themselves to be post lesbian-feminists, or indeed, post-lesbian?' Yorke surveys anthologies and poems to identify a continuing and distinct lesbian voice. In 'The Passion of Remembrance', she finds that Dorothea Smartt 'conveys lesbian particularity, contradicts conventional systems of morality and provocatively contests orthodox condemnation ... she creates for herself an intensely satisfying fantasy of sexual connection'.[20] Yorke reads 'Riddle Game' by Gillian Spraggs as multi-sexed, celebrating all sexualities but with an identifiably 'lesbian bliss' (p. 84). Additional poets in the continuum between suppressed, coded, and explicit lesbian lyrics include U.A. Fanthorpe (1929–2005), Maureen Duffy, and Suniti Namjoshi.

Twenty-first-century poems on breast cancer sit on the platforms of both female self-expression and feminizing humanity, indicating advances in conceptualizing both women and the condition. In *Illness as Metaphor and AIDS and its Metaphors* (1991), Susan Sontag observes how metaphors determine the experience of shameful afflictions and 'cancer is a rare and still scandalous subject for poetry', especially since it hits the private parts of the body.[21] Julia Darling (1956–2005) contributed towards changing attitudes in and towards breast cancer by writing plays, diaries, newspaper columns, and poems. In the *Guardian* (2004), she explained what poetry can uniquely do:

> Poetry uses images to make us see things in a fresh way. So in the case of the physical body, poetry shows us pictures and metaphors that we can use, rather like visualisations. In my case I chose to imagine my body as a house, and wrote many poems during my treatment about 'living in the new extension' or about my fears. Poetry helped me to step out of the difficult present and to use my imagination to be somewhere else.[22]

In Darling's sonnet 'Chemotherapy' (2003), that was widely circulated via anthologies and internet blogs, the speaker moves from 'I did not imagine being bald / at forty-four' to an enhanced awareness of life's gifts.[23] Similarly, in Jo Shapcott's prize-winning sequence on breast cancer, 'Of Mutability' (2010), she is a person living with a cellular condition, rather than a victim in its grip. Her lyrics reflect the more widespread scientific understanding of the disease that has helped to demythologize it. Here we see women poets 'feminising humanity' by combining what is intensely personal and female with what is also a social concern.

Lyrics on depression register and produce parallel advances in social attitudes. Kay's pithy collection on personal health and the health services, *Off Colour* (1988), includes 'Characteristics of Sadness' that captures intense misery with her domestic image: 'but inside this house it stinks'.[24] Again, in Gwyneth Lewis's sonnet 'Angel of Depression', metaphor manages the core psychological issues of self-blame for burdening others: 'it tears the breath from my solar plexus, grinds / my face in the ever-resilient dirt'.[25] Here, women are clearly at home in the most traditional of lyric forms, the sonnet, redefining 'house' as both women's and every-person's domain.

Lyrical performances and dialogues

From 1970 onwards, intellectually ferocious lyric innovators also tore at and restitched the literary/feminist seam. As Wendy Mulford explains: 'In avant-garde, experimental or Language Poetry (to throw in three assorted and not particularly helpful labels), there is no unified lyric voice – its claims are exploded ... In its place, we ... follow the text in all its provisionality, its multiple meanings, its erasures, silences, chora.'[26] Resonating with modernist Gertrude Stein's self-reflexively disruptive syntax, the title of Mulford's poem '1.' stands for the genderless pronoun 'One' and also its opposite, a definitive 'I', the female lyric subject. The poem enacts the process of self-realization that negotiates these two poles:

> is a writing of the self a writing of writing?
> and is a writing of writing a writing of the self?
> double u one.
> mark one.[27]

Such 'play and gesture' (Mulford, 1990, p. 263) with 'double u', meaning 'W' for Woman and also 'double you', a divided female self, along with 'one', the generic pronoun, brilliantly harness and devalue poststructuralism's disregard for authentic expression.

Mulford's motives for writing and founding Street Editions Press were expressly political: 'I want to join my voice with the voices of other *women* struggling to destruct [sic] the lie of culture.'[28] Street Editions published Denise Riley's first two volumes, *Marxism for Infants* (1977) and *No Fee* (1978); in refusing culture's dominant versions of femininity they resonate with her feminist activism of the time. Her emblematic 'A note on sex and "the reclaiming of language"' (1985) shows the radical poetics that Riley would continue over the next 30 years:

> The work is
> e.g. to write 'she' and for that to be a statement
> of fact only, and not a strong image
> of everything which is not-you, which sees you.[29]

As here, she pits lyric expression against discursive self-reflexivity: third- and second-person pronouns mark an absent or elusive 'I'; the idioms and syntax of non-fiction jar with the disjunctive syntax; and an assertive, albeit objectified, subjectivity – 'you' – is offset by a denial of representation – 'not-you'. For the next three decades Riley continued to problematize the theoretical and creative divide, exploring the impulses towards and away from expressing female subjectivity, 'alive to both the dangers of the rhetorical inscription of gendered power relations in the lyric form and yet its possibilities as testimonial'.[30] The wrestle with writing within and outside the lyric form permeates her writing, as evoked in 'Lyric' (1983) that begins, 'Stammering it fights to get / held and to never get held'.[31] Such ambivalent treatment of the lyric can be read alongside Riley's theoretical writings on subjectivity, language, and politics in *Am I that Name?: Feminism and the Category of 'Women' in History* (1988) and *The Words of Selves: Identification, Solidarity, Irony* (2000). In 1996, she was chosen for *Penguin Modern Poets 10*.[32] After *Selected Poems* in 2000, her next published poem, 'A Part Song', won the Forward Prize for Best Single Poem in 2012; its heart-wrenching treatment of a mother's grief at the loss of a son exemplifies Riley's ongoing search to harness emotion to lyric expression as explored in her critical work *Impersonal Passion: Language as Affect* (2004).

Cambridge-based Mulford and Riley were joined and succeeded by Veronica Forrest-Thomson, Carlyle Reedy, Maggie O'Sullivan, and Geraldine Monk. In her Introduction to *Out of Everywhere: Linguistically Innovative Poetry by Women in North America and the UK* (1996), O'Sullivan explains that formally adventurous work was often left out of both men's and women's canons, because men did not know of it and women did not think it relevant. Following on from the Anglo-American modernist pioneers such as Stein, H.D., or Mina Loy, O'Sullivan insists that these innovators have 'committed themselves to excavating *language* in all its multiple voices and tongues, known and unknown'.[33] Furthermore, their experiments in crossing poetic discourses with different media both foreground and transgress the limits of page writing.

Progressively polylingual poetics are exemplified by Caroline Bergvall, a French-Norwegian-British writer, who works across art forms. Her investigative projects around new literacies, language use, and cultural belonging assault all borders of time, place, identity, and medium. In 'The Not Tale (Funeral)', she conflates historical and contemporary narratives through the depiction of a woman being burned in a funeral pyre:

> Nor what
> nor how
> nor what she spak, nor what was her desire – [34]

Like Bergvall, Lucy English, Sri-Lankan born and London-based, proves how culturally complex and mobile writers are particularly adept at crossing artistic boundaries. Novelist, performance poet, and academic, and a finalist in the first BBC Radio 4 Poetry Slam in 2007, English organized 'MIX', a conference in Transmedia Writing and Digital Creativity in 2012. Carrie Etter's anthology *Infinite Difference: Other Poetries by UK Women Poets* (2010) features such established writers as Mulford and Bergvall along with newer names, such as Harriet Tarlo and Zoë Skoulding, to consolidate women's vital participation in poetic transliteracy.

Other strategies for re-presenting female voices include 'ex/centricity' and dramatization. Selima Hill and Shapcott disturb recognizable social and artistic norms with what Ian Gregson calls 'postmodern estrangement', citing Viktor Shklovsky: 'The technique of art is to make objects "Unfamiliar".'[35] Shapcott signals the inadequacy of familiar language for exploring female subjectivity by adopting various personae of otherness, from Superman to a goat: 'I lived for the push / of goat muscle and goat bone, the smell of goat fur, / goat breath and goat sex.'[36] The context here is the rush hour on a tube train that launches Shapcott's imaginative shape-shifting: 'It may be that I feel the self is enclosing, and I like the idea that you can pass out of it, and get into other places, other imaginations, other skins.'[37] Both Shapcott and Hill write amusingly ironic 'Cow' monologues that defamiliarize negative epithets for, and their conjunctive stereotypes of, women. Hill's 'Cow' opens with 'I want to be a cow / and not my mother's daughter' (France, p. 157), and Shapcott's sequence begins with 'The Mad Cow talks back': 'I'm not mad. It just seems that way.'[38] From her first of 15 volumes, *Saying Hello at the Station* (1984), to her most recent, *People Who Like Meatballs* (2012), Hill forges a surreal landscape to juxtapose the grim realities of marital betrayal, family relationships, and mental illness with absurdist fantasy. *Accumulation of Small Acts of Kindness* (1989) was a sequence on a woman's breakdown and return to health: 'I'm menstruating on a stranger's blankets. / Sorrow like a silver spool unwinds. // The sun is hot. My head is full of silence / attracting hordes of angry bees like bells.'[39] The dense symbolism, evocative of Plath's unsettling imagery, indicates psychological disturbance that is both acutely individual but also common to many readers. Most crucially, in airing it here in defamiliarizing language, Hill helps to strip both menstruation and mental suffering of social shame.

With Duffy at the helm, women's dramatic monologues exemplify the reach and crossover of stage and page. Duffy fractured the stability of a unitary lyric voice with searingly funny and pointed dramatic monologues that became her trademark. In her bestselling *The World's Wife* (1999), the revisionist monologues by the wives of famous men typically both fed and parodied a separatist female culture and poetics. In the more lyrical dramatic monologues in her earlier collections, such as 'Warming her Pearls', 'Standing Female Nude', or 'Small Female Skull', the voice constructs a poignantly end-of-century woman who is both tough and vulnerable, independent and longing for love. In 'Adultery' or 'Who Loves You', both speaker and addressee could be interchangeably male, female, heterosexual or same-sex. Less compassionately than Duffy, Rita Ann Higgins and Lavinia Greenlaw lay the cruelty and falsity of machismo under the microscope in such monologues as 'The Did-You-Come-Yets of the Western World' (France, pp. 151–2) and 'Hurting Small Animals' respectively.[40] Often compared to her witty elder Wendy Cope, Sophie Hannah frequently asserts and undercuts female autonomy, as manifested by contractual sex, for example:

'I know the rules and hear myself agree / Not to invest beyond this one night stand.'[41] The contradictions of 'girl power' are both mimicked and interrogated in 'Rondeau Redoublé', a clever pastiche of the French verse form of that name. Among its strict rules, it requires certain rhymes to be masculine and feminine. Playing the form off against the narrative, the poem documents ambivalent sentiments about the loss of gender roles in romantic courtship.

Dramatic monologues validate the regional and racial voices that permeated British culture from the early 1980s. Scottish Lochhead paved the way for Jamie and Kay in blending oral dialects with literary vocabularies. With a Nigerian father and adopted by white Glaswegians, Kay's most anthologized piece, 'In My Country', expresses the poignancy and potency of cultural duality. It captures the double displacement of second-generation immigrants while the metaphor of river and sea shaking hands evokes an ideal of racial harmony. In her landmark multivocal sequence *The Adoption Papers* (1991), Kay blends lyric with drama to enact the parallel and intersecting voices of the adopted child, birth mother, and adoptive mother. Elsewhere, she bridges literary and popular cultures with her dramatic monologues of the comic-strip character Maw Broon, to laugh with and at the hard-pressed wife and mother: 'A' could break. A' could jist give in' (1998, pp. 46–7). Bilingual Menna Elfyn and Lewis represent the linguistic silences, conflicts, and choices involved when the 'mother' tongue is threatened by the colonizing English language. In 'Welsh Espionage' (1995), Lewis brilliantly hints at sexual abuse to reconstruct the shame that accompanied learning English in secret: 'Welsh was my mother tongue, English was his. / He taught her the body by fetishist quiz, / father and daughter on the bottom stair.'[42] Northern Irish Medbh McGuckian and Sinéad Morrissey lead a strong band who invigorate national myths and motifs to challenge the grand narratives of patriarchal history and religion.

British Asian poets Imtiaz Dharker, Moniza Alvi, Sujata Bhatt, Khalvati, and Raman Mundair helped depict their dual identity as a condition of enrichment. In 'They say, "she must be from another country"', Dharker's 'other country' is both the land of origin and the host country to which she migrated:

> And I'll be happy to say,
> 'I never learned your customs.
> I don't remember your language
> or know your ways.
> I must be
> from another country.'[43]

Dharker's provocative multivocality corresponds to Homi Bhabha's concept of the third space of enunciation, the means by which identity is not trapped in binary formulations of centre and margin.[44] Dharker's first collection, *Purdah* (1988), revealed how poetry was an act of rebellion against the literal and figurative veiling of the female body. Writing in English as a strategy of liberation was a controversial motif in *Postcards from god* (1997): 'Watch the word cavort luxuriously strut / My independence across whole continents of / Sheets.'[45] Her fourth collection, *The Terrorist at my Table* (2006), continued her unique synthesis of race and gender politics, addressing from a micro-perspective cultural rituals, such as honour killing, and global events, such as the attack on New York's World Trade Center, 11 September 2001. Like Dharker, Mundair combines her poems with visual sketches, is frequently multivocal, and uses her cultural liminality to comment on significant conventions, such as wearing a sari, and events, such as the racially incited murder of Stephen Lawrence in 1993 ('Elegy for Two Boys').[46]

Poetry as performance

While women's page poetry tackled public and global matters with increasing authority, black women inheriting Caribbean traditions had long been cultural commentators, bringing elements of music and theatre to their hugely popular performances. Grace Nichols was a luminary, proudly projecting her group's struggles for recognition and equality with empowering pathos and entertaining humour:

> Maybe this poem is to say,
> that I like to see
> we black women
> full-of-we-selves walking
>
> Crushing out
> with each dancing step
> the twisted self-negating
> history
> we've inherited
>   Crushing out
>   with each dancing step.[47]

Since her first collection, *I is a Long-Memoried Woman* (1983), Guyanese-born Nichols has switched between Standard English, Nation Language, and Creole: 'As someone from the Caribbean, I feel very multicultural and have been affected by all the different strands in that culture – African, Amerindian, Asian, European.'[48] Nichols connects with both the more page-orientated Olive Senior, Amryl Johnson (1944–2001), Lorna Goodison, and Merle Collins, and the more stage-orientated Valerie Bloom and Jean 'Binta' Breeze. Jamaican-born 'Binta' Breeze and Bloom excel in dub traditions, political satires, and dramatized lyrics or elegies. The Ghanaian Scottish Maud Sulter (1960–2008) and Nigerian British Patience Agbabi frequently explode cultural prejudices and stereotypes. Agbabi draws easily on English literary canons, popular culture, and oral forms, notably the rhythms of reggae and rap. With Adeola Agbebiyi, Agbabi conceived *Fo(u)r Women*, a dynamic piece first performed in London's Institute of Contemporary Arts in 1996. It distinguished Black British from African American experience and expression, centred women who love women, and explored 'the interaction of skin tone and gender in the construction of power and identity'.[49] As Agbebiyi claims, 'The UK Black Experience is a perfect example of hybridity, with diaspora stories coming from all over the globe mixing with the local hybrid culture, creating exciting new forms of art content and practice' (p. 89). In a published discussion on poetry and performance, Agbabi noted how black poets were typecast as 'natural performers' and thus placed apart from serious literature, protesting that her poems also work on the page.[50] 'Binta' Breeze agreed that not enough had been written on the Black British experience and found 'no difficulties between page or stage' since poetry 'is about language and how language is used'.[51]

Malaysian-born Francesca Beard with her one-woman show 'Chinese Whispers', produced by Britain's foremost performance poetry organization, Apples and Snakes, further hybridizes labels about identity and artistic forms. SuAndi also proves how performance can be a distinct genre that intrinsically defines itself against the literary. She has released three spoken-word recordings and her work has been shown on Channel 4 television. Coming from a Nigerian family and growing up in a working-class environment in the north-west of England, SuAndi models how 'marginality' has little resonance in new poetic mainstreams. Proudly declaring, 'I am Black British', she draws on the rhythms and humour of the Liverpool poets along with African narrative traditions. All these poets register how in performance poetry the body mediates a female 'I', asserting the female subject as a confident representative of communal experience. Sometimes the communal experience is specifically female, sometimes specifically racial, often both, and sometimes global: 'I believe the poet is the timekeeper of society. I believe the poet is life's narrator, commentator and often its critic.'[52]

In the closing couplet to 'Prologue', Agbabi proclaims women poets' creative freedom at the end of the twentieth century: 'Give me a page and I'll cut form on it / Give me a stage and I'll perform on it.'[53] As a Black British Oxford-educated, bisexual, page and performance poet, Agbabi exhibits the rejuvenating hybridity that characterizes prominent figures of her generation. Women's centrality to powerfully multivocal new British mainstreams was hard won by both the consciousness-raising and the linguistically radical pioneers in the 1970s. Alongside these, a senior generation who asserted their literary credentials before their gender showed that woman and poet were not mutually exclusive. These strong models – Stevenson, Fainlight, Adcock, and Rumens – exercised the rigours of poetic form and enabled following generations to take more risks in lyric expression and self-dramatization, vibrantly cross-dressing literary forms with other media.

At the cusp of the twenty-first century, Maguire expressed her sense of a respected female tradition: 'As a result of the new wave of feminism which took root in the late 60s, I happen to be living at a moment during which, for the first time in history, it's been acceptable – even positive – to be a woman poet!'[54] One consensus, however, is around the need for good critical works, as Maura Dooley succinctly put it: 'Women are published, read and heard, but their work is not discussed' (p. 12). Speaking about performance poetry in 1999, 'Binta' Breeze complained: 'I find that people don't often critique the work. Everybody wants interviews with you about your personal life' (p. 29). In 2004, Kate Clanchy, whose collection on motherhood exposed a continuing antipathy towards blatantly female-centric poetry, echoed the point: 'It's the critical response that determines how we are historicised and how we are anthologised and how we are remembered: how we're put into literary history.'[55]

Notes

1. For example, Stella and Frank Chipasula, eds, *The Heinemann Book of African Women's Poetry* (London: Heinemann, 1995); Eunice De Souza, ed., *Nine Indian Women Poets: An Anthology* (Oxford University Press, 1997); Catherine Kerrigan, ed., *An Anthology of Scottish Women Poets* (Edinburgh University Press, 1991); Rosemary Palmeira, ed., *In the Gold of the Flesh: Poems of Birth and Motherhood* (London: The Women's Press, 1990); Gillian Spraggs, ed., *Love Shook My Senses: Lesbian Love Poems* (London: The Women's Press, 1998).
2. Linda France, ed., *Sixty Women Poets* (Newcastle upon Tyne: Bloodaxe, 1993), p. 18.
3. Eva Salzman and Amy Wack, eds, *Women's Work: Modern Women Poets Writing in English* (Bridgend: Seren, 2008), p. 7.
4. Rebecca O'Rourke, 'Mediums, Messengers and Noisy Amateurs', *Women: A Cultural Review*, 1:3 (Winter 1990), pp. 275–86.
5. See lists of poets at http://books.guardian.co.uk/nextgenerationpoets/01231558,00.html, accessed 18 July 2013.
6. Peter Forbes, 'Beyond the Bell Jar', *Poetry Review*, 86:4 (Winter 1996/97), p. 3.
7. Carol Rumens, 'My Leaky Coracle', *Poetry Review*, 86:4 (Winter 1996/97), p. 4, pp. 26–7; Elizabeth Lowry, 'Relentlessly Feminine: The Flawed Values of *Sixty Women Poets*', *Thumbscrew*, 2 (Spring 1995), pp. 30–42.
8. Charlotte Higgins, 'Oxford Professor of Poetry Ruth Padel Resigns after Smear Allegations', *Guardian*, 25 May 2009, www.theguardian.com/books/2009/may/25/ruth-padel-resigns-oxford-poetry-professor, accessed 7 April 2015; Alison Flood, 'Carol Ann Duffy is "Wrong" about Poetry Says Geoffrey Hill', *Guardian*, 31 January 2012, www.theguardian.com/books/2012/jan/31/carol-ann-duffy-oxford-professory-poetry, accessed 4 November 2013.
9. Adrienne Rich, 'When We Dead Awaken: Writing as Re-Vision' (1971), *On Lies, Secrets, and Silence: Selected Prose 1966–78* (London: Virago, 1980), p. 39, p. 44.

10. Kathleen Jamie, *Don't Ask Me What I Mean: Poets in Their own Words*, ed. Clare Brown and Don Paterson (London: Picador, 2003), pp. 127–8.
11. Carol Ann Duffy, *The World's Wife* (London: Picador, 1999), p. 3.
12. Clair Wills, 'Marking Time: Fanny Howe's Poetics of Transcendence', *Contemporary Women's Poetry: Reading/Writing/Practice*, ed. Alison Mark and Deryn Rees-Jones (Basingstoke: Macmillan, 2000), pp. 119–20.
13. Jane Holland in *Making for Planet Alice: New Women Poets*, ed. Maura Dooley (Newcastle upon Tyne: Bloodaxe, 1997), p. 97.
14. Stef Pixner in *Bread and Roses: Women's Poetry of the 19th and 20th Centuries*, ed. Diana Scott (London: Virago, 1992), pp. 230–2.
15. Sarah Maguire, 'Poetry Makes Nothing Happen', *Strong Words: Modern Poets on Modern Poetry*, ed. W.N. Herbert and Matthew Hollis (Tarset: Bloodaxe, 2000), p. 250.
16. Pascale Petit, 'Self-Portrait with Fire Ants', *The Zoo Father* (Bridgend: Seren, 2004), p. 9.
17. 'Selector's Comment', *PBS Bulletin*, 206 (Autumn 2005), p. 5.
18. Carol Ann Duffy, *PBS Bulletin*, 206 (Autumn 2005), p. 5.
19. Eavan Boland, 'The Woman Poet: Her Dilemma' (1987), reprinted in *Object Lessons: The Life of the Woman and the Poet in Our Time* (Manchester: Carcanet, 1995), pp. 239–54.
20. Liz Yorke, 'British Lesbian Poetics', *Feminist Review*, 62 (Summer 1999), p. 84.
21. Susan Sontag, *Illness as Metaphor and AIDS and its Metaphors* (Harmondsworth: Penguin, 1991), p. 20.
22. Julia Darling, 'My Joints are Rusty Cranes', *Guardian*, 5 August 2004, www.theguardian.com/books/2004/aug/05/health.poetry, accessed 4 November 2013.
23. Julia Darling, *Sudden Collapses in Public Places* (Todmorden: Arc, 2003), p. 50.
24. Jackie Kay, *Off Colour* (Tarset: Bloodaxe, 1998), p. 50.
25. Gwyneth Lewis, 'Angel of Depression', *Chaotic Angels: Poems in English* (Tarset: Bloodaxe, 2005), p. 185.
26. Wendy Mulford, '"Curved, Odd ... Irregular": A Vision of Contemporary Poetry by Women', *Women: A Cultural Review*, 1:3 (1990), p. 263.
27. Wendy Mulford, '1.', *and suddenly, supposing: selected poems* (Buckfastleigh: Etruscan Books, 2002), p. 64.
28. Wendy Mulford, 'Notes on Writing: A Marxist/Feminist Viewpoint', *On Gender and Writing*, ed. Michelene Wandor (London: Pandora, 1983), p. 33 (Mulford's emphasis).
29. Denise Riley, *Dry Air* (London: Virago, 1985), p. 7.
30. Carol Watts, 'Beyond Interpellation? Affect, Embodiment and the Poetics of Denise Riley', in Mark and Rees-Jones, p. 158.
31. Denise Riley, *Mop Mop Georgette: New and Selected Poems 1986–93* (Cambridge: Reality Street Editions, 1993), p. 62.
32. Douglas Oliver, Denise Riley, and Iain Sinclair, *Penguin Modern Poets 10* (Harmondsworth: Penguin, 1996).
33. Maggie O'Sullivan, 'To the Reader', *Out of Everywhere: Linguistically Innovative Poetry by Women in North America and the UK* (London and Suffolk: Reality Street Editions, 1996), n.p.
34. Caroline Bergvall, *Shorter Chaucer Tales* (2006), www.poetryfoundation.org/poetrymagazine/poem/237058#poem, accessed 1 May 2013.
35. Viktor Shklovsky in Ian Gregson, *Contemporary Poetry and Postmodernism: Dialogue and Estrangement* (Basingstoke: Macmillan, 1996), p. 2.

36. Jo Shapcott, *Phrase Book* (Oxford University Press, 1992), p. 11.
37. Janet Phillips, 'The Shape-Shifter: An Interview with Jo Shapcott', *Poetry Review*, 91:1 (2001), p. 21.
38. Shapcott, *Phrase Book*, p. 41.
39. Selima Hill in *Modern Women Poets*, ed. Deryn Rees-Jones (Tarset: Bloodaxe, 2005), p. 240.
40. Lavinia Greenlaw in *New Women Poets*, ed. Carol Rumens (Newcastle upon Tyne: Bloodaxe, 1990), p. 165.
41. Sophie Hannah, 'Rondeau Redoublé', *Leaving and Leaving You* (Manchester: Carcanet Press, 1999), p. 15.
42. Gwyneth Lewis, 'Welsh Espionage', *Chaotic Angels: Poems in English* (Tarset: Bloodaxe, 2005), p. 43.
43. Imtiaz Dharker, *I Speak for the Devil* (Tarset: Bloodaxe, 2001), pp. 30–1.
44. Homi K. Bhabha, *The Location of Culture* (London: Routledge, 2001), pp. 36–9.
45. Imtiaz Dharker, 'Choice', *Postcards from god* (Newcastle upon Tyne: Bloodaxe, 1997), pp. 49–50.
46. Raman Mundair, *Lovers, Liars, Conjurers and Thieves* (Leeds: Peepal Tree Press, 2003), pp. 79–80.
47. Grace Nichols, 'Of course when they ask for poems about the "Realities" of black women', *Lazy Thoughts of a Lazy Woman and Other Poems* (London: Virago, 1989), pp. 52–4.
48. Grace Nichols in *Six Women Poets*, ed. Carol Rumens (Oxford University Press, 1992), p. 33.
49. Adeola Agbebiyi, *Voicing Identities, Reframing Difference(s): The Case of Fo(u)r Women*, ed. Jane de Gay and Lisbeth Goodman (Bristol and Portland, Oreg.: Intellect Books, 2003), pp. 89–98.
50. Patience Agbabi, 'A Round Table Discussion on Poetry and Performance', *Feminist Review*, 62 (Summer 1999), p. 40.
51. Jean 'Binta' Breeze, 'A Round Table Discussion on Poetry and Performance', *Feminist Review*, 62 (Summer 1999), p. 29.
52. SuAndi, 'Reflection', Moving Manchester: Writers' Gallery, www.lancs.ac.uk/fass/projects/writersgallery/content/SuAndi.html, accessed 24 July 2013.
53. Patience Agbabi, *Transformatrix* (London: Payback Press, 2000), p. 9.
54. Sarah Maguire in *Binary Myths: Conversations with Contemporary Poets*, ed. Andy Brown (Exeter: Stride Publications, 1998), pp. 23–5.
55. Kate Clanchy, 'Cool in my Forties', *Horizon Review* 2 (Salt Publishing 2004), www.saltpublishing.com/horizon/issues/02/text/bertram_vicki_interview.html, accessed 30 April 2013.

3

Mrs Worthington's Daughters: Drama

Gabriele Griffin

Women's engagement with drama and performance has a long tradition but it was in the 1970s that this tradition, shaped by the emergence of second-wave feminism, gained new urgency and drive, leading to an explosion of theatre and performance work by women which has continued unabated until the present.[1] As feminist playwright Caryl Churchill has stated:

> [E]ven in the spring of 1973, when a group of us were meeting to plan the first Women's Theatre Festival (at the Almost Free Theatre in London in the autumn of 1973), we weren't short of plays from which to choose for the three-month season. The submerged women playwrights were there – as they appear always to have been.[2]

That feminist-inspired explosion manifested itself in a concomitant expansion of feminist publishing so that the documentation and availability of women's theatre work, beyond the consumption of theatre as lived experience, became a real possibility: Methuen's *Plays by Women* series (1982–94) which ran to ten volumes was but one example of this.

The period of the 1970s to the post-2000s has seen significant changes in the drama-scape in Britain, closely aligned with wider socio-economic, political, and cultural changes. Politically, there were shifts from the Left to the Right under Britain's first female Prime Minister Margaret Thatcher (1979–90), to New Labour under Tony Blair (1997–2007), and to the Right again in the context of the rise of new religious fundamentalisms in the post-2000s and of a sustained economic crisis from 2008. These shifts have found their expression in changing arts policies and artistic productions.[3] These expressions range from a significant expansion of arts venues in the 1970s and early 1980s and a concomitant rise of touring theatre companies which provided fora for the work of women playwrights, directors, and actresses alike, to later cuts in Arts Council funding that led to the disbanding of many touring companies, and to the increasing commercialization of performance venues desperately seeking more income. These changes also, simultaneously and slowly, led to a steady increase of women in theatre in roles such as directors. Women moved from being extramural to becoming intramural so that in 2013 the Royal Court in London, the 'writer's theatre' dedicated to promoting new work, appointed Vicky Featherstone as its new artistic director. A different kind of London venue, the Tricycle Theatre – renowned both for its engagement with theatre work by writers from diverse ethnic communities, and for its productions of so-called *verbatim* theatre, theatre that depicts politically sensitive material drawn from public inquiries, Royal Commissions, and other forms of public investigation – appointed Indhu Rubasingham as its artistic director in 2012. These are but two examples of the greater incorporation of women into the arts world, and specifically in theatre, since the 1970s when no such scene could be envisaged and when, indeed, intramurality was less on women's minds than taking theatre to public spaces where it had not previously been seen, and to audiences who did not necessarily routinely attend theatre.

The 1970s: political theatre and the politics of theatre

Noël Coward's 1947 injunction to Mrs Worthington *not* to put her daughter on the stage was thoroughly disregarded by women in the 1970s who used performance in seven core ways, all strongly associated with feminist demands, namely to:

1. make women visible
2. take space (public and private) and make it their own
3. reclaim forgotten or buried histories of women's cultural production
4. foreground women's concerns
5. highlight how the personal was political
6. utilize cultural forms for political demands/ends
7. enable women to be assertively creative in contexts from which they were, or had traditionally been, debarred.

Much women's theatre and performance of the 1970s and indeed the early 1980s was strongly political. It was made by women invested in left-wing feminist politics and centred, at the level of content, on foregrounding women's issues. It refused androcentric cultural forms, modes of organizing and expression, and was frequently experimental in style, disrupting linear narratives, refusing the conventional structures of so-called well-made plays, playing with language. An in-yer-face attitude became the trade mark of much of this work, as well as taking that work to public spaces such as the street. Feminist political imperatives are evident in the names of the companies that were formed during this period such as the Sadista Sisters,[4] Monstrous Regiment [of Women], Beryl and the Perils, Cunning Stunts, Sphinx, Siren

Theatre Company, Spare Tyre, Clean Break, Women's Theatre Group,[5] Les Oeufs Malades. These names were intended to produce what Michel Foucault described as a 'reverse discourse', designed to take on and revalue words and phrases used to derogate women.[6] The names indicate a reclaiming of and an identification with all that is abjected in women: their demands, their size, their desires, their feminine specificities; a resistance to being told what to do and instead to own a doing that flies in the face of 'decorous femininity'; and a sense of engaging with traditions and histories of viewing women as mysterious, disturbing, and in need of containment. The diverse feminist touring companies had quite different kinds of aims: Les Oeufs Malades, for example, was established to produce the work of Bryony Lavery, one of the *grandes dames* of feminist theatre in Britain who continues to work in theatre.[7] Mrs Worthington's Daughters, on the other hand, was set up to produce forgotten plays by forgotten women playwrights, not least because funding was available for such work: 'the "plays from the past scheme" was intended as a reliable income. At the time reclaiming women's "herstory" was very popular, but no one was doing it in the theatre so we got funding quite easily.'[8]

In many ways, Methuen's first *Plays by Women* volume exemplifies all this. Edited by Michelene Wandor, one of a number of feminist playwrights to emerge in the 1970s and early 1980s, it opens with Monstrous Regiment's second touring production, *Vinegar Tom*, by Churchill. This play centres on the exploration of the persecution of women as witches, a topic extensively discussed in feminist circles trying to understand the various forms of oppression women had faced through the ages. The volume ends with Wandor's *Aurora Leigh*, based on the eponymous poetical work by the Victorian poet Elizabeth Barrett Browning, and concerned with women's struggle for presence and a voice in a male-dominated world. Both plays dealt with historical topics and figures, seeking to reclaim their meaning within new feminist frames.

The contexts for these productions are typical for their time. Churchill, for instance, remembered: 'I first met Monstrous Regiment on a march, abortion I think, early in 1976' (Wandor, p. 39). Coming together in a feminist political protest context, playwright and company forged links through their mutual interest in rethinking witches. Through a process of discussions and workshopping the play then emerged. Workshopping as a practice constituted a form of democratized theatre practice, enabling women performers to articulate their experiences, and giving plays shape through the dialogue between playwright and performers. It was closely aligned with other similar practices such as consciousness-raising and community theatre, both of which were regarded as liberatory and empowering.

Wandor, in a different vein from Churchill, had decided to send her play to three venerable, male-dominated British arts institutions, 'BBC radio, the National Theatre and the Royal Shakespeare Company', because

'I wanted the play done by people who had a tradition of dealing with dramatic verse' (p. 135). She had no luck since, as she put it, 'in 1977 the theatre was still riddled with gender-blindness. Very few women writers were having their work performed, "feminism" was a dirty word in most theatre criticism, and theatres were not ... acknowledging the relative absence of plays either by women or from women's point of view' (p. 135). So Wandor 'mentioned the play to a fringe group called Mrs Worthington's Daughters' who had formed in 1978 and who toured it so successfully in the autumn of 1979 that it was then bought by BBC Radio 3 and as a result subsequently also had a rehearsed reading at the National Theatre (p. 135). A similar fate of being conceived in a marginalized theatre space (relative to the building-based venues situated in London) and then transferring to 'capital' sites befell *Tissue*, the third play in Methuen's first *Plays by Women* volume, which centres on breast cancer and the impact of having a mastectomy. Commissioned by Birmingham Arts Lab from Louise Page, a feminist socialist playwright who remains a stalwart of the British arts scene writing for stage and for television, it was workshopped with the company and opened at the Studio Theatre of Coventry Belgrade on 3 May 1978, before transferring to the ICA Theatre in London and then in turn being produced for BBC Radio 4 by one of its long-standing women producers, Vanessa Whitburn. A few years later, Deborah Levy's play *Heresies* (1987) was put on by the Royal Shakespeare Company (RSC), directed by Lily Susan Todd.[9]

There are several points here: women's work for theatre tended to move from the arts margins to the centre; connections such as Levy's with Todd, who in turn had connections with the RSC, were important along the way; women's theatre work encountered and had to overcome significant gender biases and was powerfully invested in placing women's experiences centre-stage. This, importantly, included the production of plays with all-female casts as is the case for two of the four plays in the first Methuen volume. It is also the case that most long-standing feminist theatre practitioners have worked across different media, including radio, television, and the stage, and this from the 1970s onwards, not least for pecuniary reasons.

Dusa, Fish, Stas and Vi by Pam Gems (1925–2011), the fourth play in the first Methuen volume, is emblematic of a particular strand of plays that emerged in the late 1970s and early 1980s, as identity politics, and in particular notions of 'global sisterhood', came under strain from diverse groups of women asserting their sense of difference from middle-class white women whom they regarded as dominating certain scenes.[10] These plays brought together women from different backgrounds in order to explore their competing demands and needs. Thus *Dusa, Fish, Stas and Vi*, produced by Nancy Meckler, a then emerging and relatively rare woman theatre director, at the Hampstead Theatre in 1976, featured a mother abandoned by her husband and tellingly described in the 'Notes on the Characters' as having two children but 'not overtly "motherly", because she has two children, i.e., she is not soppy, or pea-brained or henlike. She *is* split, displaying the angst and vulnerability of the breeding bitch; also the restless boredom' (Wandor, p. 47). The language used here indicates both cliché and bias as well as a refusal of conventional feminine roles – it is doubtful that such vocabulary would be used now in a feminist play to describe a woman. This character is set against three other women: Fish, a woman of upper-class origin who has become a socialist political activist; Stas, a woman who works as a physiotherapist and simultaneously 'is a hostess at night, sleeping with men for high fees' in order to save money to study marine biology (Wandor, p. 47); and Violet, an anorexic teenage hippy figure. These women form a community of sorts through coming together in Fish's flat but are all very different in terms of class, though not, for example, race. They are bound together by certain mutual dependencies and imperfect efforts at mutual support as well as by their highly heteronormative construction as women exploited and/or victimized by men. The underlying idea of presenting all-female spaces continued to be explored in women's theatre work throughout the 1980s, but the question of differences among women and the meaning of those differences steadily came to the fore.

The 1980s: having it all?

One play which epitomizes the 1980s is Churchill's *Top Girls* (1980–82). This play, with its all-female cast,[11] has two halves, the first dedicated to a dinner party of women from different periods of history, all recounting their experiences of oppression by men, the other exploring the relationship between two women: a glamorous professional who has handed over her 'slow' daughter to be raised by her sister, who is a stay-at-home mum.[12] The play raised questions about an issue which is now more commonly termed the 'work/life balance' and whether or not women can 'have it all' – career and motherhood. That question, not even an option for many working-class women and not usually asked in relation to men, became newly urgent as women in the UK in growing numbers started to work full-time, partly for personal fulfilment and to be economically independent, increasingly from financial necessity.[13] The discussions about the im/possibility of 'having it all' began to explore a shift in both public (feminist) rhetoric and public policy which occurred during the 1980s from an emphasis on 'change' to an emphasis on 'choice'. Change here refers to the desire for the transformation of women's lives, with women often being conceived as victims, while 'choice' suggests agency and individual responsibility. Where 1970s feminism and hence women's theatre work had advocated for change, increasingly – and heralding the advent of neoliberalism – the focus shifted to notions of 'choice': the choices women had or did not have, the ones they made. This shift both de-emphasized structural factors as contributing to women's situation, and produced notions of individual and individualized responsibility, atomizing women's relations.

Importantly, *Top Girls* questioned assumptions about women's 'natural' proclivity to mother, a question that had already been raised by two of the best-known plays on daughter–mother relations that acted as antecedents of feminist work of the 1970s: *A Taste of Honey* (1958) by Shelagh Delaney (1938–2011) and Ann Jellicoe's *The Sport of My Mad Mother* (1958). I mention these to counteract the notion that the chronologized structure of this chapter signifies either progression or neatly differentiated categorization.[14] Women's use of street theatre in the 1970s to make political points, for instance, has antecedents in the suffrage plays of the 1920s which, tellingly, were (re)published by Methuen in 1985.[15]

The questioning of conventional gender roles, a key dimension of feminist work, went hand in hand with the questioning of other cultural conventions, including those of representation. That issue emerged partly from interrogations of the specificities of gender – to what extent did being a woman mean doing things differently from men, based, not least, on women's particular biological make-up – and partly on the politically inspired desire for change in women's situation.[16] Theatrically, the questioning of conventions effected both the script and the actual performance styles, with the former becoming more fragmented and the latter more physical and less speech-driven. Well-made sentences gave way to fragmentary speech styles, incomplete sentences, overlaps in speech signalled by slashes on the page, and other devices, all designed to at once and in some ways paradoxically make the use of language in theatre both more 'naturalistic' and less conventional. This is as evident in Churchill's scripts as it is in those of Deborah Levy, for example. As Lily Susan Todd, director of the first production of Levy's play *Pax* which was commissioned by the Women's Theatre Group in 1984, wrote: 'When I received *Pax*, I knew I was looking at something truly innovative ... it wasn't like anything I'd ever directed before. The play was made in a new language and I knew it was going to require all my art, in alliance with that of Anna Furse who had special skill in physical theatre, to create and sustain a concrete stage life for *Pax*.'[17]

A whole range of female playwrights such as Timberlake Wertenbaker, Sarah Daniels, April De Angelis, and Kay Adshead emerged in the 1980s who dealt with the gendered issues raised above. They frequently utilized historical material, as Wertenbaker did for instance in *New Anatomies* (n.d.), *The Grace of Mary Traverse* (1985), and *Our Country's Good* (1988), thus excavating women's forgotten *her*stories in order to raise questions about the (dis)continuities of women's experiences across time and space.[18] This process led to the 'unmaking of mimesis', as Elin Diamond's work proclaimed, in relation to the social realism that had ruled much drama in the UK from the 1940s onwards, and it aligned some of the new women's theatre work more closely with the Theatre of the Absurd and with Brechtian theatre.[19]

These performance frames eschewed the 'naturalistic' in favour of a defamiliarized form of production – designed to make the audience see and think anew. That defamiliarization as aesthetic and performance practice went together with the defamiliarization of female characters in terms of conventional feminine roles.

Unlike some of the work of the 1970s and very early 1980s that constructed women as victims of oppression, female playwrights during the 1980s increasingly constructed women as agentic in their own lives. Adshead's *Thatcher's Women* (1988), for instance, deals with sex-working around Kings Cross in London and the issue of different women's relative economic need which pitted them against each other, evident for example in women from the north of England suffering the effects of deindustrialization and unemployment relative to those from the capital itself. Practices that 1970s feminists had frequently viewed as expressions of women's oppression were by the 1980s recast as practical solutions to pressing socio-economic problems – not exactly condoned but neither entirely ruled out of court. Grace Daley's *Rose's Story* (1983), for instance, centred on teenage motherhood and a young black girl's choice to keep her baby, and her move away from her parents' deeply religious but simultaneously utterly uncharitable and punitive house into a mother–baby home. The pitting of mothers' lives and experiences against daughters' continued as a major theme; it was brought together strikingly in Jackie Kay's *Chiaroscuro* of 1986, commissioned by the Theatre of Black Women, which features a group of four women from radically different geographic and racial backgrounds who, as a way of exploring their own identities, begin by remembering their mothers' lives and how they, the daughters, came to be named. This play and the volume in which it was published[20] heralded two of the three key developments in women's drama that became particularly prominent in the 1990s and which I shall discuss below: the exploration of sexualized identities and the emergence of queer; the arrival of in-yer-face theatre; and the explosion of drama by and for women from diverse ethnic backgrounds.

The 1990s: sex and violence?

The writings of American lesbian-feminist theatre critics Jill Dolan and Sue-Ellen Case as well as that of gender activist/performer Kate Bornstein articulated one of the key preoccupations of especially late 1980s and early 1990s theatre,[21] that of gender bending, cross-dressing, and lesbian/queer identities.[22] One important theatre group associated with this period was Split Britches, a US company that dated back to the 1980s but became well known in the UK only in the 1990s when they toured the country, performing at London's then foremost lesbian and gay performance space, the Drill Hall (now sadly defunct). Lois Weaver, co-founder of Split Britches, eventually became a Professor of Drama at Queen Mary, University of London.

Another American queer performance group that toured queer conferences in Britain and performed mainly in London and Manchester was Dorothy Talk.[23] Queer performance went hand in hand with the recovery of older gender-bending performance traditions, in particular cross-dressing and burlesque. The Drill Hall in London repeatedly hosted one of Britain's best-known and somewhat controversial female performers, Claire Dowie. Her gender-bending work, in both its refusal of conventional lesbian-feminist lines and its embrace of gender uncertainty, articulated in one-hander performances such as *Why Is John Lennon Wearing a Skirt?* (1991), *Leaking from Every Orifice* (1993), *Drag Act* (1993), and *Easy Access (for the Boys)* (1998), acted as a trademark for the new production of gender in performance where sexual identity remained in flux.[24]

The questioning of identities, in this instance in relation to gender and sexuality, which these plays entailed became much more problematically radicalized in the drama of 'the nasty nineties' described by Aleks Sierz as 'in-yer-face' theatre,[25] a 'theatre of sensation' which, employing 'shock tactics' and 'questioning moral norms', 'affront[ed] the ruling ideas of what can or should be shown onstage; it also tap[ped] into more primitive feelings, smashing taboos, mentioning the forbidden, creating discomfort'.[26] In-yer-face theatre, though mainly boys' own (that is, dominated by male playwrights), was also strongly associated with the work of certain women playwrights such as Sarah Kane (1971–99), American lesbian playwright Phyllis Nagy (who lived for a time in the UK), as well as Judy Upton and to some extent Rebecca Prichard. The plays in question frequently featured rape, including anal rape and rape utilizing objects, aggression more generally, extreme, often onstage violence and mutilation, and expletive language. Raising concerns that had begun to surface in the course of Margaret Thatcher's premiership about the evisceration of moral values, these plays were postfeminist in the sense that they were no longer preoccupied with women's rights or with equality but instead engaged with primal expressions of anger and rage, non-directional and all-encompassing. The plays used women's bodies, but not just women's bodies, as both vehicle and objects for these emotions. The plays were aligned with the rising presence of sexual exploitation, of violence and of gang culture in popular cultural productions such as video games but also on film and television more generally. They also came to the fore during the period of genocidal intra-European wars in the former Yugoslavia in which violent and aggressive behaviour, mainly by men against both women and men, became an almost unchallenged norm, highlighting the impotence of liberal states to prevent mass cruelty and destruction. This was replayed in Kane's *Blasted* (1995), whilst the violence of gang culture found its expression in Rebecca Prichard's *Yard Gal* (1997–98), for example.[27]

Against a certain affect-laden nihilism in this kind of theatre, a completely different type of work also emerged: that of women of diverse ethnic origins, specifically Black and South Asian women. Often young, they were frequently but not invariably the UK-born daughters of first- or second-generation migrants, mostly educated in the UK, and beginning to articulate much more extensively the (gendered) experience of racism in Britain. Repeatedly working together with Black and Asian theatre companies such as Black Theatre Co-operative and Kali, run by Black and South Asian women such as Yvonne Brewster, Paulette Randall, and Rukhsana Ahmad, playwrights Shelley Silas, Nina Patel, Tanika Gupta, Meera Syal, Winsome Pinnock, Maya Chowdhry, Dolly Dhingra, Jacqueline Rudet, Zindika, Valerie Mason-John, and many others saw their work promoted in a range of sites.[28] Their plays, part of the canon of 'postcolonial theatre' that began to become prominent, invariably spoke of the struggles of diaspora and migration, of women's roles within the family, of cross-generational and intra- as well as intercommunity antagonisms, of the problematic of racism, and, importantly, the experiences of being mixed-race.[29] Both Mason-John and Zindika, for example, construct female characters in their work who break down as a consequence of the difficulty of living a mixed-race existence, unaccepted as fully black or white and struggling to belong. Aurora Press produced a range of volumes that collected this work.[30] Black and South Asian women playwrights such as Chowdhry or Kay also engaged with questions of sexual identity, in many ethnic communities still something of a taboo topic,[31] and with the Islamicization of contemporary cultures, a topic that gained new intensity in the 2000s.

The 2000s and beyond

Women's work for theatre since 2000 has been affected by four major developments: the impacts of 9/11 and the London bombings of 7/7, which have resulted in drama dealing with trauma, witnessing, inter-ethnic and inter-/intra-faith relations; the diversification of performance media through the rapid development of new media which has impacted on performance production, dissemination, and the documenting and preservation of ephemeral performances; the impacts of globalization; and the effects of the post-2008 recession on arts funding. The last three issues point to a further important development: the renewed extramuralization of performance as women (and men) work across different media, in new spaces, and with new audiences.

Nonetheless, many of the playwrights and concerns that emerged in the 1990s continued during the 2000s. Tanika Gupta's *Sanctuary* (2002), for instance, dealt with genocide and its aftermath whilst Atiha Sen Gupta's *What Fatima Did ...* (2009) raised the question of female veiling and anti-Muslim sentiment. Importantly, both were set in England, reinforcing the fact that post-9/11 and post the 7/7 London bombings, multiculturalism as it had been practised and praised in the UK throughout the 1990s was coming under pressure as an effective means of fostering social cohesion, both across and within communities. Tanika Gupta's *Fragile Land* (2003) was a contribution to this debate. Nothing made these issues more explicit, however, than the incidents surrounding Gurpreet Kaur Bhatti's *Behzti (Dishonour)* (2004), a play for the Birmingham Rep, one of the regional UK theatres that, like the West Yorkshire Playhouse, the Corner House in Manchester, the Tricycle Theatre and the Royal Theatre Stratford in London, had promoted work from diverse ethnic communities. *Behzti* centred on the problematic and dishonourable treatment of women within the Sikh community, featuring the rape of a young woman by the Chairman of a gurdwara (a Sikh community and religious centre). The play provoked significant protests from (young) men within the community,[32] supposedly because the rape was set in a gurdwara, leading to immediate closure on opening and to its author going into hiding.[33] This event formed part of an increasing public debate about censorship in the arts and beyond, particularly, but not only, around the Islamic religion.[34] Judith Jones and Beatrix Campbell's *And All the Children Cried* (2002), directed by veteran feminist Annie Castledine,[35] had also been the subject of considerable public debate – but not a gendered riot-style protest – since it centred on Myra Hindley,[36] the female partner in the so-called Moors murders. However, as Lyn Gardner, long-time arts critic, said in her sympathetic critique of the play, 'there is nothing salacious in its investigation into the psyches and circumstances of women who kill children'.[37]

Whilst female playwrights, new and emerging as well as established ones such as those above, relied on building-based theatres to produce their work, by the 2000s many of the feminist touring companies that were established in the 1970s and early 1980s had died away, not least because of the reduction in funding from the Arts Council of England. Susan Croft has established an ongoing web-based project, 'Unfinished Histories', to document their work.[38] Companies with specific briefs such as Clean Break Theatre Company, who specialize in work with female prisoners, or Kali, who promote South Asian work, have found it easier to survive than those with generic women-centred concerns. A smallish group of individual women playwrights, for example Moira Buffini, Polly Stenham, Nina Raine, Bola Agbaje, Anya Reiss, and Laura Wade, have benefited from being associated with the Royal Court Theatre in London which has done much to promote young women playwrights.[39] But, as the Arts Council of England suggests in its Strategic Framework for the Arts 2011–15:

> Definitions of theatre have been stretched beyond those used a generation ago. Outdoor festivals such as Latitude showcase theatre, and increasingly theatre can be found in unexpected places, such as under railway arches, in docks, on the streets and in disused office buildings. Experiments have begun in digital broadcasting: NT Live reached 50,000

> people worldwide with *Phèdre*. There has been an increase in the amount of participatory work among people of all ages and in the number of people volunteering within theatre organisations ... The encouragement of diversity among artists and audiences is slowly forging change, but there is much still to be done.[40]

The image produced here is of theatre moving extramurally again, especially to relate to greater ranges of audiences but also making use of new technologies for the same purpose and to disseminate its work more widely. In some ways this draws on prior extramural performance work such as street theatre, the performance art of the 1960s and 1970s, and post-2000 performance art both online and offline to which women have extensively contributed. An interesting example of this was *Peace Camp* (2012) by Deborah Warner and Fiona Shaw, simultaneously installation and recitation, set in 'eight remote locations around Britain'.[41]

The changes described above are cast by the Arts Council in the frame of a shifting 'business model':

> The traditional theatre business models are being rethought. Theatres ... are working more collaboratively, increasing their capacity ... to take [theatre] to more people. Partnerships between commercial and subsidised theatre businesses have increased in range and number. Kneehigh's production of *Brief Encounter* was created with the Birmingham Rep, remounted with support from Royal and Derngate in Northampton, presented in the West End and toured by a commercial producer.[42]

I quote this at length because it points to trends in contemporary production that reinforce the commercialization of theatre, with inevitable consequences for its practitioners who, like Syal, may try their hands at musicals such as *Bombay Dreams* (2002) to garner new audiences. Such diversification signals the prominence of the middlebrow in contemporary cultural production; women have been significant participants in this and, since the 1980s, *inter alia* as writers and producers for television. One need only think of the work of Lynda La Plante, encouraged by Verity Lambert, Head of Commissioning at Thames Television, who wrote the series *Prime Suspect,* starring Helen Mirren.

Audiences more generally now consume theatre and performance in different ways, and especially online sites such as YouTube have made it possible for viewers to sample work from across the globe so that a woman in Britain may easily watch past and contemporary drama produced in the US and elsewhere. One useful consequence of this is that work that has tended to remain undocumented, which made it easy to 'hide women from history', is now much more readily conserved online. A good example of this is the work of Bobby Baker who has made one-woman performance events for decades. Baker's work has continuously been characterized by engagement with specifically female forms of experience, the absurdities of which she exposes in searing and painfully visceral depictions of her own life.[43] *Diary Drawings: Mental Illness and Me* (2010), funded by the Wellcome Trust, took the form of an exhibition as well as a book of drawings that articulate her long-term experiences with mental illness. Many of Baker's performances are available on YouTube.[44]

Viewing as practice has also expanded significantly, ranging from mass-gathered audiences at festivals such as Wilderness to atomized experiences in front of one's computer.[45] Performance now travels online and offline: Amelia Jones, writing about queer performance art, tells us that *Judas Cradle* 'conceived and performed by Ron Athey and Juliana Snapper, with sound design by Amanda Piaseki and costume design by Susan Mattheson ... was commissioned by Fierce! Festival with support from Arts Council England' – but she first saw it in Ljubljana.[46] This raises questions about the aesthetics, ethics, and politics of contemporary drama which acquires new meanings in different contexts but also becomes decontextualized – globalized? – through its very mobility. It also suggests the new networking society in which opportunities for women in drama have grown even as they are still not quite there in and on equal terms.

Notes

1. See, for example, Catherine Burroughs, *Women in British Romantic Theatre: Drama, Performance and Society 1790–1840* (Cambridge University Press, 2000); Kate Newey, *Women's Theatre Writing in Victorian Britain* (Basingstoke: Palgrave Macmillan, 2005); Mary A. Schofield and Cecilia Macheski, eds, *Curtain Calls: British and American Women and the Theatre, 1660–1820* (Athens: Ohio University Press, 1991). Also Susan Croft, *She Also Wrote Plays* (London: Faber and Faber, 2001).
2. Caryl Churchill, 'Introduction', *Plays by Women,* Vol. 1, ed. Michelene Wandor (London: Methuen, 1982), p. 9.
3. See the historical account of the Arts Council of England, www.artscouncil.org.uk/who-we-are/history-arts-council/, accessed 7 July 2013.
4. See http://sadistasisters.blogspot.co.uk/, accessed 7 July 2013, for details.
5. See www.thefword.org.uk/reviews/2008/12/cunning_stunts, accessed 7 July 2013, for details of some of these groups' work.
6. Michel Foucault, *The History of Sexuality*, Vol. 1, trans. Robert Hurley (London: Allen Lane, 1978), p. 76.
7. On 28 February 2013, for example, her play *Thursday* about the 7 July 2005 bombings in London premiered in Adelaide, Australia.
8. See Liz Goodman, *Contemporary Feminist Theatres: To Each Her Own* (London: Routledge, 1993), p. 7.
9. See www.unfinishedhistories.com/interviews/interviewees/lily-susan-todd, accessed 25 September 2014, for details of Todd's very interesting career.
10. Pam Gems remained a significant feminist figure on the British theatre scene. She died in 2011. See www.pamgemsplays.com/Pam_Gems_Plays/Pam_Gems_Plays.html, accessed 11 June 2013, for details of her work.

11. Plays with all-female casts remained common until the middle of the 1980s. See, for example, the collection *Pulp and Other Plays by Tasha Fairbanks*, ed. Gabriele Griffin and Elaine Aston (London: Harwood Press, 1996).
12. That dinner party has its feminist antecedent in Judy Chicago's piece *The Dinner Party* (1974–79) – see https://www.brooklynmuseum.org/exhibitions/dinner_party/, accessed 12 July 2013.
13. In 1970, 52 per cent of women of working age in the UK were in employment – by 2000 this had risen to 70 per cent (see Jason Strelitz, 'Tackling Disadvantage', p. 61, report for the Joseph Rowntree Foundation, at www.jrf.org.uk/sites/files/jrf/1859350909-4.pdf, accessed 12 July 2013).
14. For a theoretical elaboration of this point, see Clare Hemmings, *Why Stories Matter* (Durham, NC: Duke University Press, 2011).
15. Candida Lacey, Dale Spender, and Carole Haymen, eds, *How the Vote Was Won and Other Suffrage Plays* (London: Methuen, 1985).
16. The theoretical 'backdrop' for this was the highly influential notion of *écriture féminine* or 'writing the body', explored in particular by feminist theoreticians inspired by psychoanalysis such as Luce Irigaray, Hélène Cixous, and Julia Kristeva.
17. Deborah Levy, *Plays 1* (London: Methuen, 2000), p. 3.
18. Timberlake Wertenbaker, *Plays 1* (London: Faber and Faber, 1996).
19. Elin Diamond, *Unmaking Mimesis* (London: Routledge, 1997).
20. Jill Davis, ed., *Lesbian Plays* (London: Methuen, 1987).
21. Jill Dolan, *Presence and Desire: Essays on Gender, Sexuality and Performance* (Ann Arbor: University of Michigan Press, 1993); Sue-Ellen Case, ed., *Split Britches: Lesbian Practice, Feminist Perfomance* (London: Routledge, 1996); Kate Bornstein, *Gender Outlaw: On Men, Women and the Rest of Us* (London: Routledge, 1994).
22. For British commentators on and performers of this, see Nina Rapi and Maya Chowdhry, eds, *Acts of Passion: Sexuality, Gender, and Performance* (London: Routledge, 1998), and Lesley Ferris, *Crossing the Stage: Controversies on Cross-Dressing* (London: Routledge, 1993).
23. See their play *Walking on Peas* in Gabriele Griffin and Elaine Aston, eds, *Subversions: Playing with History in Women's Theatre* (Amsterdam: Harwood Academic Publishers, 1997).
24. Claire Dowie, *Why Is John Lennon Wearing a Skirt and Other Stand-Up Theatre Plays* (London: Methuen, 1996); Claire Dowie, *Easy Access (for the Boys) and All Over Lovely* (London: Methuen, 1998).
25. www.inyerface-theatre.com, accessed 19 July 2013, is the relevant online archive.
26. Aleks Sierz, *In-Yer-Face Theatre: British Drama Today* (London: Faber and Faber, 2001).
27. Sarah Kane, *Complete Plays* (London: Methuen, 2001); Rebecca Prichard, *Yard Gal* (London: Faber and Faber, 1997).
28. See Gabriele Griffin, *Contemporary Black and Asian Women Playwrights* (Cambridge University Press, 2003) for an extended discussion of these.
29. See Helen Gilbert and Joanne Tompkins, *Post-Colonial Drama* (London: Routledge, 1996).
30. For example, Kadija George, ed., *Six Plays by Black and Asian Women* (London: Aurora Metro Press, 1993); Cheryl Robson, ed., *Seven Plays by Women* (London: Aurora Metro Press, 1993).
31. See Ann Pellegrini's *Performance Anxieties: Staging Psychoanalysis, Staging Race* (New York: Routledge, 1997) as a useful exploration of this.
32. The media images of the riot-style protests outside the theatre show only men.

33. See Gabriele Griffin, 'Gagging: Gender, Performance and the Politics of Intervention', *Contemporary Theatre Review*, 17:4 (2007), pp. 541–9. Kaur Bhatti herself commented on this experience in a subsequent play, *Behud (Beyond Belief)*, which opened at the Soho Theatre in 2010.
34. The *Contemporary Theatre Review* issue (2007), 17:4, was devoted to exploring this.
35. She also edited the last volumes (nine and ten) in Methuen's *Plays by Women* series.
36. Myra Hindley was arrested with her boyfriend Ian Brady in October 1965. They became infamous as the 'Moors murderers' for burying at least three of their victims on Saddleworth Moor in Yorkshire, UK.
37. Lyn Gardner, 'And All the Children Cried', *Guardian*, 27 April 2002, www.guardian.co.uk/stage/2002/apr/27/theatre.artsfeatures, accessed 17 July 2013.
38. www.unfinishedhistories.com/, accessed 17 July 2013.
39. See Kate Kellaway, 'Royal Court Theatre Prepares to Bid Farewell to King Dominic', *Guardian*, 10 March 2013, www.guardian.co.uk/stage/2013/mar/10/royal-court-bids-farewell?INTCMP=SRCH, accessed 4 March 2013.
40. Arts Council of England, *Achieving Great Art for All: Theatre – Achievements, Challenges and Opportunities*, consultation paper appendix, www.artscouncil.org.uk/what-we-do/supporting-artforms/theatre/, accessed 17 July 2013.
41. See http://artsbeat.blogs.nytimes.com/2012/07/20/deborah-warner-and-fiona-shaw-bring-peace-camp-to-england/, accessed 19 July 2013, for details.
42. Emma Rice co-runs Kneehigh.
43. Baker also represents an example of a woman artist who has worked across media.
44. See, for example, *How To Shop, Box Story, A Model Family, Pull Yourself Together Harleem, Kitchen Show, How to Live* – all available on YouTube, see www.youtube.com/results?search_query=Bobby+Baker, accessed 17 July 2013.
45. See www.wildernessfestival.com/theme/staged-plays-cirque-traditionnel-promenade-performance/, accessed 18 July 2013, for theatre performance details of the 2013 festival.
46. Amelia Jones, 'Holy Body: Erotic Ethics in Ron Athey and Juliana Snapper's *Judas Cradle*', *TDR*, 50:1 (2006), pp. 159–69.

4
Media Old and New

Deborah Chambers

The vibrancy of women's literary writing in the UK from the 1970s to the present is matched by the diversity of women's journalistic writing over the same period. The unstable boundary between news and literary journalism, made fluid by rapid social, cultural, and technological change, makes the field difficult to define. Consequently, journalism is often treated as a devalued cultural form.[1] Yet the importance of this area is indicated by the considerable number of successful novelists who began their careers as journalists – Angela Carter (1940–92), Helen Fielding, and Zoë Heller, for instance – and by literary authors who moved into journalism, such as Jeanette Winterson, Zadie Smith, and Bidisha.[2]

As Richard Keeble explains, the term 'journalist' originally referred to writers who published in periodicals, who were distinguished from authors of literature.[3] Early eighteenth-century forms of journalism identified with newspapers and popular culture were associated with vulgarity and sleaze. Yet they evolved to include literary essays, polemical writing, legislative reports, and work in 'serious journals of opinion' (Keeble, p. 3).[4] Those who thought that journalism occupied a marginal position compared to 'aristocratic writers of literature' often adopted a confrontational tone (Keeble, p. 4), with journalists in the 1800s such as William Hazlitt vigorously defending the craft of literary journalism among other forms of creativity.[5] While associations with sleaze and questions about the seriousness of this tradition initially acted as barriers to women, this polemical style has since underpinned and characterized the emergence of a creative, subversive, and flourishing form of woman-centred writing. This chapter examines the influences of women writers in both newspaper and literary journalism in Britain. It demonstrates how passionate, strongly worded, and often controversial arguments became the hallmark of the writing of recent feminist, campaigning, literary and tabloid women journalists.

The 'women's page' and human interest stories

In the late nineteenth century, journalism was a male-dominated and hierarchical profession. However, when newspapers began to depend on advertising revenue from the 1880s, a new form of 'women's journalism' emerged to attract women readers. Consigned to the 'society' pages, women developed a style of news restricted to reports on weddings, changing fashions, and feature articles on domestic issues.[6] For educated, middle-class women who saw journalism as an attractive career, the profession provided an escape from the confinement of domestic space. Yet, ironically, they found themselves restricted to news about that space. Women's pages were commonplace in the tabloid popular press by the 1950s. Later in the same decade broadsheets such as the *Guardian* followed suit to attract advertisers. Women's reportage was segregated through separation of their feature writing from front-page reports on politics and foreign news written by men. This division was based on a distinction between 'soft' and 'hard' news.[7] While 'hard news' was associated with politics and conflict, 'soft news' stories were 'often defined as having a "woman's angle" and regarded as "fluff"'.[8]

Nevertheless, these women's pages offered women an important entrance into the profession. Male reporters refused to cover the 'four F's': family,

Figure 1 Sarah Raphael's *Women's Page Contributors to the* Guardian (1994) © National Portrait Gallery

food, fashion, and furnishing. Although the woman's page conceived 'women's issues' as apolitical, this section was 'the one place where they had the power to define news'.[9] This history offers important insights into an understanding of the trend, led by women from the 1970s, of devoting considerable portions of newspapers to lifestyle, fashion, gossip, celebrity news, and reviews. Yet, at the same time, ignited by second-wave feminism, serious news relating to women's lives was also being published on these pages by the early 1970s.

Despite being typecast, female journalists were establishing a more informal style that paved the way for exploring the relationship between the personal and the political. For example, feminist and journalist Mary Stott (1907–2002), editor of the *Guardian*'s women's pages from 1957 to 1972, moved beyond social events and fashion advice to include social and political issues. Many issues aired by Stott on these pages prompted direct action. She featured the lives of 'ordinary' working- and middle-class women, producing articles that encouraged women to form supportive networks and generate solidarity across class, ages, and cultures.[10] With an accent on human interest stories, the women's page often challenged the conventional values of domesticity with reports and features on women's health, children's issues, rape law, domestic violence, and women's wages.

A dilemma was expressed by Polly Toynbee, who wrote for the woman's page in the *Guardian* from 1977 to 1988:

> Although it was a great honour, I'm ashamed to admit that, like many others, I hesitated before joining. Although I was always a feminist and never a feminism-denier, I worried I'd be branded a single-issue women's columnist, a bit frivolous, no longer fit for the men's newsroom. Would I ever get back to the 'mainstream'? Lurking somewhere beneath was that old fear of being branded as a bra-burning harridan. Well, I stayed for 11 years, some of the best years of my working life, and it changed my view of the world.[11]

Despite its contradictions, then, the rise of the women's page and related features advanced the careers of women writers and provided a vital space for publicizing feminist issues. At the same time, independent 1970s radical publications such as *Spare Rib* and *Trouble and Strife* offered an alternative to mass-market women's magazines and played a key role in disseminating ideas central to the Women's Liberation Movement. As well as co-founding Virago, Rosie Boycott founded the radical feminist magazine *Spare Rib* with Marsha Rowe. Launched in 1972 and run as a collective, *Spare Rib* scrutinized women's traditional roles and explored alternatives. Various streams of the movement, such as socialist, radical, revolutionary, lesbian, liberal, and black feminism were hotly debated among its pages. The magazine folded in 1993 due to financial difficulties related to its principle of excluding commercial advertising.

In April 2013 Charlotte Raven announced her intention to relaunch *Spare Rib* as a glossy new title with free-to-access website and a tagline – 'Life not lifestyle' – designed to distinguish it from 'the PR and celebrity-filled women's magazines' on the market. Raven said it would offer 'top tips on keeping our female friends when all around are goading us into "bitch fests" and "catfights" – instead of cupcake recipes'.[12] Significantly, the new magazine promised to be the first to be run as a members' organization. This decision highlights the moral and professional dilemmas associated with the financing of UK titles, particularly for feminist, minority ethnic, and left-wing publishers likely to rely on small circulations and to be critical of today's new media advertising and PR systems. After copyright issues over the name, the magazine was launched on the web on 3 October 2013 under the title *Feminist Times*. However, on 14 July 2014, funding problems meant that it was put 'on ice'.[13]

Pioneering media women and campaigning journalists

In the 1970s mainstream press, women were moving beyond the 'women's page' to become feature writers and columnists. Yet they were expected to contribute something distinctive from their male colleagues. Human interest journalism, characterized by highly personalized styles, was evolving in two key ways. First, several successful women columnists and media pioneers gained fame and notoriety as the 'bitches from Fleet Street'. Second, many women journalists brought a feminist approach to their writing, with some becoming campaigners for reform laws on issues pertaining to women's lives.

Pioneering media women

The first category of women whose recognition is based on provocative styles of working or writing involves columnists pouring scorn on public figures and assertive women media managers. Women journalists who become leaders in their fields are regularly stereotyped by male colleagues and presented as highly controversial figures. They are all too often demonized as hard-hitting media moguls. This is confirmed by the public responses to prominent figures such as Jean Rook (1931–91), Ann Leslie, Lynn Barber, Suzanne Moore, Julie Burchill, Janet Street-Porter, and Rebekah Brooks (associated with the *News of the World* hacking scandal but acquitted of all charges at the trial in June 2014).

Rook led the way for a string of successful women columnists described by Carol Sarler as 'Fleet Street's bitch goddesses'.[14] She was hailed as 'The First Lady of Fleet Street' for her opinion column in the *Daily Express*. She also admitted that she was the inspiration for *Private Eye*'s parodic portrait of fictional female columnist 'Glenda Slagg' which caricatured Rook as a brassy-styled 'scurrilous hackett'.[15] Becoming fashion editor for the *Sun* in 1964, Rook expressed great pride in succeeding in a male-dominated industry. She described how she 'clawed and scrambled' her way to become 'Britain's bitchiest, best known, loved and loathed woman journalist' (Massingberd, p. 203). During the height of her career in the 1970s, Rook was renowned for her withering comments about public figures. She suggested that the Queen should pluck her eyebrows, called Sarah Ferguson (then Duchess of York) the 'Duchess of Pork',[16] and referred to Prince Philip as a 'sponger'.[17] Rook was unable to come to terms with what she dubbed 'hairy-legged feminism' (Booth, p. 5), and carved out a style of writing for women columnists that was valued by male editors.[18] She summarized her work by stating:

> My readers look for the worst in me. They love me to sink my teeth and typewriter keys into some public figure they're dying to have a go at themselves, more especially if it's some sacred cow – or bull – who's never criticized by journalists who won't kick a man when he's up.[19]

In a similar vein, Barber has been labelled the 'Demon Barber of Fleet Street' for her entertaining yet intimidating interviews with and reviews about public figures. An interview Barber conducted with conceptual artists Jake and Dinos Chapman was manifestly fraught. The Chapman Brothers warned they would kill her if they ever met again.[20] Barber was sued in 2011 for libel and malicious falsehood in response to her *Daily Telegraph* review of Sarah Thornton's book *Seven Days in the Artworld* (2008).[21] And when artist Lucien Freud responded to Barber's invitation to lunch, he wrote, 'I do eat lunch but I see no reason why I should be shat on by a stranger.'[22] Barber has been feature writer for several major newspapers since the 1980s and won six British press awards. Her memoir of a teenage love affair, *An Education* (2009), began as a short piece on a related idea written for *Granta,* and was made into a film by Nick Hornby in 2009.[23]

The confrontational style spearheaded by Rook also characterizes the work of Suzanne Moore, indicated by the title of a collection of her reprinted features, *Looking for Trouble* (1991). Moore famously ran into trouble when she entered into a public spat with Germaine Greer in 1995 and made contentious remarks about the transsexual community in the *New Statesman* in 2013.[24] However, she established her significance as a feminist columnist in articles that address topics such as the fashion industry, single mothers, and screen violence. Rejecting the view that the interface of the personal and political results in 'the tabloidization of serious matters', she seeks to convey 'the other side of the story' and to question 'why things mean what they do or how they have got to be defined that way'.[25]

Leslie's role as a pioneering woman journalist has led to her reporting on momentous global events. These include the fall of the Berlin Wall in

1989, the release of Mandela in 1990, and the failed attempt to overthrow Gorbachev in 1991. Emphasizing human interest angles in her reporting, Leslie has received many awards for her work at the *Daily Mail* and was made a Dame in 2006. While moving up the career ladder, she was confronted by male hostility. Her determination to succeed as a foreign correspondent was fuelled by responses from the 'macho thugs' on the foreign desk at the *Express* in the 1960s who thought a 'girlie' was incapable of foreign reporting.[26] She left the *Express* in 1967 after being rejected for the New York bureau job on the grounds of being thought capable of interviewing only politicians' wives rather than politicians themselves. By establishing vigorous, provocative styles, these writers convey ground-breaking qualities in raising the profile of women in mainstream journalism. However, their relationship to feminism differs considerably. While Rook and Leslie have never claimed to be feminists, Barber explores gender and power through sexual themes, Moore writes with 'an implicit feminist agenda' (Moore, p. xii), and Burchill is a self-declared 'militant feminist'.[27]

Women campaigning journalists

Campaigning journalists such as Marjorie Proops (1911–96), Jill Tweedie (1936–93), and Toynbee have courted controversy in ways that differ from the pioneering women and confrontational columnists above. By advancing the maxim 'the personal is political', campaigners have championed women's causes and shaped debates within the women's pages and beyond. Proops, who started her career in 1939 as a fashion correspondent, began her *Daily Mirror* column in 1971. As the 'problem page' editor, she became the most famous agony aunt in the UK and was awarded an OBE in 1969. Proops's column had a major impact on newspaper content and approach. She used it to campaign for several causes including rape victims. Proops advocated contraception, sex education, and tolerance towards homosexuality. Recognition of Proops's contribution to the paper's success led to promotion as assistant editor of the *Mirror* in 1978. Following Proops, Tweedie wrote a column for the *Guardian* for over 22 years from 1969 to 1988 and became an influential writer and broadcaster. She was among the first to write about major feminist subjects in the *Guardian* women's page, including the treatment of women during childbirth, rape in marriage, bride burning in India, and female circumcision.

The collection of awards bestowed on Toynbee proves that her 11-year stint on the *Guardian* women's page formed a major platform for a successful career, despite her initial concerns. After dropping out of Oxford she moved into journalism and worked at the *Observer*. In 1998 Toynbee won the Orwell Prize for journalism and was named 'Columnist of the Year' at the British Press Awards 2007. Described as 'the queen of leftist journalists', Toynbee is a social democrat and supporter of the Labour Party, whose politics informs her writing.[28] For example, her book *Hard Work: Life in Low-Paid*

Britain (2003) was highly critical of low-paid jobs in Britain. Women journalists who branched out from fashion, household tips, and recipes achieved recognition and received awards as column and feature writers by addressing significant political and personal women's issues from a feminist perspective. These writers have challenged the stubborn distinctions between 'hard' and 'soft' news. This new politicized style of column writing reveals the immense skill involved in publicizing complex political issues.

Beatrix Campbell has led a long and distinguished career as a left-wing feminist journalist. As well as publishing in the *New Statesman, New Socialist,* the *Guardian,* and the *Independent,* she has made a series of documentary films including *Listen to the Children* (1990), which addresses child abuse. Active in the Women's Liberation Movement, she joined the Communist Party of Great Britain when it was transforming its official trade union ideology to embrace a more feminist and multicultural agenda, and was a founder of the feminist journal *Red Rag* (1973–80). *Wigan Pier Revisited* (1984), winner of the Cheltenham Festival Literary Prize, records the rise in poverty and unemployment in Thatcher's Britain. Her other books include *Goliath: Britain's Dangerous Places* (1993), *Diana, Princess of Wales: How Sexual Politics Shook the Monarchy* (1998), and *End of Equality* (2014). Campbell is a member of the Free Communications Group and campaigns against monopoly ownership of the mass media. Like many political writers, she has attracted controversy. When working as sub-editor on the *Morning Star* newspaper, she was criticized for receiving state-subsidized holidays to Communist East Germany. However, Campbell was also named Campaigning Journalist of the Year in 1989 by the 300 Group (an organization that seeks to increase the number of women in Parliament) and was awarded an OBE for her services to equality in 2009.

Zoë Williams is another journalist known for her left-wing, feminist views. Drawing on personal experience, she has published political commentary, columns, interviews, and reviews in the *Guardian, New Statesman, Spectator,* and *London Evening Standard,* for which she has also written a diary about being a single woman in the city. Her book *What Not to Expect When You're Expecting* (2012), inspired by her own pregnancy, offers a humorous antidote to standard parenting books by critiquing the medical establishment, middle-class campaigning groups that promote breastfeeding, and 'the sacred myths propagated by self-righteous parents'.[29] Williams was named Columnist of the Year 2010 at the WorkWorld Media Awards.

A freelance journalist and self-identified political lesbian feminist, Julie Bindel's provocative style – exemplified by articles such as 'Why I hate men' and 'Why men hate me' – divides opinion.[30] She first published in the *Independent* in 1998 on prostitution and then wrote a column for the *Guardian* in 2001 addressing gay and lesbian issues, articulating opposition to the sex industry, prostitution, and violence against women, highlighting victims of domestic violence, and advocating child protection. Bindel also co-founded Justice for Women (JFW) in 1990, an organization that supports women who have fought back against or killed violent male partners.

Campaigning journalists confirm the diversity of feminist writers' political positions in advancing women's causes. For instance, Yasmin Alibhai-Brown is recognized for her incisive commentary on issues of race and religion. She moved into journalism in her mid-thirties after working as a teacher, mostly with immigrants and refugees. She has written for the *New Statesman* and several broadsheets, and now contributes a weekly column to the *Independent*. In 2002 Alibhai-Brown won the George Orwell Prize for political journalism. As well as writing about immigration, race, and multicultural society, she has published several books which explore the themes addressed in her journalism, including *Mixed Feelings: The Complex Lives of Mixed Race Britons* (2001). Alibhai-Brown severed her connections with the Labour Party over the war in Iraq in 2003. Appointed a Member of the British Empire (MBE) in 2001, Alibhai-Brown returned her award two years later when Benjamin Zephaniah publicly refused an OBE. She has criticized the British honours system as 'beyond repair'.[31] The courting of controversy while publicizing women's issues is a major attribute that campaigning women share in common with pioneering women journalists.

Women's literary journalism

A polemical style characterizes the writing of several women literary journalists. This quality of feminist writing coincides with the multiple aims of journalism, ranging from democratic considerations to entertainment and argument. Yet literary journalism still holds a precarious position within literary culture and the academic world. The journalism of novelists, poets, and playwrights is often undervalued and this is particularly true for female authors. Their writing has crossed the boundaries of essay, review, polemic, literature. During the 1970s, literary journalism was affirmed as a new genre through 'New Journalism', involving fiction as well as social commentary.[32] Blurring the boundaries between journalism and literature through a personalized and subjective style, this 'New Journalism' suited many women journalists concerned with the human interest story and the politicization of personal issues, and anticipated the postfeminist confessional style that gave birth to chick lit.[33]

The work of Angela Carter epitomizes the qualities of literary journalism with its accent on creativity, play, and imagination. Although Carter is known best for her strikingly original novels and short stories with their flamboyant prose and outlandish characters, she began her career as a journalist and is author of several cultural commentaries. Carter moved into journalism unintentionally, persuaded in her thirties to write for *New Society* by editor Paul Barker.[34] This gave her an opportunity to experiment with her ideas. She wrote book reviews, travel pieces, a memoir, and academic essays. Her journalistic work formed two collections: *Nothing Sacred* (1982) and *Expletives Deleted* (1992), which were published together in *Shaking a Leg: Collected Journalism and Writings* (1998).

Carter wrote essays and reviews for *New Society*, the *Guardian*, and *London Magazine* on a wide range of literary and cultural topics. Her journalism covered subjects that resonated with her fiction, including feminism, sexuality, war, pornography, sadomasochism, fashion, food, protest, and fantasy. The strength of Carter's feminist writing was derived from her mocking humour rather than a solemn style. In 1983 she wrote an irreverent piece on childbirth called 'Notes from a Maternity Ward', which was strikingly unsympathetic to notions of early bonding or of labour as an elevating experience.[35] Carter's journalism was strongly influenced by her fiction which, in turn, was shaped by surrealism and magical realism. Carter cannot be categorized as a novelist who dipped into journalism. Her journalism and fiction were both informed by her involvement in the Women's Movement.[36] She made an immense contribution to journalism and to contemporary scholarly debates about feminism, aesthetics, and postmodern writing practices.[37]

Acknowledging the influence of Carter, feminist critic Bidisha wrote her first novel, *Seahorses* (1998), at age 16, writes for the *Guardian*, and works as a television and radio presenter for the BBC. She specializes in the arts and culture, social justice, international human rights issues, and international affairs. She demonstrates the vital importance of human interest storytelling to the recording of the lives of ordinary people caught up in conflict. Her book, *Beyond the Wall: Writing a Path through Palestine* (2012), is a Middle Eastern reportage. She states that 'there is a realisation that the most profound effects of any conflict and oppression are borne by those faceless, voiceless, "ordinary" people who somehow survive and bear the consequences for generations'.[38] Bidisha aspires to counter the relentless bias of Western journalists who draw on racist and colonial stereotypes when writing about the Middle East, and maintains that conflict reporting requires a combination of styles: 'deep and immediate, factual and analytical, narrative and news-oriented' (Graham). She campaigns for women's rights through reports on violence against women. Bidisha recalls in an interview that 'endemic leering, following, harassment and general disrespect for women at a public street level was completely obvious' when she was in Palestine. However, despite the sexual assault of journalist Lara Logan in Egypt, Bidisha asserts that women journalists should not be barred from reporting on conflict (Graham).

Within the broad spectrum of women's literary journalism is Helen Fielding, who became a household name after the publication of her novel *Bridget Jones's Diary* (1996). The book spearheaded a new genre of women's writing known as 'chick lit'. Importantly, *Bridget Jones's Diary* emerged from Fielding's anonymous column in the *Independent* in 1995. This comic, confessional style drew on Fielding's personal experiences to chronicle the trials and tribulations of urban, 30-something women. It progressed into three novels, two of which have been made into films. This new 'girl column' corresponded with writing by journalists such as Heller for the *Sunday Times* and by Candace Bushnell for the *New York Observer*. Bushnell's column led to the books and films *Sex and the City*. The loosely autobiographical style of the confessional girl column evolved into a new style of postfeminist 'new girl writing' coinciding with the 'Girl Power' celebrated by the Spice Girls pop group. Caricaturing a new kind of singleton feminine identity publicized in the 1990s, the genre is characterized by revelations of women's personal anxieties, sexual triumphs, personal preoccupations, and bad habits associated with alcohol binges and fashion fetishes. Heller, among others, warns of the potential for stereotyping and ghettoizing women journalists through writing that celebrates feminine individualism and consumerism.[39]

Further exemplars of a tradition of 'cross-over' writing include the award-winning novelist Zadie Smith, who has contributed to the *New York Review of Books* and *Harper's Magazine*, and authors such as Jenny Diski, Marina Warner, and two-time Booker Prize winner Hilary Mantel, who all regularly contribute to the *London Review of Books*. Mantel's journalism is characterized by her critique of literary sexism. For example, she defended Kate Atkinson's first novel, *Behind the Scenes at the Museum* (1995), which beat Salman Rushdie's *The Moor's Last Sigh* (1995) to win the Whitbread Book of the Year. In the *London Review of Books*, Mantel wrote:

> On the day after Kate Atkinson's first novel won the Whitbread Prize, the *Guardian's* headline read: 'Rushdie makes it a losing double.' Thus Rushdie is reminded of his disappointments, Atkinson gets no credit, and the uninformed reader assumes that this year's Whitbread is a damp squib. But read on. 'A 44-year-old chambermaid won one of Britain's leading literary awards last night.'[40]

Mantel explained that Atkinson, who studied literary fiction up to postgraduate level, once took a holiday job as a chambermaid, 'and the other menial occupations cited were those which any would-be writer takes up to pay the bills – and which, in the case of young men, are thought to broaden experience and convey prole credentials'.

In a 2013 lecture titled 'Royal Bodies', on royal consorts in Tudor times, given at the British Museum, Mantel caused a media furore by daring to describe Kate Middleton, the Duchess of Cambridge, as 'a shop-window mannequin, with no personality of her own, entirely defined by what she wore'.[41] Her remarks were consistently misread, provoking a backlash from newspapers such as the *Daily Mail*.[42] The response to Mantel's comments exemplified the hostility faced by women in the British media. It also indicated 'lazy journalism and raging hypocrisy', according to Hadley Freeman:

'Mantel was discussing how the royal family and the media manipulate women; it is of little surprise that the media would attack her back.'[43]

Burchill, one of Britain's 'most acerbic newspaper columnists', demonstrates that the 'cross-over' works both ways.[44] Having begun her career in journalism, she is now also a novelist. *Sugar Rush* (2004), about a teenage lesbian, was adapted into a Channel 4 drama in 2005. Likewise, Caitlin Moran was originally a music journalist, then a broadcaster, television critic, and columnist for the *Times* but developed her bestselling feminist polemic *How to Be a Woman* (2011) into an autobiographical novel, *How to Build a Girl* (2014).

Digital media communities

The 1970s to the present is often viewed as a golden age for women journalists yet several enduring inconsistencies highlight gender disparities in journalism and the media. A report by Women in Journalism in 2012 revealed that men continue to dominate British news media: 'In a typical month, 78 percent of newspaper articles are written by men, 72 percent of "Question Time" contributors are men and 84 percent of reporters and guests on *Radio 4's* Today programme are men.'[45] The Centre for Women and Democracy report, *Sex and Power 2013: Who Runs Britain?*, notes that women constituted only 5 per cent of editors of national newspapers in 2012, down by 4 per cent since 2003.[46] Similarly, statistics published in 2010 and 2012 by the organization VIDA, which represents women in the literary arts, confirm that women remain under-represented in the literary press as the subjects and authors of reviews.[47] *Granta* is the only journal that has a majority of female contributors. In contrast, the *London Review of Books* has one of the more unbalanced ratios of male-to-female bylines in the VIDA count.

However, recent changes in the technologies of publishing are providing new openings. The growing presence of women in media opinion forums – including blogs, Facebook, Twitter, and wikis – indicates some potentially democratizing effects of new media, which has offered women opportunities to move into digital self-publishing. An example of news-orientated websites that specialize in publicizing and understanding women's issues is *Women's e-news*, an agenda-setting online news network that addresses topics of importance to women.[48] *Women's e-news* covers such issues as the role of women in revolutions in the Middle East, gang rapes in India, abortion debates, and women's education worldwide. *Women's e-news* also supports the *Global Connect! Gender Justice Writing Project*, which aims to provide opportunities for local media and writers to improve their knowledge and understanding in reporting on gender justice issues.

This era of digital journalism cultivates new genres alongside new kinds of website, blogs, and chatrooms. Through the technical affordances of user-generated content, new technologies of publishing are transforming the relationship between reader and writer. Online news, literature, comments, and criticism are forming a more democratic network of information that challenges conventional author/reader distinctions. These developments prompt assertions of online 'communities'.[49] Such evocations may seem idealistic in the light of recent high-profile cases about the online harassment of female journalists. Reporting on the regular online abuse that Laurie Penny experiences in reaction to her journalistic opinions, she states, 'An opinion, it seems, is the short skirt of the internet. Having one and flaunting it is somehow asking an amorphous mass of almost-entirely male keyboard-bashers to tell you how they'd like to rape, kill and urinate on you.'[50]

Notwithstanding the extensive online abuse experienced by women, internet-based publishing groups promote the principle of community. *BlogHer* is a leading publishing network described as 'a community and media company created in partnership with women in social media'.[51] Formed in 2005 to address the lack of women bloggers at the time, *BlogHer* now comprises the largest community of women bloggers, with 55 million unique visitors a month. Among the top five feminist websites in the UK is *The F Word*, created in 2001, which acts as a resource for UK-based feminists, with numerous contributors addressing issues such as sexuality, working mothers, and the nature of feminism. *The F Word* provides well-informed features, news, and reviews that celebrate women's writing as well as women's art, film, and music. These online communities are crucial in providing support for aspiring as well as established women writers. While women's contributions to news in traditional media forms such as newspapers, television, and radio have not reached parity,[52] a marked increase in women's presence in new media opinion forums is confirmed by the 2012 OpEd Project Byline survey.[53]

This chapter demonstrates that journalism has played a fundamental role in providing a space for women's creative writing and the publicizing of gender issues. Remarkably, although early women journalists were confined to 'soft news', they broadened news agendas to create a personalized and human interest style of reporting. Comprising a subaltern space, the 'woman's page' simultaneously confirmed and subverted gendered distinctions between 'hard' and 'soft' news. A political journalist of the calibre of Toynbee suggests that women are now integrated into a gender-free profession. Similarly, women's literary journalism now plays a key role in destabilizing conventional boundaries between 'literature' and 'reportage', forming a central cultural field where public debate has been shaped by feminism and women's experiences.

Despite these achievements, women writers' involvement in mainstream journalism raises questions about whether their association with 'the subjective' advances or confines women. After all, the subjective approach of 1970s New Journalism sustained rather than challenged the dominance of men such as Tom Wolfe and Truman Capote. Despite significant advances, women's status in journalism remains precarious with women continuing to be in a minority in the literary press, as writers of newspaper articles, and as editors of newspapers. Certain dimensions of women's writing are developing in exciting new ways through the hybridization of genres and audiences and through intersections between old and new media. Yet women's journalism is increasingly being squeezed into the kind of celebrity news, apolitical confessional styles, and post-*Cosmopolitan* sexual entrepreneurship that promote a postfeminist rhetoric.[54] Newspaper supplements, lifestyle news, magazine features, chick lit, and 'mommy porn' are areas dominated by female journalists.[55] Embedded in hyper-consumerist popular media discourses, a dominant postfeminist sensibility is being evoked. While celebrating the agency and choice associated with a 'new femininity', these modes of writing sideline issues of gender and power (Gill and Scharff, p. 2). The status of women journalists is distinguished and constrained in both new and recurring ways.

Notes

1. See Catherine Clay, 'Book Review: Women Making News: Gender and Journalism in Modern Britain', *Feminist Theory*, 8:3 (2007), pp. 353–4; Michelle Elizabeth Tusan, *Women Making News: Gender and Journalism in Modern Britain* (Urbana: University of Illinois Press, 2005).
2. See John Hartsock, '"Literary Journalism" as an Epistemological Moving Object within a Larger "Quantum Narrative"', *Journal of Communication Research*, 23:4 (1999), pp. 432–47.
3. Richard Keeble, 'Introduction: On Journalism, Creativity and the Imagination', *The Journalistic Imagination: Literary Journalists from Defoe to Capote and Carter*, ed. Richard Keeble and Sharon Wheeler (London: Routledge, 2007), p. 3.
4. Michael Schudson, *Discovering the News* (New York: Basic Books, 1981).
5. See Kirsten Daly, 'William Hazlitt: Poetry, Drama and Literary Journalism', in Keeble and Wheeler, pp. 29–43.
6. See Deborah Chambers, Linda Steiner, and Carole Fleming, *Women and Journalism* (London: Routledge, 2004).
7. Gaye Tuchman, *Making News* (New York: The Free Press, 1978), pp. 47–8.
8. John Hartley, *Understanding News* (London: Methuen, 1982), p. 38.
9. Dustin Harp, 'Newspapers' Transition from Women's to Style Pages: What Were They Thinking?', *Journalism*, 7:2 (2006), p. 213.
10. See Fiona McCarthy, 'Obituary: Mary Stott', *Guardian*, 18 September 2002, www.guardian.co.uk/news/2002/sep/18/guardianobituaries.gender, accessed 28 April 2013.
11. Polly Toynbee, 'Why Does the Guardian Still Need a Woman's Page? Because the Feminist Revolution is Only Half Made', *Guardian*, 18 July 2007, www.guardian.co.uk/commentisfree/2007/jul/18/gender.pressandpublishing, accessed 28 April 2013.
12. Ben Dowell, 'Spare Rib Magazine to be Relaunched by Charlotte Raven', *Guardian*, 25 April 2013, www.guardian.co.uk/media/2013/apr/25/sarah-raven-relaunch-spare-rib, accessed 27 April 2013.

13. Roy Greenslade, 'Feminist Times "Put on Ice" after Failure of Crowdfunding', *Guardian,* 14 July 2014, www.theguardian.com/media/greenslade/2014/jul/14/digital-media-feminism, accessed 2 November 2014.
14. Carol Sarler, 'Unleashed and Unrepentant: Fleet Street's Bitch Goddesses', *Independent,* 13 July 2008, www.independent.co.uk/news/media/unleashed-and-unrepentant-fleet-streets-bitch-goddesses-866278.html, accessed 26 April 2013.
15. Hugh Massingberd, *The Daily Telegraph Third Book of Obituaries: Entertainers,* Vol. 3 (London: Pan Books, 1998), p. 203.
16. M. Paton, 'Obituary: Jean Rook', *Independent,* 6 September 1991, p. 126.
17. J. Booth, 'The British Don't Like Too Many Changes: They Like to be Left Alone', *Sunday Telegraph,* 31 March 2002, p. 5.
18. See Joan Smith, 'What's My Line', *Guardian,* 15 September 1994, p. 13.
19. Jean Rook, *Rook's Eye View* (Worthing: Littlehampton Books Services, 1979).
20. Lynn Barber, 'How I Suffered for Art's Sake', *Observer,* 1 October 2006, www.guardian.co.uk/artanddesign/2006/oct/01/art.turnerprize2006, accessed 28 April 2013.
21. England and Wales High Court (Queen's Bench Division) decisions, www.bailii.org/ew/cases/EWHC/QB/2011/1884.html, accessed 26 April 2013.
22. Lucy Holden, 'The Interview: Lynn Barber', *Leeds Student,* 1 February 2013, www.leedsstudent.org/2013-02-01/ls2/lifestyle/the-interview-lynn-barber, accessed 26 April 2013.
23. Lynn Barber, *An Education* (Harmondsworth: Penguin, 2009); Lynn Barber, 'An Education', *Granta,* 82 (1993), pp. 203–23.
24. Rachelle Thackray, 'Germaine Smacks her Sister', *Independent on Sunday,* 21 February 1999, www.independent.co.uk/news/germaine-smacks-her-sisters-1072156.html, accessed 10 November 2013; 'Seeing Red: The Power of Female Anger', *New Statesman,* 8 January 2013, www.newstatesman.com/politics/2013/01/seeing-red-power-female-anger, accessed 2 November 2014.
25. Suzanne Moore, *Head Over Heels* (London: Viking, 1996), p. xii, p. xiv.
26. Anne Leslie, 'If You Ask Me', *Press Gazette: Journalism Today,* 3 December 2007, www.pressgazette.co.uk/node/39606, accessed 22 April 2013.
27. Author profile on *Goodreads,* www.goodreads.com/author/show/152275.Julie_Burchill, accessed 8 November 2013.
28. Andy McSmith, 'Polly Toynbee: Reborn, as a Lady of the Right', *Independent,* 26 November 2006, www.independent.co.uk/news/people/profiles/polly-toynbee-reborn-as-a-lady-of-the-right-425833.html, accessed 25 January 2014.
29. Jane Sandeman, 'How to be a "Dudelike" Mum' (review of 'Zoë Williams, *Bring it on, Baby*), *Spiked,* 30 July 2010, www.spiked-online.com/review_of_books/article/9371#.VCp8mU1waUk, accessed 30 September 2014.
30. Julie Bindel, 'Why I Hate Men', *Guardian,* 2 November 2006, www.guardian.co.uk/commentisfree/2006/nov/02/whyihatemen, accessed 21 April 2013; 'Why Men Hate Me', *Guardian,* 24 December 2007, www.guardian.co.uk/commentisfree/2007/dec/24/juliescomplaintformonday, accessed 21 April 2013.
31. Yasmin Alibhai-Brown, 'These Shamless Honours Dishonour Us All', *Independent,* 19 June 2006, www.independent.co.uk/voices/commentators/yasmin-alibhai-brown/yasmin-alibhaibrown-these-shameless-honours-dishonour-us-all-404665.html, accessed 28 April 2013.
32. See E. Dennise Everette and William L. Rivers, *Other Voices: The New Journalism in America* (San Francisco: Canfield Press, 1974).
33. John Hollowell, *Fact and Fiction: The New Journalism and the Nonfiction Novel* (Chapel Hill: University of North Carolina Press, 1977), see Chapters 2 and 6.

34. See Blake Morrison, 'Polemics with a Giggle: The Posthumous Literary Career of Angela Carter Continues with a Collection of her Journalism', *Independent*, 6 July 1997, www.independent.co.uk/arts-entertainment/books/polemics-with-a-giggle-1249378.html, accessed 24 April 2013.
35. Angela Carter, 'Notes from a Maternity Ward', *Shaking a Leg: Collected Journalism and Writings*, ed. Jenny Uglow (London: Vintage, 1998), pp. 29–30.
36. See Linden Peach, 'The Journalist as Philosopher and Cultural Critic: The Case of Angela Carter', in Keeble and Wheeler, pp. 145–58.
37. See Maggie Tonkin, *Angela Carter and Decadence: Critical Fictions/Fictional Critiques* (Basingstoke: Palgrave Macmillan, 2012).
38. Sarah Graham, 'Interview: Bidisha', *The Student Journals*, 28 October 2012, www.studentjournals.co.uk/features/interviews/1772-interview-bidisha, accessed 27 April 2012.
39. Zoë Heller, 'Girl Columns', *Secrets of the Press: Journalists on Journalism*, ed. Stephen Glover (Harmondsworth: Penguin, 1999), pp. 10–17.
40. Hilary Mantel, 'Shop!', *London Review of Books*, 4 April 1996, pp. 23–4.
41. Hilary Mantel, 'Royal Bodies', *London Review of Books*, 21 February 2013, pp. 3–7.
42. BBC News, 'Author Hilary Mantel Defends Kate Middleton Comments', 8 March 2013, www.bbc.co.uk/news/entertainment-arts-21710158, accessed 10 June 2013; Adam Sherwin, 'David Cameron Defends Kate over Hilary Mantel's "Shop-Window Mannequin" Remarks', *Independent*, 19 February 2013, www.independent.co.uk/arts-entertainment/books/news/david-cameron-defends-kate-over-hilary-mantels-shopwindow-mannequin-remarks-8501237.html, accessed 10 June 2013.
43. Hadley Freeman, 'Hilary Mantel v Kate: A Story of Lazy Journalism and Raging Hypocrisy', *Guardian*, 19 February 2013, www.guardian.co.uk/commentisfree/2013/feb/19/hilary-mantel-duchess-cambridge-scandal, accessed 10 June 2013.
44. Stephen Brook, 'Burchill Bows out of Journalism', *Guardian*, 21 June 2007, www.guardian.co.uk/media/2007/jun/21/pressandpublishing.uknews, accessed 13 June 2013.
45. Jane Martinson, Kira Cochrane, Sue Ryan, Tracey Corrigan, and Fiona Bawdon, *Seen but not Heard: How Women Make Front Page News*, 15 October 2012, Womeninjournalism.co.uk, womeninjournalism.co.uk/wp-content/uploads/2012/10/Seen_but_not_heard.pdf, accessed 24 April 2013.
46. Centre for Women and Democracy, *Sex and Power 2013: Who Runs Britain?* 28 February 2013, www.fawcettsociety.org.uk/wp-content/uploads/2013/02/Sex-and-Power-2013-FINAL-REPORT.pdf, accessed 8 June 2013.
47. 'The 2012 Count', VIDA: Women in Literary Arts, www.vidaweb.org/the-count, accessed 24 April 2013.
48. See http://womensenews.org/.
49. See Margaret Beetham, 'Periodicals and the New Media: Women and Imagined Communities', *Women's International Forum*, 29 (2006), p. 238.
50. Laurie Penny, 'A Woman's Opinion is the Mini-Skirt of the Internet', *Independent*, 4 November 2011, www.independent.co.uk/voices/commentators/laurie-penny-a-womans-opinion-is-the-miniskirt-of-the-internet-6256946.html, accessed 10 June 2013. See also Laurie Penny's e-book, *Cybersexism: Sex, Gender, and Power on the Internet* (2013).
51. BlogHer can be accessed at www.blogher.com/about-this-network.
52. Global Media Monitoring Project, *Who Makes the News?* (2010), compiled by Sarah Macharia, Dermot O'Connor, and Lilian Ndangam, http://whomakesthenews.org/images/stories/restricted/global/global_en.pdf, accessed 25 April 2013.

53. Tarin Yaeger, 'Who Narrates the World? The OpEd Project 2012 Byline Report' (2012), http://theopedproject.org/index.php?option=com_content&view=article&id=817&Itemid=103, accessed 25 April 2013.
54. See Rosalind Gill and Christina Scharff, 'Introduction', *New Femininities*, ed. Gill and Scharff (Basingstoke: Palgrave Macmillan, 2011), pp. 1–20.
55. Lynn Comella, 'Fifty Shades of Erotic Stimulus', *Feminist Media Studies*, 13:3 (2013), pp. 563–6.

5
Publishing and Prizes

Gail Low

Feminist activists, thinkers, theoreticians, writers, and critics of second- and third-wave feminism have probed representations of femininity, questioned social limits, and imagined the fullness of women's potentiality. In addition, the feminist work done since the 1970s reveals that the Women's Movement continues to be a transnational phenomenon whose influence, ideas, and narratives are not bounded by geographical location; that the battle of genders is one not only of politics and economics but also of words and culture; that the institutional contexts – educational and publishing – helped foment an audience for women's writing and writing about women. The task of this chapter is to account for some of that material history and to examine aspects of the developing literary infrastructure in Britain. Its focus is particularly on publishing and associated activities, literary prizes, and on the tension between politics and commerce that governs recent history.

In *Mixed Media* (2004), Simone Murray observes that the establishment of women's presses was motivated by a political agenda which saw a continuity between forms of marginalization and a belief that mainstream presses were not neutral in their withholding – or support – of women's writing.[1] The most effective way to promote women's voices was, arguably, to own the actual means of production and to form independent presses supportive of women's writing. Anne McDermid, a London-based literary agent, asserted that despite the success of some women in mainstream publishing, women 'should be in control from beginning to end'; similarly, Ursula Owen of Virago Press declared that while, in a perfect world, one would not 'need women's publishing companies or women's pages', Virago's presence was and is part of that 'very long and difficult process' of establishing that objective.[2] Sheba Feminist Publishers asserted that the distinctiveness of women's experiences and the 'persistent bias' towards 'white, heterosexual, and middle class values' resulted in 'women turning to women's presses'.[3] Many women writers, Lilian Mohin notes in *One Foot on the Mountain* (1979), choose not to publish with commercial publishers because 'they know they challenge male conceptions of reality and of worth and/or because they do not wish to enhance the coffers or the reputations of establishment publishers'.[4] Such debates over the politics of representation paved the way for the flowering of women's presses in the 1970s. But those cultural interventions played out very differently in different publishing imprints and houses, stretching from the not-for-profit collectives to organizations aiming to compete with mainstream publishers in the literary marketplace.

Big sister presses

Virago, formed in 1972, is one of the earliest and the best known of the presses associated with the exceptional flowering of women's writing and publishing in the 1970s and 1980s.[5] Set up by Carmen Callil, Rosie Boycott, and Marsha Rowe, the latter two being editors of the feminist magazine *Spare Rib*, and joined by Ursula Owen and Harriet Spicer and, subsequently, Alexandra Pringle and Lennie Goodings, Virago's aim was 'to publish books that celebrated and illuminated women's history, lives and tradition ... [to] make women's writing central ... to provide a place for women to publish and be published in a context where others understood what they were writing about'.[6] Between 1972 and 1976, Virago issued its first nine titles as an editorially independent imprint funded by Quartet books. *Fenwomen: A Portrait of Women in an English Village* (1975), Mary Chamberlain's social and oral history of a village in the Cambridgeshire Fens, launched the list. The focus on working women, framed within a broadly Fabian, Labour, or Socialist perspective, was to be developed with the successful non-fiction reprint list inspired by Sheila Rowbottom's *Hidden from History* (1974). Titles included *Life As We Have Known It: By Co-operative Working Women* (1977), edited by Margaret Llewelyn Davies (1861–1944); *Round About a Pound a Week* (1979) by Maud Pember Reeves (1865–1953); Barbara Taylor's *Eve and the New Jerusalem* (1984); Beatrix Campbell's *Wigan Pier Revisited* (1984); and Carolyn Steedman's ground-breaking *Landscape for a Good Woman* (1986), which addressed working-class life through its portrait of a mother and daughter.

Callil has remarked on the productive symbiosis between higher educational and extramural courses, and the reprint list; academics suggested books for publication and also taught the published Virago titles (Callil, 'Women', p. 187). A similar cross-fertilization took place with the Modern Classics series, 'dedicated to the rediscovery and celebration of women writers, challenging the narrow [and exclusionary] definition of a Classic'.[7] The latter, intended to discover and celebrate forgotten women writers and 'to demonstrate the existence of a female tradition in fiction', proposed a women's literary tradition where women novelists were aware of the work of their literary mothers.[8] In invoking such a female literary tradition, Elaine Showalter's influence over the formative years of the series is evident. *A Literature of Their Own* (1977), Callil records, led directly to the revival of forgotten women writers of the nineteenth and earlier twentieth centuries such as May Sinclair (1863–1946), Dorothy Richardson (1873–1957), Katherine Mansfield (1888–1923), Rosamond Lehmann (1901–90), and Stevie Smith (1902–71).[9] The Modern Classics Series advisory group also contained other influential writers and academics in the Women's Movement, including Sally Alexander, Germaine Greer, Liz Calder, Angela Carter (1940–92), and the Spare Rib Collective. The relationship between publishing and academia provided Virago with a ready audience that not only understood and encouraged the company's ideological project and translated such support into real sales but also, as Murray suggests, with a 'political analysis and intellectual vocabulary' by which Virago could articulate its publishing mission (p. 43).

Launched in 1976 with Antonia White's *Frost in May*, the Modern Classics was a B-format trade paperback series, part-modelled on the successes of Allan Lane's Penguin revolution. With their 'racing green' covers adorned with fine-art reproductions and apple colophon, the Modern Classics offered a distinctive and attractive middle-class tastefulness in contrast to the identikit mass-market branding of the original Penguin output; they became synonymous with the Virago brand itself. Though the concept of the 'classic' text and canon formation were much disputed in feminist criticism, Joan Scanlon and Julia Swindells suggest that the idea of 'classics' provided Virago with a mainstreaming strategy, signifying, perhaps, a form of literary writing that could pass as 'undisputed (and timeless common ground)' (p. 218), especially in a period when feminist publishers were generally seen as producing 'disturbing and unmarketable' work (p. 219). In this manner, 'the political project of discovering and reprinting neglected works by women meshed seamlessly with a more broad-based commitment to publishing works of "literary merit"' (p. 219).

While conceived as a means to rediscover forgotten and out-of-print texts by women, the Modern Classics series also published contemporary women's writing as 'classics' in the making: for example, five novels by Carter; Pat Barker's novels of working-class women's lives, *Union Street* (1982) and *The Century's Daughter* (1986), later retitled *Liza's England*; and the popular and bestselling five-volume autobiography of the African American poet Maya Angelou. Virago also published Carter's controversial polemic on sex, *The Sadeian Woman* (1979), Zoë Fairbairns's dystopian science fiction, *Benefits* (1979) – in the Virago New Fiction imprint – and her family saga beginning with *Stand We at Last* (1983). The Virago `V' imprint, designed for a younger reading public, published Sarah Waters's historical novels with strong women leads, *Tipping the Velvet* (1998), *Affinity* (1999), *Fingersmith* (2002), *The Night Watch* (2006), *The Little Stranger* (2009), and *The Paying Guests* (2014), all of which have been commercially very successful.

Virago's association with the Canadian novelist Margaret Atwood has also lent the imprint feminist longevity and international credentials; her body of work has appeared in both the Modern Classics and Virago New Fiction since her paperback rights were acquired from André Deutsch in 1979. More widely, the Modern Classics and Virago New Fiction series sought to internationalize its list. Notably, Virago reissued *Their Eyes Were Watching God* (1937; 1986) by American Zora Neale Hurston (1891–1960) and has published important South Asian writers such as Shashi Deshpande, *That Long Silence* (1988) and *The Binding Vine* (1993); South African writers such as Nadine Gordimer (1923–2014), *Occasion for Loving* (1983) and *The Lying Days* (1983); and Zoë Wicomb, *You Can't Get Lost in Cape Town* (1987). Australian-born Janette Turner Hospital's novel *Borderline* was published in 1990 and diasporian writers such as Attia Hosain (1913–98) – *Phoenix Fled* (1988) and *Sunlight on a Broken Column* (1989) – and Amryl Johnson (1944–2001) in her account of her return to Trinidad, *Sequins for a Jagged Hem* (1988), further illustrate Virago's reach.

The inclusion of writers from outside the UK addressed accusations that Virago published only white, middle-class texts for readers drawn from the same socio-economic group. Callil acknowledges in an article in 1986 that the boom in black women's writing published by rival presses clearly necessitated a response.[10] At the same time, Virago's inclusion of international writers enabled the press to establish itself, increasingly, as a cosmopolitan publisher in an Anglophone literary field that itself was gradually becoming more denationalized and international. This move is crucial in what today is an increasingly transnational and globalized Anglophone world republic of letters where prestige, as Pascale Cassanova has argued, is marked by a nexus of writing and cosmopolitan writers who remain relatively autonomous of national geopolitical cultural spaces.[11] By the time of the launch of the reprint library in 1977, Virago had already staged a management buy-out from Quartet in order to pursue its editorial independence. The pattern of incorporation into larger publishers (such as Chatto, The Bodley Head, Cape, and Little, Brown), part-ownership, and management buy-outs would also be repeated across the next two decades as Virago's fortunes and politics straddled a desire to expand, to be mainstream, and also to retain financial and editorial autonomy. Virago, now part of Hachette Livre, a subsidiary of the French media conglomerate Lagardere, styles itself as an *international* publisher of books by women.

For much of the 1980s, The Women's Press acted as a supportive rival to Virago. In 1977, Stephanie Dowrick, an editor and publisher who had previously worked with George Harrap and New English Library, convinced Quartet and its owner Naim Attallah to fund the setting up of The Women's Press. Like Virago, The Women's Press was formed with a consciousness-raising agenda and an explicit ideological link to the Women's Movement, and an advisory group of feminist academics and media personnel.[12] Unlike Virago, though, The Women's Press, under Ros de Lanerolle (1932–93), adopted a 'Live Authors, Live Issues' initiative to emphasize a focus on contemporary writing that addressed the pressing cultural, social, and political issues of the day. It also adopted a diversity agenda, publishing Third World women's texts, radical feminist texts, and writing by women of colour who did not at that time have much presence in the cultural mainstream.[13] In contrast to Virago, the use by The Women's Press of a domestic iron as colophon – and their books' central spine of, initially, black and white stripes to represent an iron's electric cord – original illustrations, paintings or photo-montage, gave their covers a distinctive contemporary edginess.

The most high-profile author at The Women's Press in the 1980s was American Alice Walker, whose *The Color Purple* (1982) was a bestseller on both sides of the Atlantic and influenced a generation of Black British writers.[14] In an interview, de Lanerolle recorded that one dramatic effect of publishing Walker was 'a steady flow' of unsolicited manuscripts by black women; this resulted in the press taking seriously the work of black and Third World and international women's books.[15] In their pioneering Women's Press anthology, *Watchers and Seekers: Creative Writing by Black Women in Britain* (1987), Rhonda Cobham and Merle Collins write that the 'discovery of Afro-American women writers [was] a turning point in ... [the] creative development' of the Black British women who located themselves in a wider Black Atlantic culture.[16] In the context of the history of immigration and a heightened racial politics in Britain, even writers such as Leena Dhingra, a member of the Asian Writers Collective, and Meiling Jin, of Chinese/Guyanese ancestry, understood themselves as 'part of a wider Black community' (p. 8). Susheila Nasta's foundational collection of essays, *Motherlands* (1991), cemented the intellectual commitment to a diversity agenda; it also contained many of the feminists who would later form an influential academic generation in postcolonial literary studies.

The variety of output – political history, feminist thought, and fiction in a range of genres – is striking. The Press produced two important early anthologies of the Women's Liberation Movement, *No Turning Back: Writings from the Women's Liberation Movement, 1975–80* (1981), edited by the Feminist Anthology Collective, and *Sweeping Statements: Writings from the Women's Liberation Movement, 1981–83* (1984), edited by Hannah Kanter, Sarah LeFanu, Shaila Shah, and Carole Spedding. It provided a platform for radical feminist thinking, issuing the work of American writers such as Mary Daly (1928–2010) and Andrea Dworkin (1946–2005). In fiction, it published Michèle Roberts's first two novels, *A Piece of the Night* (1978) and *The Visitation* (1983), and Tsitsi Dangarembga's *Nervous Conditions* (1988). Genre-based writing has also been important in two dedicated series at The Women's Press: a science fiction series of original and reprinted titles 'to present exciting and provocative feminist images of the future' to challenge men's domination of the genre, and a crime fiction series which initiated the writing careers of Val McDermid and UK-based Gillian Slovo, as well as promoting the work of North American crime writers.[17] A series of novels for teenagers, *Livewire*, launched in 1987, thrived for a time and is, perhaps, best remembered for publishing Malorie Blackman's collection of short stories, *Not so Stupid!: Incredible Short Stories* (1990). The Women's Press also initiated a book club to encourage readers to buy at a reduced cost women's writing published by them and other houses.

The financial difficulties that beset Virago and which led to a pattern of incorporation into larger companies and management buy-outs played itself out differently at The Women's Press. The Press has only ever been an independent imprint within Quartet Books with its financial balance sheet underwritten by Attallah's holding company, Namara Ltd. If Attallah's reputation as a die-hard patriarch did not sit well with the image of a radical press, the corporate affiliation did enable a progressive publishing programme. However, the marriage of convenience came all but unstuck in 1990 in a boardroom struggle over the direction of the Press. Attallah alleged that the commitment of The Women's Press to diversity had everything to do with falling sales revenue; when a management buy-out was refused, de Lanerolle left, together with some of the senior management staff at the Press. The Women's Press as a publishing imprint would weather the storm but the difficulties highlighted the precariousness of corporate alliances for independent presses whose commercial and ideological agendas do not always sit well together; the direction of the list did change. More pertinently, while The Women's Press is still listed as a publisher and one can still buy backlisted titles of its Classics, the imprint has been slowly wound down for a number of years with no new titles for some time now; it has all but ceased to exist within Quartet Books.

The audience for women's writing within academia, fuelled by the emergence of Women's Studies programmes at higher educational institutions in the eighties and the synergies that developed between publishing and academia, also led to the formation of Pandora Press in 1981, a feminist non-fiction imprint within Routledge, Kegan & Paul, with Philippa Brewster at its helm. While the Press's main focus was non-fiction, with titles such as Hilda Scott's *Working Your Way to the Bottom – the Feminization of Poverty* (1984) and critical analyses of popular culture such as *Boxed In: Women and Television* (1987), edited by Helen Baehr and Gillian Dyer, Pandora also issued original fiction, for example Miriam Tlali's *Soweto Stories* (1989) and the critically and commercially successful *Oranges Are Not the Only Fruit* (1985) by Jeanette Winterson. In addition, Pandora also undertook reprints of writers of earlier periods such as Elizabeth Gaskell and, later, Australian women writers. As an imprint housed within a succession of mainstream commercial presses, Pandora had, possibly, less control over its list than Virago or The Women's Press, and its fortunes waxed and waned as ownership changed hands, and as each successive owner brought different demands to the table. In recessionary conditions and under HarperCollins, some of the titles within the imprint also altered from the earlier more explicit politicized agenda to a more generalized women's issues agenda. Brewster attempted an unsuccessful management buy-out in 1991 after which she was made redundant; Winterson would also very publicly leave Pandora under HarperCollins. Pandora titles now appear under, or in conjunction with, the small independent Rivers Oram Press as part of the latter's backlist of titles. However, academic gender and Women's Studies titles now form a stable, if niche, presence in mainstream higher educational publishing catalogues of conglomerates such as Taylor and Francis Education or Macmillan Science and Education.

The wider picture: collectives and multiculturalism

While Virago and The Women's Press are the biggest and best known of the women's presses that started life in the 1970s, small collectives were also important to the rise of feminist publishing. Many began as women meeting together for support and/or for writing activity. Only later did they seek an outlet for their work. Writing collectives were, in the main, run as egalitarian, self-help, consciousness-raising networks where women read, wrote, and critiqued each other's work constructively; they also functioned as forums for debates on feminist aesthetics. In her memoir of the 1970s, *Paper Houses* (2007), Roberts writes of how women at that time experimented 'with different kinds of narrative voices, uncovering new raw, angry subject matter' inspired by the group.[18] Members of collectives sometimes wrote collaboratively. For example, *Tales I Tell My Mother* (1978) was conceived as a 'unique experiment' to break out of the mould of a writer working creatively in splendid isolation; it launched the careers of Fairbairns, Valerie Miner, Sara Maitland, Roberts, and Michelene Wandor.[19]

Feminist collectives enabled the development of a writing community and identity based on the politics of shared experience, where all aspects of women's lives – work, leisure, play, class, sexuality, motherhood, development – were validated. As the Minority Press Group report indicated, collectives were 'part of a process' of encouraging women to 'take themselves seriously as writers, [and] of consciously adopting that identity for themselves' (Cadman, Chester, and Pivot, p. 12). For some, that identity politics was revolutionary. Onlywomen Press, for instance, was established as a separatist organization, 'a women's liberation publishing and printing group', and as part of a 'feminist communication network and, ultimately, [for] a feminist revolution'.[20] The formation of the Press in 1974 as both a printer and publisher enabled it to cross-subsidize and be wholly self-reliant, controlling all aspects of production.

However, there was no easy consensus as to what constituted a feminist (or even female) aesthetic. In *One Foot on the Mountain,* Onlywomen Press's foundational feminist poetry anthology, there is an exhortation to see and write 'counter' to 'prevailing views' (p. 5), but the relationship between language and subjectivity is contentious. Mohin, also a founding editor at the same Press, writes self-consciously of the variability of the poetry in the collection, some seemingly all too 'inaccessible' or too 'obvious' when judged by 'traditional academic standards of poetic craft'; however, she also records that debates about craft and subject matter would lead to 'new definitions, identities, connections' (p. 5). Such a particular and recurring tension in the feminist cultural politics of the 1970s and 1980s registers, as Claire Buck argues, the pull between art practices defined by agit-prop politics and social realism, (high) modernist aesthetics, and the growing influence of a newly minted poststructuralist deconstruction of subjectivity as the 1980s progressed.[21]

Collectives were important in creating an audience for women's short fiction and, especially, women's poetry, often excluded from both the mainstream and alternative, underground poetry scenes, performances, anthologies, and collections in 1970s Britain, or only given a token presence.[22] Playbook 2 published *Cutlass and Earrings* in 1977, edited by Wandor and Roberts, while Roberts, Stef Pixner, Tina Reid, and Ann Oosthuizen brought out *Licking the Bed Clean: Five Feminist Poets* under Teeth Imprints in 1978. Other important regional women's presses inaugurated on a co-operative basis include Stramullion in Edinburgh, formed in 1979 and now defunct, and Honno in Aberystwyth, established later in 1986, part-funded by the Welsh Book Council, and still actively publishing Welsh women's writing in English and Welsh. Anthologies were a staple of feminist publishing co-operatives in the 1970s and 1980s; they performed acts of canon-formation or canon-intervention, bringing together different perspectives and initiating dialogue across varied experiences and between participants. The brevity of the anthologized pieces, Gail Chester observes, also allowed women to juggle writing efforts with diverse other responsibilities.[23] Of the 40 titles Onlywomen Press published by 2002, 11 were anthologies, particularly of poetry and fiction, including not only *One Foot on the Mountain* but also *Beautiful Barbarians: Lesbian Feminist Poetry* (1986), also edited by Mohin.

One Foot openly acknowledges the omission of black women in its survey of a decade of feminist poetry in a way that now seems surprising. Criticisms of such gaps had in the 1980s led to the formation of presses that sought particularly to address the marginality of Black and ethnic minority women writers and the specificity of their experiences not figured in the cultural politics of either the feminist mainstream or the anti-racist Left. In addition to the output of The Women's Press, many smaller independent presses and collectives formed to fill this gap. Sheba was established in 1980 as a not-for-profit workers' co-operative, to prioritize 'writing by women of colour, or lesbians, or working-class women'.[24] Their commitment to diversity resulted in two significant works by Black and diasporian women writers based in Britain, *A Dangerous Knowing: Four Black Women Poets* (1984), including the work of Barbara Burford (1944–2010), Gabriela Pearse, Grace Nichols, and Jackie Kay, and *Charting the Journey: Writings by Black and Third World Women* (1988), edited by Shabnam Grewal, Jackie Kay, Liliane Landor, Gail Lewis, and Pratibha Parmar. But a marked difference in the conceptualization of identity in these books is evident. In the former's Introduction, the collection is described as a 'unique and historical' literary and publishing moment that for the first time collects together work written by four 'British based Black women'. In this preface, neither the terms 'black' nor 'women' are self-consciously invoked, though the 'complexities of Black Women's lives' are acknowledged.[25] However, a conceptual sophistication characterizes *Charting the Journey*'s theorization of identity; for example, Black is described as a 'contradictory' idea and process, defined in terms of colour and yet 'transcendant [sic]' of it.[26] Roots, in relation to diverse cultural kinships, are counterpointed by *routes*, or women's 'geographical, social and political journey[s]' (p. 2). Bemoaning 'guilt tripping' and the 'collective adornment of moral and political superiority' on the basis of 'merely being a Black woman', the editors advocate instead an affiliative blackness that does not hide contradictions, divisions, or difference (p. 3). In this way, self and collective representation in *Charting* and similar collections was fully cognizant of the cultural politics debates inflected by academic poststructuralist and postcolonial theorizations of identity and diaspora.[27] In line with the transnational dimension of feminist cultural work, Sheba also published prominent Black American writers such as Audre Lorde (1934–92) and Jewelle Gomez, and the cultural theorist bell hooks in Britain. This internationalism references a specific history of black Atlantic cultures of influence and exchange, but one that is staged and recreated as a contemporary black Atlantic identity in Britain.

Other notable smaller houses that sprung up to address similar issues include Centerprise Publications, which published *Words from the Women's Café* (1993), edited by Bernadette Halpin and Dorotthea Smartt, and including poets Patience Agbabi and Valerie Mason-John; Kanak House, the publishing arm of the Intef Institute, an organization of African Caribbean arts and culture formed in 1975, and best remembered for Grace Nichols's award-winning *i is a long memoried woman* (1983); Karia Press, a small organization established by Buzz Johnson that published iconic African Caribbean diasporian women activists such as Claudia Jones (1915–64) and also brought out an anthology of Caribbean poetry edited by Merle Collins; Ogwugwu Afo started by Buchi Emecheta to publish her own work, *Double Yoke* (1982), *The Rape of Savi* (1983), and her autobiography, *Head Above Water* (1986); Tamarind, established by Verna Wilkins in 1987 to address the question of diversity in the publishing of books for children;[28] and the Asian Women's Writers Workshop inaugurated in 1984.[29] The workshop mutated into the more organized and funded Asian Women Writers Collective, staging public readings and also putting together anthologies, notably through

The Women's Press – *Right of Way* (1988) – and Virago Press – *Flaming Spirit* (1994).[30]

Many of the concerns and patterns of development outlined here are echoed in the history of Mango Publishing, formed in 1995 as a partnership primarily between Joan Anim-Addo and Diana Birch to promote literary works by writers from British, Caribbean, and Latin American literary traditions both in English and in translation. In an interview, Anim-Addo recalls falling into publishing simply because the Lewisham collective she was part of was asked repeatedly if their work was available in print.[31] Mango's approach of working around a kitchen table is akin to publishing as a cottage industry but the house has issued some valuable and important books; its list includes poetry by leading contemporary authors, short story anthologies, novels, and autobiographical work, some not originally written in English, and an essay collection by Beryl Gilroy (1924–2001), *Leaves in the Wind* (1998). The production of writing within shared domestic spaces has been a recurring feature of women's collectives in this period.

Not all of these small presses published women's writing exclusively; some such as Bogle L'Ouverture, Allison and Busby, and New Beacon, set up in the mid- and late 1960s, have held an important place in Black British and African Caribbean literature. Allison and Busby was founded by Margaret Busby and Clive Allison (1944–2011) in 1967 to produce affordable paperback poetry; publications in its inaugural year included Libby Houston's *A Stained Glass Raree Show* and work by James Reeves and James Grady. Allison and Busby's list was eclectic, including international writers of fiction, non-fiction, poetry, and children's books (including books by Jill Murphy), but they would be best remembered for reissuing the work of C.L.R. James (1901–89) and Nuruddin Farah, and publishing Buchi Emecheta. Busby, who has the distinction of being the first black woman publisher in Britain, also edited and published the influential anthology *Daughters of Africa* (1992), a literary ancestry of Black women's writing, stretching across continents and historical periods, and including different concerns and genres, from orature to fiction, and from poetry to politics.[32]

Both Bogle L'Ouverture and New Beacon were set up by migrant intellectuals from the Caribbean; both combined publishing activities with the creation of a specialist bookshop which also functioned as a meeting space for cultural, political, and intellectual activity. Bogle L'Ouverture, established by Jessica Huntley (1927–2013) and Eric Huntley in 1969, and New Beacon Books, by John La Rose (1927–2006) and Sarah White in 1966, were presses begun in the living rooms of their houses, before moving to rented premises that functioned also as bookshops. The two presses were strongly committed to a left anti-colonial politics, (re)publishing between them a generation of Caribbean writing, including Erna Brodber's *Jane and Louisa Will Soon Come Home* (1980) and Anne Walmsley's *The Caribbean Artists*

Movement, 1966–1972: A Literary and Cultural History (1992). Both used the shop premises as a storefront, a national and international mail-order service, and as a lively meeting place for readings, lectures, debates, discussion, and workshops that spoke to the politics and concerns of the black community in Britain. In addition, Bogle and New Beacon collaborated on the first International Book Fair of Radical Black and Third World Books in 1982. Under La Rose and White, the London-based fair met annually until 1995 to promote and sell books, and to encourage literary and creative activity, educational and cultural work among the black community becoming, as Brian Alleyne argues, genuinely a 'democratizing' public space that served to undo the 'barriers between intellectuals and the [general] public ... and between genres/fields of intellectual and artistic endeavour'.[33]

Bogle and New Beacon continue a vein of radical and feminist bookshops that included Compendium, Collets, Silver Moon, Sisterwrite, Central Books, and Gay's the Word in London, Grassroots in Manchester, News from Nowhere in Liverpool, Frontline in Leicester, Greenleaf in Bristol, and Mushroom in Nottingham. As publishing and bookselling has steadily become more commercially oriented, and as independents are swallowed up by larger companies or can no longer compete with them, many of these bookshops no longer exist. The demise of the Net Book Agreement in 1996, which protected bookshops and small presses by fixing the recommended retail price, also led to the collapse of independent presses such as Sheba; others such as Virago are now part of larger international conglomerates. Thus, the Alliance of Radical Booksellers today presides over a much diminished community but its members are organizations with strong political loyalties and commitments.[34]

Prizes

Prizes are an 'influential way of bringing outstanding writers to the attention of readers'.[35] Pierre Bourdieu famously compared the function of annual literary awards and ceremonies to *haute couture* fashion collections but not everything can be reduced to financial capital or prestige, or the translations between different modes of capital.[36] Prizes, book clubs, and commendations by programmes such as BBC Radio 4's *Open Book* have become increasingly important not only to establishing a book's excellence but also to generating publicity and sales. James English suggests that the prize is 'an instrument of cultural exchange' in a terrain in which art, money, artists, patrons, bureaucrats, functionaries, and administrators of culture are all 'significant players'.[37] Since its establishment in 1969, the Man Booker, Britain's best-known prize for literary fiction, has been awarded to nearly twice as many men as women. Female winners include Nadine Gordimer (1974), Iris Murdoch (1978), Ruth Prawer Jhabvala (1975),

A.S. Byatt (1990), Arundhati Roy (1997), Kiran Desai (2006), and Hilary Mantel (2009 and 2012). However, the repeated marginalization of women writers is reflected in the somewhat sexist 'spinsterish' term 'Booker Bridesmaid', coined for Beryl Bainbridge, who was nominated five times but never won.

The Booker's failure to recognize women writers was a persistent problem. Although, in 1992, women published more books than men (60/40 percentage split), only 10 per cent of novelists shortlisted for the Booker were women; in 1991 the Booker shortlist featured no women writers. In response to what was seen as a bias in the literary establishment towards men, illustrated by that all-male Booker shortlist, a group of journalists, writers, publishers, booksellers, and agents decided to set up an all-women prize of equal status to the Booker. There was already a women-only prize, the Fawcett Society Book Prize (1982–97), awarded to the book that had done most to further understanding of women's lives and experiences in the year preceding the award. Alternating annually between fiction and non-fiction, prize-winners include Stevie Davies, Shena Mackay, Pat Barker, Carolyn Steedman, and Marina Warner. Established in 1996, the Orange Prize for Fiction was open to any full-length novel written in English by a woman of any nationality and published for the first time in the UK. Orange withdrew its sponsorship in 2012, and in 2013 the Women's Prize for Fiction was funded privately. A new sponsorship deal resulted in the relaunch of the prize as the Baileys Prize for Fiction in 2014.

The question of whether in the late twentieth- and twenty-first century a women-only prize for writing is needed periodically prompts heated debates about reverse sexism and literary apartheids, about ghettoization, and changed circumstances. The huge popularity of women writers such as Mantel and J.K. Rowling, the wide influence of women in publishing and marketing such as Amanda Ross of the Richard and Judy Book Club, or Gail Rebuck, Chair of Penguin Random House, the predominance of women on the 2013 Booker shortlist and the all-women 2013 Costa Book Awards shortlist suggest to some that the battle has been won. Prizes, of course, not only represent literary value *per se*; the transfer of different kinds of capital – economic, social, cultural, symbolic, and journalistic – is vital to a literary marketplace that relies both on differentiation and validation for its wares, and for creating a niche target group of readers. As a result, there are many prizes today, each speaking to different sets of concerns: The Commonwealth Writers Prize (now awarded for short stories), Scottish Book of the Year, The Guardian Fiction Prize, the T.S. Eliot Poetry Prize, the Forward Prize for Poetry, the Costa Book Award, the SI Leeds Literary Prize for Black and Asian Women Writers, the Green Carnation Prize; many, though not all, of these demand that the book is published or first published in the UK.

There are equally as many sponsors, writers, and readers that form specific markets and audiences for awards; prizes help publicize and sell books, adding to the notes and material already available to book groups and individual readers by publishers and publicists. In the performative rituals of award ceremonies, the media circus, book promotions and readings that accompany the award, communities of readers and writers are forged. As could be seen in the consciousness-raising days of women's collectives, readers, needless to say, also read against the grain, and use books for non-textual social, communal, and political activities of their own.

Politics and commerce are integral to women's writing and publishing. The political effectiveness of the Women's Movement since the 1970s has always been a transnational phenomenon not bounded by geographical location, but the internationalism of women's writing is also part and parcel of a larger commercial world republic of letters. Sexual politics includes words and culture but these are forged within institutional and organizational contexts; cultural politics has created audiences for women's writing, but segmentation of the marketplace and need for differentiation have also contributed to the establishment of niche genres, markets, and publishers of women's writing, not all of whom are politicized in the manner of 1970s women's movements. In conclusion, what is evident in such a brief account is how culture, politics, and commerce intermesh in the literary infrastructures that attend women's literary work.

Notes

1. Simone Murray, *Mixed Media: Feminist Presses and Publishing Politics* (London: Pluto Press, 2004).
2. Quoted in Eileen Cadman, Gail Chester, and Agnes Pivot, *Rolling Our Own: Women as Printers, Publishers and Distributors* (London: Minority Press, 1981), p. 26. Quoted in Joan Scanlon and Julia Swindells, 'Bad Apple', *The Trouble and Strife Reader*, ed. Deborah Cameron and Julia Swindells (London: Bloomsbury, 2009), p. 217.
3. http://mith.umd.edu/WomensStudies/ReferenceRoom/Publications/about-sheba-press.html, accessed 17 July 2013.
4. Lilian Mohin, *One Foot on the Mountain* (London: Onlywomen Press, 1979), p. 12.
5. There is some dispute as to whether the foundation of the press is 1972 or 1973. See Murray, p. 35.
6. Carmen Callil, 'Women, Publishing and Power', *Writing: A Women's Business*, ed. Judy Simons and Kate Fullbrook (Manchester University Press, 1998), p. 185.
7. Virago timeline, www.virago.co.uk/the-history-of-virago/, accessed 14 July 2013.
8. 'Virago Modern Classics' advertisement, n.d.
9. Carmen Callil, 'Virago Reprints', *Times Literary Supplement*, 12 September 1980, p. 1001.
10. Carmen Callil, 'The Future of Feminist Publishing', *The Bookseller,* 1 March 1986, pp. 850–2.
11. Pascale Casanova, *The World Republic of Letters* (Cambridge, Mass.: Harvard University Press, 2004), p. 108.
12. See The Women's Press, 'Feminism and Publishing', *News From Neasden*, 11, (1979), pp. 32–4.

13. Ros de Lanerolle, 'Publishing Against the "Other Censorship"', *Index on Censorship* (October 1990), pp. 8–9.
14. My capitalization of 'Black' indicates a broadly inclusive figuring of different peoples who experience racial discrimination. Current particularly in the 1980s, this is a term that included peoples of African, Caribbean, and South Asian descent. Where the lower case of 'black' is used, a more neutrally 'descriptive' and sociological usage applies. However, terms and what they signify change. See www.britsoc.co.uk/equality/.
15. Elizabeth Young, 'The Business of Feminism: Issues in London Feminist Publishing', *Frontiers*, 10:3 (1989), p. 4.
16. Rhonda Cobham and Merle Collins, eds, *Watchers and Seekers* (London: The Women's Press, 1987), p. 8.
17. The Women's Press publicity blurb for Science Fiction, incorporated into Joanna Russ, *The Female Man* (London: The Women's Press, 1975).
18. Michèle Roberts, *Paper Houses* (London: Virago, 2008), p. 130.
19. Nicci Gerrard, *Into the Mainstream: How Feminism Has Changed Women's Writing* (London: Pandora, 1989), p. 68.
20. Publicity blurb, Inside cover, *One Foot on the Mountain*.
21. Claire Buck, 'Poetry and the Women's Movement in Postwar Britain', *Contemporary British Poetry*, ed. James Acheson and Romana Huk (Albany: State University of New York Press, 1996), pp. 103–4.
22. Alvin Alvarez, *The New Poetry* (Harmondsworth: Penguin, 1966).
23. Gail Chester, 'The Anthology as a Medium for Feminist Debate in the UK', *Women's Studies International Forum*, 25:2 (2002), p. 196.
24. http://mith.umd.edu/WomensStudies/ReferenceRoom/Publications/about-sheba-press.html, accessed 5 November 2013.
25. Pratibha Parmar and Sona Osman, 'Introduction', *A Dangerous Knowing: Four Black Women Poets*, ed. Barbara Burford, Gabriela Pearse, Grace Nichols, and Jackie Kay (London: Sheba Feminist Press, 1984), p. vii.
26. Shabnam Grewal, Jackie Kay, Liliane Landor, Gail Lewis, and Pratibha Parmar, *Charting the Journey: Writings by Black and Third World Women* (London: Sheba Feminist Press, 1988), p. 1.
27. Some of these debates about black identities were put into motion by the innovative work of the black film collectives in the 1980s: see Lynne Jackson and Jean Rasenberger, 'Young, British and Black', *Cineaste*, 16:4 (1988), pp. 24–5; Kobena Mercer, ed., *Black Film, British Cinema*: ICA Documents 7 (London: ICA, 1988); Lisa Appignanesi, ed., *Identity*: *The Real Me*: ICA Documents 6 (London: ICA, 1988).
28. See Kadija Sesay, 'Publishing, Books', *Companion to Contemporary Black British Culture*, ed. Alison Donnell (London: Routledge, 2002), pp. 247–50, and 'Publishing', *The Oxford Companion to Black British History*, ed. David Dabydeen, John Gilmore, and Cecily Jones (Oxford University Press, 2008), pp. 380–4.
29. Asian Women Writers Collective, *Flaming Spirit* (London: Virago, 1994), p. xiii.
30. South Asian Diaspora Literature and Arts Archives, www.vads.ac.uk/large.php?uid=47321&sos=0&pic3=aw1-8, accessed 27 November 2013.
31. Interview with author, 17 October 2011.
32. Amy Goodman, 'Women's Voices from Africa: A Conversation with Margaret Busby', www.democracynow.org/2006/3/8/womens_voices_from_africa_a_conversation, accessed 27 November 2013.

33. Brian Allenyne, *Radicals Against Race: Black Activism and Cultural Politics* (London: Bloomsbury, 2002), p. 61.
34. See www.radicalbooksellers.co.uk/, accessed 30 December 2013.
35. Kate Mosse, 'History', www.womensprizeforfiction.co.uk/about/history, accessed 1 December 2013.
36. Pierre Bourdieu, *The Field of Cultural Production* (Cambridge: Polity, 1993), p. 100.
37. James English, *The Economy of Prestige* (Cambridge, Mass. and London: Harvard University Press, 2005), p. 12.

Part II
Feminism and Fiction: Evolution and Dissent

6
The *Grandes Dames*: Writers of Longevity

Maroula Joannou

This chapter focuses on the *grandes dames* of literature: Beryl Bainbridge (1932–2010), Anita Brookner, A.S. Byatt, Margaret Drabble, Doris Lessing (1919–2013), Iris Murdoch (1919–99), Margaret Forster, Barbara Pym (1913–80), and Muriel Spark (1918–2006). The oldest is Pym, born before the First World War. Spark was born at the end of the war, Lessing and Murdoch just after it, followed by Brookner in 1928. The remaining four – Bainbridge, Byatt, Forster, and Drabble – were children during the Second World War. Their adolescent memories were of the deferential conservative Britain of the 1950s which was to give way to the more permissive society of the 1960s. With the exception of Bainbridge and Brookner, whose writing careers were launched in the 1970s and 1980s respectively, the books that initially established the literary reputations of these writers were, largely, published in the 1960s: Spark, *The Prime of Miss Jean Brodie* (1963); Lessing, *The Golden Notebook* (1962); Drabble, *The Millstone* (1965); Forster, *Georgie Girl* (1965); and Murdoch, *A Severed Head* (1961). Pym's *Excellent Women* (1952) was even earlier, and other texts of the 1950s were highly significant in the published *oeuvre* of some authors, for example Murdoch's *Under the Net* (1954), and Lessing's *The Grass is Singing* (1950) and *Martha Quest* (1952).

Viewed in total, their work constitutes a formidable exploration of the aspirations, concerns, and anxieties of the second half of the twentieth century and of the twenty-first. This is evident in, for instance, the coming-of-age novel sequence of Byatt and the matrilineal fictions of Drabble and Forster, in which the personal fortunes and social histories are traced over many years and linked to their characters' lives. While some writers have remained remarkably consistent in style and subject matter, the longevity of their production has allowed for consistent engagement with specific themes such as alienation, isolation, and the loss of spiritual values, as well as considerable formal and generic variety. Lessing, for instance, moves between realist, dystopian, and science fictions; Bainbridge changes from fiction about her present day to historical fiction; Brookner shifts from female characters to focalization through male characters.

The term *'grandes dames'* is ambivalent. These women are distinguished writers who have become established literary figures and who have all been conferred with numerous honours and awards in public recognition of their literary achievements. Bainbridge, Byatt, Drabble, Murdoch, and Spark are all Dames of the British Empire and Brookner is a Commander of the British Empire. However, the laurels acquired in maturity should not distract from the dissidence that is sometimes discernible in their writing, nor from the deeply felt sense of themselves as situated on the margins of mainstream society in Britain; this is particularly marked in those writers with an exilic consciousness (Lessing, Murdoch, and Spark). Moreover, their own sense of themselves as outsiders can appear to sit uncomfortably alongside the widespread public perception of these women as established literary figures. For example, Lessing, while accepting a Nobel Laureate for Literature, declined the title of Dame of the British Empire offered in 1992, citing her history of support for the liberation movements and anti-racist struggles in Africa: 'Thank you for offering me this honour: I am very pleased. But for some time now I have been wondering, "But where is this British Empire?"' When young she had done her best 'to undo that bit of the British Empire I found myself in: that is, old Southern Rhodesia'.[1]

Feminism and the female literary tradition

The *grandes dames* demonstrate that there is no simple equation between feminist fiction and women's writing although all have benefited from a female readership and feminist critique of their work. Suspicious of political activism, of 'women's fiction', and often wary of feminist criticism, they have, with a few notable exceptions, maintained a cautious distance from, or in some instances explicit hostility to, the politics of organized feminism. This is due in part to their formative attitudes to gender and sexuality having taken shape before the Women's Liberation Movement of the late 1960s and the 1970s and such legislative milestones as the Divorce Reform Act (1969), the Equal Pay Act (1970), and the Sex Discrimination Act (1975). Until second-wave feminists demanded that the personal be recognized as political, the gendered inequalities of the home, workplace, and personal relationships were frequently accepted as part of the 'natural' order of things and left without question. Bainbridge explains her antipathy to feminism:

> I've never been drawn to the feminist movement. I was brought up to believe that men had little to do with the home or children – except to bring in the money. I've never been put down by a man, unless I deserved it, and have never felt inferior. It seems to me that a mutually beneficial relationship between a man and woman requires the man to be dominant. A sensible woman will allow the man to think he is the most important partner.[2]

Both Murdoch and Byatt defended the notion of the universality of human experience in accordance with the dominant intellectual assumptions and practices in their respective academic disciplines of Philosophy and English Literature after the war. In all her 27 works of fiction, Murdoch has no female central protagonist and displays little interest in depicting the specificity of women's experience: 'About writing as a man, this is instinctive. I identify more with my male characters than my female characters ... I think I want to write about things on the whole where it doesn't matter whether you're male or female, in which case you'd better be male because a male represents ordinary human beings, unfortunately, as things stand at the moment, whereas a woman is always a woman!'[3]

In an Introduction to her first novel, *The Shadow of the Sun* (1964), reissued in 1991, Byatt recollects the sexual discrimination encountered at university in the 1950s when her research grant was withdrawn on marriage while men in her position had theirs increased so that they could support their families: 'We had fought, much harder than the men, who outnumbered us eleven to one, to be allowed to study at Cambridge, and we were fatally torn, when thinking of our futures, hopes of marriage, and hopes of something, some work, beyond getting to university at all. Men could have both, work and love, but it seemed that women couldn't.'[4] Byatt explains how she jettisoned her aspirations to become 'at once, a passionate woman and a passionate intellectual' and adopted the term 'lamination' to describe the deliberate separation of the two layers of her identity as a 'strategy for survival'.[5] She feels that she was born too late to identify with the Women's Movement and that literature has 'always been my way out, my escape from the limits of being female. I don't want to have to get back in.'[6]

Irrespective of their individual positions in relation to feminist theory and practice, the fiction of this group is steeped in intertexual references displaying intimate knowledge of women's literary traditions, recognition of the primary importance of emotional relationships between women, and acknowledgement of important literary debts. Examples include Drabble's friendship with Lessing, Byatt's admiration for George Eliot, and Pym's indebtedness to Jane Austen. Brookner, too, while adamant that she is not a feminist, creates fictive structures of sensibility entirely compatible with the writings and values of the feminists she disowns. *Hotel du Lac* (1984) is dedicated to her mentor and friend Rosamond Lehmann, 'because I hoped it might be the kind of novel she would find to her taste'.[7] The central protagonist bears 'a striking physical resemblance to Virginia Woolf', who is a benevolent unseen presence in the novel: 'Edith thought with shame of her small injustices, of her unworthy words to those excellent women who had befriended her ... She bent her head, overcome by a sense of unworthiness. I have taken the name of Virginia Woolf in vain, she thought.'[8]

Among the best-known casualties of the changing literary mores in this period is Pym, who had enjoyed considerable success in the 1950s, particularly with *Excellent Women.* Although it was not noticeably different in subject matter to her previous work, *An Unsuitable Attachment* (1982) was rejected in 1963 by Jonathan Cape who had published all six of Pym's previous books. The reasons were never fully specified but *An Unsuitable Attachment* with its well-mannered canon's daughter, Ianthe Broome, a typical Pym protagonist with her penchant for sensible clothes, good antique furniture, and church tours of Rome, was almost certainly considered too dated to appeal to contemporary taste. The subsequent eclipse of her literary reputation that left Pym without a publisher for 14 years ended when she was named among the most underrated writers of the twentieth century by both David Cecil and Philip Larkin in a symposium organized by *The Times Literary Supplement* in 1977. *Quartet in Autumn* was published the same year and *The Sweet Dove Died*, which had been rejected initially, followed in 1978. *An Unsuitable Attachment* was published after Pym's death from cancer in 1980, as was *An Academic Question* (1986), first written in 1970–72.

Following closely in Pym's footsteps in the attempt to make old-fashioned (usually feminine) virtue appear interesting for a late twentieth-century readership was Brookner. Her lonely, fastidious, intelligent women – it was not until *Lewis Percy* (1989) that her focalization was to be through a man – are generally more sophisticated than Pym's while often displaying a similarly wry sense of humour and a knowingly self-deprecating attitude towards the self. Finely discriminating about art and literature, they are equally astute about the vicissitudes of their own lives: in her first novel, *A Start in Life* (1981), Dr Ruth Weiss, who 'at forty, knew that her life had been ruined by literature', is writing a book on women in Balzac's novels.[9] The question that concerns Brookner in her writing, no less than it obsesses Edith Hope, the romantic novelist in *Hotel du Lac*, is 'what behaviour most becomes a woman, the question around which she had written most of her novels' (p. 40).

Further questions preoccupy and inform the writing of this group of writers. What do we know of our mothers' lives? How can we escape from or honour their legacy? Must we resemble our mothers more as we grow older? How can we live our lives as mothers and daughters at the same time? These questions, asked variously in *A Room of One's Own* (1929) by Virginia Woolf (1882–1941), Alice Walker's *In Search of Our Mothers' Gardens* (1984), and Lorna Goodison's *I Am Becoming My Mother* (1986), are notably present in the fiction of Drabble and her exact contemporary Forster. Their writing offers prescient insights into the experience of maternity and the lives and aspirations of intelligent women struggling to juggle relationships with siblings and women friends, with love affairs, marriage, motherhood, and work. Drabble's novels *A Summer Bird Cage* (1963), *The Garrick Year* (1964), *The Millstone,* and *Jerusalem the Golden* (1967) anticipated the Women's Liberation Movement which formalized women's demands for equal pay, equal educational and employment opportunities, 24-hour nurseries, free contraception, and abortion on demand. Like *The Millstone,* Forster's *Georgie Girl,* published in the same year, is one of the iconic novels about London in the 1960s. Georgie is besotted with a baby that the biological mother does not want to keep. This is at a time when unmarried motherhood was too heavily stigmatized for women to contemplate with equanimity, even those with the confidence, social status, and financial security of Rosamond Stacey in *The Millstone.*

Forster has published social history and literary biography alongside fiction: *Daphne du Maurier* (1993) and *Elizabeth Barrett Browning* (1988). *Hidden Lives* (1995) tells the stories of three generations of women in her own family, her grandmother, Margaret Ann, her mother Lilian, and the author herself, and includes such 'shameful' family secrets as illegitimacy. *Significant Sisters* (1984) is a study of a hundred years of feminist activism from 1839 to 1939. In several novels, including *The Battle for Christabel* (1991), *The Memory Box* (2000), and *Over* (2007), Forster's focus is on women attempting to come to terms with loss, grief, and personal trauma by sifting through their memories and trying to understand the effects of the past. In *The Battle for Christabel* an orphaned little girl is caught in a tug-of-war between her maternal grandmother and her foster mother whose stories unravel during the adoption proceedings. In *The Memory Box,* Catherine is prompted by objects left to her to discover what she can about her birth mother's life by tracking down her cold-hearted relatives. *Over* is about how men and women differ in their expressions of grief as Louise leaves home to start a new life after the accidental death of her daughter, failing to realize that her own way of coping is as damaging to her family as her husband's obsessive quest to hold others responsible for Miranda's death. In *The Unknown Bridesmaid* (2013), Julia, a child psychologist who specializes in behavioural difficulties, is jolted into revisiting an unhappy incident in her own troubled childhood to come to a better understanding of herself. Forster's interest in family, memory, and tracing the lives of ordinary women in the twentieth century from birth to death come together in her fictionalized memoir, *Diary of an Ordinary Woman* (2003). We are initially invited to believe that 95-year-old Millicent King (revealed to be fictitious) has read and admired *Hidden Lives* and presented Forster with the diaries from 1914 to 1995 to edit for posterity. Written in part in diary form, the novel scrupulously records the minutiae of family life and the social and political changes of the twentieth century, the significance of which Millicent is hardly aware.

Tess Cosslett defines the matrilineal narrative as 'one which either tells the stories of several generations of women at once, or which shows how the identity of a central character is crucially formed by her female ancestors'.[10] Matrilineal narrative takes the reader backwards and forwards in time. A key discovery made in Byatt's erudite historical romance, *Possession* (1991), a phenomenal bestseller despite being as intellectually challenging as any of its Victorian antecedents, is that the Victorian poet Christabel LaMotte, into whose life Maud Bailey is researching, is the scholar's own great-great-great-grandmother. Thereafter, the novel is predicated on Maud's desire to understand her family history. One recurring feature of such narratives is the emotional relationship between mother and daughter, fraught, unhappy, loving, ambivalent, grateful, or resentful as the case may be. In *The Witch of Exmoor* (1996) Drabble avoids romanticizing the primary bond between mother and daughter. Her ageing protagonist is emotionally rooted in the feminist struggles of the 1960s and retreats to the country to write her memoirs and to do battle with her three middle-aged children concerned with their genetic and material inheritance. As Adrienne Rich puts it, 'We are, none of us, "either" mothers or daughters; to our amazement, confusion, and greater complexity, we are both' and mothering and non-mothering are both charged concepts for us because *'whichever we did has been turned against us'*.[11] Their mother's life was an unhappy object lesson for both Drabble and her older sister (A.S. Byatt), who writes of her mother's 'perpetual rage, depression, and frustration' which she was to come to recognize as the driving force that made sure none of her daughters became housebound: 'we wanted "not to be like her"' (Byatt, 1991, p. ix). In *Babel Tower* (1996), Frederica reflects, 'I always resented my own mother's passive quietness. It was not a life. It was what I do not want. It is what I have got.'[12]

The central controlling metaphor of Drabble's *The Peppered Moth* (2000) is the Biston Betularia, a species of speckled moth with a distinctive pattern of evolution that offers an interpretative framework for three generations of women whose lives have taken very different turns. Scientists believe that some variants of this moth acquired dark wings as camouflage in order to survive in a polluted industrial environment while the lighter coloured specimens unable to adapt to their habitat became virtually extinct. Like the black moth, the clever Bessie appears to merge inconspicuously with the drab surroundings of the grim provincial town to which she returns as a teacher after the failed promise of metamorphosis at university. But she becomes increasingly bitter, frustrated and disgruntled with her dull marriage and wasted academic potential. Bessie is a fictionalized version of Drabble's own mother: *'This is a novel about my mother, Kathleen Marie Bloor ... Maybe I should have tried to write a factual memoir of her life, but I have written this instead.'*[13]

Both Chrissie, Bessie's daughter, and Faro, her granddaughter, escape provincial life. But many years later the sophisticated, intellectually curious Faro, trying to work out who she is and what she wants from life, is ineluctably drawn back to the small northern town to listen to a scientific talk about matrilineal descent and mitochondrial DNA, the genetic substance peculiar to women that passes on patterns of behaviour from one generation to the next. Dr Hawthorn hopes to enlist the help of the women in the audience to answer some of his scientific questions about their genetic inheritance and to understand the resemblances between mother and daughter to which

Drabble pointedly directs the readers' attention: 'Can you tell from whom they may descend, can you discern the form of their common ancestor? Will Dr Hawthorn be able to reveal their origins to them, and if he can, will they want to know?' (p. 2).

Home and away

Spark, Murdoch, and Lessing, none of whom were English by birth, thought of themselves as outsiders and wrote about the exilic condition. As Murdoch told John Haffenden, 'I feel as I grow older that we were wanderers, and I've only recently realized that I'm a kind of exile, a displaced person. I identify with exiles.'[14] Lessing always thought of Rhodesia (Zimbabwe) as 'home' but became a *persona non grata* for many years in the country of her birth due to her opposition to its white racist policies. Born in Dublin to Irish parents, Murdoch was taken as a baby to London. Her family, 'Irish on both sides for 300 years never assimilated into English life, staying a small enclosed unit, never gaining many – if any – English friends' (Haffenden, p. 33). As her biographer Peter Conradi puts it, there is a 'lifetime's investment in Irishness visible in every decade' of Murdoch's life as a writer.[15] Born and educated in Edinburgh, the setting for *The Prime of Miss Jean Brodie,* Spark lived in Rhodesia, London, New York, Rome, and Tuscany. Bryan Cheyette describes her as an 'essentially diasporic writer with a fluid sense of self'.[16]

Bainbridge grew up in a household beset by domestic squabbles and claimed her father as the basis for some of her male protagonists, including Captain Scott – even though 'Scott went to the South Pole and my father never went further than the corner shop.'[17] Although she lived much of her adult life in London, Bainbridge remained emotionally rooted in Liverpool. In *English Journey* (1984), she wrote that, although she had left the city some 20 years earlier, 'I am so tied to it by the past, by memories of family and beginnings, that I still think of it as home.'[18] Her early novels *Harriet Said* (1972), *The Dressmaker* (1973), and *The Bottle Factory Outing* (1974) reflected the dismally repressive world she had known: 'All my childhood was spent with people who were disappointed. They'd married the wrong person, failed in employment, been manipulated by others.' Moreover, family, friends and acquaintances 'were either dead common or a cut above themselves' (1984, p. 99). *The Dressmaker,* set in Liverpool in the war, 'was about my two aunts, Margaret and Nellie, plus a plot' in which the torso of a two-timing American serviceman is dumped in the river. 'Then came *The Bottle Factory Outing,* because for a while I worked in a bottling factory here, and the story was all true, apart from the murder plot' (Guppy, p. 255).

Women writers old enough to remember the hopes and aspirations of the postwar settlement were often critical as the centre of gravity of British politics moved to the right, alienating those with egalitarian politics on the liberal left. Some whose writing was deeply rooted in nineteenth-century realist traditions were acutely aware that their own literary sensibilities appeared out of sorts with altered times. Drabble, editor of *The Oxford Companion to English Literature* (1995), commented, 'I'd rather be at the end of a dying tradition, which I admire, than at the beginning of a tradition which I deplore.'[19] Drabble, associated with what came disparagingly to be known as the 'Hampstead novel' (fiction focused on the lives and finer feelings of the cultured metropolitan middle class), was an outspoken critic of the Gulf War and of the Americanization of British society. She explained, 'they [the politicians] shift but I don't! My position is very familiar to *Guardian* readers. I don't feel there's a party that represents me now.'[20]

Both Drabble and Byatt employ the novel sequence as a way of tracing change over time. Drabble's *The Radiant Way* (1987), the first of a trilogy consisting of *A Natural Curiosity* (1989) and *The Gates of Ivory* (1991), starts with three middle-aged friends (her women protagonists got older as the novelist aged herself) who have followed very different life paths. Esther, an art historian, Liz, a psychiatrist, and Alix, an outreach worker, meet at a New Year's Eve party in 1979 after the election of Thatcher's Conservative government. Britain is soon to be riven with disharmony and social division as rampant individualism takes over from the co-operative ethos that underwrote the creation of the welfare state. *The Radiant Way* was the title of a book for primary school children and its optimism symbolized the confidence of the progressive postwar social consensus. *A Natural Curiosity* follows Alix in her quest to understand the mentality of a vicious serial killer to its roots in his dysfunctional family. *The Gates of Ivory* deals with Liz's attempts to establish the whereabouts of a missing friend. His personal effects lead her to an excursion to the killing fields of the Khmer Rouge in Cambodia.

Byatt's novel sequence, comprised of *The Virgin in the Garden* (1978), *Still Life* (1985), *Babel Tower*, and *A Whistling Woman* (2002), is an ambitious work of historiography that took a quarter of a century to complete. The tetralogy explores the changing anatomy of England in the 1950s and 1960s alongside the changing lives of intelligent young women like Frederica Potter. Byatt begins with *The Virgin in the Garden* and the hope of a New Elizabethan age initiated by the coronation of the young Queen Elizabeth II in 1953. The Suez crisis of 1956 erupts in Frederica's third year at university and was to end the postwar illusion of national unity, splitting the country into two irreconcilable warring camps. At the start of *Still Life* Frederica is leaving grammar school for university. Intellectually gifted and curious, she is unsure about a career and considers a future writing 'witty, critical journalism, maybe even a new urban novel like those of Iris Murdoch'.[21] Underlying the representation of girls' education in the 'condition-of-England' novels of both Byatt and Drabble is the question, 'education for what?' Byatt writes of an earlier historical time before contraception was freely available, when very few, privileged girls attended university, and the pursuit of academic success was often presented as joyless and austere. Moreover, the examples set by mothers, school mistresses, and female dons presented the enjoyment of sexuality, femininity, and intellectual work as all but impossible, and career, marriage, and motherhood as conflicting, alternative, or sequential rather than compatible roles. The entrapment of intelligent woman in domesticity is Byatt's *bête noir*. In contrast to Frederica, her older sister, Stephanie, settles for motherhood and married life in the provinces after graduation, unhappily relinquishing the intellectual stimulation to which university accustomed her and which she still craves. The tragic early death that befalls Stephanie in *Still Life* symbolizes what Byatt clearly sees as the wasted potential of a life misspent.

The events in *Babel Tower* and *A Whistling Woman* take place in the 1960s in a Britain altered beyond recognition by social, political, and technical change. Frederica, a young, unhappily married mother, is able to divorce and acquire a lover and a job as a television presenter in London. The possibility of combining love and a fulfilling new career in middle life would have appeared impossible for most educated women a mere decade earlier, and the opportunities open to Frederica as a divorcee reflect the social transformations on which each part of the novel sequence looks forward or back. The prologue to *Still Life* is set in 1980, far in advance of the events the novel depicts, and the prologue to *The Virgin in the Garden* in 1968, moving the reader forward in time and to the National Portrait Gallery where Dame Flora Robson's performance of Elizabeth I is attended by Frederica and her former schoolteacher who recollects his own verse-drama about the Virgin Queen produced in 1953 at Frederica's school.

Literary responses to the nightmares of the twentieth century

Lessing, Murdoch, and others who had survived the great traumas of the century – fascism, the Second World War, the Holocaust, the Atomic bomb – reflected upon the horrors through which they had lived. As Byatt writes of her women at university in the 1950s in *Still Life*: 'They were – we were – a generation who had characteristically ... lived through a convulsive and exhausting piece of history ... Most had felt creeping terror about human nature itself, faced with the pictures and documents of Belsen and Auschwitz, Hiroshima and Nagasaki, for which some parents sought to protect their young' (p. 280). The recognition that it had not been possible for the forces of reason to withstand the forces of barbarism that Hitler unleashed marked a significant shift in the contemporary imagination as writers were forced to contemplate the abyss.

After *The Golden Notebook*, Lessing became disillusioned with the organized Left, began to explore spirituality and Sufism, and gravitated to futuristic visionary forms of writing. *Shikasta* (1979) is the first volume in the *Canopus in Argos: Archives* consisting of *Three, Four, and Five* (1980), *The Sirian Experiments* (1980), *The Making of the Representative for Planet 8* (1982), and *Documents Relating to the Sentimental Agents in the Volyen Empire* (1983). Lessing's concerns here, as in *Briefing for a Descent into Hell* (1971) and *Memoirs of a Survivor* (1975), are largely terrestrial rather than extraterrestrial. Her interest in the technologies of the future is minimal as opposed to her interest in the moral and philosophical questions the imaginary future enables her to explore. Lessing envisaged *Canopus in Argos: Archives* 'as a framework that enables me to tell (I hope) a beguiling tale or two; to put questions, both to myself and to others; to explore ideas and sociological possibilities'.[22]

Canopus in Argus: Archives uses Shikasta (planet earth) to warn the twentieth century about the consequences of its own folly and emphasizes that in order for their world to survive human beings must become receptive to ways of feeling and thinking that are not their own. Shikasta is the name allocated by the colonizer, the victorious galactic empire Canopus; the defeated galactic power Sirius is permitted to conduct other experiments in the South. The future in *Shikasta* is the very near future, the late twentieth century, near enough to the present for Lessing's ideological project to be recognizable to the reader. If galactic visitors have a purpose – and images of surveillance proliferate – it is to enable human beings to see the universe differently. In *Shikasta,* the final days of the planet ruined by the arms race, weapons of mass destruction, war, pestilence, and environmental catastrophe are recounted by Johor, a benevolent emissary who surveys the excesses of the twentieth century with bemused incomprehension: 'Looking from outside at this planet it was as if at a totally crazed species.'[23] *The Sirian Experiments* is narrated from the viewpoint of Ambien 11 of the Sirian colonial service whose complacent misconceptions about the superiority of the Empire Sirius are shaken as she struggles to take in more of the universe. Her restricted vision reflects the limited ability of highly evolved species to encompass their place in the wider scheme of things. The difficult truth with which the narrator must come to terms is that the detested Canopean Empire is by far the more advanced of the two.

The images of Belsen concentration camp profoundly affected Bainbridge and may help to account for her violent and macabre plots. Spark, of English Protestant descent through her mother and Jewish descent through her father, was present at the trials in Jerusalem of the Nazi war criminal Adolf Eichmann. Her mordant subject matter and experimental fictive techniques (one short story, 'The Seraph and the Zambezi' (1951), has been described as 'possibly the first example by a British author of what became known as magic realism') bear witness to the inadequacy of language to describe the evils that the trial had brought to light.[24] The Holocaust also influenced Murdoch, who was employed by the United Nations Relief and Rehabilitation Administration and worked with Jews fleeing persecution in Austria.

The deracinated, dispossessed, and displaced come to occupy an important place in her fiction, in which the refugee figures often as a barometer of the human condition. In contrast to later Jewish writers, such as Linda Grant and Naomi Alderman, who explore the legacy of the Holocaust and the specificity of Jewish experience in Britain, Brookner scarcely uses the word 'Jewish', and does not accentuate Jewish culture or refer explicitly to the Holocaust, elisions that may intimate the difficulties of writing about trauma explicitly as well as the absence of an established Jewish literary tradition in Britain. Nonetheless, many of her characters are the children of European immigrants to Britain and are clearly recognizable as Jewish in origin: for example, the two central characters in *Latecomers* (1988) who arrive in Britain on the *Kindertransport* from Germany.

Murdoch's philosophically searching fiction and preoccupation with questions of good and evil are also a response to the Second World War. Like the French avant-garde *nouveau roman* (the work of Alain Robbe-Grillet and Nathalie Sarraute were important influences on Spark as well as Murdoch), her novels suggest new ways of grappling with alienation, isolation, and the predicaments of the modern world. Murdoch's fiction is continuous with her interest in moral philosophy and her preoccupation with ethical choice. Finding herself intellectually at odds with logical positivism and the dominant Anglo-American analytical philosophical tradition, Murdoch introduced the English reader to Sartre in her book *Sartre: Romantic Rationalist* (1953). In France the novels of Sartre and Camus were widely read and discussed but, until Murdoch became the doyenne of a new kind of intellectually serious philosophical novel published after the war, England had no equivalent history of professional philosophers publishing literary fiction. Over the course of time, Murdoch's fiction came to be influenced by Marxism, Christian and Buddhist mysticism, Platonism, Freud, and spirituality. Isaiah Berlin famously derided her as 'a lady not known for the clarity of her views' (Conradi, p. 301).

Murdoch's Booker Prize-winning novel *The Sea, The Sea* (1998) dramatizes her notion of life as a moral struggle between the egotistical self which seeks power and domination and the moral imagination which aspires to respect the autonomy of others. Drawing on *The Tempest,* Murdoch grapples, as she does in *The Flight from the Enchanter* (1956), *The Black Prince* (1981), and *The Philosopher's Pupil* (1984), with the misuses of power by megalomaniacs, delusional states of jealousy, and extreme romantic infatuation. Charles Arrowby, a Prospero-like figure, abjures the enchantment of the London stage to retire to an isolated house by the sea professing that his objective in later life is to learn how to be good. However, his one-time sweetheart, held captive in the house, contests his fantasy about their past as Murdoch explores a maze of moral arguments pertaining to Arrowby's preposterous delusion that his controlling behaviour is in the best interests of those whom he manipulates.

The metaphysical, the surreal, and the grotesque

In their different ways both Spark and Bainbridge explore the macabre, including representations of death and the workings of the subconscious, using unsettling imagery and incongruous juxtapositions of subject matter. A defining moment in Spark's life was her conversion to Roman Catholicism in the 1950s. In an interview with Martin McQuillan, Spark insisted that 'I am a Catholic and I'm a believing Catholic' but that 'I don't set out to be a Catholic apologist in any form.'[25] As Hélène Cixous puts it, 'Unlike her co-religionists, whose view of the world reflects their attachment to traditional humanist values and their distance from the world they deem decadent, Spark underscores the irreparable duplicity of the universe, where ordinary things coexist with supernatural ones in hideous harmony' (McQuillan, p. 205). While secular naratives are open to religious interpretations in much of Spark's earlier fiction, *The Abbess of Crewe* (1974) signals an important shift of direction; religious dissemblings have secular parallels and political lessons to be imparted. Like Bainbridge, Spark yokes together incongruous elements from the satirical, the metaphysical, the absurd, the grotesque, and the mundane. In the surreal world of her fiction the devil is as likely to make his presence felt in a street in Peckham or Kensington as anywhere else. In *The Driver's Seat* (1971), advertised in publicity material as a 'metaphysical shocker', Spark has the central character apparently orchestrate her own murder at the hands of a man who has emerged from an asylum without once offering the reader the opportunity to enter the character's mind. The novel expresses in fictional terms Spark's objections to luxuriating in 'the victim-oppressor complex' and to the writer partaking in the 'cult of the victim', which she discusses in a key essay, 'The Desegregation of Art' (1971).[26] Subtitled *A Modern Morality Tale*, the novella *The Abbess of Crewe,* a fictional reworking of the Watergate scandal set in an English convent, is at once absurdist parable and literary satire.[27] Like Nixon, Sister Alexandra has introduced electronic surveillance into her office. Her supporters arrange for a break-in to the sewing box where her rival conceals incriminating letters. In Spark's mischievous hands the weighty Watergate affair becomes a *reductio ad absurdum*: all that is stolen in the robbery is a tiny thimble.

In her final psychological thriller, *Aiding and Abetting* (2000), no fewer than two highly disturbed characters purport to be Lord Lucan, the fugitive English aristocrat accused of the murder of his children's nanny in 1974 and never brought to justice. As Drew Milne puts it, 'Criminal acts that remain fictional allow Spark to trace analogies between legal understandings of crime and religious conceptions of sin.'[28] Dr Hildegard Wolf, the soi-disant psychotherapist at whose expensive private clinic in Paris both Lucans have arrived, one referred by a priest, is herself a charlatan. A notorious stigmatic who duped the gullible in Munich using another name, she is anxious to avoid detection while leading a double life as a clinical practitioner. When one of the Lord Lucans threatens to turn the last of Spark's monstrous egoists over to the police, the distinctions between innocence and guilt, pursuer and pursued, and good and evil become increasingly unclear. As in *The Abbess of Crewe,* what interests Spark in this psychological black comedy is human depravity, the nature of evil, and the psychic life of those who have chosen to enter into latter-day pacts with the devil.

Bainbridge's fictions traffic in the macabre and the perverse, whether she is dealing with historical fiction or present time; in *Injury Time* (1977), for example, the hostess is bizarrely kidnapped by intruders in the course of her own dinner party. Characters are often fickle and psychologically damaged and their behaviour hardly open to rational explication. *Sweet William* (1975) is based on her relationship with her second husband, a plausible lothario whose capacity for lying when juggling his multiple sexual entanglements is arguably matched only by the protagonist's own capacity for self-deception. Her plots, like Spark's, are surrealistic and scattered with sudden accidents and grotesque deaths. In *Master Georgie* (1998), a medical student stumbles accidentally into a Liverpool brothel to find his father dead from a heart attack. The macabre has a long history in Bainbridge's work. Her first novel, *Harriet Said,* was written in 1958 but rejected by publishers who found its subject matter too gruesome. The story is derived from newspaper clippings about two disturbed adolescent girls in New Zealand, the one egging the other on to murder. *Watson's Apology* (1984) is based on a Victorian murder eclipsed by the notorious Ripper murders in London. John Shelby Watson, a teacher, cleric, and poet manqué, brutally murders his wife Anne after returning from church in 1871: 'My marriage has destroyed me,' he thought. 'I am buried under trivialities.'[29] The voice of his hapless victim remains largely unheard.

Although Bainbridge switched from writing modern novels about women like herself to writing historical dramas exploring men and masculinity, the penchant for unexpected acts of violence and sudden deaths that she shares with Spark links the historical fiction to earlier texts like *The Bottle Factory Outing* where, on the factory workers' annual excursion, a dead woman's body is disposed of in a wine barrel destined for Portugal. The turning point in her career was *Young Adolf* (1978), which dramatizes a bizarre episode in 1912 when the young Hitler visited his brother in Liverpool and worked as a bell boy in the Adelphi Hotel. In this surrealist plot, Bainbridge stops just short of holding a dysfunctional family or a joyless Liverpool directly responsible for unleashing the evils for which Hitler was to be remembered. *The Birthday Boys* (1996) is a fictionalized account of the ill-fated Scott Polar expedition which finishes with a 1912 birthday celebration and one of Bainbridge's many portrayals of suicide. Also set in 1912, *Every Man for Himself* (1996) is centred on the maiden and only voyage of the *Titanic.* On the top deck there is untold luxury, but below, culpable negligence, disregard for safety, and an unprepared crew. The answer to the question,

'Have you not learnt that it's every man for himself?' is provided when the ship finds its nemesis, and long before that.[30]

Unlike the nineteenth and early twentieth centuries, to which Bainbridge turned for inspiration, the late twentieth and twenty-first centuries afforded writers no shared understanding of what constitutes the 'real' or the imaginative depiction of contingent reality to which they aspired. On the contrary, the complexities of the postwar world gave rise to complex generic and stylistic practices and techniques. Murdoch translated existential philosophy into aesthetic practice, reconfiguring the concerns and procedures of philosophy to deal with questions of freedom in her fiction, and Spark used the surreal, the grotesque, and bleak comedy to investigate religious questions of good and evil. Drabble's 'condition-of-England' novels depicted the consequences of 'every man for himself', the economic watchword of Thatcherite individualism, through the mimetic rendition of the minutiae of social relationships during Thatcher's time in power. Lessing's futuristic dystopias, however, moved beyond England to Armageddon and global destabilization in the philosophical denial that it was possible to represent the dangers that threatened the modern world using the literary conventions of the Victorian novel. The intellectual enquiry of these and other writers of longevity is far-ranging and sophisticated in its scope and it can also be innovative in its relationship to the literary past. As Angela Carter put it, 'most intellectual development depends on new readings of old texts. I am all for putting new wine in old bottles, especially if the pressure of the new wine makes the old bottles explode.'[31]

Notes

1. Quoted in Alison Flood, 'Doris Lessing Donates Revelatory Letter to University', *Guardian*, 22 October 2008, www.guardian.co.uk/books/2008/oct/22/doris.lessing-letters, accessed 8 April 2013.
2. Shusha Guppy, interview, 'Beryl Bainbridge: The Art of Fiction No. 164', *Paris Review*, 157 (Winter 2000), p. 259.
3. Iris Murdoch quoted in Deborah Johnston, *Iris Murdoch* (Hemel Hempstead: Harvester Press, 1987), p. xii.
4. A.S. Byatt, 'Introduction', *The Shadow of the Sun* (London: Vintage, 1991), p. ix.
5. Nicholas Tredell, 'A.S. Byatt', *Conversations with Critics*, ed. Nicholas Tredell (Manchester: Carcanet, 1994), p. 69.
6. A.S. Byatt, interview with Juliet Dusinberre, *Women Writers Talking*, ed. Janet Todd (New York: Holmes S. Meier, 1983), p. 186.
7. Anita Brookner, 'Rosamond Lehmann', *Spectator*, 17 March 1990, p. 21.
8. Anita Brookner, *Hotel du Lac* (London: Jonathan Cape, 1984), p. 88.
9. Anita Brookner, *A Start in Life* (London: Jonathan Cape, 1981), p. 1.
10. Tess Cosslett, 'Matrilineal Narratives Revisited', *Feminism and Autobiography: Texts, Theories, Methods*, ed. Tess Cosslett, Celia Lury, and Penny Summerfield (London: Routledge, 2000), pp. 142–3.
11. Adrienne Rich, *Of Woman Born: Motherhood as Experience and Institution* (1976; London: Virago, 1992), p. 253.

12. A.S. Byatt, *Babel Tower* (London: Chatto & Windus, 1996), p. 126.
13. Margaret Drabble, 'Afterword', *The Peppered Moth* (London: Viking, 2001), p. 390.
14. 'John Haffenden Talks to Iris Murdoch', *Literary Review*, 58 (April 1983), p. 33.
15. Peter Conradi, *Iris Murdoch: A Life* (London: HarperCollins, 2001), p. 29.
16. Bryan Cheyette, 'Imagined Communities: Contemporary Jewish Writers in Great Britain', *Under Postcolonial Eyes: Figuring the 'Jew' in Contemporary British Writing*, ed. Efraim Sicher and Linda Weinhouse (Lincoln: University of Nebraska Press, 2012), p. 96.
17. Quoted in Janet Watts, 'Dame Beryl Bainbridge Obituary', *Guardian*, 3 July 2010, p. 39.
18. Beryl Bainbridge, *English Journey or the Road to Milton Keynes* (London: Duckworth, 1984), p. 84.
19. Quoted in Bernard Bergonzi, *The Situation of the Novel* (London: Macmillan, 1979), p. 65.
20. Quoted in Lisa Allardice, 'A Life in Writing: Margaret Drabble', *Guardian*, 18 June 2011, p. 12.
21. A.S. Byatt, *Still Life* (London: Chatto & Windus, 1985), p. 283; Byatt wrote a critical study of Murdoch entitled *Degrees of Freedom* (1965).
22. Doris Lessing, 'Preface', *The Sirian Experiments: The Report by Ambien 11 of the Five* (London: Jonathan Cape, 1981), p. 198.
23. Doris Lessing, *Shikasta: Re: Colonised Planet 5* (London: Jonathan Cape, 1981), p. 90.
24. Martin Stannard, *Muriel Spark: The Biography* (London: Weidenfeld and Nicolson, 2009), p. 124.
25. Muriel Spark, '"The Same Informed Air": An Interview with Muriel Spark', *Theorizing Muriel Spark: Gender, Race, Deconstruction*, ed. Martin McQuillan (Basingstoke: Palgrave Macmillan, 2002), p. 217.
26. Muriel Spark, 'The Desegregation of Art', *Proceedings of the American Academy of Arts and Letters* (New York: The Blashfield Foundation, 1971), pp. 23–4.
27. The Watergate scandal takes its name from an office complex in Washington, DC which was the headquarters of the Democratic National Committee. A break-in in 1972, a subsequent cover-up, and the involvement of the White House led to the resignation of Republican President Richard Nixon in August 1974.
28. Drew Milne, 'Muriel Spark's Crimes of Wit', *The Edinburgh Companion to Muriel Spark*, ed. Michael Gardiner and Willy Maley (Edinburgh University Press, 2010), p. 116.
29. Beryl Bainbridge, *Watson's Apology* (London: Duckworth, 1984), p. 21.
30. Beryl Bainbridge, *Every Man for Himself* (London: Duckworth, 1996), p. 154.
31. Angela Carter, 'Notes from the Frontline', *On Gender and Writing*, ed. Michelene Wandor (London: Pandora, 1983), p. 69.

7

'The Monstrous Regiment': Literature and the Women's Liberation Movement

Imelda Whelehan

The Women's Liberation Movement produced feminist writers and readers. It inspired specialist publishers and small presses, as well as academic study, bolstering further interest in women's writing. The relationship between artistic creation, political identity, and commerce was both mutually strengthening and deeply problematic. Writers explored what the feminist slogan 'the personal is political' might mean; readers consumed fiction that encapsulated their own experiences in its focus on the previously unrepresented aspects of women's private lives. This second wave of feminism created 'monsters' in the eyes of detractors, and feminists exploited the 'monstrous' in a sustained challenge to the notion of appropriate 'feminine' behaviours. One feminist theatre group took the moniker 'Monstrous Regiment', thus subverting John Knox's famous sixteenth-century tract attacking female power. Other misogynist terms, such as 'Virago' and 'Shrew', were rehabilitated and celebrated by feminists with deliberate irony.

This chapter explores the period immediately following the birth of second-wave feminism. It offers a brief prehistory of British feminist thought and characterizes the features of its political activism. Not all writers discussed were actively involved in feminist politics, or regarded themselves as feminist writers, but they captured the spirit of the age whether in realist, magic realist, or utopian terms. Literary forms like the *bildungsroman* were extraordinarily popular in the UK and US, demonstrating an insatiable hunger for detailed, often painful accounts of 'ordinary' women's lives. These early feminist years can appear simple yet inspirational: the rhetoric of sisterhood suggested the possibility of a singular, shared vision of change. In reality, dissent and disagreement rocked a movement perceived as dominated by white, middle-class, heterosexual women. Disagreement was a productive although painful feature of the British Women's Liberation Movement, as analyses of women's oppression generated diverse conclusions about its core characteristics. A movement from euphoric (if illusory) sisterhood, through identity politics and feminist 'sex wars' was part of the legacy of the British Women's Liberation Movement for writers and their readers.[1] While the relationship between literature and politics remains troubled, the significance of literature for feminism, and feminism for literature, was profound.

The emergence of British feminism

British feminists drew inspiration from a rich tradition of feminist writings, with *A Room of One's Own* (1929) by Virginia Woolf (1882–1941) and *The Second Sex* (1949) by Simone de Beauvoir (1908–86) occupying a special place. Just as *The Feminine Mystique* (1963) by Betty Friedan (1921–2006) anticipated US radical feminism, British writers, particularly among the Marxist intelligentsia, anticipated a new era of gender politics. In 'Women: The Longest Revolution' (1966), Juliet Mitchell argued that women were marginalized by twentieth-century socialism, despite Engels's analysis of the family at the end of the nineteenth century. Mitchell asserts that women's position as the kernel of the family unit, in a 'universe of their own', naturalizes relationships to childcare and domestic labour.[2] She outlines the key structuring elements of women's social role as production, reproduction, sexuality, and the socialization of children, identifying a persistent familial ideology, even as families shrink in size.

In *The Captive Wife* (1966), Hannah Gavron (1936–65) interviewed young mothers living in London. Although her sample group was small, she explicitly compared middle- and working-class married women's lives, highlighting their general ignorance about their husbands' incomes, as well as an overwhelming tendency for women to cease paid work after childbirth. She argues that motherhood has the most significant impact on these women's lives 'because it changed them from being a new kind of woman to being the traditional woman. It meant in particular a loss of independence.'[3] Like Mitchell, Gavron acknowledges the persistence of a familial ideology, which conflicts with these women's values and aspirations – 'the freedom that the "new woman" has been encouraged to expect from her childhood and education' (p. 146). This captivity persists even in the face of rapidly changing social aspirations and educational achievement among young women, and, she suggests, can only be counteracted by greater provision of nurseries and the wider socialization of childcare.

The prison-house of motherhood is the topic of a number of British novels, pointing us from the 1960s into the 1970s and comparable to US 'mad housewife' novels.[4] In *The Pumpkin Eater* (1962) by Penelope Mortimer (1918–99), the key 'problem' identified is that the unnamed narrator has too many children. The reason for her breakdown, she insists, is that 'nothing happened', foreshadowing Friedan's identification of 'the problem that has no name', that is, the overwhelming malaise felt by scores of middle-class housewives.[5] From her husband and analyst's point of view, the narrator's problem is that she is excessively maternal, neglecting the duty of a modern wife to be her husband's lover. To placate her husband she aborts a pregnancy and agrees to sterilization, only to discover that he has impregnated his lover. Her post-operative abdomen gapes, 'as though my wound were laughing at me' (p. 111), emphasizing the finality of her operation. Her retreat to their country home, a secluded tower, brings a Freudian phallic counterpoint to the narrator's identification with the womb, while connoting imprisonment, also suggested by the novel's nursery rhyme title.

The Pumpkin Eater concludes with a promise of reconciliation, something that distinguishes it from later novels with more explicit feminist content. Fay Weldon's *Down Among the Women* (1971) suggests the battle lines between men and women are continually redrawn. While Weldon's relationship to feminism is problematic, the 'sources of [her] indignation' are 'the same as they are for other women in the Women's Movement who are better fitted to analyse and to see how things can be changed'.[6] The novel portrays a group of women linked to the rhythms of home life, as men come and go, love and father children, provide money, or abandon families. A conjunction of third- and first-person narratives takes on a choric quality through which prophetic truisms are communicated: 'Down among the women you don't get to hear about man maltreated; what you hear about is man seducer, man betrayer, man deserter, man the monster.'[7] As for the women: 'We are the cleaners. We sweep the floors which tomorrow will be dusty. We cook the food and clean the lavatory pan ... We make the world go round. Someone's got to do it' (p. 83). There is a circular sameness in their lives which obscures or devalues their individuality to represent one or another injustice against women, as mistresses become wronged wives and identify profoundly with those wronged before them. Wanda is a matriarchal figure, the first of the group to be abandoned and to seek new life through lovers and the first to experience the ambiguity of maternal love. She is followed by her husband's subsequent wife, her daughter, her daughter's friends; their stories are both mundane and tragic, but endlessly repetitive. Some hope resides in the strength of granddaughter Byzantia, who chides her mother for seeing the world in relation to men: '[h]ow trivial, with the world in the state it's in' (p. 233).

Second-wave feminism is most often associated with the US, and some of the early activities and writings of the Women's Liberation Movement, particularly the protests in 1968 and 1969 at the Miss Universe contest held in Atlantic City, and pamphlets such as Kate Millett's 1968 essay-length precursor to *Sexual Politics* (1970), had a significant influence on the development of British feminism.[8] In the UK, 1968 marked the fiftieth anniversary of women's suffrage, so debates about women's social position were in vogue. The first Women's Liberation Conference, held at Ruskin College, Oxford, in 1970 was the unexpectedly successful public announcement of a new era of British feminism. A year later the Women's Liberation Movement developed Four Demands: equal pay for equal work, equal education and opportunities, free contraception and abortion on demand, and 24-hour nurseries. These demands, expanded to seven by 1978, guided British feminist activism and were conveniently reprinted in the *Spare Rib* diary.[9] *Shrew* magazine (1969–74) intended to present feminist ideas to people outside the movement, while local and regional newsletters connected disparate women's groups, producing publications and events on a shoestring, in the absence of any central body to compare with the US National Organization for Women.[10] Crucially, British feminism was socialist in character, both class-conscious and concerned with the welfare state. However, it received less newspaper coverage than its US counterparts, and articles tended to focus on celebrity figures, at the expense of covering UK groups' broader political agendas.[11] A number of campaigns challenged the commodification and representation of women, adding a radical feminist edge to this primarily socialist movement. The 1970 Miss World protest in London – 'the first militant confrontation with the law by women since the suffragettes' – owed much to Atlantic City.[12] According to the *Daily Mail*, 'if any single event proved that 1970 was the year Women's Lib got itself moving it was that incident during the Miss World contest when a battling horde of feminists forced poor Bob Hope to close his eyes and think of Vietnam'.[13]

Patriarchal Attitudes (1970) by Eva Figes (1932–2012), published just a few months before *The Female Eunuch* (1970), was a result of her frustration with Beauvoir's writings and her dissatisfaction with Friedan's blueprint for the future. Figes offers a cultural history of the treatment of Western women since the Middle Ages to show that 'patriarchal attitudes can survive intellectual change'.[14] The more women demanded the right to share the benefits of the capitalist system, the more subtle forces prevented them: 'Freudian analysis appeared on the intellectual horizon to provide a subtle psychological taboo' (p. 135). Figes presents a trenchant critique of the structure of contemporary marriage, arguing that children are erroneously positioned as its chief justification, and her proposition that the state should take more of the economic burden of childrearing shows a close compatibility with the socialist class-infused analysis of the British Women's Liberation Movement.

Writing feminism, being feminist

The relationship of feminist creative writing to the Women's Liberation Movement was inevitably complex. Political feminism developed in a culture that valued collaborative writing and collective anonymity, whereas creative writing – as the cover of this volume suggests – tends to be an individual act that requires isolation and resists set ideological parameters. Writers whose feminism informed their fiction had to negotiate these subtle political realities. While freedom of authorial expression was cherished, there is the question of political obligation and whether there are authentic and inauthentic ways to depict feminism. Writers engage with feminism in ways that expose tensions between collective visions and the individual's struggle to comprehend their own place in this imagined world order. Michèle Roberts recalls that she experienced fiction writing as a guilty indulgence: '[w]riting a novel, a private, individual project, still felt necessarily a secret activity. I salved my conscience by going to lots of meetings called by local tenants' groups and women's groups.'[15] Meanwhile writers like Weldon covered themes of deep feminist relevance but with no sense of direct political obligation to the Women's Liberation Movement.

While feminist politics attempted to confront and analyse contradictions, fiction allowed women to dramatize them. Throughout the 1970s the *bildungsroman* charted the coming to consciousness that the Women's Liberation Movement encouraged through activism, favouring realist accounts of women's lives, which often depicted the protagonists failing to achieve their ideals. This raised the question of what makes a *feminist* text. For Sara Maitland, her activism inspired her fiction, but 'I always thought that one of the things a feminist could do in fiction which is difficult in other forms of writing is introduce some of the real contradictions without being heretical ... I felt a kind of freedom in writing fiction, a freedom to say it's not that simple.'[16] Such 'freedoms', while essential to the health and range of feminist fiction, suggest a lack of fit with the politics of the Women's Liberation Movement, which in its early stages was looking for some way of garnering consensus. Accordingly, while numerous writers expressed their commitment to feminist politics, their fiction was where they challenged and problematized the core demands to which they also subscribed.

Writing collectives suggested a new approach to authorship and one, comprising Roberts, Zoë Fairbairns, Michelene Wandor, Maitland, and Valerie Miner, resulted in *Tales I Tell My Mother* (1978). Its subtitle – *A Collection of Feminist Short Stories* – is a statement of intent, and the discussion pieces that introduce each section suggest the fruitfulness of exchange; yet each story asserts the dominance of individual expression and underscores a disconnection between fiction and polemic. Roberts's *A Piece of the Night* (1978) takes impetus from one of her stories in this volume, and indicates increased freedom to challenge orthodoxies beyond the collective.[17] Whereas the stories offer snapshots of engagement with feminist politics, focusing on consciousness-raising groups, motherhood, friendship, sex, and class, Roberts's novel develops a more problematic perspective on the process of coming to consciousness and living one's beliefs. It becomes apparent through flashback that Julie Fanchot's marriage has ended, she is living in a women's commune, and is involved in a troubled relationship with her lover, Jenny. Her relationship with her mother is coloured by childhood anxieties of separation, and she returns to France looking for nurturance and to 'reclaim my place with her, become her child again'.[18] At the same time she antagonizes her mother by announcing her sexuality and symbolically emblazoning her feminism on her mother's birthday cake.

Her teenage religious vocation, resulting from an infatuation with a nun, persuades her of the advantages of female separatism: 'I lusted for power which girls and women do not have in this world; I would have it, by going beyond womanhood into sanctity' (p. 53).

Life in the commune subverts this vision as Julie encounters daily jealousies sharing Jenny's affections and managing her daughter's insecurities. The experience of marriage and childbirth politicizes Julie as she encounters crushing boredom and the lack of value attributed to domestic labour, and imagines violently confronting her husband: 'I wanted to tumble my unscholarly evidence all over his desk, women's domestic labour I wanted to scream, how about that for stains on your academic purity?' (p. 87). Julie's life story is interspersed with that of Amy, companion to wealthy relative Harriet, whose journal she discovers. It becomes clear that the dead nun at the novel's opening is Amy, whose relationship with Harriet was, we imagine, a romantic friendship, and Julie decides her novel will portray the rest of Amy's life, 'beginning ... where she left off' (p. 184). This act of imaginatively reconstructing the lives of women past is a crucial part of the feminist project of remembering, just as it is important for Julie to participate in and share her experiences through consciousness-raising: 'The women sit in circles talking. They are passing telegrams along battle-lines ... recognizing allies under the disguise of femininity, no longer smuggling ammunition over back garden walls, no longer corpses in the church and mouths of men' (p. 186).

While the interpretation and documentation of contemporary reality was an important feature of feminist writing, fantasy also shaped fiction and politics. It is important to imagine the world you want, or do not want, in order to challenge the way things are. Fairbairns's dystopian *Benefits* (1979) explores how changes to the welfare state in favour of women might backfire, by dramatizing one of Women's Liberation Movement's more controversial campaigns – Wages for Housework. Fairbairns wrote the novel to ask, 'what would actually happen to you, me and the woman next door, if a British government introduced a wage for mothers?'[19] This issue split the movement: for some it was the obvious solution to the problem of 'surplus value' in that it acknowledged housework as labour. On the other hand, to pay women for domestic work would be to further entrench traditional gender divisions. The title refers explicitly to Child Benefit (formerly Family Allowance, introduced in 1946) given to all mothers regardless of income, a cornerstone of the welfare state.

Fairbairns's protagonist, journalist Lynn Byers, is drawn into feminist activism, via the *Guardian* women's page and *Spare Rib*, supporting women occupying a derelict tower block. The non-hierarchical collective frustrates her and she complains, 'there seemed to be no mechanism for making decisions, even if there had been agreement'.[20] The novel charts a country in social and economic disarray, becoming increasingly sexualized: 'Hairy rubber cunts were sold in supermarkets ... and pornography publishers produced education supplements that could be torn out and given to children' (p. 37). A new political party, FAMILY, advocates traditional values and operates a punitive anti-feminist scrutiny of women's lives. Benefit has its own momentum, ultimately resulting in the exclusion of women from paid employment, with 'unfit' mothers compulsorily fitted with invasive contraceptive devices. Lynn's daughter, born with cystic fibrosis, is one such 'unfit' mother and seeks underground feminist help to conceive in an increasingly eugenicist environment. Women's right to choose, a fundamental feminist principle, is subverted under this regime; reminiscent of George Orwell's *Nineteen Eighty-Four* (1949), oppositional language is appropriated to establishment purposes, so that 'sexism' is redefined as 'hatred of women in their natural role' (p. 145). The continued operation of clandestine feminist groups provides a ray of hope, and Lynn is forced to recognize that their structurelessness is a key to their survival.

Feminist literary criticism and the women's writing industry

Collectives and small presses played their part in aiding communication to a broader reading public. Early British Women's Liberation Movement documents were anthologized in *The Body Politic: Writings from the Women's Liberation Movement, 1969–1972* (1972), compiled by Wandor, and *Conditions of Illusion: Papers from the Women's Movement* (1974), edited by Sandra Allen, Lee Sanders, and Jan Wallis, collections which focus on motherhood, sexuality, work, class, and welfare. It is only in the third anthology, *No Turning Back: Writings from the Women's Liberation Movement, 1975–80* (1981), published by the more commercial Women's Press, that the 'flourishing of women's music, theatre, writing groups, printing presses and publishing houses' is fully acknowledged as essential to political development.[21] Commercial presses with a feminist conscience operated in a 'borderland position' between the activist tradition of feminist collectivity and the publishing mainstream.[22] This position is exemplified by opposing perspectives on Virago: 'feminists tended to regard Virago as having more to do with publishing than with activist feminist politics while, simultaneously, publishers suspiciously regarded Virago as a feminist cabal' (p. 38). The Women's Press, with its male majority shareholder, was controversial, but it possessed 'the cultural element of a consciousness-raising dynamic', particularly in its commitment to publishing the work of women of colour.[23] Feminist publishing and feminist criticism benefited from intellectual cross-fertilization: Elaine Showalter's *A Literature of Their Own* (1979) influenced Virago's developing Modern Classics list and the wider availability of writings by women supported burgeoning Women's Studies courses in academia.[24]

The increasing diversity of literature by women continued in parallel with the development of British academic feminism. *Feminist Review* began in 1979 as a collective with the conviction that '[f]eminist research and theory should not be locked in educational institutions but should be available as a necessary part of feminist politics'.[25] While it became a more mainstream academic publication, early emphasis was on accessibility and a commitment to preventing the division of 'theory' from 'practice'. Focus on *contemporary* women's writing is surprisingly rare, but Rebecca O'Rourke reflects on the importance of criticism in guiding feminist reading, or even creating a 'feminist text'. She notes that recent literature 'offers only resistances, never change',[26] whilst observing that feminist criticism seems more comfortable analysing pre-twentieth-century writing. Rosalind Coward's response to O'Rourke focuses on the burning question 'Are Women's Novels Feminist Novels?', arguing that '[m]any are suspicious of the commercial success of "the novel that changes lives" and are eager to demonstrate how these novels are ultimately "not feminist"'.[27] Coward revisits the question of the value of culture to politics and suggests a materialist analysis of publishers is required, as well as an interrogation of how the institution of literary criticism makes qualitative distinctions between low and highbrow. Yet Coward dismisses the feminist impact of bestselling novels and in doing so foregrounds the value of literary fiction to feminism. The tension remains between ideas and their fictional representation: how we define a 'feminist text' and whether such work has any political use value.

In a movement that romanticized sisterhood, successful authors of both fiction and non-fiction were viewed suspiciously.[28] For Rita Felski, feminist literature has a dual purpose: 'One of the most important achievements of the women's movement has been to repoliticize art on the level of production and reception, and to question ruling ideologies of the text as a self-contained artifact.'[29] The ways in which feminist fiction was circulated, understood, and criticized went some way to challenging these ideologies. Lisa Hogeland anticipates a period of emerging 'feminist literacy', from an interpretive community where '[f]eminist criticism's utopian project of total social transformation rested on an enormous faith in the power of texts to make change', undercutting Coward's comment above.[30]

However, Showalter, interviewed after the publication of *A Literature of Their Own*, asserts that '[a] consciously feminist novel is a dreary exercise. The heroine is put through her paces. Topics that could be treated in your consciousness raising group are dramatized ... It's awfully predictable even though it's moving because these are stages most of us have gone through.'[31] A clear definition of feminist writing appears to underpin this statement but is not forthcoming. Showalter prefers novels like *The Bell Jar* (1963) by Sylvia Plath (1932–63) where 'it's the contradictions that engage us so powerfully' (p. 29), and concludes, '[f]eminists have a responsibility to writers more than writers do to feminists' (p. 29). These comments go some way to explaining Showalter's focus on the nineteenth century over the contemporary scene; for her the tension between artistic expression (via the lone creative voice) and a 'collective cultural task' remains unresolved.[32]

Showalter heralds a vibrant liberal-feminist trend in literary criticism that looks backwards, doing the important work of unearthing or revisioning 'lost' feminist classics, whilst strategically avoiding the more searching questions the Women's Liberation Movement was asking of its writers. However, the final 20 pages of *A Literature of Their Own* are devoted to the contemporary, with reference to authors such as Doris Lessing (1919–2013), Muriel Spark (1918–2006), Margaret Drabble, and Mortimer. In Drabble's *The Millstone* (1965), for example, Showalter sees the germs of 'feminine surrender' in Rosamund's awareness of the commonality of her fate with other pregnant women, but the novel anticipates the politicization of women's bodies and experiences facilitated by the Women's Liberation Movement (p. 305). It marks a transition between narratives about marriage and motherhood, and feminist accounts of female self-definition, as Rosamund's unshakeable belief that she can care for her child and pursue her career are confirmed when she secures a university position. Her initial dis-identification with other mothers changes to a recognition that motherhood, in medical and social terms, is already inscribed. While acknowledging that she is 'trapped in a human limit', there is little hint of surrender.[33] Rosamund successfully pursues an academic career, acutely aware of the privileges of her class, and the material benefits that allow her, like Woolf, to enjoy a room and income of one's own.

For Showalter in 1977, British feminism was still waiting patiently for Shakespeare's sister, but she overlooked the possibility that writers like Drabble were inaugurating the kinds of contributions Woolf envisaged by grasping 'the habit of freedom and the courage to write exactly what we think'.[34] Toril Moi's bestselling *Sexual/Textual Politics* (1985) further entrenched the idea that 'Anglo-American feminist criticism', as she dubbed it, was 'not quite political enough' in its compatibility with a male-oriented humanist tradition.[35] While she is right to identify a strong liberal strand in this critical approach, she all too summarily dismisses its radical impact on academic institutions. For all the tension between feminist criticism, literature, and politics, it was not simply the case that one resided in the academy, another was found in all good book shops, while the last was taking it to the streets. As Cora Kaplan reminds us, feminist literary texts 'were part of the ongoing debate of the social movement of which we were part'.[36] The key legacy of early feminist critics was that they transformed academic literary study for good and contributed to theoretical perspectives that further problematized the relationship between writer and reader, critic and academic institution, teacher and student.

Difference, diversity, and division: feminist writings from the late 1970s

While socialism added class consciousness and analysis of the state to British feminist politics, 'it is radical feminism which has given the women's movement its greatest charge of energy'.[37] Radical feminism challenged representation and objectification, inaugurated the consciousness-raising tradition, and provided challenging definitions of patriarchy. For some, socialist women were part of the problem, threatening to disrupt the movement by using the Women's Liberation Movement to recruit left-wing groups.[38] The tensions between British socialist and radical feminism are best exemplified by writers like Pat Barker whose early novels – *Union Street* (1982), *Blow Your House Down* (1984), and *Liza's England* (1986) – are carefully drawn portraits of social and economic hardship in England's north. *Union Street* depicts vignettes of characters at different life stages, from young rape victim, the mother who buries the remains of her daughter's late abortion, to the elderly woman seeking a quiet spot to die. A far cry from the *bildungsroman*, these novels show lives circumscribed by lack of choice, poverty, domestic violence, and pregnancy where children are not always welcome or loved. *Blow Your House Down* channels the widespread panic and controversy around the 'Yorkshire Ripper' case and final arrest of Peter Sutcliffe in 1981.[39] Barker depicts a community of women, describing the circumstances surrounding their 'choice' to sell their bodies for sex, and problematizing the erroneous distinction between 'deserving' and 'innocent' victims of male violence. The novel emphasizes that 'prostitute' is a label that can be applied to any woman: simply walking the street is enough to attract 'business'.

Liza's England centres on 80-year-old Liza, virtually bedridden and about to be evicted. Her box of memorabilia contains her family history, each item recalling a story she has been told about previous generations. Her antagonistic relationship with her mother is replicated with that of her own daughter as if 'both were links in a chain of women stretching back through the centuries into the wombs of women whose names they didn't know'.[40] This linearity, and indeed circularity, of female experience from youth to old age is a recurring theme in Barker's work, best symbolized by the touch of Kelly and Alice's hands in *Union Street*. Barker's achievement is to convey a transhistorical sisterhood of experience while individuating each woman's life, and shocking, violent actions are communicated with gritty realism. While the men remain relative outsiders to domestic cycles of housework and birth, Liza's husband Frank has his own deep-seated traumas. A survivor of the First World War, he is haunted by his schoolfriends' voices which he channels in séances to alleviate his survivor's guilt. This is a political novel with a socialist-feminist conscience, but its cyclical historical sweep supports a radical feminist definition of patriarchy. Liza's community seems immune to the march of progress, their lives circumscribed by ever-narrowing opportunities for social advancement in Thatcher's Britain. The local youths who cause Liza's death in a botched robbery are themselves trapped in a cycle of unemployment and lack of opportunities. Barker's particular brand of realism bridges polemic and imagination, where utopia is still distant.

During the 1980s, the ethnocentric, heterosexual, and bourgeois focus of the Women's Liberation Movement was challenged. Hazel Carby notes that for black feminists the dominant analyses of the family, patriarchy, and reproduction are deeply problematic as the 'metropolitan centres of the West define the questions to be asked of other social systems and, at the same time, provide the measure against which all "foreign" practices are gauged'.[41] 'Sisterhood' perpetuated ethnocentric concepts and practices, as well as endorsing offensive parallels between women's oppression and colonization. Racism is still perceived to be the problem of those who suffer abuse rather than those who perpetuate it, and feminist identity politics threatened to tear the Women's Movement apart, by creating a 'hierarchy of oppression', but it necessarily challenged mainstream feminists to own their sins of omission and embrace competing voices.[42]

Writing by women of colour breaks down the category of the 'black' woman writer in order to account for cultural specificities, location, and politics, and depicts the harsh realities of British racism. Buchi Emecheta's *In the Ditch* (1972) tells the story of Nigerian-born Adah, housed with her five children in a London tower block. As Adah signs on the dole she asks, 'Why was it that everybody would always judge one black person by the way another black person behaved?'[43] Hyacinth, in Joan Riley's *The Unbelonging* (1985), also suffers from such generalized judgements while negotiating her own sense of hybridity: she feels a foreigner in England but when she returns to Jamaica as an adult, she finds that the country bears no relation to the place of her nostalgic childhood dreams. Sent to England to live with her abusive father, she is ultimately a victim of a welfare state built on racist assumptions about her social and academic potential.

Ravinder Randhawa's *A Wicked Old Woman* (1987), 'arguably the first *explicitly* Asian British novel', focuses on Kulwant's experiences as the first Asian child in her British school, and its impact on her subsequent life.[44] Randhawa, responsible for setting up the Asian Women Writers Workshop in 1984, depicts a young woman torn between the cultural traditions of her Punjabi family, while trying to pass as 'English' at school.[45] Her white boyfriend proposes marriage, jolting a realization that she has stepped far beyond her inter-cultural comfort zone: 'No more trying to walk in the middle ... She'd messed it all up because she had wanted everything, wanted to be Indian and English.'[46] The 'old' woman we encounter at the beginning is not yet 50 years old, and uses her aged disguise to behave badly. Residing between two worlds, she enjoys the discomfort of others as they try to 'place' her. Another character, Ammi, never learnt to speak or write English and suffers persistent nightmares that can only be quelled by her daughters' stories of the women at Greenham Common Peace Camp, and she rallies her community to make them food. The Greenham protests, begun in 1981, foregrounded a cultural feminist dimension to radical politics, in that women's supposedly nurturing and peaceable natures were summoned to resist the threat of nuclear proliferation. A kind of cultural feminist vision of women's virtues seems to prevail in this novel, particularly around Rani, who killed a white man in self-defence, and is championed by the other women because '[t]hat skin of yours means we all go to the dock with you' (p. 204).

While debates about 'compulsory heterosexuality' and political lesbianism raged within feminist politics, Jeanette Winterson's *Oranges Are Not the Only Fruit* (1985) resisted the bleakness of the lesbian coming-out novel whose associations stretch back to *The Well of Loneliness* (1928) by Radclyffe Hall (1880–1943). Winterson's novel shares some striking similarities with American author Rita Mae Brown's *Rubyfruit Jungle* (1973). Both are first-person confessional narratives of working-class girls whose birth heritage is concealed from them. In both cases, they invent themselves and Jeanette is empowered, strengthened by her eccentric upbringing within an unofficial matriarchy: 'The women in our church were strong and organised. If you want to talk in terms of power I had enough to keep Mussolini happy.'[47] This utopia of female self-sufficiency is destroyed when Jeanette's relationship with her girlfriend Melanie is discovered and her mother relinquishes power to the minister, in an attempt to force Jeanette to conform to a heterosexual norm. This is a portrait of the artist on the threshold of greatness; but for all the informal 'sisterhoods' in the novel, Jeanette's sexuality is portrayed as a product of her individual personality. Her success lies in escaping the thrall of her adopted family and getting to university, despite the triple yoke of class, gender, and sexual orientation.

The feminist 'sex wars' left scars on feminism as pro- and anti-porn positions became imbued with questions of freedom of speech, to the point that it became difficult to explore female desire without occupying the territory of either of these positions. Angela Carter (1940–92), however, navigated a feminist path between them, regarding femininity as one of the 'social fictions' she demythologizes in her work.[48] *The Passion of New Eve* (1977) anticipates Judith Butler's queer theoretical analysis of gender performativity in Evelyn/Eve, whose journey is from male sexual exploiter to female victim. The setting is a post-apocalyptic civil war, a magic realist landscape where the reader is never sure exactly how modern California came to lie in ruins. There are hints of racial and feminist protests as Evelyn is prevented from taking up his academic position on arrival in the US. Feminist radicalism takes a terrorist bent: 'Female sharp-shooters took to sniping from concealed windows at men who lingered too long in front of posters outside blue movie theatres.'[49] Mother's (a guerrilla/goddess figure) desert army resembles single-breasted Amazonian warriors, and Evelyn/Eve becomes their most important project: the creation of the perfect woman and womb. The novel is dominated by the larger-than-life screen presence of Tristessa St Ange, an embodiment of perfect Hollywood femininity. Hiding in a fairytale castle (complete with waxworks of Jean Harlow, James Dean, and Marilyn Monroe),

Tristessa's secret identity as a biological male is revealed as Eve and she are forced to couple. For Carter, the emergence of feminist radical politics meant that 'all that was holy was in the process of being profaned' and her own forays into the profane raised some thorny questions for feminists of her generation (1983, p. 70).

As women's writing courses became more widespread, Carter's novels joined a feminist 'canon'. In the academy, debates about what constitutes a feminist text continued, but in the 1980s literariness was an assumed prerequisite. The 1990s heralded broader interest in readerly textual pleasures and spawned research into women's popular fiction as a site of feminist negotiation. Feminism makes a surprise appearance in Shirley Conran's *Lace* (1982), a novel which focuses on four women who share a secret about which of them is the mother of movie star Lili. One of the four, Kate, joins a consciousness-raising group in 1969, but is immediately disenchanted by what she witnesses: 'The sisters never seemed to talk about practical considerations; discussion was either directed to experience-sharing or else utopian theorizing.'[50] Her practical solution is to develop a magazine, a blend of *Cosmopolitan* and *Ms*, moving from sisterhood to celebration of individualist female economic power. It is easy to overlook the fact that Kate's motivations emerge from her experience of a powerful sorority who forged their own free-market feminism out of the ruins of the Women's Liberation Movement. As Felski acknowledges, 'the money, sex and power genre would not be possible without feminism', particularly in the way it positions women as independent, desiring subjects.[51] Ultimately such novels do not provide an enlightened model of feminist sexuality, but are, like Carter's work, a response to profound critical gaps in feminist approaches to sex and desire. *Lace* uses aspirational fantasy to fuse postfeminist female power with a re-enactment of pre-feminist manifestations of femininity, resulting in a liberal feminist, individualist rearticulation of radical and socialist feminist core principles. The lifestyle magazine embracing female financial power renders the career woman close to Carter's reimaginings of Sade's Juliette in *The Sadeian Woman* (1979): 'She plays to win, this one; she knows the score. Her femininity is part of the armoury of self-interest.'[52]

Radical politics assumes material transformation as well as imaginative leaps. Writing about her experiences at the *Guardian* newspaper, Jill Tweedie (1936–93) beautifully exemplifies the tensions between feminism and fiction, theory and life, asserting feminists 'were the officers and we were the foot soldiers slogging through mud, they gave the orders, we tried to carry them out and often failed, hung about as we were with delinquent husbands and intractable children collected in the unenlightened past, who unaccountably refused to respond to theories'.[53] This division between the model feminist of theory and the 'real' woman immersed in the quotidian messiness of life is dramatized by Tweedie in the personae of Mary and Martha, evangelical separatist versus flawed aspirational feminist in the column

'Letters from a Fainthearted Feminist'.[54] It may be, as Maria Lauret observes, that since the 1980s 'feminist fiction, like feminism itself, has diversified into a multiplicity of textual practices and political concerns to the point where, as a designation of an oppositional literary movement, it has probably outlived its usefulness'.[55] Nevertheless, feminism's political legacy to women's writing lies in the continuing intellectual challenges it provides to writers who explore the tensions and connections between creativity and feminist transformational politics.

Notes

1. The flashpoint of these 'sex wars' is usually located as the Barnard Conference on Sexuality in 1982. In the 'sex wars', divisions between anti-porn and anti-censorship (or 'sex positive') campaigners demonstrated deep rifts within the Women's Liberation Movement around pornography, sadomasochism, and sex work.
2. Juliet Mitchell, 'Women: The Longest Revolution', *New Left Review*, 1:40 (November–December 1966), p. 11.
3. Hannah Gavron, *The Captive Wife* (Harmondsworth: Penguin, 1966), p. 137.
4. For a detailed discussion of 'mad housewife' novels see Imelda Whelehan, *The Feminist Bestseller: From* Sex and the Single Girl *to* Sex and the City (Basingstoke: Palgrave Macmillan, 2005).
5. Penelope Mortimer, *The Pumpkin Eater* (Harmondsworth: Penguin, 1964), p. 46.
6. Fay Weldon, 'Me and My Shadows', *On Gender and Writing*, ed. Michelene Wandor (London: Pandora, 1983), p. 164.
7. Fay Weldon, *Down Among the Women* (Harmondsworth: Penguin, 1973), p. 61.
8. See www.jofreeman.com/photos/MissAm1969.html.
9. Zoë Fairbairns, 'Saying What We Want', *The Feminist Seventies*, ed. Helen Graham, Ann Kaloski, Ali Neilson, and Emma Robertson (York: Raw Nerve Books, 2003), p. 101. *Spare Rib* was first published in December 1972.
10. Eve Setch, 'The Face of Metropolitan Feminism: The London Women's Liberation Workshop, 1969–79', *Twentieth Century British History*, 13:2 (2002), p. 173.
11. Kaitlynn Mendes, 'Framing Feminism: News Coverage of the Women's Movement in British and American Newspapers, 1968–1982', *Social Movement Studies*, 10:1 (2011), p. 86.
12. Anon., 'Miss World', *The Body Politic*, ed. Michelene Wandor (London: Stage 1, 1972), p. 254.
13. Patricia Ashdown Sharp quoted in Angela Neustatter, *Hyenas in Petticoats: A Look at Twenty Years of Feminism* (Harmondsworth: Penguin, 1990), p. 26.
14. Eva Figes, *Patriarchal Attitudes* (London: Virago, 1978), p. 111.
15. Michèle Roberts, *Paper Houses* (London: Virago, 2007), p. 126.
16. 'Women Writing', Jean Radford interviews Michèle Roberts and Sara Maitland, *Spare Rib*, 76 (November 1978), p. 16.
17. Zoë Fairbairns et al., 'Martha and Mary Raise Consciousness from the Dead', *Tales I Tell My Mother* (London: Journeyman Press, 1978), pp. 71–9.
18. Michèle Roberts, *A Piece of the Night* (London: The Women's Press, 1978), p. 16.
19. Zoë Fairbairns, 'On Writing *Benefits*', *No Turning Back: Writings from the Women's Liberation Movement 1975–80*, ed. Feminist Anthology Collective (London: The Women's Press, 1981), p. 255.

20. Zoë Fairbairns, *Benefits* (London: Virago, 1979), p. 11.
21. Feminist Anthology Collective, 'Introduction', *No Turning Back: Writings from the Women's Liberation Movement 1975–80* (London: The Women's Press, 1981), p. 1.
22. Simone Murray, *Mixed Media: Feminist Presses and Publishing Politics* (London: Pluto, 2004), p. 32.
23. The Women's Press, 'Feminism and Publishing', *News from Neasden* No. 11, 1979, pp. 32–4.
24. Carmen Callil, 'Virago Reprints: Redressing the Balance', *Times Literary Supplement*, 12 September 1980, p. 1001.
25. 'Editorial', *Feminist Review*, 1 (1979), p. 1.
26. Rebecca O'Rourke, 'Summer Reading', *Feminist Review*, 2 (1979), p. 117, p. 1.
27. Rosalind Coward, '"This Novel Changes Lives": Are Women's Novels Feminist Novels? A Response to Rebecca O'Rourke's Article "Summer Reading"', *Feminist Review*, 5 (1980), p. 53.
28. For an account of this phenomenon in a US context, see Alice Echols, *Daring to be Bad: Radical Feminism in America 1967–1975* (Minneapolis: University of Minnesota Press, 1989), p. 206.
29. Rita Felski, *Beyond Feminist Aesthetics* (London: Hutchinson Radius, 1989), p. 175.
30. Lisa Maria Hogeland, *Feminism and its Fictions* (Philadelphia: University of Pennsylvania Press, 1998), pp. 12–13.
31. 'A Literature of Our Own', Elaine Showalter interviewed by Rozsika Parker and Amanda Sebestyen, *Spare Rib*, 78 (January 1979), p. 29.
32. Elaine Showalter, *A Literature of Their Own* (London: Virago, 1984), p. 318.
33. Margaret Drabble, *The Millstone* (Harmondsworth: Penguin, 1968), p. 58.
34. Virginia Woolf, *A Room of One's Own* (1929; London: Triad Grafton, 1977), p. 108.
35. Toril Moi, *Sexual/Textual Politics: Feminist Literary Theory* (London: Methuen, 1985), p. 87.
36. Cora Kaplan, 'Feminist Criticism Twenty Years On', *From My Guy to Sci-Fi: Genre and Women's Writing in the Postmodern World*, ed. Helen Carr (London: Pandora, 1989), p. 18.
37. Terry Lovell, ed., *British Feminist Thought: A Reader* (Oxford: Blackwell, 1990), p. 4.
38. Selma James, 'From the Mother Country: One English Woman's Words on the US and British Women's Movements', *Off Our Backs*, 2:7 (31 March 1972), n.p.
39. Peter Sutcliffe was convicted of 13 counts of murder and seven of attempted murder.
40. Pat Barker, *Liza's England* (London: Virago, 1996), p. 211.
41. Hazel V. Carby, 'White Woman Listen! Black Feminism and the Boundaries of Sisterhood', *Black British Cultural Studies*, ed. Houston A. Baker Jr, Manthia Diawara, and Ruth H. Lindeborg (University of Chicago Press, 1996), p. 66.
42. Pratibha Parmar, 'Other Kinds of Dreams', *Feminist Review*, 31 (Spring 1989), p. 58.
43. Buchi Emecheta, *In the Ditch* (London: Flamingo, 1988), p. 58.
44. Susheila Nasta, *Home Truths: Fictions of the South Asian Diaspora in Britain* (Basingstoke: Palgrave, 2002), p. 182. Nasta notes that 'British Asian' comes into currency in 1988 after the Commission for Racial Equality's recommendation that the British Asian population no longer be classified as 'black'.
45. Funded by the Greater London Council. See Miriam Ticktin, 'Contemporary British Asian Women's Writing: Social Movement or Literary Tradition?', *Women: A Cultural Review*, 7:1 (1996), p. 69.
46. Ravinder Randhawa, *A Wicked Old Woman* (London: The Women's Press, 1987), p. 29.

47. Jeanette Winterson, *Oranges Are Not the Only Fruit* (London: Pandora, 1985), p. 124.
48. Angela Carter, 'Notes From the Front Line', in Wandor (1983), p. 70.
49. Angela Carter, *The Passion of New Eve* (London: Virago, 1982), p. 13.
50. Shirley Conran, *Lace* (Harmondsworth: Penguin, 1982), p. 495.
51. Rita Felski, *Doing Time: Feminist Theory and Postmodern Culture* (New York University Press, 2000), p. 109.
52. Angela Carter, *The Sadeian Woman: An Exercise in Cultural History* (London: Virago, 1979), p. 117.
53. Jill Tweedie, 'Strange Places', in Wandor (1983), p. 114.
54. Published as a book by Robson Books in 1982.
55. Maria Lauret, *Liberating Literature: Feminist Fiction in America* (London: Routledge, 1994), p. 187.

8

Writing the F-Word: Girl Power, the Third Wave, and Postfeminism

Rebecca Munford

The 1990s witnessed the beginnings of feminism's transformation into the 'f-word', a word too indeterminate, too risky, and too offensive to be fully articulated. Feminist thinking in the 1990s called into question assumptions about the category 'woman', putting pressure on notions of a unified subject of 'feminism'. Influenced by postmodern notions of subjectivity, and informed by developments in the fields of poststructuralist, postcolonial, and queer theory, third-wave feminism offered a response to the perceived limitations of second-wave feminism. The term 'third-wave feminism' was popularized by Rebecca Walker, who announced in a 1992 article for *Ms. Magazine*, written in response to the Anita Hill/Clarence Thomas hearings in the US, 'I am not a postfeminism feminist. I am the third wave.'[1] Distancing herself from popular postfeminist accounts of the demise or 'death' of feminism, Walker's self-identification as 'third waver' affirmed the enduring vitality of feminist politics. Her use of the wave metaphor, however, performs a double function: at the same time as it conveys continuity and connection, it also articulates difference and dissociation. Installing the generational vocabulary that has characterized many of its subsequent expressions, Walker's pronouncement about third-wave feminism intimates a movement away from the second wave and asserts a reinvigorated feminist politics.

The third wave's eagerness to signal its departure from second-wave understandings of gender and identity is reflected in a desire to offer new definitions of femininity, sexuality, and the body. According to Imelda Whelehan, third-wave feminists 'profit from a pre-established discourse of feminism with an embarrassment of riches, in terms of theoretical and political explorations, and one of the frustrations they experience is the need to articulate their own experiences of their postmodern world'.[2] Emphasizing multiplicity, contradiction, and difference in their formulations of contemporary identity, third-wave writers often adopt a confessional style that tends to privilege individual over collective experience – a move heralded by Walker's insistent use of the first person ('I am the third wave'). As Walker puts it in the introduction to her collection *To Be Real: Telling the Truth and Changing the Face of Feminism* (1995), '[f]or us the lines between Us and Them are often blurred, and as a result we find ourselves seeking to create identities that accommodate ambiguity and our multiple positionalities: including more than excluding, exploring more than defining, searching more than arriving' (p. xxxiii).

Thus, although third-wave feminists seek to convey the agency and empowerment of the 'new' feminist subject in terms that sustain visible links with second-wave feminism, this articulation all too often reflects back a shadowy image of what is perceived to be the moribund politics of an earlier generation. An anxiety about the authoritarianism of second-wave feminism similarly informs Natasha Walter's *The New Feminism* (1998), in which she argues that '[t]his generation of feminists must free itself from the spectre of political correctness'.[3] For Walter, one of the most deleterious aspects of second-wave feminist critique is its insistence on the idea of a heterosexual culture that 'sees women only as victims' (p. 112) and, as such, effaces a 'powerful tradition' of women giving voice to their own social, artistic, and erotic stories (p. 113). Such thinking has informed the conceptualization of a dichotomy between 'victim' and 'power' feminism that is often formulated along distinctly generational lines and positions second-wave feminism as both prescriptive and puritanical.[4]

In such configurations, second-wave feminism's language of sisterhood is displaced by a vocabulary of daughterly protest, with the mother–daughter metaphor becoming a central motif in contemporary accounts of feminist history and politics. Hence, the move to redress second-wave narratives of victimization finds popular expression in the generational rhetoric of 'girl power' and the rehabilitation of 'girl culture' in third-wave feminist and postfeminist accounts of identity. In the 1990s, 'the girl' emerged as a pre-eminent figure of popular culture and the embodiment of a new female subjectivity. Promulgated most bombastically in mainstream British culture by the Spice Girls, girl power was enacted with a more overtly political inflection earlier in the decade by members of the US Riot Grrrl movement. A celebration of girl power is also central to third-wave Girlie culture. According to Jennifer Baumgardner and Amy Richards, 'Girlies are adult women, usually in their mid-twenties to late thirties, whose feminist principles are based on a reclaiming of girl culture (or feminine accoutrements that were tossed out with sexism during the Second Wave), be it Barbie, housekeeping, or girl talk' (p. 400). In its various configurations, then, girl power signifies a mode of female independence and empowerment that is grounded in a playful reappropriation of aspects of traditional femininity and 'girlishness' – one that harnesses the voice of the daughter and distances itself from the overbearing 'gigantic mother' that, as Gloria Steinem points out, is seen to personify second-wave feminism.[5]

Celebrations of girlishness are likewise a prominent feature of postfeminist discourse. Although it is generally associated with the anti-feminist backlash of the 1980s and the girl power discourses of the 1990s, the term 'postfeminism' has literary origins. It was first used nearly one hundred years ago by a group of female literary radicals in Greenwich Village, New York. In *The Grounding of Modern Feminism* (1987), Nancy F. Cott explains that the literary group founded a new journal on the principle that 'we're interested in people now – not in men and women'; pledging to be 'pro-woman without being anti-man', the group described its stance as 'postfeminist'.[6] In its contemporary configuration, however, postfeminism has been enthusiastically appropriated by a media culture eager to announce the death of feminism. Popular culture has become an especially fertile site for promulgating the idea that the achievements of second-wave feminism have so pervaded our social, economic, and political structures that its politics are not only extraneous to the concerns of modern women but also somewhat irksome. Rather than a straightforward 'backlash' against feminism, postfeminist discourse acknowledges some of the (sexual, economic, and social) changes and freedoms that are a result of second-wave feminist activism at the same time as it announces its secession from feminist politics.

In *The Aftermath of Feminism* (2009), Angela McRobbie argues that postfeminist texts – for example, Helen Fielding's *Bridget Jones's Diary* (1996) and television series such as *Ally McBeal* (1997–2002) and *Sex and the City* (1998–2004) – deploy images of girlishness and 'tropes of freedom and choice' to position feminism as 'decisively aged' and 'redundant'.[7] In this way, she suggests, postfeminist discourse 'positively draws on and invokes feminism as that which can be taken into account, to suggest that equality is achieved, in order to install a whole repertoire of new meanings which emphasize that it is no longer needed, it is a spent force' (p. 12). Not only do postfeminist texts consign feminism and feminist endeavour to history but, time and time again, they turn the pre-feminist past into a repository of strangely desirable and glamorized images of traditional femininity. In this respect, popular culture has come to be haunted by what might be described as a 'postfeminist mystique' that works to reanimate the very models of femininity that were investigated and debunked by second-wave feminists.[8]

Chick lit and the return to femininity

In the literary sphere, popular representations of 'girlishness' in the 1990s tend to signify a somewhat ambivalent relation to feminism, one that is articulated most visibly in the realms of chick lit. The publication of Fielding's *Bridget Jones's Diary* heralded the explosion of a new and highly successful genre in Britain and America. Concerned with the trials and tribulations of the girlish, usually single, urban-dwelling professional woman in her late twenties or early thirties, chick lit novels appearing in the 1990s and 2000s evinced a notably postfeminist sensibility in the pages nestled beneath their distinctive pastel-coloured dust jackets.[9] Employing confessional, first-person narratives, chick lit explores the experiences of young women enjoying sexual and financial freedoms in a contemporary world in which the 'ghost of feminism' seems always to be 'hovering' (McRobbie, p. 22). The postfeminist 'chick' recognizes the opportunities afforded by second-wave feminist activity, but is reluctant to relinquish either the trappings of traditional femininity or the scripts of heterosexual romance.

Chick lit's reorientation of notions of freedom and agency towards the sphere of traditional femininity and girlishness – exemplified by Becky Bloomwood's obsession with fashion and shopping in Sophie Kinsella's *The Secret Dreamworld of a Shopaholic* (2000) – may be at the root of the censorious and often dismissive response of critics. Famously denounced by Beryl Bainbridge (1932–2010) as 'a froth sort of thing', and by Doris Lessing (1919–2013) as 'instantly forgettable', chick lit has been denigrated for its superficiality and frivolity.[10] Writing in *The Whole Woman* (1999), Germaine Greer lambasts *Bridget Jones's Diary* as an 'updated version of the old Mills & Boon scenario where girl eats heart out over (not-so-rich) Mr Wrong until (extremely-rich) Mr Right makes his play on the second last page' and laments the novel's spawning of 'a gaggle of imitations in print and on screen, all featuring sassy career women who are insecure, needy, anxious about their body-image and disappointed in love'.[11] Countering such responses, Suzanne Ferriss and Mallory Young argue that the genre requires serious critical attention precisely because it 'brings into focus many of the issues facing contemporary women and contemporary culture – issues of identity, of race and class, of femininity and feminism, of consumerism and self-image' (pp. 2–3). Indeed, far from 'forgettable', chick lit has made an indelible mark on the literary landscape of the 1990s and early 2000s, as evidenced by the popularity of such titles as Jill Mansell's *Perfect Timing* (1997), Jenny Colgan's *Amanda's Wedding* (2000), Jane Green's *Jemima J.* (2000) and *Straight Talking* (2003), Allison Pearson's *I Don't Know How She Does It* (2002), Kinsella's expanding *Shopaholic* series (2001–), and the continuation of Fielding's *Bridget Jones* opus with the publication of *Mad About the Boy* in 2013.

In spite of its claims to capture the distinctiveness of the contemporary moment, chick lit makes use of intertextual references to nineteenth-century writers such as Jane Austen, Charlotte Brontë, and Edith Wharton to locate itself self-consciously in a tradition of women's writing. Shari Benstock points out that the genre's 'use of the diary form, journals, letters, and e-mail links it to the epistolary tradition and to the novel that emerged out of private modes of writing commonly associated with women'.[12] She argues that just as new technologies, such as telephone, radio, telegraph, and cinema, informed modernist style, so too do 'e-mail and instant messaging function in chick lit to capture the rapid, clipped pace of contemporary life and conversation' (p. 255). Benstock's observation not only contextualizes the aesthetic particularities of chick lit, but also signals the manifestation of what Yvonne Tasker and Diane Negra describe as postfeminism's 'distinct preoccupation with the temporal'.[13] For Whelehan, meanwhile, chick lit has especial affinities with the American 'feminist bestsellers' of the 1970s, such as Erica Jong's *Fear of Flying* (1973), Marge Piercy's *Woman on the Edge of Time* (1976), and *The Women's Room* (1977) by Marilyn French (1929–2009), which similarly employ a confessional style to explore women's experiences in relation to the discourses of second-wave feminism. Both types of fiction, Whelehan suggests, 'are in dialogue with feminism, the former directly – often through the avowed feminism of its heroines – and the latter more obliquely by the way its heroines often seem to be wrestling with a nascent feminist consciousness set against their quest for The One' (p. 5).

This fraught relation to feminism permeates novels such as Colgan's *Amanda's Wedding*, where Melanie feels guilty that she is 'the worst feminist of all time' and Fran is characterized as a 'man-hater'.[14] But chick lit's ambivalent feminist vocabulary finds particularly pronounced expression in *Bridget Jones's Diary*, a text in which, as Whelehan puts it, 'feminism lurks in the background like a guilty conscience' (p. 176). Across the pages of her diary entries, Bridget reflects in an ironic manner on the personal and professional aspirations and frustrations that characterize her experiences as a single woman. This narrative is inflected by her antagonistic relation to her mother and her girlish self-identification. She is, by her own admission, 'a child of *Cosmopolitan* culture' who has been 'traumatized by supermodels and too many quizzes', and knows that neither her 'personality nor [her] body is up to it if left to its own devices', but she is partial too to a 'delicious night of drunken feminist ranting' with her girlfriends.[15] Still, as the use of the word 'ranting' here intimates, Bridget and her friends have an uneasy relation to feminism; after all, as Bridget remarks about one particularly 'strident evening' with Jude and Sharon, 'there is nothing so unattractive to a man as strident feminism' (p. 20). Bridget's confusion about her identity turns, then, on the tension inflecting her sense of self as both a 'feminist' and a 'feminine' subject, positions she sees as irreconcilable. On one hand, her humorous ventriloquization of beauty discourse suggests a knowing, postmodern notion of identity, one that offers a critique of the disciplinary practices of femininity: 'Being a woman is worse than being a farmer – there is so much harvesting and crop spraying to be done ... The whole performance is so highly tuned you only need to neglect it for a few days for the whole thing to go to seed' (p. 30). On the other hand, her diary inscribes those very disciplinary practices into her daily regime (each diary entry begins with a confession about her calorie, cigarette, and alcohol intakes). In spite of Bridget's feminist awareness, she remains unable – or unwilling – to relinquish the trappings of traditional femininity that seem inexorably tied to the prospect of finding romantic fulfilment, represented by the Austenian Mark Darcy. Indeed, the text's loose adaptation of Austen's *Pride and Prejudice* (1813) bespeaks a nostalgia for an uncomplicated antediluvian pre-feminist identity when courtship was not complicated by feminism's vocabulary of autonomy and empowerment.[16]

If the self-conscious temporality of the diary form draws attention to Bridget's position as a postfeminist subject at a distance from the 'strident feminism' of a past generation, it also voices an anxiety about the girlish woman's ability to 'keep time'. Tasker and Negra argue that in postfeminist texts 'women's lives are regularly conceived of as time starved, women themselves are overworked, rushed, harassed, subject to their "biological clocks" to such a degree that female adulthood is defined as a state of chronic temporal crisis' (p. 9). Bridget's constant lateness for professional and social occasions is not simply another instance of the chaos she seeks to regulate by exercising greater self-control; it also gestures to the more unsettling implications of the career girl's deferral of her obligations to heteronormative definitions of femininity. As Una exclaims, 'You career girls! I don't know! Can't put it off for ever, you know. Tick-tock-tick-tock' (p. 11). In its depiction of the 'singleton', the novel brings into focus the single woman as a culturally legitimate sexual identity for young women, but one that is shot through with uncertainties and anxieties about the social position of the uncoupled woman.

Chick lit's exploration of the pressures placed upon the postfeminist woman to 'have it all' finds renewed emphasis in its spin-off, 'mum lit' or 'yummy mummy lit'. Following Maeve Haran's *Having it All* (1992), in which Liz, a beleaguered television executive, is under pressure to negotiate the demands of her professional and family lives, texts such as Pearson's *I Don't Know How She Does It*, Polly Williams's *The Rise and Fall of a Yummy Mummy* (2006) and *How to be Married* (2010), Fiona Neill's *The Secret Life of a Slummy Mummy* (2007), and Niamh Greene's *Secret Diary of a Demented Housewife* (2007) explore the feelings of guilt and inadequacy attending the harried woman's attempts to balance her familial and professional responsibilities. In *I Don't Know How She Does It*, Kate Reddy's struggle to navigate her double life as high-powered career girl and wife and mother leaves her feeling ghostly and insubstantial. 'Don't hate me if I stop work, will you?', she implores in an email to another working mother. 'I know we said how we all need to keep going to prove it can be done. It's just I used to think that maybe my job was killing me and now I'm scared I died and didn't notice.'[17] Far from being ready/Reddy, Kate experiences a temporal crisis that is resolved only through her return to the home and fulfilment of her role as mother and housewife (a role that is reiterated rather than mitigated by the opportunity to take on a dolls' house business). It is by reasserting a pre-feminist notion of domestic femininity that the postfeminist woman is able to keep to time once again.

Girl trouble

If 'the girl' tends to reaffirm domesticity as the proper realm of female subjectivity in chick lit, she acts as a more troublesome figure in recent experimental women's writing. In Ali Smith's *The Accidental* (2005), the beautiful, enigmatic Amber arrives, unexpectedly, at the door of the Smart family's holiday cottage in Norfolk and slips across the threshold into their disconnected and disaffected middle-class lives. The novel is divided into three parts – 'The Beginning', 'The Middle', and 'The End' – each of which unfolds through the successive, retrospective free indirect discourse of 12-year-old Astrid, her 17-year-old brother Magnus, her adulterous step-father Michael, and her mother Eve, author of 'autobiotruefictinterviews' which reimagine the life stories of people 'who died before his or her time in the Second World War'.[18] Set against the backdrop of the invasion of Iraq, *The Accidental* is a text profoundly concerned with anxieties about temporality and the status of history. Eve may be preoccupied with reinventing and reliving the past in her Second World War life histories, but she is unable to look directly at photographs of historical moments that are 'really happening' – represented most pressingly by newspaper coverage of the abuse of Iraqi prisoners of war (p. 285). In turn, her troubled daughter Astrid, who is obsessed with recording daybreak on her Sony digital camera, sees herself as 'newer' than the rest of her family who 'are all more part of the old century than she is' (p. 11). In so doing, she offers a counter to the girlish 'now-ness' that structures the diary of Bridget Jones.

Born in 1968, a landmark year of radical cultural reappraisal, Amber functions as an at once disruptive and illuminating force for each member of the family.[19] With her watch stopped at seven o'clock, she inhabits a position of temporal uncertainty, one that turns, at least in part, on her ambiguous location on the equivocal boundary between 'girl' and 'woman'. Seen through Astrid's eyes, she is 'kind of a woman but more like a girl' (p. 21), while Magnus perceives in Amber the image of 'a beautiful used girl off an internet site' (p. 55). For Michael, she is a frustrating sexual fantasy who moves between maturity and girlishness over the course of a single thought: 'That woman, Amber, had just pushed her plate away, pushed her chair back, long-limbed and insouciant and insolent as a girl' (p. 57). He identifies her, more anxiously, as 'one of those older women still determinedly being a girl; all those eighties feministy still-political women were terribly interested in what Eve did' (p. 64). It is Eve, however, who most insistently refers to Amber as 'the girl', even though she is 'only about ten years younger' than her, and wonders too if 'she could be a tramp' or a 'gypsy kind of person' (p. 98). Simultaneously girlish and old-fashioned, Amber is a strangely itinerant and 'untimely' figure who disrupts both the linear unfolding of the narrative and the mother–daughter chronology represented by Eve and Astrid.[20] If *The Accidental* shares common ground with third-wave feminism's interest in time and temporality, it suggests that fixed notions of gender and generation cannot be preserved in Amber.

Smith's interest in the fluidity of categories of gender and generation is also explored in *Girl Meets Boy* (2007), a novel in which girl trouble becomes 'boy-girl' trouble. Narrated by two sisters, Anthea and Imogen, Smith's novel reimagines Ovid's myth of Iphis, the story of a girl who is brought up as a boy to protect her from her father's infanticidal intentions and then metamorphoses into a boy on her wedding night so that she can marry her lover, Ianthe. The narrative opens with an image of the girls' sex-changing, suffragette grandfather – 'Let me tell you about when I was a girl, our grandfather says' – and incorporates into its narratives references to both first-wave feminist history (specifically the Cat and Mouse Act of 1913 and cross-dressing) and aspects of girl culture (such as *Spice World* and *Buffy the Vampire Slayer*), which locate the text's queer themes in the context of a broader feminist history.[21] Recasting Ovid's story about 'boy-girl' Iphis in its portrayal of the relationship between Andrea and Robin, *Girl Meets Boy* gestures also to a reinterpretation of Ovid informed by queer theory: 'Ovid's very fluid, as writers go, much more than most. He knows, more than most, that the imagination doesn't have a gender' (p. 97). Ovid's 'boy-girl' is figured by the indeterminate Robin, an eco-warrior and feminist activist: 'She had the swagger of a girl. She blushed like a boy ... She made love like a boy. She made love like a girl. She was so boyish it was girlish, so girlish it was boyish' (p. 84). Unsettling the meanings attached to the girlish and the boyish, *Girl Meets Boy* reimagines the narrative structures of romantic love that legitimize fixed notions of gender. Moreover, its queer recasting of Jane Eyre's celebrated enunciation, 'Reader, I married him/her' (p. 149), cuts across the cultural authority of second-wave feminist literary criticism's canonical interpretations of female agency.[22]

Such articulations of 'gender trouble' have their roots in the rich body of writing that emerged in the 1990s to contest heterosexual discourses of sex and gender. The shift from lesbian-feminist to queer politics, heralded in the work of theorists such as Judith Butler and Eve Kosofsky Sedgwick, ignited a literary interest in the multiplicity, ambiguity, and incoherence of genders. As Butler proposes in *Gender Trouble* (1990), if gender is a matter of 'becoming' rather than 'being', it 'ought not to be conceived as a noun or a substantial thing or a static cultural marker, but rather as an incessant and repeated action of some sort'.[23] Texts such as Jeanette Winterson's *Written on the Body* (1992) and *Art and Lies* (1994) and Patricia Duncker's *The Deadly Space Between* (2002) resist normative categories of identity in their exploration of the narrative territories of queer desire. The ambiguously gendered, bisexual narrator in *Written on the Body*, for example, refuses the heteronormative conventions of the romance narrative that would necessitate 'hearing the same story every time' – even if, in another echo of Brontë's *Jane Eyre* (1847), Louise, the object of the narrator's desire, is cast as 'a heroine from a Gothic novel, mistress of her house, yet capable of setting fire to it and fleeing in the night with one bag'.[24] In Duncker's *The Deadly Space Between*, a novel bustling with references to Freud and Mary Shelley's *Frankenstein* (1818), the triangular relationship between Toby, his mother Iso, and her lover, the enigmatic and captivating Roehm, heightens the queer dimensions of Oedipal desire. An interrogation of the 'fictive construction' of 'man' and 'woman' as 'abiding substances' (Butler, p. 32) also informs explorations of transsexual and transgender experience in texts such as Rose Tremain's *Sacred Country* (1992), Jackie Kay's *Trumpet* (1998), and Duncker's *James Miranda Barry* (1999).

Butler's theories of performativity have provided an especially apposite context for Sarah Waters's neo-Victorian fictions of the 1990s, in particular her representation of male impersonation in *Tipping the Velvet* (1998). Sharing common ground with third-wave feminism's emphasis on dissonant and ambiguous identities as well as an uneasy attitude to generational relationships, Waters's fiction is notable too for its depictions of deceitful and treacherous relations between women. Kaye Mitchell points out that Waters's work engages with gender politics and 'evinces a feminist interest in women's lives, bodies, histories and relationships', but its presentation of female characters and relationships between women is complex and contradictory rather than straightforwardly celebratory.[25] In *Affinity* (1999), for example, Margaret perceives a spiritual and erotic connection with Selina Dawes that promises escape from the castigatory surveillance of her mother and domestic expectations about heterosexual womanhood. But, in the end, it is the fraudulence and trickery of Selina and her lover, Ruth Vigers, that leave her feeling diminished and dematerialized. Although Waters's neo-Victorian novel plays with spectral metaphors to bring lesbian desire to the centre of the narrative, affinities between women are marked by duplicity and dissimulation in ways that complicate feminist assumptions about sisterhood. Nonetheless, while postfeminist writing of the 1990s, exemplified by chick lit, frames its obsession with the past in a manner that risks re-inscribing pre-feminist sensibilities, Waters's neo-Victorian fiction manifests a third-wave feminist consciousness that – through its mapping of 'women's ongoing search for self-definition' – remains firmly grounded in a knowledge and understanding of feminist history.[26]

Relations to history and the past are also central threads in the work of writers such as Andrea Levy and Bernardine Evaristo, whose semi-autobiographical depictions of young women searching for self-definition are informed by feminist and postcolonial perspectives. Levy's *Every Light in the House Burnin'* (1994), *Never Far from Nowhere* (1996), and *Fruit of the Lemon* (1999) are *bildungsromane* about the experiences of British-born girls of Jamaican immigrant parents growing up in North London. The protagonists negotiate their sense of identity and belonging in relation to the complex crossings of race, gender, and class. For Faith, the protagonist of *Fruit of the Lemon*, these fraught intersections are thrown into sharp relief by the race-blind assumptions of second-wave feminism. Listening to a Jamaican dub poet in the Victorian Crown and Castle pub as part of 'The Comedy Cabaret', Faith becomes acutely aware that she and the poet are the 'only black people' in a 'room of white people'.[27] In this moment of alienated affinity, the poet comes to stand in for 'every black man – ever', for her father and brother, as well as 'the unknown black faces in our photo album' (p. 92). It is not, however, simply the disparaging response of her friend Marion's father to the dub poet that angers Faith. Rather, it is Marion's recourse to her 'white working-class origins' to explain her father's racism as a 'cultural thing' that brings into focus the extent to which race is marginalized and deferred in a second-wave feminist analysis of oppression. This is exemplified by Marion's Marxist-feminist assurance that 'all racism would be swept away after the revolution. As a feminist we were all sisters – black and white' (p. 94).

London similarly appears as a 'war zone' for sexual and racial conflicts in Bernardine Evaristo's experimental novel-in-verse, *Lara* (1997 and 2009).[28] Spanning 150 years, seven generations, and three continents, *Lara* explores the experiences, in the 1960s and 1970s, of its eponymous protagonist, the daughter of a black Nigerian father and a white Anglo-Irish mother. For Lara, feminism plays a decisive role in her negotiation of the racially and sexually subjugating structures of patriarchal culture: 'Marriage? / I love the F-word too much, you know ... freedom' (p. 143). Wandering the streets of London she is 'a walking irradiated diatribe' who sees 'the rapist in every homme, worms in every phallus, / the bigot in all whites, the victim in every black / woman' (p. 145). In Evaristo's London, the heart of the British Empire is reconfigured as a postcolonial space with 'the "Great" Tippexed out of it' (p. 188), in which the diverse, transcultural futures of the 'f-word' might be articulated.

Regenerating feminism

Moving away from an exclusive focus on women and women's issues, and manifesting a more oblique relation to the 'f-word', fiction by women writers in the 1990s often muddies the relationship between women's writing and feminist politics posited by literary feminism of the 1970s. The 'prevalence of male protagonists' in Tremain's writing, for instance, leads Sarah Sceats to speculate that her fiction 'might be considered less than feminist',[29] while writers such as A.L. Kennedy have proclaimed that they 'never got the feminist thing'.[30] In spite of these authorial and critical anxieties about the status of the 'f-word', the work of such writers often remains shaped by a feminist consciousness, even if feminism finds expression in more dispersed and dissonant forms. Kennedy's *So I am Glad* (1995), a novel about perverse desires and ghostly intimacies, interrogates notions of romantic love, which makes Jennifer feel 'up to the waist in a lukewarm sump of thin, over-scented emotions', with self-conscious reference to the narrative conventions of romance fiction.[31] According to Glenda Norquay, Kennedy 'is clearly writing in a context that is informed by feminism. In her work there is a recognition of the social constructions of femininity which have held women in particular roles and positions of powerlessness.'[32] For Norquay, the central female characters in Kennedy's novels of the 1990s – Margaret in *Looking for the Possible Dance* (1993), Jennifer in *So I am Glad*, and Mary in *Everything You Need* (1999) – could be described as 'post-feminist, working with an explicit recognition of the ways in which their own lives might be mapped out differently from women of a previous generation' (p. 144). Linking this assertion to a movement in Kennedy's work away from the concerns of realist fiction towards a more interior, fragmented, and ludic aesthetic, Norquay's use of the term 'post-feminism' indicates the emergence of a 'different, but equally important form of feminism, which emerges out of poststructuralist feminism' (p. 144).[33]

Inhabiting the domestic territories of marriage, sex, and pregnancy, Helen Simpson's short story collections of the 1990s and early 2000s, *Four Bare Legs in a Bed* (1990), *Dear George and Other Stories* (1995), *Hey Yeah Right Get a Life* (2000), use dark humour and ambivalent narrative voices to render unstable straightforward understandings of both feminine and feminist identities. In 'The Immaculate Bridegroom', Dawn's enactment of a fairytale wedding, wearing 'magnolia petal slippers whispering in the cathedral hush beneath wild silk underskirts, enormously hooped', is unimpeded by the absence of a bridegroom.[34] 'To Her Unready Boyfriend' mimics the address of Andrew Marvell's 'To His Coy Mistress' (1681), as a woman, 'dogged by [the] rhythmic noise' (p. 65) of her biological clock, implores her boyfriend to come to bed 'unprotected' (p. 68). Simpson's satire is especially pronounced in a later story, 'Night Thoughts', published in *Granta*'s 'The F Word' issue (2011), dedicated to the relationship between gender, power, and feminism in the twenty-first century. Using free indirect discourse, the story chronicles the nocturnal anxieties of an insomniac husband frustrated by the pressures of housework, the giant posters of 'ribbed abs, honed six-packs, buff biceps' tyrannizing his route to work, his wife's 'impersonal demands for sex' and 'obdurate refusal to talk, ever', and his fears about the impossibility of social change in a 'woman-shaped' world.[35] Playing with clichéd cultural anxieties about feminist desires to reverse rather than redress gender inequities, Simpson's use of a male narrative voice up-ends conventional gender roles to denaturalize the patriarchal order of things.

The move to explore male subjectivity and constructions of masculinity is exemplified by Pat Barker's *Regeneration* trilogy. Turning to what Margaretta Jolly describes as 'the masculinised sphere of the pub, battlefield, hospital or government', Barker's writing in the 1990s appears to mark a stark departure from her socialist-feminist fictions of the previous decade, such as *Union Street* (1982) and *Blow Your House Down* (1984), which were characterized by their unflinching portrayals of male violence, prostitution, and the poverty and disaffection experienced by working-class women and girls in the north-east of England.[36] Barker's critically acclaimed *Regeneration* trilogy – *Regeneration* (1991), *The Eye in the Door* (1993), and *The Ghost Road* (1995) – focuses on the treatment of soldiers, including Siegfried Sassoon, Wilfred Owen, and the fictional Billy Prior, suffering from various neurological disorders, by the military physician W.H.R. Rivers at Craiglockhart War Hospital during World War One. In these historical fictions, Barker recasts her examination of psychical and corporeal injury, and violence and victimization, in the context of wartime trauma. Although the fictional worlds of the early novels and the trilogy might seem at a distance from one another, both are concerned with the ideological and material structures shaping experiences of gender, sexuality, and class. In the *Regeneration* trilogy, Rivers's analysis and treatment of his patients, as well as his own self-analysis, become a lens through which wartime ideas about masculinity and manhood are scrutinized. Reflecting on his clinical practice, Rivers observes that his patients had 'been trained to identify emotional repression as the essence of manliness. Men who broke down, or cried, admitted to feeling fear, were sissies, weaklings, failures. Not *men*.'[37] The military subject is revealed as one schooled in the disciplinary practices of masculinity – or what in *The Ghost Road* is referred to in a different context as 'lesson[s] in manliness'.[38] If wartime ideology worked to reify codes of heterosexual masculinity, it also unsettled them, placing gender and sexuality in crisis, undoing 'manliness', and transforming men into 'not *men*'.

The vocabulary of haunting and ghostliness that gives form to the texts' articulation of history as trauma, and of the compulsive return of the past, is used to expose the debility of a masculine identity only partially inhabited by the shell-shocked soldiers. Feelings of emasculation and impotence are conveyed through images of the vulnerable male body. In *Regeneration*, Anderson dreams that, upon returning home inadvertently naked, he is tied up and straitjacketed using a pair of corsets. Elsewhere in the novel, Burns, stumbling through the muddy landscape after leaving Craiglockhart, discovers a tree laden with dead animals. Laying the corpses out on the ground around him, he removes his clothes; standing naked at the centre of this deathly tableau, he 'cup[s] his genitals, not because he was ashamed, but because they looked incongruous, they didn't seem to belong with the rest of him' (p. 39). Stripped of its military uniform, the male body presents a loss of masculinity. As Rivers reflects, the 'war that had promised so much in the way of "manly" activity had actually delivered "feminine" passivity, and on a scale that their mothers and sisters had scarcely known. No wonder they broke down' (pp. 107–8). Through an anatomization of the impact of World War One on ideas about masculinity and manhood, *Regeneration* explores the ways in which war exposes the fragility of gender boundaries.

Like much historical fiction, the *Regeneration* trilogy not only offers a revisionist view of the past, but also turns to history to illuminate contemporary debates about gender, sexuality, and class. Concerned with the damaging effects of patriarchal power structures for both men and women, Barker's work bespeaks the shifting meanings attached to masculinity in the twentieth century. In an interview in 1991, Barker expressed her desire 'to protest the idea that feminist writing and feminism are exclusively about women. I think it's about the way in which gender stereotypes distort the personal development of both sexes and make people less creative and happy than they otherwise might be.'[39] According to Jolly, it is precisely the tension in Barker's 'double status as feminist and mainstream writer' that illuminates 'the influence that feminism has had within the literary establishment and the concomitant testing of feminism from within' (p. 60). The power of the *Regeneration* trilogy, she proposes, lies in the way that Barker's 'celebrated "socialist-realist" style balances critique of social relations as they are with sympathy for both oppressor and oppressed. Historically, this is an important direction for fiction in the 1990s, so often complacently touted as an example of "post-feminism"' (p. 60). In this respect, Barker's work does not reflect the waning or dissolution of feminist ideas but, rather, their expansion to incorporate a broader analysis of gender politics.

In conclusion, while the meanings attached to third-wave feminism and postfeminism accrued mainly in the sphere of popular culture, they find their fictional articulation in the responses of women writers to the shifting and multifarious valences of feminism. In its exploration of the tensions surrounding traditional feminine identities, women's writing that emerges in the 1990s variously interrogates, resists, and redefines feminist politics, complicating dominant understandings of the relationship between gender and power. Privileging multiplicity and fragmentation in its reimagining of identities, it is inhabited by a convergence of voices moving across generational and gender boundaries. Much fiction of the period conveys a particular interest in the relationship between identity and time – a concern that manifests in the diaries of chick lit, the spectral temporality of work by Smith and Kennedy, the transhistorical crossings of Evaristo, and the historical fiction of writers such as Tremain, Waters, and Barker. Expanding the capacity of the 'f-word' to incorporate the complexities and contradictions of contemporary definitions of identity, women's writing in the 1990s and beyond engages with and animates feminist discourse in distinct and disparate, but nonetheless compelling, ways.

Notes

1. In 1991, Clarence Thomas was nominated for the Supreme Court by President George W. Bush. The proceedings were challenged by Anita Hill who had worked with Thomas and who made allegations of sexual harassment. Rebecca Walker, 'Becoming the Third Wave', *Ms.* (January 1992), p. 41. The meanings attached to third-wave feminism were developed in the proliferation of (mainly American) texts published from the mid-1990s onwards. See, for example, Rebecca Walker's *To Be Real: Telling the Truth and Changing the Face of Feminism* (New York: Anchor, 1995); Barbara Findlen's *Listen Up: Voices from the Next Feminist Generation* (Seattle:

Seal, 1995); Leslie Heywood and Jennifer Drake's *Third Wave Agenda: Being Feminist, Doing Feminism* (Minneapolis: Minnesota University Press, 1997); and Jennifer Baumgardner and Amy Richards's *Manifesta: Young Women, Feminism, and the Future* (New York: Farrar, Straus and Giroux, 2000).

2. Imelda Whelehan, *The Feminist Bestseller: From* Sex and the Single Girl *to* Sex and the City (Basingstoke: Palgrave Macmillan, 2005), p. 169.
3. Natasha Walter, *The New Feminism* (London: Virago, 1999), pp. 4–5.
4. Walter's criticism of second-wave feminist narratives of victimization has a correlative in the cultural commentary of prominent American writers such as Naomi Wolf, Katie Roiphe, Christina Hoff Sommers, and Camille Paglia.
5. Gloria Steinem, 'Foreword', in Walker, p. xix.
6. Nancy F. Cott, *The Grounding of Modern Feminism* (New Haven: Yale University Press, 1987), p. 282.
7. Angela McRobbie, *The Aftermath of Feminism: Gender, Culture and Social Change* (London: Sage, 2009), p. 11.
8. For a discussion of the 'postfeminist mystique' and the contemporary fascination with resuscitating seemingly anachronistic models of femininity, see Rebecca Munford and Melanie Waters, *Feminism and Popular Culture: Investigating the Postfeminist Mystique* (London: I.B. Tauris, 2013), pp. 9–12.
9. It seems that the term was first used by Cris Mazza and Jeffrey DeShell, editors of *Chick-Lit: Postfeminist Fiction* (Carbondale: FC2, 1995), in an ironic way 'to refer to postfeminist attitudes' (p. 9). While early chick lit novels tended to privilege the experience of white, middle-class, heterosexual women, the contours of the genre have expanded to incorporate subgenres such as 'Ethnick lit', 'Sistah lit', and 'Chica lit'. See Suzanne Ferriss and Mallory Young, 'Introduction', *Chick Lit: The New Woman's Fiction*, ed. Suzanne Ferriss and Mallory Young (New York: Routledge, 2006), p. 9, p. 6.
10. *Today Programme*, BBC Radio 4 (23 August 2001).
11. Germaine Greer, *The Whole Woman* (London: Anchor, 2000), p. 314.
12. Shari Benstock, 'Afterword: The New Woman's Fiction', in Ferriss and Young, p. 255.
13. Yvonne Tasker and Diane Negra, 'Introduction: Feminist Politics and Postfeminist Culture', *Interrogating Postfeminism: Gender and the Politics of Popular Culture*, ed. Yvonne Tasker and Diane Negra (Durham, NC: Duke University Press, 2007), p. 9.
14. Jenny Colgan, *Amanda's Wedding* (London: HarperCollins, 2011), p. 82, p. 304.
15. Helen Fielding, *Bridget Jones's Diary* (London: Picador, 1996), p. 59.
16. In its nostalgic mode, postfeminist discourse has found a peculiarly hospitable residence in the profusion of Jane Austen sequels and spin-offs that appeared from the mid-1990s onwards.
17. Allison Pearson, *I Don't Know How She Does It* (London: Vintage, 2003), p. 329.
18. Ali Smith, *The Accidental* (Harmondsworth: Penguin, 2006), p. 81.
19. Angela Carter, for example, proposes: 'I can date to that time and to some of those debates and that sense of heightened awareness of the society around me in the summer of 1968, my own questioning of the nature of my reality as a *woman*' (p. 70; emphasis in original). Angela Carter, 'Notes from the Front Line', *On Gender and Writing*, ed. Michelene Wandor (London: Pandora, 1983), pp. 69–77.
20. According to Jane Elliot, 'debates about generational rhetoric and the different waves of feminism are often underpinned by the question of which version of feminism was more appropriately situated in time: third-wave feminists often accused second-wave feminist analysis of being out of date, and second-wave

feminists accused third-wave feminists of anachronistically reinventing the wheel' (p. 1700). Insofar as it disrupts the chronology of the generational model, Smith's novel interrupts the 'contemporary moment' with what Elliot describes as a 'practice of the untimely' (p. 1701). See Jane Elliot, 'The Currency of Feminist Theory', *PMLA*, 121:5 (2006), 1697–703.

21. Ali Smith, *Girl Meets Boy* (Edinburgh: Canongate, 2007), p. 3.
22. This is exemplified by Sandra M. Gilbert and Susan Gubar, *The Madwoman in the Attic: The Woman Writer and the Nineteenth-Century Literary Imagination* (New Haven: Yale University Press, 1979).
23. Judith Butler, *Gender Trouble: Feminism and the Subversion of Identity* (1990; New York: Routledge, 1999), p. 143.
24. Jeanette Winterson, *Written on the Body* (London: Vintage, 1993), p. 49.
25. Kaye Mitchell, 'Introduction', *Sarah Waters*, ed. Kaye Mitchell (London: Bloomsbury, 2013), p. 10.
26. Lucie Armitt, 'Dark Departures: Contemporary Women's Writing after the Gothic', *Postfeminist Gothic*, ed. Benjamin A. Brabon and Stéphanie Genz (Basingstoke: Palgrave Macmillan, 2007), p. 28.
27. Andrea Levy, *Fruit of the Lemon* (London: Review, 1999), p. 92.
28. Bernardine Evaristo, *Lara* (Tarset: Bloodaxe Books, 2009), p. 145. *Lara* initially appeared in 1997 but was republished in a rewritten and much expanded version 12 years later.
29. Sarah Sceats, 'Appetite, Desire and Belonging in the Novels of Rose Tremain', *The Contemporary British Novel Since 1980*, ed. James Acheson and Sarah C.E. Ross (Edinburgh University Press, 2005), p. 165.
30. 'Interview with A.L. Kennedy', *Edinburgh Review*, 101 (1999), p. 107.
31. A.L. Kennedy, *So I am Glad* (London: Vintage, 2004), p. 217.
32. Glenda Norquay, '"Partial to Intensity": The Novels of A.L. Kennedy', in Acheson and Ross, p. 144.
33. This definition is consonant with Ann Brooks's notion of postfeminism as a theoretical category that expresses 'a stage in the constant evolutionary movement of feminism ... encompassing the intersection of feminism with a number of other anti-foundationalist movements including postmodernism, post-structuralism and post-colonialism' (p. 1). See *Postfeminisms: Feminism, Cultural Theory and Cultural Forms* (London: Routledge, 1997).
34. Helen Simpson, *Dear George and Other Stories* (London: Vintage, 2001), p. 105.
35. Helen Simpson, 'Night Thoughts', *Granta: The F Word*, 115 (2011), p. 119, p. 121, p. 125.
36. Margaretta Jolly, 'After Feminism: Pat Barker, Penelope Lively and the Contemporary Novel', *British Culture of the Postwar: An Introduction to Literature and Society, 1945–1999*, ed. Alistair Davies and Alan Sinfield (London: Routledge, 2000), p. 59.
37. Pat Barker, *Regeneration* (Harmondsworth: Penguin, 1992), p. 48.
38. Pat Barker, *The Ghost Road* (Harmondsworth: Penguin, 1996), p. 96.
39. Donna Perry, 'Going Home Again: An Interview with Pat Barker', *The Literary Review: An International Journal of Contemporary Writing*, 34:2 (1991), p. 244.

Part III
Gender and Genre

9

The Gothic: Danger, Discontent, and Desire

Sue Zlosnik

The famous 1974 assertion by Angela Carter (1940–92) that 'we live in Gothic times' seems to carry even more force now as the appetite for Gothic stories and style in popular culture continues unabated and Gothic studies are firmly embedded in many university departments.[1] For some critics it is not surprising that the twentieth-century accumulation of wars and violence offers an inspiration for and a reinforcement of 'an age in which a Gothic aesthetic flourishes'.[2] 'Gothic' has proved to be a slippery term, however. Long regarded as denoting a historically defined genre confined to the latter part of the eighteenth century and early decades of the nineteenth, Gothic began to be understood, from David Punter's ground-breaking work in 1980 onwards, as a mode of expression enduring into the present day.[3] It is now widely accepted that Gothic adapts its forms according to cultural context. It can also be argued that even the Gothic sensibility (its preoccupation with 'horror, madness, monstrosity, death, disease, terror, evil, and weird sexuality') is inflected differently in different texts and performances so that its tendency to excess becomes on occasion the stuff of comedy rather than terror.[4] Characterized above all by transgression and an ambiguous relationship with everyday reality, Gothic shifts according to recognized social boundaries.

Among these boundaries are the cultural constraints of gender. It is no coincidence that the rise of Gothic studies in academia was contemporaneous with the emergence of second-wave feminism and the ensuing development of feminist literary theory and criticism in the 1960s and 1970s. As David Richter notes, feminism was 'perhaps the most obvious force at work' in transforming 'a field that was neglected at best – and at worst a bastion of bibliophilic cranks' into 'a very important area of study'.[5] In the mid-1970s, Ellen Moers coined the term 'Female Gothic', which, although not closely defined, identified a tradition of women's writing reaching back to the late eighteenth century.[6] In this tradition, the predominant characteristic of the Gothic, 'fear', manifests itself in the specifically female terrors experienced by women in patriarchal society, what Helene Meyers calls 'femicidal fears'.[7]

A repeated feature is the reworking of the folktale 'Bluebeard', most recently in Helen Oyeyemi's *Mr Fox* (2012). Charlotte Brontë's *Jane Eyre* (1847), itself a version of 'Bluebeard', has surfaced again and again through the twentieth and twenty-first centuries. As well as providing a persistent plot line for popular romance (in numerous Mills and Boon novels, for example), it has provoked powerful fictional dialogue in works such as *Rebecca* (1938) by Daphne du Maurier (1907–89), *Wide Sargasso Sea* (1965) by Jean Rhys (1890–1979), which disrupted assumptions about gender and ethnicity, and Diane Setterfield's metafictive *The Thirteenth Tale* (2006). Following the initial influence of second-wave feminism, increasingly sophisticated feminist theorists challenged androcentric assumptions and heteronormativity, questioning conventional configurations of gender. At the same time, women writers continued to turn towards the Gothic to examine female discontents and explore other ways of being for women in a world of rapid social and technological development and changing attitudes towards gender and sexuality. Many writers have at times written in a Gothic vein: for example, Beryl Bainbridge (1932–2010), Muriel Spark (1918–2006), Jeanette Winterson, Nicola Barker, A.S. Byatt, Iris Murdoch (1919–99). In the late twentieth century, too, crime fiction by writers such as P.D. James (1920–2014) and Ruth Rendell (1930–2015) has also taken a Gothic turn.

Wives and mothers

It is Gothic fiction's hybridity, its blend of the dark fantastic with the hard truths of a recognizable world, that makes it such a powerful vehicle for challenging entrenched stereotypes. Late twentieth-century Gothic texts by women writers create a disturbing world in which what had been accepted as 'normal' appears 'uncanny'. Often the focus, as in earlier Female Gothic, is the domestic sphere, the 'Bluebeard' trope persisting in the representation of marital confinement. Angela Carter's *The Magic Toyshop* (1967) explores female desire and women's economic dependency; it represents the home as a place of entrapment through its retelling of the Bluebeard tale, locating events in a London suburb of the 1950s. Her volume of short stories, *The Bloody Chamber* (1979), uses traditional tales as the basis for narratives that expose oppression and query the nature of female identity. In the title story, Carter rewrites the closure of the traditional Bluebeard plot. Its naïve young heroine, overwhelmed by erotic desire, is shown to be complicit in her subordination, playing the masochist to her sadistic husband; the story demonstrates how masochism is culturally associated with the female subject position in a patriarchal society. 'Home' becomes the most dangerous place of all as the forbidden room and its grisly contents are revealed. It is the plot's denouement in Carter's version of the story that disturbs conventional expectations of gendered behaviour: the heroine is rescued not by her three brothers, as in the traditional folk version, but by a gun-wielding mother who appears just as her daughter is about to be beheaded. It has been noted that Carter does not offer closures that move out of the heterosexual frame.[8] Instead there is here a redefinition of heterosexual relations as the saved heroine finds happiness with a 'new man', a sensitive and kind piano-tuner who, like Rochester at the end of *Jane Eyre*, is blind and thus symbolically deprived of predatory masculinity. Moreover, his inability to see is related to the anger women felt during the 1960s and 1970s as they realized their cultural positioning as objects of the male gaze.[9]

The negative effects of femininity and the expectations placed upon women find expression in Hilary Mantel's early work, much of which is distinctly Gothic. *Eight Months on Ghazzah Street* (1988), for example, accentuates the isolation of the domestic space by placing a British woman in a culture she finds alien and misogynistic. Having gone to Saudi Arabia with her husband for his work and thereby abandoning her own career as a cartographer, she becomes in effect a prisoner in a stifling apartment in Jeddah. She finds Saudi society indecipherable, the streets threatening, and the expatriate community oppressive; when acquaintances begin to die in unexplained ways, she becomes consumed by a nameless terror. This is her reward for being a dutiful wife; whereas her husband is not represented as a predatory Bluebeard figure, his indifference to her anguish is part of her plight. Mantel's novel is notable for its powerfully menacing atmosphere in which the everyday becomes uncanny. In that sense it is more Gothic than Canadian Margaret Atwood's dystopic fantasy *The Handmaid's Tale* (1985), which also plays upon Western anxieties about the reversal of progress towards gender equality.

In the 1980s, the influence of feminist thinkers in France, such as Hélène Cixous, Luce Irigaray, and Julia Kristeva, moved feminist criticism and theory beyond a concern with 'images of women' to consider the psychological, philosophical, and discursive foundations of gender identity. For Irigaray, the masculinity underpinning Western culture is founded upon the repression of the maternal and characterized by persistent patriarchal anxiety about the return of an avenging monstrous mother figure. One memorable Gothic text that enacts this anxiety is du Maurier's 'Don't Look Now' (1971), which contains some of the themes that a new generation of women writers were to take up: the loss of a child; the limitations of a masculine rationality; vengeful feminine monstrosity. Here that monstrosity appears in the shape of the female dwarf who kills the male protagonist in the final twist of the story.[10]

In the Gothic fiction of Susan Hill, the child is often an uncanny figure and conventional images of motherhood are overturned. Her ghost stories mock Victorian and Edwardian narratives, use their conventions to critique the history from which they emerged, and expose the limitations of a masculine perspective through their male narrators.[11] Two novellas published almost a decade apart –*The Woman in Black* (1983) and *The Mist in the Mirror* (1992) – unsettle assumptions about Victorian family values, often invoked by Conservative politicians in the 1980s. *The Woman in Black,* a tale about the ghostly revenge of a bereaved mother, has enjoyed a vigorous afterlife in adaptations for radio, television, the stage, and the screen. This success points to its inherently dramatic character, with strange apparitions and sudden shocks. Its framing (the 'ancient tradition' of telling ghost stories on Christmas Eve)[12] and the remote fog-bound setting evoke the ghost stories of M.R. James while its title echoes *The Woman in White* (1859) by Wilkie Collins. However, whereas the eponymous woman in Collins's novel is a victim, Hill's substitution of 'black' for 'white' in her title suggests the contrary. In Hill's tale, it is the male narrator (a lawyer, representing bourgeois convention) who is traumatized by his encounter with a child's ghostly cries and the apparition of 'the woman in black'; she is the phantom of an unmarried mother who had had her child taken from her and then witnessed his death in an accident at an early age. The terrifying climactic scene of this novella takes place in an eerie house, in a barred nursery which functions as a kind of bloody chamber where, in this twist of the Bluebeard tale, the narrator regresses to infancy and the figure of the mother becomes the source of horror.[13] Haunting is not confined to this location, however, and the 'woman in black' appears a year later as an avenging demon in the apparently safe world of a London park. Just before, the narrator's own wife and baby son are killed in an accident, the circumstances of which echo the earlier tragedy.

Female doubles and the reclamation of monstrosity

The *doppelgänger* or double has been a persistent motif in Gothic fiction since the early nineteenth century, the most famous example appearing in Robert Louis Stevenson's *Strange Case of Dr Jekyll and Mr Hyde* (1886). The double is present in Brontë's *Jane Eyre,* with many critics now reading the first Mrs Rochester as Jane's *alter ego.*[14] Since 1970, women writers of Gothic fiction have adapted the trope of the double in various ways. Emma Tennant, for example, subverts the two most famous male-authored Gothic tales of doubling. In *The Bad Sister* (1978), a novel about a Scottish landowner's two daughters (one legitimate and one illegitimate) and their father's murder, she evokes James Hogg's *The Private Memoirs and Confessions of a Justified Sinner* (1824). As in the source text, this may be the story of an evil *alter ego,* a *doppelgänger.* There is no authoritative narrative point of view in Tennant's novel, which is framed, as in Hogg's original, by an anonymous 'editor'. Two versions offer alternative explanations for events in *The Bad Sister*: the delusions of mental illness or an alternative reality peopled by wild women led by the charismatic Meg, a lesbian vampire. Tennant's novel is a vividly imagined excursion into what feminist critics of the time, following Elaine Showalter, called the 'wild zone'.[15] In this 'no-man's land', conventional femininity, defined as passivity, is overturned as the death of the Father is enacted. Over a decade later, Tennant turned to Stevenson's novella in *Two Women of London* (1989). Her latter-day *Strange Case* reworks the original for a Britain in which inequalities had become starker after ten years of 'Thatcherism', exposing the fragility of female social identity.[16] Structured by a detective plot with a murder, the novel explores the connection between Eliza Jekyll, talented and elegant gallery director, and Mrs Hyde, downtrodden, slovenly and prematurely aged single mother who turn out to be the same woman.

In Mantel's *An Experiment in Love* (1995), the enigmatic *doppelgänger* is revealed to be truly malevolent. This is a tale of two young students in which one thrives seemingly at the expense of the other, growing larger while the impoverished narrator shrinks into herself, collapsing from near starvation compounded by emotional distress. Intimations of another reality just beyond the vividly realized quotidian detail are disturbingly represented. In this powerful Gothic female *bildungsroman*, the *alter ego* is apparently capable of anything – even, it would seem, causing the death of a third girl by locking her in a burning hall of residence. As these examples suggest, Bertha Mason's metaphorical daughters were much in evidence in the late twentieth century, manifesting the 'hunger, rebellion and rage' of *Jane Eyre*.[17]

Female embodiment and monstrosity are key themes in Mantel's tale of doubling. French feminism in its emphasis on the body has rendered significant insights for scholars of the Gothic, especially Kristeva's concept of 'the abject', developed in *Powers of Horror* (1982). Horror and revulsion, Kristeva argues, are an echo of our early anxieties surrounding the separation from the mother that involve insecurity about materiality and the borders of the self. The abject is that which 'disturbs identity, system, order ... [t]he in-between, the ambiguous, the composite'.[18] The abject figure is monstrous or grotesque, qualities attributed in many Gothic texts to older or transgressive women in reworkings of the archetypal witch figure.

The Gothic proved an effective way for late twentieth-century women writers both to represent anxieties about female embodiment and to challenge cultural myths of female monstrosity. In contrast with du Maurier's terrifying dwarf, the 'abnormal' female body is represented in carnivalesque mode by some writers, such as Carter, whose Fevvers in *Nights at the Circus* (1984) is a celebratory figure with a physical aberration in the form of wings that symbolize liberatory potential for women. More grotesque and of supernaturally massive proportions, Jeanette Winterson's seventeenth-century Dog Woman in *Sexing the Cherry* (1988) becomes an empowering *doppelgänger* for a present-day female eco-warrior battling global capitalism. Winterson's later novel, *The Daylight Gate* (2012), retells the brutal story of the seventeenth-century persecution of the Pendle witches in a way that humanizes its subjects while exploring transgressive desire.

One of the most famous examples of the reclamation of female monstrosity is Fay Weldon's *The Life and Loves of a She-Devil* (1983) which enacts in comic vein multiple transgressions in its portrayal of a woman who rejects the role of victim. In the beginning, Ruth Patchett has the traditional physical attributes of a witch (excessive height, jutting jaw, sunken eyes, and hooked nose) but is trapped in the role of housewife and mother. The label 'she-devil', used as an insult by her husband, triggers her revolt as she embraces this new role with gusto, burning down the marital home and taking elaborate revenge on her husband and his lover. Rejoicing in the decline and death of the latter, she undergoes cosmetic surgery to transform her own body into an exact double of the dead woman and by the end of the novel all roles are reversed. Whether this ruthless transformation should be understood as an uncomfortable collusion with patriarchal values or a defamiliarization of the accepted order remains open to debate.

While Weldon's novel reflects the growing popularity of surgery among women to achieve a physical ideal and raises questions about women's complicity with masculine fantasies of the perfect feminine body, it also predicts a world in which the concept of stable identity is put under erasure through cosmetic manipulation of the body and in which gender is seen as performance rather than biological essence. Situating itself within emerging discourses of the body, *The Life and Loves of a She-Devil* can thus be seen as both a reactive and a prophetic text. Like Carter's work – *The Passion of New Eve* (1977), for example – it anticipates the theories of Judith Butler and Judith Halberstam, both of whom consider gender identity as performance rather than essence.[19] Weldon's sensitivity to the implications of scientific developments in relation to the instability of female identity is also evident in *The Cloning of Joanna May* (1987), which gives a new and darkly comic twist to the Gothic motif of the double. The multiple *doppelgängers* in this novel derive from a manipulation of technology to further the interests of Joanna's husband, a classic Gothic scientist figure. While their discovery of each other leads to sisterhood not conflict, the novel is dominated by anxiety about the ubiquitous fallout from the Chernobyl nuclear disaster of 1986 and the fear of the grotesque bodily metamorphoses that might ensue. Thus monstrosity is removed from the abject feminine to a malfunctioning patriarchal technology.

Haunted spaces, haunted selves

In contemporary British women's fiction, haunting has become a recurrent trope in which abject female figures frequently feature. Ghosts often represent the return of repressed trauma, both personal and historical. Mantel's *Beyond Black* (2005) has a drab contemporary setting, the satellite towns around the London orbital M25, and is focused on a moment of national crisis, the death of Princess Diana in 1997. This novel turns a female grotesque into a Gothic heroine of sensibility in excess. The obese Alison Hart is a professional psychic who is haunted by the spirits of brutal men from her past, now deceased. Her daily life is one in which the boundary between ordinary experience and a banal hereafter is constantly destabilized, her authenticity never called into doubt by the narrator. Only when she is able to bring into consciousness a violent trauma from her childhood can she exorcize her personal demons and replace them with benign female spirit guides. Like Weldon, Mantel understands the power of the comic turn in the Gothic: 1990s managerialism is reflected in an afterlife that involves going on courses and being 'made up' to management by (Old) Nick himself.[20] Far from comic, however, are the details of Alison's childhood abuse (again, another emerging theme of the times) and the depiction of the wraiths who are so dislocated and dispossessed as a result of their modern lives that in death they cluster under motorway flyovers, unsure of where to haunt.

In contrast, Sarah Waters's *The Little Stranger* (2009) places the haunted house at the centre of a novel about changing Britain in the late 1940s. A modern day House of Usher, decayed Hundreds Hall is evocative of ruined Thornfield and Manderley, suggesting an echo of the *Jane Eyre* tradition.[21] The novel's plot, though, takes a different turn, the source of its haunting unclear. Hundreds is a troubled space in more senses than one. The novel's unreliable male narrator, Dr Faraday, claims the objectivity of the medical profession, even while it becomes apparent that he is deeply implicated in the disturbing events that unfold. Of working-class origin, he covets the social privilege that Hundreds has represented to him since childhood when his mother was a servant there. Feeling his precarious social status and income threatened by socialist developments, he is a troubled man. Although he is inclined to accept a colleague's Freudian explanation of the haunting as emanating from an internalized 'little stranger', he does not recognize that he may be its source. The novel's central female figure, the daughter of the house, Caroline, embodies the closing down of alternatives for women in the postwar period. Her refusal to comply with Faraday's plan to acquire Hundreds by marrying her (preferring to return to a life of independent activity such as she enjoyed in the Wrens during the war) hints at an alternative desire that is ended by her mysterious death. This is possibly at the hands of her rejected suitor who then becomes, by default, the caretaker of the crumbling house.

The climax of *The Little Stranger* offers a reminder of the Gothic's affinity with 'queerness'. The fate of Caroline is evocative of Terry Castle's concept of the 'apparitional lesbian', developed in her book of the same name in which she argues that lesbians have been compelled to inhabit a 'recessive, indeterminate, misted over space' in literature.[22] Another writer who makes manifest the traditional metaphoric 'ghosting' of lesbian desire in literature is Ali Smith. *Hotel World* (2001), for example, begins with the disembodied voice of a young woman who has been killed in a freak accident at one of the 'Global Hotels' chain. She is one of five different voices, each from a different woman somehow connected with the hotel; separately and together, they represent aspects of female identity and experience in the modern world. The dead voice is accorded the same narrative status as those of the living women and it is through this voice that the occlusion of lesbian desire is expressed. The dead girl had left a watch to be mended and reflects on her attraction to the female assistant in the jeweller's shop; that the nascent attraction was reciprocated is confirmed at the end of the novel when the assistant takes the unclaimed watch to wear herself and reflects on a missed opportunity, feeling 'small wings moving against the inside of her chest, or something in there anyway, turning, tightened, working'.[23]

A complex pattern of transgressive sexual desire that chimes with emerging queer discourses is evident in Patricia Duncker's fiction. *The Deadly Space Between* (2002) is a ghost story with a new dynamic: it is a reworking of the Freudian family romance, representing the Father as a sinister phantasmal figure and subverting Freud's Oedipal account of family relationships and the construction of subjectivity. The 18-year-old narrator, Toby, has been brought up by his single mother, Iso, with support from her older lesbian sister and her partner. He experiences and acts upon incestuous desire for Iso; meanwhile he is both fascinated by and jealous of his mother's mysterious lover, the enigmatic Roehm, who, it is implied, is his father, and for whom he also harbours an incestuous desire.[24] In the icy setting of a Swiss glacier, reminiscent of the ultimate destination of Frankenstein and his monster, the final pages of the novel reveal the dead body of Roehm to be that of a Swiss botanist who had perished over two hundred years earlier. Thus the oppressive return of the Oedipal Father may be seen as enacted through a ghost, suggesting that Toby's narrative inhabits the realms of fantasy.

The affirmation of otherness and difference in Queer Gothic is also a feature of Oyeyemi's and Pauline Melville's Postcolonial Gothic, in which ghosts may represent the trauma and legacy of an imperial past as well as the anxieties of a dual cultural heritage. There has been considerable critical debate about the relationship between such postcolonial texts and the Gothic tradition, the inception and history of which has been Western and bourgeois.[25] For British women writers, the further inflection of gender adds another dimension to the representation of otherness. Pauline Melville was born in Guyana to an English mother and a Guyanese father of partly Amerindian descent and is well known for novels that draw on this background, such as *The Ventriloquist's Tale* (1997) and *Eating Air* (2009). Melville's most Gothic work is found in her short stories, which often express anxieties about identity, both ethnic and gendered. The collection *Shape-shifter* (1990) contains a chilling story with a title suggesting an accusation of complicity, 'You Left the Door Open'. This describes an attack on a woman in her own home by a male intruder whose ontological status remains ambiguous. In one sense 'real', he is also demonic, claiming the identity of a nineteenth-century murderer but also assuming the identity of a character created by the victim for a cabaret show, a male *doppelgänger* who turns on his female creator.[26] *The Migration of Ghosts* (1998) includes stories that are all in some way about cultural displacement and dislocation. In 'The President's Exile' a newly dead South American dictator, unaware of his own demise, revisits the scenes of his ruthless rise to power (beginning with a realistically rendered London School of Economics). The story leaves him asleep in his own country but implies he will 'wake again'.[27] The collection's title story seems to suggest that ghosts are an intrinsic part of a culture, the expatriate central character reflecting that he would forever feel displaced in Brazil 'because he did not know the ghosts' (p. 196).

The tensions of a dual cultural heritage are also expressed through the Gothic writing of Oyeyemi, who is Nigerian but grew up in London. In *The Icarus Girl* (2005), a powerful tale of haunting, Oyeyemi blends the Gothic tradition of the destructive *doppelgänger* with African mythology and the story of a dead twin to make vivid the anguish of its child heroine's sense of dislocation. Its eight-year-old heroine, Jessamy, child of a Nigerian mother and English father (both of whom are loving and well educated) finds her London childhood difficult. On a trip to visit her grandfather in Nigeria, she encounters what she thinks is another little girl, whom she names Tilly Tilly and who mysteriously follows her back to England, with disruptive consequences. *White is for Witching* (2009) is a contemporary haunted-house story. A family bereaved of its mother inhabits the ancestral maternal home in Dover, a place where new immigrants land and the displaced wait in the limbo of a detention centre. The daughter, Miri, is the victim of mental illness and a rare eating disorder. Set in uneasy balance with this condition is a vivid and distressing haunting by her female forbears who meld with the malign spirit of the house itself and eventually destroy her. A new housekeeper of Yoruba descent understands the power of the spirits in the way that her predecessors could not but this cannot save Miri any more than her lesbian relationship with a lover at Cambridge can. This lover is herself emblematic of dislocation, a black girl adopted by white working-class parents, who experiences the house in Dover as a malign force. As mentioned at the start of this chapter, Oyeyemi's most recent novel, *Mr Fox* (2012), is another reworking of the traditional tale of Bluebeard. Although, as Oyeyemi has explained, she began the book after reading du Maurier's *Rebecca,* the 'linear suspense story' she intended to write 'based on Bluebeard, complete with locked doors and a brooding, irresistible wife-killer' was rapidly abandoned so that she 'ended up going on a jaunt through a Bluebeard kaleidoscope'. Playful in tone, *Mr Fox* is in Oyeyemi's own words 'about the power of stories'.[28]

In conclusion, British women's Gothic writing since 1970 shows the power of stories, challenging patriarchal plots, and imagining alterative possibilities for women. Like the tradition of the Gothic itself, it constantly shifts shape, responding to changing boundaries and figuring new forms of transgression.

Notes

1. Angela Carter, 'Afterword', *Fireworks: Nine Profane Pieces* (1974; London: Quartet Books, 1976), p. 122.
2. Lucie Armitt, *Twentieth-Century Gothic* (Cardiff: University of Wales Press, 2011), p. 81.
3. David Punter, *The Literature of Terror: A History of Gothic Fictions from 1765 to the Present Day* (London: Longman, 1980).
4. See Bradford Morrow and Patrick McGrath, Introduction to *The New Gothic* (New York: Random House, 1991), p. xiv. On comedy, see Avril Horner and Sue Zlosnik, *Gothic and the Comic Turn* (Basingstoke: Palgrave Macmillan, 2005).
5. David Richter, *The Progress of Romance: Literary Historiography and the Gothic Novel* (Columbus: Ohio State University Press, 1996), p. 2.
6. Ellen Moers, *Literary Women* (New York: Doubleday, 1976), Ch. 5.
7. Helene Meyers, *Femicidal Fears: Narratives of the Female Gothic Experience* (Albany: State University of New York Press, 2001).
8. See Patricia Duncker, 'Re-imagining the Fairy Tales: Angela Carter's Bloody Chambers', *Literature and History*, 10:1 (1984), pp. 3–14.
9. See Laura Mulvey's influential essay 'Visual Pleasure and Narrative Cinema', *Screen,* 16:3 (1975), pp. 6–18.
10. Daphne du Maurier, 'Don't Look Now', *Not After Midnight* (London: Gollancz, 1971). For a detailed reading of this story, see Avril Horner and Sue Zlosnik, *Daphne du Maurier: Writing, Identity and the Gothic Imagination* (Basingstoke: Palgrave Macmillan, 1998).
11. Linda Hutcheon, *A Theory of Parody: The Teachings of Twentieth-Century Art Forms* (London: Methuen, 1995), p. 6.
12. Susan Hill, *The Woman in Black* (London: Vintage, 1983), p. 18.
13. Anne Quéma makes this point in 'Family and Symbolic Violence in *The Mist in the Mirror*', *Gothic Studies*, 8:2 (2006), p. 125.
14. See Sandra M. Gilbert and Susan Gubar, *The Madwoman in the Attic: The Woman Writer and the Nineteenth-Century Literary Imagination* (New Haven: Yale University Press, 1979), pp. 336–71 for an influential reading of *Jane Eyre* in these terms.
15. Elaine Showalter, 'Feminist Criticism in the Wilderness', *Critical Inquiry*, 8 (1981), pp. 179–205.
16. The term 'Thatcherism' was first coined by Stuart Hall in 'The Great Moving Right Show', *Marxism Today* (January 1979), pp. 14–20.
17. Matthew Arnold, *Letters of Matthew Arnold,* ed. George W.E. Russell (London: Macmillan, 1896), Vol. 1, p. 34. Cited in Gilbert and Gubar, p. 337.
18. Julia Kristeva, *Powers of Horror: An Essay on Abjection,* trans. Leon S. Roudiez (New York: Columbia University Press, 1982), p. 4.
19. See Judith Butler, *Gender Trouble: Feminism and the Subversion of Identity* (New York: Chapman and Hall, 1990) and Judith Halberstam, *Female Masculinity* (Durham, NC: Duke University Press, 1998).
20. Hilary Mantel, *Beyond Black* (London: Fourth Estate, 2005), p. 379, p. 387.
21. In Edgar Allan Poe's short story 'The Fall of the House of Usher' (1839), the main character is Roderick, also the name of one of Waters's central characters.

22. Terry Castle, *The Apparitional Lesbian: Female Homosexuality and Modern Culture* (New York: Columbia University Press, 1993), p. 30.
23. Ali Smith, *Hotel World* (Harmondsworth: Penguin, 2002), p. 235.
24. For a discussion of intertextuality in the novel in relation to literary reworkings of the Oedipal narrative see Anne Quéma, 'The Political Uncanny of the Family: Patricia Duncker's *The Deadly Space Between* and The Civil Partnership Act', *Gothic Kinship*, ed. Agnes Andeweg and Sue Zlosnik (Manchester University Press, 2013), pp. 132–56.
25. See Alison Rudd, *Postcolonial Gothic Fictions from the Caribbean, Canada, Australia and New Zealand* (Cardiff: University of Wales Press, 2010) and Glennis Byron, ed., *Global Gothic* (Manchester University Press, 2013).
26. Pauline Melville, 'You Left the Door Open', *Shape-shifter* (London: The Women's Press, 1990), pp. 148–75.
27. Pauline Melville, *The Migration of Ghosts* (London: Bloomsbury, 1998), p. 24.
28. Helen Oyeyemi, 'Paperback Q&A: Helen Oyeyemi on *Mr Fox*', *Guardian,* 12 June 2012, www.guardian.co.uk/books/2012/jun/12/helen-oyeyemi-mr-fox, accessed 25 April 2013.

10
Changing the Story: Fairy Tale, Fantasy, Myth

Elizabeth Wanning Harries

Many recent British women writers believe that we need 'new versions – but only *versions* – of the old, deep tales that are twisted into our souls'.[1] Tales from the Bible, Greek mythology, British history, and various fairytale collections lie beneath some of their most imaginative and compelling work. Sometimes they depend primarily on glancing references to fairy tales and myths, like Kate Atkinson in *Behind the Scenes at the Museum* (1995) and *Human Croquet* (1997). Sometimes they recast Greek tragedies and other plays: a few examples include Timberlake Wertenbaker's translations of Sophocles and Euripides as well as her reworking of the Philomela story in *The Love of the Nightingale* (1989), Caryl Churchill's translation of Seneca's *Thyestes* (2001), Liz Lochhead's translation of Molière's *Tartuffe* into Scots (1986). Sometimes they recast Biblical stories, as Michèle Roberts does in *The Wild Girl* (1984), republished as *The Secret Gospel of Mary Magdalene* (2007), and *Impossible Saints* (1998), or like Jeanette Winterson in her first novel *Oranges Are Not the Only Fruit* (1985). Sometimes they rewrite nineteenth-century novels that inspire retelling after retelling. Lochhead returns to Mary Shelley's *Frankenstein* (1818) in her play *Blood and Ice* (1985) and in her volume of poetry *Dreaming Frankenstein* (1984). Emma Tennant reimagines many nineteenth-century British novels (*Jane Eyre, Wuthering Heights, Dr Jekyll and Mr Hyde,* and several novels by Jane Austen), often more than once. All of these returns – whether glancing references, translations, or rewritings – suggest a fascination with the work of earlier women and work that seems to call out for feminist revision. As Dorothy Macmillan says, 'The telling and retelling of stories may well be the central project of contemporary women's writing.'[2]

Marina Warner, both fiction writer and critic, focused on fairy tales and their tellers in *From the Beast to the Blonde* (1994), arguing that 'fairy tale provides motifs in common, a sign language and an image store that can be interpreted and re-interpreted'.[3] In a world that seems to have lost most shared symbolic languages, fairy tales are a useful reference point – well known, but also endlessly fertile and provocative. Women writers have often interrupted or questioned gendered patterns that seem immutable (the obedient heroine, the girl and the threatening beast, the 'happily ever after' ending).

More recently, critics have begun to show how narrative theory can enrich our understanding of retold tales as a deliberate turn to intertextuality. Intertextuality depends on a kind of double reading that keeps two or more related texts constantly in mind, foregrounding narrative engagement with earlier texts. To give one example, Sara Maitland's story 'The Wicked Stepmother's Lament' retells the story of Cinderella from the stepmother's point of view. In order to understand the reasoning behind her self-justifications, you have to remember the story as Charles Perrault and most British versions give it. Think of it as a palimpsest – one text superimposed upon another that is still visible underneath the newer one. Though many rewritings can be seen as critiques of earlier texts, they do not obliterate them, but present a different way of telling the story. As Stephen Benson says, 'A source narrative is retold in order to draw out the submerged voice, a voice which functions not to erase the tale of which it is a part but to cut across, comment on, and recast it – just as ... it is implicitly already traversed by related variants.'[4] Benson wants to show that fairy tales and myths are part of 'a fluid tale pool' (p. 181). Though we tend to see them as static and fixed, they have a long history and often many older variants that modify or question what we know as the standard version. The many challenging, often explicitly feminist versions written by women since 1970 are best understood as part of this long tradition, as well as part of the literary response to the second wave of feminism that also began in the late 1960s and early 1970s.

Twisting fairy tales

The dominant strand in the tangle of retellings is the insistent reworking of fairytale material. In 1971 the American poet Anne Sexton (1928–74) published *Transformations,* a collection of poems based on the Grimms' tales, and the fairytale flood was set in motion. Though many poems based on ancient myths and fairy tales had been written before that, Sexton's collection – followed by another key American text, Olga Broumas's fairytale poems in *Beginning with O* (1977), and then Angela Carter's short story collection *The Bloody Chamber* (1979) – led to many new versions of old tales.

Carter's dazzling tales in *The Bloody Chamber* probably initiated this proliferation in Britain. As she explained, her intention was 'to extract the latent content of the traditional stories and to use it as the beginning of new stories'.[5] This 'latent content' could be the secret, selfish wishes of the granddaughter in 'Little Red Riding Hood', or the complicity of Bluebeard's apparently innocent wife in her own seduction, or Beauty's recognition of her own sexual attraction to the beast. Refusing the easy option of giving more 'agency' to a central female character, Carter looks for darker motivations and more unsettling possibilities. Her choices have been controversial: many critics, focusing on the links between her tales and her book about the Marquis de Sade, *The Sadeian Woman* (1979), published in the same year, found them both disturbing and insufficiently 'feminist'.[6] But Carter, who was deeply versed in fairytale material of all kinds and had translated Perrault's tales, wanted to look beneath the apparently neutral narrative surface of traditional tales, to explore psychological possibilities, to change the story in radical ways. As Susannah Clapp has said, 'Playing with style, making fairy tale and fantasy tell new truths, were at the root of her stories.'[7] Her collection inspired many other writers to explore the tales we all thought we knew.

In the early 1980s, several volumes appeared in Britain that were inspired by fairy tales: Judith Kazantzis's *The Wicked Queen* (1980), Lochhead's *The Grimm Sisters* (1981), Carol Rumens's *Scenes from the Gingerbread House* (1981), Suniti Namjoshi's *Feminist Fables* (1981).[8] Sometimes the old stories seem to offer a framework for exploration of personal experience. As Rumens says in her Introduction:

> This gingerbread house was in a rather urban forest – Forest Hill, south-east London, in fact. Red-brick, Edwardian, end-of-terrace, it belonged to my maternal grandparents and was where, with my own parents, I spent my early childhood ... I have tried to open doors to a few of its rooms, and to explore them with an adult objectivity that is still rooted in earlier feelings.[9]

Rumens's memories – 'The grown-ups had their secrets / I had my rhymes and riddles, / my own room growing inside me' – reverberate within the metaphorical gingerbread house.[10] Penelope Shuttle, too, in a poem from 1983, makes the house a double of her own, and signals its threats:

> Our smart house new-painted chocolate-brown
> makes me think too closely of the Märchen,
> of Hansel and Gretel and the tasty roof;
> of the maiden with no hands;
> and all the dangerous defenceless ones
> in those old and far-off tales[11]

One impulse, then, that runs through the early responses to Sexton and Carter is to recast the tales as signposts in attempts to understand one's own past. Carolyn Steedman, in her *Landscape for a Good Woman: A Story of Two Lives* (1986), uses Hans Christian Andersen's tales, particularly 'The Little Mermaid' and 'The Snow Queen', as part of her biographical/autobiographical project.

Lochhead, in a 1990 interview, suggests another reason for her own turn to myth and history:

> [In *The Grimm Sisters*] I began to tell familiar stories from another angle. I didn't want the women to be the object in the stories, but the subject. And so there's irony there. And since then I've been fascinated by familiar stories and myths and legends.[12]

Her new, allusive method – writing 'from another angle' – has become the dominant way women writers respond to old, familiar stories. They change the subject.[13] They tease new versions out of the gaps in older versions, or sometimes out of the inconsistencies between them. The crucial 'irony' comes from the friction between familiar versions of the tales and writers' new angles on them.

In *The Grimm Sisters,* Lochhead calls her most sharply inventive rewritings 'twists'. In 'Rapunzstiltskin', for example, Rapunzel tolerates her lover as he 'was shimmying in & out / every other day, as though / he owned the place', but then tears herself in two (like Rumpelstiltskin) when he comes up with the 'right' answer to a question she never explicitly asks.[14] We see similar 'twists' in Carter's complex tales, or Namjoshi's compressed fables, or in Kazantzis's title poem in *The Wicked Queen*:

> I call, mirror, mirror
> narrowing my eyes
> like a renowned painter laying in the first stroke.[15]

This 'fairest of them all' uses her mirror not simply to reflect and confirm her beauty, as in many versions of 'Snow White', but to help her create it, 'with all / these beauty aids'. Kazantzis's sardonic voice calls all the earlier versions into question.

Carol Ann Duffy's poetry – particularly her popular collection *The World's Wife* (1999) – develops this revisionary practice further. As her speaker in 'Mrs. Beast' says, 'These myths going round, these legends, fairytales, / I'll put them straight'.[16] 'Putting them straight' in Duffy's work means not only giving a voice to the supposed wives of many legendary figures, from Eurydice and Medusa to 'Queen Kong', but also giving them a voice that is often tough, slangy, sexy, and crude. Mrs Rip Van Winkle, for example, has happily substituted painting and travelling for sex in her husband's hundred-year absence, but then 'I came home with this pastel of Niagara / and he was sitting up in bed rattling Viagra' (p. 53). Or Salome, who 'flung back the sticky red sheets, / and there, like I said – and ain't life a bitch – / was his head on a platter' (p. 57). Duffy's startling quasi-autobiographical poem that opens the collection, 'Little Red-Cap', explores the appeal of the wolf for the 16-year-old girl, particularly the back

> of his lair where a whole wall was crimson, gold, aglow with books.
> Words, words, words were truly alive on the tongue, in the head,
> warm, beating, frantic, winged; music and blood. (p. 4)

She discovers, however, that the wolf sings 'the same old song at the moon' year after year (p. 4), and at the end she resorts to the violence of the Grimms' tale:

> I took an axe to the wolf
> as he slept, one chop, scrotum to throat, and saw
> the glistening, virgin white of my grandmother's bones.
> I filled his old belly with stones. I stitched him up.
> Out of the forest I come with my flowers, singing, all alone. (p. 4)

'Little Red-Cap' is Duffy's declaration of independence as a poet: 'singing, all alone' (p. 4). Her appointment as Poet Laureate in 2009 – the first woman and openly gay poet to be so honoured – endorses this creative independence and reflects her wide readership. Her poem is also, implicitly, a declaration of her immutable connection to her 'grandmother's bones', to her female ancestors and forbears, and to the many 'wives' who people her book. Like many other poets who have preceded and followed her, Duffy draws inspiration from the old tales, even as she changes them. Her palimpsestic poetry depends on our knowledge of those old tales and our recognition of the ways she has changed them. She and her contemporaries deliberately twist them to reveal old, often patriarchal patterns and new paths.

'Putting tales straight'

Many novelists have also returned to the old tales. Winterson always interweaves well-known stories into her fiction. In *Sexing the Cherry* (1989), she meditates on the Grimms' 'Twelve Dancing Princesses', grafting it onto a story set primarily in mid-seventeenth-century London. The sailor and explorer Jordan realizes early that:

> My own life was written invisibly, was squashed between the facts, was flying without me like the Twelve Dancing Princesses who shot from their window every night and returned home with torn dresses and worn-out slippers and remembered nothing.[17]

Jordan's gradual recovery of his life is tied up with his obsessive search for Fortunata, the twelfth of the dancing princesses, who has the gift of supernatural lightness and grace. He first glimpses her climbing down a rope which she has cut and reknotted several times during her descent. Her lightness is a counter-weight to the dark heaviness of Jordan's life along the riverbank of the Thames, where his mother, the gigantic Dog Woman, originally found him 'wrapped up in a rotting sack' (p. 3). Fortunata's brief, surreal contacts with Jordan point up the mysteries of time and space that structure the novel, superimposing a twentieth-century London on the London of Cromwell, John Tradescant the Younger, the execution of Charles I, and the Plague. The Great Fire of 1666 seems to be caused by Jordan's mother setting fire to a twentieth-century factory that is polluting the Thames, though that, like much else in the novel, remains ambiguous. As Jordan says at the end:

> The future and the present and the past exist only in our minds ... And even the most solid of things and the most real, the best-loved and the well-known, are only hand-shadows on the wall. Empty space and points of light. (p. 167)

Winterson transforms the Grimms' tale about the princesses into a set of cautionary tales about marriage and a meditation on art, time, and space, a meditation she continues in her volume of essays *Art Objects* (1995). Fortunata's legendary lightness becomes a metaphor for her own legerdemain as a writer, recasting fairy tales as part – but only part – of her complex narratives.

While A.S. Byatt has worked with old tales throughout her career, in *The Children's Book* (2009) she concentrates on the dangers of storytelling itself.[18] One of her central characters is Olive Wellwood, a successful writer of children's fiction at the end of the nineteenth century. Known as the mother of eight children, hiding her past as a coal-miner's daughter, she writes in part to support her family, but also because she is possessed by writing: 'the real world sprouted stories wherever she looked at it' (p. 90). She writes stories that are on the edge between the magical and the 'unbearable' or 'impermissible' (p. 91). She explores the underground and darkness, in her published work and in the special manuscript books she writes for each child. Her fertile imagination absorbs and often consumes her.

As the novel moves into the twentieth century, however, Olive is unable to continue writing. Family tragedies and World War One suddenly confront her with 'real world' events that she cannot transform into narrative. At the end of the novel, many of the children's generation also find themselves unable to tell stories: 'They all had things they could not speak of and could not free themselves from, stories they survived only by never telling them' (p. 675). The only writing adequate to the experience of World War One may be the bleak poems one character makes out of trench names. Another character is unable to 'describe the unspeakable' (p. 671). But Byatt continues to sketch the historical context and tie up some of her narrative threads. The final scene brings many of the survivors together at one table in 1919: 'Steam rose to meet the fine smoke from the candles, and all their faces seemed softer in their quavering light' (p. 675). Like the dinner in *To the Lighthouse* (1927) by Virginia Woolf (1882–1941), this dinner briefly brings an order out of the chaos of death and loss. Significantly, Olive Wellwood is not there. Byatt implies that her days are over, that her children's generation will eventually be the new storytellers, telling the tales they can bear to tell.

Helen Oyeyemi's *Mr Fox* (2011) is a brilliant combination of many dangerous versions of 'Bluebeard', including the British tale 'Mr Fox', the ballad 'Reynardine', the French seventeenth-century legend of 'Lustucru', Perrault's 1697 version, the Grimms' 'Fitcher's Bird' and 'The Robber Bridegroom', Yoruba legends, and many others. Oyeyemi's St John Fox, a writer whose stories always end with the death of the heroine, is visited or haunted by 'Mary Foxe', one of his readers who wants him to stop being what she calls 'a serial killer'.[19] Their initial testy exchange of letters – titled BE BOLD, BE BOLD, BUT NOT TOO BOLD, a motto from the old British 'Mr Fox' tale – takes them into an intricate game, taunting and avoiding each other. As they play, Bluebeard stories keep proliferating in the interstices between their moves. Dr Lustucru, the legendary seventeenth-century doctor who executed women for talking too much, beheads his wife: 'Dr. Lustucru's wife was not particularly talkative. But he beheaded her anyway, thinking to himself that he could replace her head when he wished for her to speak' (p. 7). The 'Fitcher's Bird' chapter turns Miss Foxe into a florist's assistant who is hoping to meet a true fairytale prince through newspaper advertisements. Her encounter with a 'Fitcher' leads to an all too realistic ending, another beheading that does not result in a transformation. The 'serial killing' goes on. Mr Fox and Mary continue their games. The novel ends, however, with a section called 'Some Foxes' – two tales about young women and their mysterious, edgy relationships with foxes in nearby forests. The third tale is just two sentences: 'I almost forgot to mention another fox I know of – a very wicked fox indeed. But you are tired of hearing about foxes now, so I won't go on' (p. 324). This turn to the reader suggests that such linked stories can never really end, that the possibilities of story are infinite.

Serious play with traditional tales – twisting the tales or putting the story straight – has been a hallmark of the most original work of the last four decades. Oyeyemi's novel shows that the fairytale vein is far from exhausted. The examples in this chapter must stand for the many stories, poems, and plays women have written since 1970 that force us to reread, rethink, and perhaps to retell.

Resurrecting crones

Many recent writers also often reimagine British myths about an ancient, gigantic woman, whether fury, harridan, spinster, *cailleach*, or crone. In her play *The Old Wives' Tale* (1977), Michelene Wandor has her 'old girls' – working-class women in North London – rehearse some of the witches' incantations from *Macbeth* for an Evening Institute performance. Shakespeare's lines give their everyday, postwar banter a deeper resonance, as when Ellie says, 'I'm a witch. I can see into the past. I don't like it much, the past, but I can see into it.'[20] Unlike the *Macbeth* witches, they can only see into the past, not the future. But taking on the role of witches forces them to reread the war years and their own histories.

Ellen Galford explores some of the mysteries of pre-Celtic goddess history in her novel *The Fires of Bride* (1986), set on a mythical Scottish island called Cailleach. Circles of stones, ancient manuscripts, ghostly visitations, and persistent questions about the past all lead to a traditional Hogmanay celebration and the untraditional unveiling of a twentieth-century goddess figure:

> A massive moon-round smiling female face beams out from an aureole of gold and silver and copper sun-bursts. She is a carnival giantess, of painted metal, with vast piratical hooped earrings dangling from someplace within her crown of metallic curls.[21]

Like Wandor's evocation of *Macbeth,* Galford's shifting goddess figures, both ancient and modern, point to a hidden history of powerful women: gigantic, sometimes menacing, but in touch with untold truths.

Lochhead, too, in *The Grimm Sisters,* often evokes crone and goddess figures. Bruegel's *Dulle Griet* or Mad Meg hangs over a speaker's mantelpiece, once a scholarly subject, now another self:

> Oh that kitchen knife, that helmet, that silent shout,
> I know Meg from the inside out....
> Oh I am wild-eyed, unkempt, hellbent, a harridan.
> My sharp tongue will shrivel any man. ('Harridan', p. 16)

In *The Grimm Sisters,* Mad Meg is accompanied by other hags and crones whose power derives from their age and indifference to convention and rules. They lash out, they undermine, they 'let rip' ('The Last Hag', p. 53). They glory in their freedom, their position outside society, and the language that they shape as their own. *(Dulle Griet* also appears in Churchill's 1982 play *Top Girls* as Dull Gret, one of the fantastic set of powerful women from history in the first scene.)

Lochhead's 'La Corbie' in her play *Mary Queen of Scots Got her Head Chopped Off* (1987) continues the line of free-thinking commentators on the world around them. This crow/crone presides over the action of the play, from opening to end, speaking in broad Scots, placing the play firmly in its Scottish setting, and evoking its national past: 'Once upon a time there were twa queens on the wan green island, and the wan green island was split intae twa kingdoms.'[22] She functions as a kind of chorus, but is 'always and quite openly, partial' (p. 7). She comments caustically on Queen Mary's suitors, on Mary's verbal duels with her cousin Queen Elizabeth I, on the complexities of being both queen and woman, and on the malign misogynist influence of John Knox. Traditional songs and chants punctuate the play, sometimes based on old ballads and lullabies and skipping rhymes: the song the Corbie sings after Lord Darnley's murder, for example, based on the old ballad 'The Twa Corbies' or the skipping rhyme 'On a mountain / stands a lady', sung by the children in the last scene, that echoes the rise and fall of queens.

Lochhead stresses the Corbie's deep roots in Scottish traditions and her foreknowledge of the scenes that are unfolding again before her. Only at Mary's execution does she refuse to look, refuse to witness the death. In the scene with the modern-day children that ends the play, she simply echoes their chant while playing with a marigold head on a stalk:

> Mary Queen of Scots got her head chopped off.
> Mary Queen of Scots got her ... head ... chopped ... off!
> – And *CORBIE flicks the golden flower-head off.* (p. 78)

This last gesture leads to the tableau of the children surrounding and threatening MAREE/MARY as the play ends. La Corbie is witness, commentator, and symbolic executioner of the queen she seems to love, if she loves anything.

Another even more outsize female figure is Churchill's Skriker, in her 1994 play of the same name, 'a shapeshifter and death portent, ancient and damaged'.[23] The Skriker's opening words are typical of her punning babble:

> Hears her boast beast a roast beef eater, daughter could spin span spick and spun the lowest form of wheat straw into gold, raw into roar, golden lion and lyonesse under the sea, dungeonesse under the castle for bad mad sad adders and takers away. (p. 243)

The Skriker combines references to fairy tales and British lore ('Rumpelstiltskin' and Arthurian legends of Lyonesse, the land under the sea near Cornwall), nursery rhymes ('This little piggy had roast beef'), the home of two British nuclear power stations ('Dungeonesse' or Dungeness), and advertisements ('spic and span'). She glories in the double meanings of words ('adders' in 'for bad mad sad adders and takers away', for example) and in the strings of rhyming and chiming words she creates. Her linguistic virtuosity is part of her shape-shifting; her words point in many different directions at once.[24] Her words and phrases are both ancient and new; they suggest her roots in the deepest past, as well as her eruption into the present lives of two young women, also damaged and depressed. Under her influence, one young woman begins to speak pound coins and the other toads, as if they were characters in Charles Perrault's tale 'Les Fées'. As the Skriker appears and disappears, in her many shapes from ancient fury to middle-aged man to child, she transforms their twentieth-century lives into something deeper and more mysterious, though still threatened.

Like Lochhead's La Corbie, the Skriker is witness to an unspeakable past. Like Winterson's Dog Woman in *Sexing the Cherry,* she is also harbinger of an equally unspeakable ecological future. The Skriker constantly refers to a world 'dry as dustpans, foul as shitpandemonium. Poison in the food chain saw massacre' (p. 271). The poisoning of the earth is part of what Churchill sees as its malign globalization, as Elin Diamond points out.[25] These gigantic women – grotesque, absurd, antiquated though they seem – give voice not only to a half-remembered past in which they played significant roles, but also to the near-certainty of a blighted future. The powerful image of the *cailleach* in Galford's novel is made out of scrap metal, recreated from the trash that litters our culture. But the Dog Woman and the Skriker do not see much hope as the toxic dust heaps rise higher and higher. The Dog Woman escapes to sea with her son Jordan. The Skriker's last words, however, are a dark eulogy for one of the broken young women: 'So Lily bit off more than she could choose. And she was dustbin' (p. 291). These writers bring their half-forgotten crones to centre stage, or to the forefront in a poem or novel. They suggest new ways to read British legends and the past. Resurrecting these mythical beings, showing their continuing power, is another way of changing the story.

Women telling new tales

The writers included here are all self-conscious about the ways they tell and revise stories, whether stories about fairytale characters or about legendary old women. In her poem 'Storyteller', that opens *The Grimm Sisters,* Lochhead talks about storytelling as an important part of many women's daily work:

> No one could say the stories were useless ...
> To tell the stories was her work.
> It was like spinning
> gathering thin air to the singlest strongest
> thread. (p. 11)

Drawing on the ancient connection between storytelling and spinning, she sets her storyteller in a traditional context. (Her women are also sewing, grating corn, patching, darning, building fires.) Though Lochhead suggests that they create their stories out of 'thin air', many of her own stories come from the 'fluid tale pool' identified by Benson. Like many of her contemporaries, Lochhead often depends on earlier tales and legends to make her meanings.

This process is always complicated, and demands active reading to be understood. In poem after poem, novel after novel, play after play, traditional tales and their variants form a substratum that informs each text, sometimes remaining deep below the surface as barely legible traces, sometimes rising to the surface as a signal of their continuing presence. Only in this context could Jeanne Marie Beaumont and Claudia Carlson put together *The Poets' Grimm* (2003), an anthology of twentieth-century poems in English based on the Grimms' tales: most of them by women, most written in the last decades of the century. As they say in their Introduction, 'there is a mutual enrichment when poets become tale (re)tellers: the poets keep the stories current and fresh, and give them back their original vivacity, rigor, and immediacy, while the stories enable the poets to tap into a vast and resonant source of symbol and cultural history'.[26]

But the most exciting retellings go beyond enrichment, raising questions about gender roles and deviations from them, exploring motives and plots to question the outdated cultural assumptions about the patterns of women's lives that lie behind them. As Salman Rushdie said of Carter, 'She opens an old story for us, like an egg, and finds the new story, the now-story we want to hear, within.'[27] Prying open old stories, pressing their weak spots, revealing their hidden secrets and possibilities, the writers I have been able to include here (and many others) have truly changed the story.

Notes

1. A.S. Byatt, *The Children's Book* (New York: Knopf, 2009), p. 514. The speaker here is August Steyning, an avant-garde theatrical producer.
2. Dorothy Porter Macmillan, 'Liz Lochhead and the Ungentle Art of Clyping', *Liz Lochhead's Voices*, ed. Robert Crawford and Anne Varty (Edinburgh University Press, 1993), p. 17.
3. Marina Warner, *From the Beast to the Blonde: On Fairy Tales and their Tellers* (New York: Farrar, Straus and Giroux, 1985), p. 417.
4. Stephen Benson, *Cycles of Influence: Fiction-Folktale-Theory* (Detroit: Wayne State University Press, 2003), p. 210.
5. Quoted in Sarah Gamble, 'Penetrating to the Heart of the Bloody Chamber: Angela Carter and the Fairy Tale', *Contemporary Fiction and the Fairy* Tale, ed. Stephen Benson (Detroit: Wayne State University Press, 2008), p. 22.
6. See Gamble's essay for an intelligent summary of this controversy.
7. Susannah Clapp, 'Diary', *London Review of Books*, 14:5 (12 March 1992), www.lrb.co.uk/v14/n05/susannah-clapp/diary, accessed 30 December 2014.
8. The first editions of both Lochhead's and Rumens's collections feature bright orange covers and crude graphics, a visual way to mark their departure from earlier work.
9. Carol Rumens, *Scenes from the Gingerbread House* (Newcastle upon Tyne: Bloodaxe, 1982), n.p. This introduction has not been reproduced in later collections of her work.
10. Carol Rumens, 'Secrets', *Poems 1968–2004* (Tarset: Bloodaxe, 2004), p. 110.

11. Penelope Shuttle, 'Märchen, or, the Earthborn' (1983), *Selected Poems* (Oxford University Press, 1998), pp. 23–4.
12. Liz Lochhead in *Sleeping with Monsters: Conversations with Scottish and Irish Women Poets*, ed. Gillean Somerville-Arjat and Rebecca Wilson (Edinburgh: Polygon, 1980), pp. 9–10.
13. See Eavan Boland's volume of essays *Object Lessons: The Life of the Woman and the Poet in Our Own Time* (Manchester: Carcanet, 1995). As she says, 'over a relatively short time – certainly no more than a generation or so – women have moved from being the objects of Irish poems to being the authors of them. It is a momentous transit. It is also a disruptive one' (p. 126).
14. Liz Lochhead, *The Grimm Sisters*, in *Dreaming Frankenstein and Collected Poems 1967–1984* (1984; Edinburgh: Polygon, 2003), pp. 89–90.
15. Judith Kazantzis, 'The Wicked Queen', *Selected Poems 1977–1992* (London: Sinclair-Stevenson, 1995), p. 17.
16. Carol Ann Duffy, *The World's Wife: Poems* (New York: Faber and Faber, 2000), p. 72.
17. Jeanette Winterson, *Sexing the Cherry* (New York: Vintage, 1991), p. 2.
18. See my article '"Ancient Forms": Myth and Fairy Tale in A.S. Byatt's Fiction', in Benson (2008), pp. 74–97.
19. Helen Oyeyemi, *Mr Fox* (New York: Penguin Riverhead, 2012), p. 4.
20. Michelene Wandor, *The Old Wives' Tale*, in *Five Plays* (London: Journeyman/Playbooks, 1984), p. 54.
21. Ellen Galford, *The Fires of Bride* (London: The Women's Press, 1986), p. 217.
22. From the revised version of Lochhead's play (London: Nick Hern Books, 2009), p. 6.
23. Caryl Churchill, *Plays: Three* (London: Nick Hern Books, 1998), p. 243.
24. In 'From *Finnegans Wake* to *The Skriker:* Morphing Language in James Joyce and Caryl Churchill', *Papers on Joyce*, 7/8 (2001/2), Derek Attridge sees Churchill as a true follower of Joyce who has created 'a distinctive language' (p. 7).
25. Elin Diamond, 'Caryl Churchill: Feeling Global', *A Companion to Modern British and Irish Drama*, ed. Mary Luckhurst (Blackwell Reference Online), www.blackwellreference.com/subscriber/tocnode.html?id=g9781405122283_chunk_g978140512228343, accessed 9 May 2013.
26. Jeanne Marie Beaumont and Claudia Carlson, eds, 'Introduction', *The Poets' Grimm* (Ashland: Story Line Press, 2003), p. xvi.
27. Salman Rushdie, 'Introduction' to Carter's *Burning Your Boats*: *The Collected Short Stories* (New York: Henry Holt, 1995), p. xiv.

11
Disputing the Past: Historical Fiction

Jeannette King

'All novels called "historical novels" before the publication of *Waverley* [were] misnamed': T.H. Lister's claim, published in the influential *Edinburgh Review* in 1832, concerns not only genre but also implicitly gender.[1] As Ina Ferris has argued, with *Waverley* Walter Scott was seen to restore masculinity to the novel, re-establishing fiction as a male domain and novel reading as a 'manly practice' (p. 80). In the process he also altered the 'generic hierarchy' (p. 1). Before Scott, reviewers regarded the predominantly female genre of fiction 'confined' to the private life, written for a predominantly female readership, as a degraded form compared to the eighteenth-century male canon. That view was perpetuated into the twentieth century, notably by Georg Lukács, whose book *The Historical Novel* (1962) also credited Scott with creating the genre. Scott's characters, 'in their psychology and destiny, always represent social trends and historical forces', unlike novels which are 'historical' only in theme and costume.[2] Suggesting that the 'authenticity' of Scott's work derives not from the local colour of his descriptions but from his ability to make the reader 're-experience the social and human motives which led men to think, feel and act just as they did in historical reality' (p. 42), Lukács emphasizes the novelist's power to contribute to the reader's understanding of history. By addressing serious political, economic, cultural, and sociological concerns, and using historical facts with accuracy, Scott established a new benchmark for realism; he, nevertheless, also showed a readiness, in Ferris's words, to 'interrogate official history' (p. 197), through his focus on the experiences of individuals. Such interrogation became a driving force for women's historical fiction of the 1970s and after, finally refuting the idea of historical fiction as an inherently masculine genre. Lukács's canon, however, is entirely male. While arguing that the historical novel 'in its origins, development, rise and decline follows inevitably upon the great social transformations of modern times' (p. 17), Lukács could not have anticipated the impact of the Women's Movement upon the genre.

Women's historical fiction since 1970 encompasses a wide range and diversity of periods, forms, and political perspectives, which the critical and/or popular success of novels set in the Tudor and Victorian periods tends to obscure. Novels dealing with the pre-Victorian period, and meriting more attention than I have time for here, include Michèle Roberts's literary historical novels *Fair Exchange* (1999) and *The Looking Glass* (2000), inspired by the lives of Mary Wollstonecraft and William Wordsworth in the first case, and Flaubert and Mallarmé in the second. Alison Fell's *The Pillow Boy of the Lady Onogoro* (1994) uniquely extends the historical novel's reach to eleventh-century Japan. The historical fiction of Penelope Fitzgerald (1916–2000) ranges widely, from Renaissance Italy in *Innocence* (1986) to eighteenth-century Germany in *The Blue Flower* (1995), based on the life of the German Romanticist known as Novalis, as well as the twentieth century.

Pat Barker's earliest fiction explores the twentieth century from the perspective of the doubly marginalized working-class woman. Liza, the heroine of *The Century's Daughter* (1986), embodies that perspective in a lifetime spanning the century. This novel shows the effect of social and economic crises on the most vulnerable, bringing into focus lives easily erased from history by poverty and environment. The title of Margaret Forster's *Diary of an Ordinary Woman* (2003) announces its similar purpose in a novel which purports to be that most 'authentic' of documents, a diary. Its editor calls Millicent King's diary a 'social document', with additional researched material providing 'bridging work'.[3] The text's status as historical document is further reinforced by Millicent's recruitment by Mass Observation, whose goal is to record 'ordinary' lives to create a 'picture of our society' (p. 207).

Historical novels which focus on women's dispossession and repression can equally be classified as postcolonial fiction when race augments the marginalizing effects of gender and class. Andrea Levy's *The Long Song* (2010) foregrounds the problematic nature of historical testimony in the forthright narrative of July, a freed female slave. July's story is framed by the narrative of her son, Thomas, who attempts to edit and sanitize his mother's tale. In *Promised Lands* (1995), Jane Rogers interrogates the colonial perspective through an account of Lieutenant William Dawes's time with the first fleet to settle convicts in New South Wales, written by twentieth-century schoolteacher Stephen. Both men are idealists but unable to deal with the social, political, and economic realities which confront them. Stephen finally recognizes the ambivalent nature of the most benign of missionary impulses in 'the colonizing power of love, which ... sees in the most intractable and opposed territory visions of peaceful and productive dominion'.[4] Jeanette Winterson's *The Daylight Gate* (2012), based on the witch trials of the seventeenth century, can be described as historical fiction or Gothic horror, with its stomach-churning accounts of torture and grotesque characters. Helen Dunmore's novels about World War Two include a ghost story, *The Greatcoat* (2012).

Men, politics, and power

The contemporary woman writer whose work most obviously suggests the Lukács model is Hilary Mantel, once described as 'the woman who made historical fiction respectable again, who ... freed it from the ... bodice-ripping romps of Philippa Gregory et al'.[5] Her first historical novel, *A Place of Greater Safety* (1992), demonstrates the shaping of men by their historical circumstances through introducing the reader to three key figures in the French Revolution – George-Jacques Danton, Maximilien Robespierre, and Camille Desmoulins – before they became inextricably associated with the Terror. But while providing a meticulously researched historical context for these characters' actions, the novel is not intended to be an historian's overview of the Revolution. Instead it presents events as seen through the prejudices and feelings of those three figures, only intermittently shifting to an impersonal perspective using the historic present to set the scene. Taking what is known about them, Mantel fills the gaps with inventions, utilizing the novelist's freedom to imagine their thoughts. Thus, she makes it possible for the reader to understand how the idealistic young Robespierre who did not believe in capital punishment, and was influenced by Rousseau, grew to regard such violence as necessary for the achievement of his revolutionary ideals, as well as – more cynically – for self-preservation. Reminding the reader that Robespierre himself said in 1793, 'History is fiction', she indicates the degree of uncertainty in the historical record which gives her own fictions their legitimacy.[6] As A.S. Byatt, herself an important writer of historical fiction, says: 'The idea that "all history is fiction" led to a new interest in fiction as history.'[7]

The first two volumes of Mantel's Thomas Cromwell trilogy, *Wolf Hall* (2009) and *Bring up the Bodies* (2012), were awarded the Man Booker prize, unprecedented for two consecutive novels. Here too, Mantel is less interested in the historian's chronology than in the way memory works: events happen in the present tense and are filtered through the main character's sensibility. These strategies create an uncertain sense of events unfolding as they occur, of a future unknown to the protagonists, and they draw attention to the turning points at which things could have gone differently. Mantel again follows the trajectory of a man from a humble background as a blacksmith's son to the second most powerful man in Henry VIII's court, from early idealism to the man for whom violence was an essential tool of statecraft. At the same time, Cromwell's attention to other people's words and motives – which gives him his power – provides insight into other figures. His perspective on Anne Boleyn, for instance, suggests her downfall is due not so much to her alleged adultery and witchcraft as to her failure to understand a world where every word uttered – however thoughtlessly, frivolously, or ironically – may be used to destroy her. These novels create a powerful sense of a world dominated by spies, professional or otherwise, and by the arbitrary exercise of power. Cromwell, himself the most brilliant of the spies, is assisted by his inscrutability, so that only the reader understands the calculation underlying his every act and word. Mantel's use of the present tense also underlines the connections between historical and modern times: the fear generated cannot be simply relegated to history, and the fear generated by much more recent tyrannies will reappear as a theme in the work of Helen Dunmore.

Such times of dramatic change and conflict as the Tudor period have an obvious interest for historical novelists, including Gregory, whose novels about 'the Boleyn girls' are the antithesis of Mantel's. Conforming to the genre of romantic historical fiction, they are categorized as 'women's fiction', focusing on the lives of the women unfortunately caught up in Tudor history, particularly their domestic and sexual lives. However important Henry's women are in Mantel's Cromwell novels, they are only seen from the outside, and Anne's successor, Jane Seymour, remains a mystery even to Cromwell. It is a mistake, though, to dismiss Gregory's novels as mere 'bodice-rippers'. These novels represent the helplessness of women as pawns in history, using the only power available to them – their beauty and wit. They illustrate Lisa Fletcher's argument that historical romance is 'a complex and ongoing discussion about gender and sexual norms', about the relationship between formations of romance and heterosexuality.[8] Nevertheless, women like Anne Boleyn are credited with an interest in the political and historical processes to which they are subject, even if failing to read them as successfully as Cromwell. While categorizing Gregory's novels as 'erotic historical', on account of their explicit sexuality, Diana Wallace is equally insistent on their social and political resonances. She regards Gregory's eighteenth-century Wideacre trilogy, for instance, as 'Marxist-feminist', connecting a Marxist analysis of 'the growth of capitalism to a feminist analysis of the relationship between women, property and ownership'.[9]

Historical fiction and feminism

Where Mantel and Gregory can be said to supplement the historical record, others can be said to challenge it. Sarah Waters, one of the most successful practitioners of the genre, argues that women have not only dominated historical fiction since the 1920s, but have used it to 'map out an alternative, female historical landscape', which often 'constitutes a radical rewriting of traditional, male-centred historical narrative'.[10] It is this body of historical fiction which has arguably been of most significance since the 1970s and is part of the wider project of second-wave feminism. It reinserts women into history not just as victims but as agents, giving them the voices they have been denied in the official records. For instance, when citing her sources for *The Wild Girl* (1984, republished as *The Secret Gospel of Mary Magdalene*), a reconstruction of the Gnostic gospel according to Mary Magdalene, Roberts acknowledges her debts to the feminist academic research of the 1970s and 1980s. Sometimes called 'hysterical history', or 'hystory/hystery', such fiction questions the claims to objectivity of more traditional accounts. By making female experience central to its narratives, it exposes gaps in the 'master narratives'. If, according to Fredric Jameson, using history responsibly means bringing to the surface of the text the 'repressed and buried reality' of class struggle, it surely also means bringing to the surface the reality of women's struggle for a voice, particularly the struggle of those oppressed by gender and/or class or race.[11]

If women's lives have been so neglected, it is usually because they are private and domestic, and therefore considered of little interest. What is often called bio-fiction can redress the balance. Byatt explains that the original impulse behind her novella *The Conjugial Angel,* published in *Angels and Insects* (1992), was 'revisionist and feminist. It would tell the untold story of Emily [Tennyson], as compared to the often-told story of Arthur [Hallam, her fiancé] and Alfred [her brother] in which Emily is a minor actress' (2000, p. 104). Emily's overwhelming private grief after Arthur's death is overshadowed by the very public display of grief that is 'In Memoriam', where Tennyson usurps her role as grieving 'widow'. Using Tennyson's own words, Byatt suggests the damaging, even humiliating effect the poem had on his sister while making his name with the Victorian public. The idea for the novella grew out of a footnote in Hallam's letters, which is symptomatic of revisionary novels. As Louisa Hadley argues, in her analysis of Janice Galloway's novel *Clara* (2002), such novels challenge the 'Great Man' approach of male-centred biography.[12] *Clara* juxtaposes the diaries of the pianist and composer Clara Schumann, largely dictated by her father and husband Robert, with Clara's imagined thoughts and impressions. Mainly concerned with the 'facts' of her musical career, the diaries construct an identity for her as a musician in which her gender is irrelevant. Clara's narrative explores the emotional dimensions of her experience, ironically conveying a sense of authenticity lacking from the diaries, and highlighting the problematic nature of all biography. Other novels construct lives for those of whom very little is known, such as Patricia Duncker's *James Miranda Barry* (1999). Duncker provides an imaginative reconstruction of the life of the eponymous 'hero', who became a surgeon general in the British army early in the nineteenth century, but was discovered after his death to be female.

Victoriana

The popularity of the Victorian period for women novelists, particularly since 1990, is arguably attributable to the scope it offers for exploring gender issues.[13] Once the concept of separate spheres for men and women became established, the private life designated as women's 'proper sphere' – above all their sexuality – was largely hidden from public view, so that the period holds obvious appeal for writers concerned to bring hidden experiences to light. Moreover, the codification of sexual difference during this time and the simultaneous subversion of patriarchal gender discourse by some Victorian women draw attention to the historicized nature of gender itself, making the Victorian period one of significant interest for feminists.

While the consolidation of patriarchal gender discourse is everywhere evident in the restrictions on women's lives represented in women's historical fiction, subversion takes different forms, one of the most common being through spiritualism. Writers as diverse as Byatt, Roberts, Waters, and Victoria Glendinning use séances to demonstrate the means by which some Victorian women could challenge the conventions. Each novelist exploits the ambivalent role of the female medium, embodying both traditional female passivity as the conductor of the spirit presence, and an atypical degree of agency in controlling the séance and acquiring a position of power and even profit in the process. Roberts's *In the Red Kitchen* (1990, republished as *Delusion* in 2008) uses historical material about the life of the Victorian medium Florence Cook as the basis for her fictional character, Flora Milk. Here spiritualism acts as both a plot function, linking ancient Egypt to Victorian England and to the modern day, and embodies traditions of thought and feeling which women may exploit or be exploited by. Thus, a novel which demonstrates how successfully women have been written out of history also suggests forms of resistance and resurrection. For the female participants, the séance provides an opportunity for the release of repressed desires and transgressive behaviour. Grief for a lost child (in *In the Red Kitchen* and Glendinning's *Electricity*, 1995), or parent (Waters's *Affinity*, 1999), or husband (*The Conjugial Angel*) can be both freely expressed and eased by reconnection with a loved one. The spirits themselves enjoy a subversive sexual licence. The spirit of Emily Tennyson's dead sailor husband uses the private language of their sexual life, allowing the medium to use language otherwise totally unacceptable in a middle-class lady. Most unsettling of all is Waters's Peter Quick, in reality Ruth the housemaid and the medium's lover. His status is complicated by the element of cross-dressing, so that his illicit touching of the female participants in the circle marks a further degree of homoerotic subversion. As in *James Miranda Barry*, cross-dressing is the ultimate form of gender subversion, foregrounding the extent to which gender is a social construction, or 'performative', to use Judith Butler's terminology and, moreover, allowing women to usurp man's privileged place.[14]

Where there is a romance plot, cross-dressing further challenges the heterosexual norm through the real or suggested erotic relationship between women. This form of subversion is fully explored in Waters's early novels, which made the genre of lesbian historical fiction such a popular and critical success. Waters suggests that lesbians have a special affinity with historical fiction, enabling them to 'queer' official versions of history by incorporating those figures previously excluded, and suggesting same-sex relationships where they had not previously been recognized (p. 176). Her novels explore what lesbian lives may have been like, in the absence of historical evidence. Nancy, the central protagonist of *Tipping the Velvet* (1998), takes on the roles of male impersonator in the music hall, rent boy, and plaything of a rich but closeted lesbian, before finding happiness with Florence. In *Affinity,* Margaret's unnamed desires make her a tragic victim, betrayed by the medium Selina Dawes, the very woman who brings Margaret's desires to the surface.

Jameson argues that neo-Victorian fiction participates in postmodernism's 'nostalgia mode', creating the past through the recreation of its surfaces, without any genuine interest in its substance.[15] For him it is mere pastiche, imitation eclipsing the original. But in a lively rebuttal, Dana Shiller claims that it reinvents the Victorians, rather than effacing them, through 'its careful reconstruction of the Victorian past' (p. 545). Likewise Byatt's intention is to rescue 'the complicated Victorian thinkers from modern diminishing parodies' and from 'disparaging mockery' (p. 79). As Hadley emphasizes, such fiction 'requires an understanding of the historical conditions to which these forms are responding', going far beyond surface verisimilitude (p. 160). Byatt's use of spiritualism, for instance, demonstrates the tension between religious faith, including belief in the afterlife, and the spirit of scientific enquiry typical of the period, embodied in the Society for Psychic Research. Byatt gives as much weight to Swedenborgianism as to Emily Tennyson's personal drama. In *Electricity,* Glendinning traces connections between the new 'male' science of electricity and the predominantly female world of the séance, through their shared discourse of attraction, repulsion, and polarity. Byatt's *Morpho Eugenia* (1992) similarly suggests the complex intellectual background to nineteenth-century natural history and exploration in a narrative about male and female aspiration, sexual relationships, and class. As Byatt points out, as a love story it is as much about pheromones as about Romantic love (*On Histories and Stories*, p. 81). All these novels engage fully with the discourses of nineteenth-century scientific and cultural life, conveying to the reader something of the period's complex mindset, rather than simply its changing fashions.

Women and war

Nor are women novelists deterred from engaging with the traditionally masculine world of war that so profoundly affected ordinary lives throughout the twentieth century. The outspoken account by Millicent, in Forster's *Diary of an Ordinary Woman,* of the growth of her sexual awareness is punctuated by references to the two World Wars; these indicate both the powerlessness of women in her position and the gradual changes for women, partly due to those wars. Where the emphasis is on men at war, one might expect feminist 'revisioning' to be less prominent. But while Barker's *Regeneration* trilogy (1991–95) is based on the well-documented lives of the poets of the First World War and the doctors who treated them, the interrogation of ideas about gender and sexuality is evident throughout. In a context where the concept of masculinity was asserted and challenged in equal measure, where the need for strong male bonds also generated a fear of homosexuality, the 'hysteria' experienced by the young officers at Craiglockhart hospital is seen as a female symptom, an outbreak of emotion which threatens to undermine that masculinity. Returning to the period in *Life Class* (2007), Barker interweaves the world of ambulance drivers at the front, and the grim reality of battlefield injuries they face, with an enquiry into the role of art in wartime. The different narrative voices of her art students, sometimes in letters from the Front, suggest the tension between the two worlds, and bring into play the frustrations of young women of the time without making them appear trivial against the anguish of the men in battle. The sequel, *Toby's Room* (2012), depicts the work that real-life art lecturer Henry Tonks undertook as a surgeon. Tonks deploys a different kind of art reconstructing the faces of disfigured soldiers, underlining the responsibility art has towards war.

In *The Paying Guests* (2014), Waters explores the impact of the First World War on social relations with unexpected intimacies becoming possible. Dunmore writes about the First World War in *Zennor in Darkness* (1993), in which D.H. Lawrence and his German wife Frieda become the victims of rumour and suspicion while living in Cornwall in 1917 because of their campaigning for peace, and Frieda's nationality. Dunmore will, however, probably be best remembered for novels set in Russia in World War Two and after. *The Siege* (2001) focuses on the first and worst winter of the Siege of Leningrad (1941–44) when Hitler's armies attempted to starve the Russian people into submission. It presents this historic event through the consciousness of 23-year-old Anna Levin, as she struggles to keep herself and her loved ones alive. A novel which conveys hunger and cold in harrowing detail, it nevertheless also captures the tenderness and determination which enabled at least some of the city's inhabitants both to survive and to retain their humanity. *The Betrayal* (2010) returns to Anna and her family in 1952, using them to convey the consequences of Stalin's paranoid totalitarianism. Recovering from the trauma of war, they experience a new despair: the people's hope for a better future, which enabled them to survive the siege, is betrayed.

In *The Night Watch* (2006), Waters brings to the Second World War her desire to uncover lesbian lives, telling her story backwards to underline the need to understand the past in order to explain the present. Roberts contributes to these perspectives on World War Two by viewing the experience of Occupation through the eyes of young French women and their families in Booker-shortlisted *Daughters of the House* (1993) and *Ignorance* (2012).

Characteristically, Roberts appeals to all the senses to evoke the experience of those difficult times, while highlighting the complicity of French nationals with Nazi anti-semitism and its legacy in contemporary France.

Realism and postmodernism

The formal aspects of historical fiction have been the subject of considerable debate. Lynn Pykett has applauded the psychological and intellectual realism of those historical novels which recreate the forms of nineteenth-century fiction. Pykett singles out for praise Barker's early novels, where matrilineal histories dramatize the struggles of working-class women for personal, political, and social emancipation, comparing them to nineteenth-century 'condition-of-England' novels, studies of the individual in society.[16] Extensive research makes possible the verisimilitude most often associated with the genre, while characters are presented by an omniscient narrator, or by a first-person narrator whose voice adds authenticity.

Other critics, however, are suspicious of such attempts to recreate the Victorian novel. Responding to Pykett, Linda Anderson argues that reclaiming history for women through neo-Victorian forms simply results in reproducing the 'history' with which that fiction has made us familiar, without challenging the 'conceptual limits' which excluded women from history in the first place. She concludes that we cannot ignore 'how that existence is textually mediated', and the imperatives of genre itself.[17] Only through the textualization of the past can women writers evade the impasse she describes. Byatt calls her attempts to 'hear the Victorian dead' ventriloquism (p. 46), evident in the 'Victorian' poetry of the fictional poets Christabel LaMotte and Randolph Ash in *Possession: A Romance* (1990). But her 'ventriloquism' is deployed through the use of parallel plots which draw attention to the text's construction, to different ways of narrating the past, and the gaps in official versions of the past. The work of her Victorian poets constitutes the research of modern-day academics, a form of detective work which leads to the discovery of significant manuscripts, and provides a plot structure common to women's historical fictions in their search for hidden truths. The use of parallel plots also enables historical and contemporary beliefs to engage with each other. Even love, so often considered a universal, is historicized by the juxtaposition of the intensity of the Victorian lovers against the view of the scholars who dismiss such feelings as belonging to outmoded ways of thinking and living.

Postmodern plot strategies are used in some of the most popular recent historical fiction. In Kate Mosse's *Labyrinth* (2005), the contemporary protagonist, prompted by archaeological discoveries in France, engages in a kind of detective work to find out more about the persecuted Cathars of Carcassone, as well as the criminal organization hunting for sacred – and valuable – Cathar texts. Alice must abandon her usual rational modes of thought to solve the mystery of the labyrinth, learning that truth is 'beyond the limits of her conscious thought'.[18] Memories of her previous incarnation as Cathar predecessor Alais introduce the reader to the parallel thirteenth-century plot dealing with the crusade against the Cathar 'heretics'. It is Alice's responsibility to live to tell this hidden story. In Maureen Duffy's *Alchemy* (2004), Jade is a professional detective and the route to the past is via a seventeenth-century manuscript. Its author, Amynta, is a cross-dressing young woman, inheritor of her father's skills as a herbalist, and so accused of the devil's work. In her, the most subversive tendencies are easily conflated – lesbianism, witchcraft, and popery. Past and present protagonists are connected by their lesbianism and their position as outsiders. When Jade discovers the memoir might not be true, that Amynta may not have existed, she feels a sense of emptiness since she has grown to identify with her. The impression of historical veracity is similarly questioned in Forster's *Diary of an Ordinary Woman* by the Author's Note, which reveals that the 'editor' neither met Millicent nor read her diaries.

Such plot structures draw attention to the engagement of women's historical fiction with the historical process itself, building on postmodern trends in historiography. History can only ever be contested versions of the past; it is not an objective truth, but fragmented, subjective, and plural, made apparently coherent by the use of narrative techniques borrowed from fiction itself. Postmodernists have a particular interest in decentring recorded history, which intersects with the concerns of feminist novelists. Unlike Lukács's model, predicated on realism, their characters are not the 'types' of the period but its opposite – the marginalized and peripheral figures which the historical record has failed to include.

Linda Hutcheon has coined the term 'historiographic metafiction' for novels which are 'both intensely self-reflective and yet paradoxically also lay claim to historical events and personages'.[19] Novels of this kind often adopt a playful approach to history, combining historical figures and events with characters and tales which escape the confines of realism. In *The Passion* (1987), the always experimental Winterson tells a fantastical tale about a cook in Napoleon's army and a gondolier's daughter. The passion of the title encompasses not only the passion of love and suffering embodied in Christ, and the passion of human sexuality, but Napoleon's apparent passion for chicken, undercutting his reputation as a great man. Winterson's *Sexing the Cherry* (1989) goes further back in time to tell a story of Rabelaisian characters caught up in the English Civil War. Rose Tremain's *Restoration* (1989) was inspired by Pepys's diaries, their earthy materiality and bawdiness. But the hedonism of her anti-hero narrator, Merivel, is counterpointed by the spirit of scientific and philosophical enquiry embodied in his Puritan friend, Pearce. Yet these novels are as much about the present as about the past. Tremain pointed out in an interview that she saw Charles II's reign as an analogy for Thatcher's Britain, embodying 'all that was shallow, showy, excessive and distracting'.[20] Winterson similarly added a note to *The Passion* in the 1990s making it explicit that the novel is about Thatcherism. Angela Carter's *Nights at the Circus* (1984) characteristically blends fantasy and reality. The story of Fevvers, the winged woman, and her increasingly fantastic adventures is situated not only in the Rabelaisian world of music hall and circus, but at a distinct historical moment when changes in women's lives seemed possible – the fin-de-siècle. Again, however, the parallel with the 1980s is implicit: Fevvers is a 'material girl'. Giving Fevvers the power to narrate her own story, moreover, allows her sense of self to triumph over the myths by which patriarchy has sought to clip women's wings. The novel illustrates what can be gained by rejecting realist parameters for imagined alternatives, as Anderson suggests.

To conclude, it will be evident that attempts to categorize women's historical fiction are fraught. But while many historical novels belong equally to other genres discussed elsewhere in this volume, all are characterized by a historical perspective which foregrounds the contingent nature of institutions and ideologies. In allowing for other versions of the past, they constitute – in Pykett's words – an attempt to recover 'a usable past', what J.H. Plumb calls 'the past as a weapon in the battle for the future' (p. 76). These alternative histories enable the reader to conceive of alternative futures.

Notes

1. Quoted in Ina Ferris, *The Achievement of Literary Authority: Gender, History and the Waverley Novels* (Ithaca: Cornell University Press, 1991), p. 7.
2. Georg Lukács, *The Historical Novel*, trans. Hannah and Stanley Mitchell (Lincoln: University of Nebraska, 1983), p. 34.
3. Margaret Forster, *Diary of an Ordinary Woman 1914–1995* (London: Vintage, 2004), p. 1, p. 7.
4. Jane Rogers, *Promised Lands* (London: Abacus, 2000), p. 160.
5. Stuart Jeffries, 'The History Woman', G2, *Guardian*, 18 October 2012, p. 6.
6. Hilary Mantel, *A Place of Greater Safety* (London: Viking, 1992), p. 29.
7. A.S. Byatt, *On Histories and Stories: Selected Essays* (London: Chatto & Windus, 2000), p. 38.
8. Lisa Fletcher, *Historical Romance Fiction: Heterosexuality and Performativity* (Aldershot: Ashgate, 2008), p. 1.
9. Diana Wallace, *The Woman's Historical Novel: British Women Writers, 1900–2000* (Basingstoke: Palgrave Macmillan, 2005), p. 190, p. 187.
10. Sarah Waters, 'Wolfskins and Togas: Maude Meagher's *The Green Scamander* and the Lesbian Historical Novel', *Women: A Cultural Review*, 7 (1996), p. 176.
11. Fredric Jameson, *The Political Unconscious: Narrative as Socially Symbolic Act* (Ithaca: Cornell University Press, 1981), p. 20.
12. Louisa Hadley, *Neo-Victorian Fiction and Historical Narrative: The Victorians and Us* (Basingstoke: Palgrave Macmillan, 2010), p. 45.
13. A large body of criticism has developed around neo-Victorian fiction. In addition to Hadley (note 12), see, for example, Alice Jenkins and Juliet John, eds, *Rereading Victorian Fiction* (Basingstoke: Palgrave Macmillan, 1999); Jeannette King,

The Victorian Woman Question in Contemporary Feminist Fiction (Basingstoke: Palgrave Macmillan, 2005); Cora Kaplan, *Victoriana: Histories, Fiction, Criticism* (Edinburgh University Press, 2007); Ann Heilmann and Mark Llewellyn, *Neo-Victorianism: The Victorians in the Twenty-First Century* (Basingstoke: Palgrave Macmillan, 2010). See also the e-journal, *Neo-Victorian Studies* (www.neovictorianstudies.com) and the *Neo-Victorian Series* (Amsterdam and New York: Rodopi), co-edited by Marie-Luise Kohlke and Christian Gutleben.

14. Judith Butler, *Gender Trouble: Feminism and the Subversion of Identity* (New York: Routledge, 1990), p. 140.
15. Quoted in Dana Shiller, 'The Redemptive Past in the Neo-Victorian Novel', *Studies in the Novel,* 29 (1997), p. 539.
16. Lynn Pykett, 'The Century's Daughters: Recent Women's Fiction and History', *Critical Quarterly*, 29 (1987), pp. 71–7.
17. Linda Anderson, *Plotting Change: Contemporary Women's Fiction* (London: Edward Arnold, 1990), p. 134.
18. Kate Mosse, *Labyrinth* (London: Orion, 2005), p. 611.
19. Linda Hutcheon, *A Poetics of Postmodernism: History, Theory, Fiction* (New York: Routledge, 1988), p. 5.
20. Rose Tremain, 'Introduction', *Restoration* (London: Vintage, 2000), p. 1.

12
Life Lines: Auto/biography and Memoir

Linda Anderson

The promise that autobiographical writing seems to hold – to lead us beyond the fictional, providing ways of intervening in political debate with personal stories of discovery and transformation – made it a particularly important form in the 1970s and 1980s. Women's autobiographical writing – encouraged as praxis as much as studied as texts – became allied with the idea of 'finding a voice', of putting an identity into words or telling a life story which challenged the ready-made stereotypes of women within a patriarchal order. The phenomenon of 'consciousness-raising', with which feminism is associated in this period, depended on an idea of telling one's unique story and being able to validate the personal as an 'authentic truth'. However, key to this use of personal stories was also the idea that the personal would provide insight into politically charged questions of gender identity, and that any story would achieve 'interactive significance' or collective resonance within the group.[1]

The personal and the political

Many feminist autobiographies from this time represent a moment of political awakening when the personal story made visible how socially instituted versions of sexual difference influenced and constrained lives. Sheila Rowbotham, mixing her account of the Women's Liberation Movement with autobiographical reflection, commented on how the recognition of her own 'colonization' came 'with the force of an electric shock':

> It jolted me into perceiving all my glimpses of myself in a different light ... I experienced a kind of joy like that which Bunyan describes when Christian's burden rolls off. I felt incomparably light-spirited. My eyes opened a bit wider.[2]

Alison Light has commented on the similarity between stories of feminist awakening and transformation and other conversion narratives. She refers to the narratives of nineteenth-century socialists for whom 'the discovery of politics was the revelation on the road to Damascus'.[3] However, as Rowbotham's own reference to Bunyan indicates, we might extend Light's analogy to a whole history of religious confession and conversion where the self, as in feminist narratives, is re-formed in terms of later insight and knowledge and the past rejected because of its incoherence and error.[4]

This intertextuality suggests the ways in which any form of life-writing is inevitably in dialogue with established paradigms and pre-existing texts. Contrary to one important historical strand of feminist thinking, therefore, writers may not be free simply to invent a self. A similar contradiction lurks in the notion that female self-discovery could converge on a shared notion of womanhood without compromising the uniqueness of individual stories and without repeating overarching stereotypes. Rita Felski notes in 1989 that feminist confession tended towards 'anxiety and self-castigation' as the corollary or accompaniment to self-affirmation, as if there was an ideal of autonomy within feminism that it was impossible to emulate.[5] Writing about Rousseau, Paul de Man argues that confession as a narrative mode actually required shame to fuel it and that there was a necessary and unavoidable connection between hiding and exhibiting the self.[6] Whilst confession seems in many ways a radical mode for the female subject, breaking taboos and silence, the intimate alliance of self-assertion and shame could rhetorically imitate the same anxiety of authorship that has traditionally attended female authors. In her autobiography, *Taking it Like a Woman* (1984), Anne Oakley is defensive about why she is writing her autobiography:

> This book is about my life, but it is also about others – for it would be arrogant to suppose I'm unique; I'm not. In those passages in the book where I write about myself I have no drive salaciously to exhibit a purely private history ... I have persevered in this task precisely because I know I am living and writing about something which is recognizable to others.[7]

Here feminism becomes a justification for autobiography but this is a feminism that is strikingly adapted to the need to conceal female self-assertion under a more socially acceptable cloak of modesty and altruism.

The urgent political necessity felt by women to offer self-narration as an alternative to denial and invisibility was important in generating and validating a diverse range of new writing in the 1970s and 1980s. Nevertheless, the fact that it could lead to a contradictory outcome, with the subject not so much recognized as unique as assimilated into a collective sense of identity, became the subject of critical anxiety. The differences elided under an idea or ideal of representativity returned, like a Freudian repressed, albeit in female form. Lauretta Ngcobo's *Let It Be Told* (1987), a collection of short autobiographical essays and reflections by 'Blackwomen' living in the UK, perfectly enshrines the dilemma. The collection itself bears witness to the moment when the communal identity of 'woman' was disputed and fractured and many women, defining themselves through class, ethnicity, race, and sexuality, seceded from the universalism implied by an overarching notion of gender. Each contribution to this collection bears witness to a unique journey into writing and different engagements with ethnicity and race – ranging from powerful recognitions of the impact of racism by Maud Sulter (1960–2008) to Grace Nichols's sense of herself as a writer as 'multi-cultural and very Caribbean'.[8] However, the introduction attempts to subordinate the multivocal nature of the collection's form and extol what is 'common':

> Few of our writings are strictly personal in the subjective sense of encompassing individual exploits. Rather, they reflect a collective subject, the common experience of Blackwomen reaching, reflecting and capturing different shades and depths and heights of moods. (p. 4)

Criticism of autobiography in the 1980s and 1990s became an important site for feminist debates around the poststructuralist notion of 'difference' and ways of thinking about the subject as mediated or constituted by texts rather than pre-existing them. Yet, it again witnessed the phenomenon of an unbidden return of ideas and structures. Even when most radically opposed to 'essentialized identities' – those thought of as innate or prior and which seemed inevitably to repeat gestures of inclusion and exclusion – feminist critics worried about the extent to which they had become complicit in denying female agency and authorship, as if escaping from one way of thinking simply locked them in another, predominantly masculine, model of thought. Nicole Ward Jouve, assuming the right to use 'I', and to speak as a critic simply 'bent on self-knowledge', lamented the critical landscape of the 1980s:

> We have lost ourselves in the endlessly diffracted light of Deconstruction. I say 'we' meaning all of us, but especially women. For we have been asked to go along with Deconstruction whilst we had not even got to the Construction stage. You must have a self before you can afford to deconstruct it.[9]

To some extent the predicament was a function of critical discourse itself. Autobiographical texts have always presented themselves as more flexible, various, and experimental than feminist theory, at once reflecting, but always exceeding, critical positions. The fact that new terms for autobiography emerged at this time – 'life-writing' but also 'auto/biography' – was also a way of registering the need to attend to the more informal ways in which autobiographical writing behaves in relation to genre, challenging us to extend our critical purview. In particular, these new terms drew attention to the importance of the 'bios' element, the historically inflected engagement with the material world, which life-writing seems to provide. Liz Stanley, approaching autobiography as a sociologist rather than a literary critic, went so far as to suggest in her book, *The Auto/biographical I* (1992) – carefully named to diminish a sense of hierarchy amongst different kinds of life-writing – that there was a thin line between the historian and the autobiographer: 'The "writing of a life" is the writing of a history, an account of the past by a particular kind of historian known as an auto/biographer.'[10] She comments later: '[I]n autobiography graph is predicated upon bio, writing upon a life, and not the other way round' (p. 110).

The personal and the historical

Looking back across the period since the 1970s, one of the strongly marked features of many autobiographical texts by British women would seem to be their consciousness of historical and generational change. *Truth, Dare or Promise* (1985), edited by Liz Heron, shares with *Let It Be Told* the same format of gathering together multiple different voices. The Introduction, however, starts with a historical premise: 'The end of the Second World War marked the start of an era, of a new period whose initial character shaped the way we live now.'[11] By making the parameters of the book historical rather than ideological (all the authors were born in Britain between 1943 and 1951), Heron is also able to celebrate diversity: all her writers may call themselves feminists but what interests her are the varied, individual narratives, 'the values and material circumstances of our parents, the place and region where we grew up, our class and ethnic identity' (p. 2). The stories can provide, not just another version of history, as Stanley suggests, but the subjective experience of change, its complexities and 'untidy contradictions' (p. 4) which 'disturb' any general account of social history with their 'singularity and uneven reflections' (p. 1).

Carolyn Steedman's chapter grew into a celebrated book, *Landscape for a Good Woman* (1986), which offered a profound reflection on the ways in which the peculiarities of autobiography, its details as well as the particular tones and longings contained in memory, can be used to question current theoretical and historical assumptions. For Steedman, as it turns out, it is not so much the austerity of her childhood which was formative as her mother's aspirations and disappointments. This is given imagistic form in the inaugural dream of her mother in a 'New Look' dress:

> She wore the New Look, a coat of beige gaberdine which fell in two swaying, graceful pleats from her waist at the back (the swaying must have come from very high heels, but I didn't notice her shoes), a hat tipped forward from hair swept up at the back ... Encouraging me to follow in this way perhaps, but moving too fast for me to believe that this was

> what she wanted, she entered a revolving door of dark, polished wood, mahogany and glass, and started to go round and round, looking out at me as she turned. I wish I knew what she was doing, and what she wanted me to do.[12]

This dream yields insight into how a child, though puzzled by what is happening around her, and without the analytic tools to make sense of it, yet becomes 'a repository for other people's history' (Heron, p. 105). By learning the significance of words like 'gaberdine' and 'mahogany', Steedman gains insight into her mother's desires. These have been shaped by generations of working-class dispossession and given focus, postwar, by the promise of 'fairness' and material possessions – clothes and furniture – which signify the class to which she wanted to belong. As a child Steedman absorbs the lesson that she is 'lucky', given the state's investment in her welfare and education, and an expensive burden, a barrier to her mother's fulfilment. Having, in her mother's view, been given so much materially, Steedman and her sister are treated by their mother as if they need nothing else, and their 'landscape of feeling' (p. 128) remains bleak and empty: 'The house was full of her terrible tiredness, her terrible resentment; and I knew it was all my fault' (p. 39). One of Steedman's achievements is thus to understand how far the subject, and its structures of feeling, are imbricated in the narratives of others.

As well as this, however, Steedman provides a way of reading remembered details and objects within autobiography as not just the indicators of social history but as offering disjunctive moments that can open up the silences and assumptions of dominant discourses. Drawing on the experiences of the bourgeois household, which are presented as 'normal' or 'neutral', these discourses cannot accommodate differences of class. One memory Steedman draws on is of her father picking bluebells and then being caught and humiliated by the forest keeper. This memory does not support a theory of patriarchy that ignores class and assumes the father's social power. The memory provides a way of moving the child she was into historical time.

Bad Blood (2001), by Lorna Sage (1943–2001), recounts her growing up in roughly the same postwar period, but also explores the ways in which historical change is uneven, inflected through the specifics of region and place, and not necessarily experienced by different generations in the same way. Sage recalls that her childhood village, Hanmer, on the Welsh border and predominantly a farming community, had not been exposed to the changes produced by the decimations of World War Two, though increasingly 'islanded' and depressed by economic decline in agriculture. The expectation in Sage's childhood that children would grow up to work on the land makes education almost irrelevant and they are 'consigned to near-illiteracy and innumeracy' by a schoolmaster who believes the children are born to fail. That this poor education is 'functional' is apparent when the jobs begin to disappear and the young people 're-educate themselves and move on'.[13]

Sage's own sense of inhabiting an 'enclave of the nineteenth century' (p. 18) is increased by the influence of her grandparents on her early childhood, particularly her grandfather, the village vicar, who teaches her to read, aged four, and thus initiates her into his world: 'I'd kneel on the threadbare rug in his study while he worked on his sermon, or talked to the odd visitor, pulling out books and puzzling over big words' (p. 15). Yet, this inheritance is complicated by the fact that he is also a drinker and a philanderer, so that to be told, as she is by her mother, that she is 'just like you're your grandfather' is an insult, meaning she is 'promiscuous, sex-obsessed' (p. 77). Sage also reveals another point of contact: as a diary-keeper her grandfather provides a line of continuity with her own writing. Pondering the question 'who is he writing *for*', Sage decides that he is writing at least partly for her grandmother, not so much justifying himself as confirming his wickedness, revelling in what makes him distinctive, and saving himself from 'the squalor of insignificance' (p. 77). Beyond this, he is also writing for her, 'reaching out a scrawny hand across the years' (p. 78). Sage is aware that she as writer is both memorializing her grandfather, and fulfilling his dearest wish: 'Here are his words, though, in print at last' (p. 78).

Sage's reflection and analysis never have the effect of diminishing the strangeness of her grandparents who inhabit a 'gothic' space and stand for 'anarchy of all sorts': 'So postwar moral rearmament, with everyone conscripted to normality and standing to attention, didn't get far in the vicarage' (p. 89). Their distance and difference seems to provide access to creativity, to a time before, which is both psychological and historical, and seems unreal or fictional. Hilary Mantel's memoir *Giving up the Ghost* (2010), again set in the postwar period, uses the idea of 'haunting' to describe her equivalent sense of being occupied by 'other people's stories, and other people's claims'.[14] For Mantel, there is something irreducibly strange about early sense impressions that are 'synaesthesic' and in excess of words (p. 23). Like Julia Kristeva's idea of a semiotic, a pre-linguistic register that goes on troubling the smooth functioning of the symbolic, these impressions never simply belong to the past, and the attempt to write about her childhood can thus never be finished.

Mantel's mother comes from a family of millworkers just as Steedman's did, and has inherited an ethos of endurance, 'accepting your place', and surrendering ambition. Later she will take to amateur dramatics, with Cinderella being her favourite part, with its paradigm of female transformation dependent on the arrival of a prince. Mantel's own account of her childhood includes an experience (or performance) of gender as one of disempowerment. Though the fifties opened up opportunities for children like Mantel who passed the 11-plus, the experience of gender is more constrained. Mantel's childhood fantasy that she will change into a boy has to be given up along with the fictional roles of knight errant or Davy Crockett. Instead she comes to inhabit a body that feels alien and out of control, and a selfhood that feels other. As memoirist, her aim is to determine her own story:

> For a long time I felt as if someone else were writing my life. I seemed not able to create or interpret myself. About the time I reached mid-life, I began to understand why this was. The book of me was indeed being written by other people: by my parents, by the child I once was, and by my own unborn children, stretching out their ghost fingers to grab the pen. I began this writing to seize the copyright in myself. (pp. 70–1)

However, for Mantel, that wresting of control by writing is always coincident with the haunting presence of the past, a multiplicity of other lives encountered or missed. Ghosts are also seen as creating a penumbra of potential in which her writing exists: 'I will always look after you, I want to say, however long you have been gone. I will always feed you, and try to keep you entertained; and you must do the same for me' (p. 252).

Family favourites[15]

In her Introduction to *Truth, Dare or Promise*, Heron comments on how the image of the family 'looms large in postwar Britain', and that its function was partly to produce a 'comforting sameness' which transcended class and sex antagonisms and diminished the importance of other structures in people's lives (p. 5). Many of the autobiographies by women who were growing up in the 1950s and 1960s bear witness to the intense battles that were waged within the family and how far removed the reality was from the idealized version, promoted as a form of social engineering. In *The Three of Us* (2009), Julia Blackburn describes a relationship with her mother that is dangerous and inappropriate, with her mother first treating her as an adult to whom she can confide sexual secrets and then attacking her as a sexual rival:

> I was having a shower when she suddenly burst into the little bathroom. She pulled back the curtain and, fully clothed, stepped in under the drenching hot water. She put her face close to mine and she began screaming accusations at me, about how I had destroyed her life for ever. I remember thinking that maybe she had a knife and she was going to kill me.[16]

Violence, this time inflicted by an older sister, is also represented in Janice Galloway's memoir *This is Not About Me* (2008), and with it the continual sense that life is unsafe. Cora, who comes back to live with her mother and sister when her marriage fails, is unstable and unpredictable and sees her younger sister, Janice, as one of the causes of her frustration and unhappiness. As the main wage earner Cora dominates the household, expects others to undertake domestic chores and terrorizes her mother. On one occasion, having set fire to Janice's hair (by accident, she claims), she ends up hitting both Janice and the mother who attempts to reprimand her, at the same time revealing a deep jealousy: 'It was her fault, she yelled. We were fine before. You and me before *she* turned up. Bloody Smart Alec thinking she's It.'[17] Galloway begins her memoir by looking at a photograph, where she sits, age five, between the two adult women, mother and sister, 'too close because the sofa is meant for two' (p. 1). That 'too close' perhaps signifies the actual lack of space in their house, their world. However, 'too close' has also been a theme within feminist theorizing of mother–daughter relations. The 'distance-less proximity' which, according to Luce Irigaray, has characterized mother–daughter relations, and relations between women in general, has arisen, so she argues, from the lack of a language which accounts for women as social subjects with their own connection with history and with change.[18]

Both Blackburn and Galloway provide a vivid picture of the damage already done to women. However, Blackburn interleaves the story of her disastrous growing up with a much more benign account of her relationship with her mother when her mother is near death. Told in italics to designate the notebook written at the time, Blackburn reports her mother's words: '*"Mother and daughter, mother and daughter" she says, practising the words*' (p. 203). This is poignant, of course, because her mother seems to have come so late to value the relationship. On the other hand, to practise the words – as Blackburn is also doing in her memoir – is important, since it signifies experimentation, moving the relation away from muteness, from bodily fusion, into language, into time and the possibility of change.

Narratable selves

Galloway ends her memoir by weighing up what it is possible to change. The cards you are dealt in life are fixed, as it were, but, she writes, 'with luck, they might be shuffled, cut, turned to best advantage. Inventiveness counts for something' (p. 339). Judith Butler has argued that whenever we try to tell the story of ourselves – whenever we turn to narrative – we are faced with the inescapable problem that there is no *one* authoritative version. Partly this is because all accounts are addressed to someone, even if only implicitly, and thus given away or 'expropriated from the domain of what is my own'.[19] But it is also the case because the 'I' cannot tell the story of its own emergence, cannot attempt to represent its own origin, without resorting to fiction. In Butler's words, 'I can tell the story of my origin and I can even tell it again and again, in several ways ... but of no single one can I say with certainty that it alone is true' (pp. 37–8). In other words, the lack of an origin does not destroy the possibility of autobiographical narrative but merely ensures that it will always ultimately point in a fictional direction.

Jeanette Winterson's memoir, *Why Be Happy When You Could Be Normal* (2011), retraces some of the same ground as her debut novel, *Oranges Are Not the Only Fruit* (1985), in particular her relationship with the abusive and eccentric adoptive mother who dominated her early life. Telling the story again, so Winterson sees it, is not a matter of substituting the facts for the fiction; rather there is an inevitable intermingling of both: 'Part fact part fiction is what life is.'[20] This is particularly the case for her as an adopted child whose origin is perhaps, even more than in the general case, obscure and problematic:

> Adopted children are self-invented because they have to be; there is an absence, a void, a question mark at the very beginning of our lives ... The baby explodes into an unknown world that is only knowable through some kind of story – of course that is how we all live, it's the narrative of our lives, but adoption drops you into the story after it has started. It's like arriving after curtain up. (p. 5)

Winterson's story shares with many other autobiographical narratives an experience of social deprivation and, though in more exaggerated form, an antagonistic relationship with a mother who, mired in the limited roles history has allowed her, cannot recognize and accept her daughter's difference and independence. As for other girls growing up in the 1950s and 1960s, education furnishes an escape to a world of expanded choice. More than most, though, Winterson revels in her self-reliance and capacity for storytelling as an act of survival, as a way of resisting the deeply skewed version of reality her mother gives her: 'I can't remember a time when I wasn't setting my story against hers. It was my survival from the very beginning ... To avoid the narrow mesh of Mrs Winterson's story I had to be able to tell my own' (p. 5).

Butler draws on Adriana Cavarero when thinking about the way the 'I' addresses itself to, or is exposed to, others in self-narration. Yet Cavarero seems to go further than Butler in proposing how telling the story of oneself actually requires others, is always 'relational': 'Someone's life-story always results from an existence, which, from the beginning has exposed her to the world – revealing her uniqueness' (p. 36). The word 'unique' is important, as is the notion that we are all 'narratable selves', whether we write our autobiographies or not, since our memories, intermittent and fragmented, will still come to us with the feeling that they *could* be narrated. Cavarero's claim about what the autobiographical story is – making 'texts' secondary and thus subverting debates about the alienation of the self in language – undoes the division between fact and fiction, history and story. The 'narratable self' is not 'a *fiction* that can distinguish itself from *reality*' (p. 34). Rather it is 'the familiar sense of every self, in the temporal extension of a life-story that is this and not another' (p. 34).

Jackie Kay's memoir, *Red Dust Road* (2011), is a moving and sometimes humorous account of her search for her birth parents, and a persuasive demonstration of the importance of stories to people's lives. Born of a Nigerian father and a mother from the Scottish Highlands, and given up for adoption as a baby, Kay learns about her adoption when she is seven and realizes she is a different colour to her parents. As with Winterson, Kay's adoption seems to create a special need to fill a void, an unknown origin for which she searches – naïvely and fruitlessly, as she also reflects:

> You cannot find yourself in two strangers who happen to share your genes. You are made already, though you don't properly know it, you are made up from a mixture of myth and gene. You are part fable, part porridge. Finding a strange, nervous, Mormon mother and finding a crazed, ranting, Born-Again father does not explain me. At least I hope not! *Please, God, thank you, God.*[21]

Kay celebrates in her memoir a capacity for storytelling. Her generous, adoptive, Glaswegian parents, both accomplished storytellers themselves, weave around her stories about her birth, compensating for the story she does not have. In the end what Kay inherits from her adoptive mother, her 'mum', is not *the* story of her origins but the ability to tell stories: 'It was a heartbreaking story and it was mine. In a way my mum and I loved it, the story of me. It was a big bond, the story' (p. 44). Kay enshrines her inheritance of stories in a chapter where she drives her parents across Scotland, a journey resonant with other, similar journeys: 'I imagine the stories as a kind of fortress ... as long as the stories are shared, swapped, strengthened and embellished, my parents will be buttressed from the worst and live on, changing still' (p. 121). Stories are inseparable from our relationships and our humanity. In a sense, Kay's memoir is layered with stories, a family of stories, which hold her in their weave.

Chimamanda Ngozi Adichie has recently called for a new form, 'a cross between fiction and memoir'.[22] Is it time to find different ways of thinking about the relation between fiction and memoir? Will this provide a new way of thinking about women's life-writing? Is the intertwined creativity of both fiction and life-writing also a celebration of women's changing selfhood? What story will women in the future tell about their lives? Or I should say 'stories' for, whatever they will be, they will surely be both manifold and unpredictable.

Notes

1. See Adriana Cavarero, *Relating Narratives: Storytelling and Selfhood*, trans. Paul A. Kottman (London: Routledge, 2000), p. 61.
2. Sheila Rowbotham, *Woman's Consciousness, Man's World* (Harmondsworth: Penguin, 1973), pp. 39–40.

3. Alison Light, 'Writing Lives', *The Cambridge History of Twentieth-Century English Literature*, ed. Laura Marcus and Peter Nicholls (Cambridge University Press, 2005), p. 754.
4. See Linda Anderson, *Autobiography* (London: Routledge, 2010), pp. 26–9.
5. Rita Felski, *Beyond Feminist Aesthetics* (Cambridge, Mass.: Harvard University Press, 1989), p. 105.
6. Paul de Man, *Allegories of Reading: Figural Language in Rousseau, Nietzsche, Rilke and Proust* (New Haven: Yale University Press, 1979), p. 286.
7. Anne Oakley, *Taking It Like a Woman* (London: Jonathan Cape, 1984), pp. 2–3.
8. Lauretta Ngcobo, ed., *Let It Be Told* (London: Virago, 1987), p. 96.
9. Nicole Ward Jouve, *White Woman Speaks With Forked Tongue: Criticism as Autobiography* (London: Routledge, 1991), p. 7.
10. Liz Stanley, *The Auto/biographical I* (Manchester University Press, 1992), p. 101.
11. Liz Heron, ed., *Truth, Dare or Promise: Girls Growing Up in the Fifties* (London: Virago, 1985), p. 1.
12. Carolyn Steedman, *Landscape for a Good Woman* (London: Virago 1986), p. 28.
13. Lorna Sage, *Bad Blood* (London: Fourth Estate, 2001), p. 21.
14. Hilary Mantel, *Giving Up the Ghost: A Memoir* (London: Fourth Estate, 2010), p. 4.
15. The radio programme *Family Favourites* took the place of *Forces Favourites* after World War Two. It was a record-request programme, the aim of which was to link families in the UK with the British Forces serving overseas. It adopted a high moral tone, refusing mention of 'sweethearts'.
16. Julia Blackburn, *The Three of Us: A Family Story* (London: Vintage, 2009), p. 202.
17. Janice Galloway, *This is Not About Me* (London: Granta, 2008), p. 179.
18. Luce Irigaray, 'The Limits of the Transference', *The Irigaray Reader*, ed. Margaret Whitford (Oxford: Blackwell, 1991), p. 181.
19. Judith Butler, *Giving an Account of Oneself* (New York: Fordham University Press, 2005), pp. 36–7.
20. Jeanette Winterson, *Why Be Happy When You Could Be Normal?* (London: Vintage, 2012), p. 6.
21. Jackie Kay, *Red Dust Road* (London: Picador, 2011), p. 47.
22. Chimamanda Ngozi Adichie, 'Facts are Stranger than Fiction', *Guardian*, 19 April 2013, www.theguardian.com/books/2013/apr/19/chimamanda-ngozi-adichie-stranger-fiction, accessed 31 March 2015.

Part IV

Writing the Nation: Difference, Diaspora, Devolution

13
Writing the Nations: Welsh, Northern Irish, and Scottish Literature

Hywel Dix

This chapter analyses how women writers in Wales, Northern Ireland, and Scotland have attempted to develop distinctive narrative voices that articulate diverse kinds of female experience in a series of literary canons that are overwhelmingly male. Beginning with Welsh women writers, it argues that their historical challenge has been to resist a strong imperative to compartmentalize different kinds of work: nationalist, ethnic, English-language, Welsh-language, and feminist.[1] As the cultural confidence of Wales has increased, so too have Welsh women writers become more confident in articulating a multiplicity of subject positions simultaneously, rather than categorizing and dividing them. The resistance to compartmentalization is also an important consideration when analysing contemporary writing by women from Northern Ireland. Drawing on Edna Longley's critique of the dominant tendency to separate all Irish culture into either nationalist or unionist categories, the chapter proposes that such binary thinking prompts female writers from Northern Ireland to develop literary strategies that bring different texts into a dialogic relationship with each other.[2] A similar set of concerns will be revealed as important elements in Scottish women's writing since 1970, but there a subtly different position will be expounded. It is argued that ideas of luck and fate are frequently and ironically presented by Scottish women writers to reveal that what is often experienced as chance is more commonly the result of contingently taken political decisions. Discussion of these concepts reveals national identity itself to be based on elective affinity and supported by a literary imagination that has become transnational.

Cultural confidence and multiple cultural identities in Wales

There is a paradox in Welsh literary culture. Wales has the popular romantic image of being a nation of poets, but in the canon of English literature the female writers of Wales are nowhere to be found.[3] With the possible exception of Gillian Clarke, who features on GCSE poetry syllabi, even the most oppositional construction of a canon of English literature will struggle to include any of Wales's contemporary women writers. In other words, Welsh women writers have been in a double bind for some time: they are excluded from the wider canon, perhaps due to the highly un-metropolitan nature of their social identities, and relatively under-emphasized even within a putative canon of Welsh writing in English dominated by Dylan Thomas (1914–53) and R.S. Thomas (1913–2000).[4] Only a recent growth in national confidence, and of specific women writers, has started to loosen this bind.

One Welsh woman writer who can be considered canonical is Bernice Rubens (1923–2004), winner of the Booker Prize for *The Elected Member* (1969). This novel narrates the story of Norman Zweck, hospitalized as a consequence of drug addiction to the consternation of his Rabbi father. In this way, *The Elected Member* foregrounds a questioning of Jewish cultural values, but the same is not true of Welsh culture. Neither the text nor its paratextual apparatus generates any sense at all of Rubens as a Welsh writer. Rubens herself seems to have been aware that to a London publisher in 1969 a Welsh novel offered little or no fashionable pedigree and accordingly suppressed that aspect in her writing.

That Welsh dimension is much more prominent in Rubens's novel *I Sent a Letter to my Love* (1975), where Amy Jones exists in a relationship of co-dependency with her disabled brother Stan for whom she cares. This portrayal of dependency opens onto a darkly comical satire of Welsh provincial life. Reading a news story about the theft of £30,000, Amy asks herself what she would do with such a sum and decides that she would go on a luxury cruise. Not only does this symbolize her dream of escaping a life of paralysis, but it also pre-empts the cruel conclusion in which Stan goes on a cruise for his honeymoon. In broader terms, it also pre-empts Rubens's later novel *Birds of Passage* (1981) about two widows who go on a cruise to celebrate their new-found freedom from men. But in *Birds of Passage* there is, once more, no Welsh context and little or no sense of Rubens as a Welsh writer. It is as if Rubens separated her Welsh and feminist selves between different novels, just as she had compartmentalized her Jewish and Welsh selves.

To read *The Elected Member* alongside *I Sent a Letter to my Love* and *Birds of Passage* is to feel an odd sense of triangulated identities, with the first a 'Jewish' novel, the second a 'Welsh' novel, and the third a 'feminist' novel. There is surprisingly little sense of intersection or interaction between these elements within any of the individual novels, which are constructed in such a way as to segregate them. All the novels date from the period surrounding the failure of the 1979 referendum on home rule in Wales, when low cultural confidence generated a sense of a precarious national identity that accordingly struggled to accommodate a duality or multiplicity of identities. In a study of devolutionary cultures around the UK, Arthur Aughey argues that one of the historical challenges facing writers in the different nations of Britain is to move beyond a logic of 'either/or' towards a relationship of plurality: 'both/and'.[5] The Welsh cultural environment in the 1960s and 1970s made it difficult for Rubens to see herself and be seen as Welsh *and* Jewish *and* feminist.

Perhaps the most significant Welsh literary theorist and political commentator of the twentieth century was the socialist intellectual Raymond Williams (1921–88), who was interested in the question of cultural confidence. Williams belonged to the first generation of working-class students who received scholarships to study at Cambridge in the 1930s and 1940s, and subsequently devoted his career to extending the educational franchise. He was enormously influential in bringing political questions into the cultural arena and hence in democratizing educational institutions and cultural practices. As a literary professor and critical thinker, Williams helped to transform the study of literature and culture, making it possible to relate the social and cultural circumstances in which a literary text is produced to the way that its content is interpreted. This could often be a quite straightforward means of bringing political questions into the cultural and literary arena.

In Scotland and Wales, for example, it had long been a commonplace that literature is a bearer of particular social, political, and cultural values – maybe even 'national values' – but Williams thought those nations were characterized by a lack of cultural confidence. Indeed, he believed this lack of confidence was one of the main reasons why the referenda on self-government in each nation in 1979 were overwhelmingly defeated and the Scottish and Welsh people chose not to govern themselves.[6] Williams himself did not survive to see the later referenda in 1997 when each nation voted in favour of self-government. Within only 18 years the resounding and apparently final 'no' of 1979 had become a tentative but clear 'yes'. The apparent rapidity of these transformations is one of the important factors in understanding contemporary British public culture, because during the period 1979–97, writers, musicians, and filmmakers contributed to the increase in cultural confidence in both Scotland and Wales, and hence to achieving those 'yes' votes in 1997. In other words, developing new ways of representing the lives of the people of those nations in literature played a part in increasing their cultural confidence and strengthening their inclination to ask for increased forms of political representation.

If Williams explicitly addressed the problem of cultural confidence in Wales and Scotland, however, for Wales's women writers his position with regard to questions of cultural empowerment is highly ambivalent. Gwyneth Roberts argues that the cost of Williams's idealized vision of working-class communities was a neglect of women's experience, and that in his fiction, female characters tend to be static.[7] This recurring feature gives rise to Morag Shiach's well-known critique of Williams: that feminists can find plenty of things to interest them in his work, but that they are unlikely to find any women.[8] One tactic available for women writers to address this shortsightedness has been the established feminist literary practice of 'writing back', and significant novels by Menna Gallie (1920–70) and Tessa Hadley can be said to have written back to Welsh industrial writing, and specifically Williams's novel *Border Country* (1960).

As an early example, Gallie's *The Small Mine* (1962) is consciously located in the tradition of Welsh industrial fiction, and includes at its mid-point one of that tradition's significant recurring conventions: the mining disaster. Gallie's innovation was to direct a greater degree of attention to female characters and women's experience. She strongly rejects the stereotype of an overbearing Welsh mother, and disperses narrative perspective across a series of different characters, both male and female. This dispersal within a single structure has enabled Katie Gramich to argue that Gallie's work as a whole is characterized by a 'duality of allegiance' – both Welsh and feminist – that is largely absent from the tradition of Welsh industrial writing.[9]

Williams's *Border Country* is about the cultural anxiety caused by a working-class boy moving from a Welsh community to Cambridge, only to be jolted back by the death of his father. Hadley's *The Master Bedroom* (2007) employs that same plot structure but focuses on female experience rather than class relations or masculinity. It opens with its female protagonist Kate Flynn travelling back from London to Cardiff to care for her dying mother. As the months pass and she finds herself still in Cardiff, she is drawn into two love affairs – one with an old school friend, David Roberts, and the other with David's son, Jamie. Like Catherine Merriman's novel *State of Desire* (1996), about a woman in her forties entering a sexual relationship with one of her son's friends, Hadley portrays a relationship that challenges dominant assumptions about gender and age.

One of the settings for Kate's liaison with David is Wales Millennium Centre, opened in Cardiff Bay in 2004 as a home for several of Wales's artistic companies. Gwyneth Lewis's poetic inscription on the walls of the Centre, 'In these stones horizons sing', has been cited as an example of the recent increase in the cultural self-confidence of Wales.[10] By contrast, Kate in Hadley's novel is distinctly uncomfortable when she attends a performance by the Welsh National Opera, believing that it is a highbrow and implicitly patriarchal event. In other words, Hadley both thematizes and questions the straightforward assumption that the establishment of the Centre unproblematically heralds an increase in cultural confidence. The 'highbrow' arts centre feels incongruous in Cardiff Bay because the surrounding area, formerly known as Butetown Docks, was traditionally a working-class and highly multicultural district.

The short fiction of Butetown writer Leonora Brito portrays a Cardiff Bay very unlike that symbolized by Wales Millennium Centre in *The Master Bedroom*. Brito is interested in how class intersects with ethnicity to create a distinctive working-class culture. Her short story collections *dat's love* (1995) and *Chequered Histories* (2006) resist a simplistic sense of nation based on ethnic absolutism in favour of an accent on the performativity of national and cultural identities. Indeed, Linden Peach suggests that by moving in her fiction from a static sense of Welsh culture to a hybrid sense of a culture always in the process of being expanded and recreated, Brito 'may have inspired a number of Welsh women writers ... concerned with the ethnic diversity of Wales'.[11] Examples of texts he suggests have been inspired by Brito are Trezza Azzopardi's *The Hiding Place* (2000) and Charlotte Williams's *Sugar and Slate* (2002).

Williams is interested in exploring how far an increase in Welsh cultural confidence has been replicated among members of Wales's ethnic minorities. In her memoir *Sugar and Slate,* she writes that growing up in North Wales with a white, Welsh-speaking mother and a black father from Guyana, she felt she had to try to stand for something but had no idea what because it seemed that 'black' stood for 'nothing'.[12] Answering the problem of what she stood for necessitated an enlarged and more nuanced definition of Welsh culture, in which Williams would 'write myself into the story as best I could' (p. 176). Her metaphor of a page being rewritten recalls Homi Bhabha's concept of cultural hybridity. To Bhabha, hybridity is a process in which a culture is made and remade over successive generations so that it is always in the process of coming into being and the subjectivities expressed within it are always also subjects in process. Hybridity implies a sense of cultural open-endedness: every time a culture is expressed it does so as if for the first time.[13] Likewise, Williams presents Welsh culture in process. When she writes about attending an aunt's funeral, she imagines the faces of centuries of Welsh soldiers whom Aunt Maggie will join in the earth. But, she reflects, those same soldiers could never have imagined her, because black people had previously had no place in the culturally sanctioned histories of Wales. Thus, when she imagines their faces, the expressions are blank (p. 177). Implicit in Williams's critique of the concept of racially pure culture is a corresponding critique of the ease with which the postcolonial model of identity has been adopted within the Welsh academy. Such a critique of Welsh culture and institutions would have been more difficult to imagine in the earlier period, when Wales's relatively fragile sense of its own culture had militated against critical self-reflection.

The increased cultural confidence and resistance to cultural division can be seen more generally in the work of Wales's recent women writers. The compartmentalization of Rubens's work contrasts with Siân James's *A Small Country* (1979), in which both Catrin's Welsh identity and female experience are validated. It contrasts also with Kym Lloyd's *The Book of Guilt* (2004), which is defiantly unsettling and uncommercial in its portrayal of private trauma, but which positively foregrounds the fact that Lloyd was 'born in Swansea' and 'lives in Hertfordshire'.[14] This may imply that the earlier necessity for writers to repress a Welsh sense of self in order to succeed in the commercial world of London publishing is no longer as strong. It is also possibly because, as Jane Aaron and M. Wynn Thomas argue, Wales has developed an increasing capacity to promote the work of its writers and artists since the years immediately surrounding the two referenda of 1979 and 1997 due to its stronger sense of political self-control.[15] This capacity is exemplified in the establishment in 2006 of the first Dylan Thomas Prize. Its conferral on Rachel Trezise for the short story collection *Fresh Apples* (2005), and the award of Wales Book of the Year to Deborah Kay Davies's collection *Grace, Tamar and Laszlo the Beautiful* (2008), suggest that there has been a broadening conception of Welsh literary culture in gender terms.[16]

Here too, however, Williams generates a powerful critique of the tendency in contemporary Wales to venerate icons and celebrities. This, she thinks, has the effect of short-circuiting the gains in cultural confidence that have been made. Williams says of the confident multicultural Wales that her work attempts to imagine into existence: 'I hope it won't be a place where we have to listen to an endless round of "first-tos" and "been-tos" boasting among ourselves: the first black Welsh man to have done this or the first black Welsh women to have been there' (p. 191).[17] In contrast to Rubens, Williams's refusal to categorize demonstrates how far Wales's women writers have come since 1970, moving from a logic of 'either/or' to embrace a logic of 'both/and'.

Female experience and intertextuality in Northern Ireland

In *The Living Stream: Literature and Revisionism in Ireland* (1994), Longley suggests that the challenge for a recent generation of female writers is to decouple particular ideals of womanhood from a nationalist culture based strongly on the Catholic church. Longley argues that political debates in the 1980s made it difficult for Irish women to assert their commitment to social issues of particular importance to them such as divorce and abortion. She argues that in a society where the 'national' is strongly equated with Catholicism, to campaign for social reforms opposed by the church is often constructed as being anti-Irish: 'the more republican, the less feminist'.[18] Irish literature has also become associated with a national canon of works; it can only explore feminist subjectivity if the dominant mode of thought that associates 'national' with 'Catholic' on the one hand, and with 'literature' on the other, is questioned. Longley suggests that Northern Irish literature be seen as dialogic and intertextual on the grounds that it opens up language to a polyphony of meaning beyond this binary thinking and to a gendered expression of subjectivity.

The critique of patriarchal authority and a dialogic interplay between past and present are both important elements in the work of Deirdre Madden, whose novel *Authenticity* (2002) offers a fictional portrayal of the ideas expressed in feminist classic *A Room of One's Own* (1929) by Virginia Woolf (1882–1941). In *Authenticity,* Madden takes Woolf's question about how women can fulfil an artistic vocation and explores differing responses from three men: artist Roderic Kennedy; his banker brother Dennis; and the art-collecting lawyer William Armstrong. This need not be seen as a surrender of feminist insight to patriarchal authority but as a sympathetic portrayal of how the pressure of holding a community together has often devolved historically upon women. Julia accepts William's invitation to make him her confidant but, when she tries to discuss with him the tragedy of witnessing her mother's early death, he is unable to meet her emotional needs and flees.

In contrast, Madden's earlier novel, *One by One in the Darkness* (1996), centres on the Troubles, a historical experience normally associated with men, but it explores the impact on three women. Ostensibly, events take place over one week, but alternate chapters narrate the sisters' lives from the start of the Troubles in the late 1960s to just before the ceasefire in 1994. As in Williams's *Border Country*, a sense of estrangement is expressed by the fact that in London Kate changes her name to Cate, signalling that her decision to leave Ulster was also a decision to become a different person. Just as Hadley in *The Master Bedroom* 'writes back' to *Border Country* from a female perspective, so Madden uses the same technique to portray the effects of the Troubles on women's lives. For example, one of Kate's childhood memories is of having sparked a bomb scare by leaving her school bag unattended in a shop and of her father buying her a magazine to console her. Given that the adult Cate works for a magazine, Madden creates a subtle link between the past and the present, hinting that in both cases the magazine provides Cate with a way out of trouble, and juxtaposes the mechanisms of officially sanctioned violence with the domestic concerns of family life. In the end, only a very uneasy reconciliation is achieved between the sisters and their mother, Emily. Madden hints that Emily's experience of having been estranged from her own mother informs her decision not to let this happen with her daughter and so she allows herself to be reconciled with Cate through the intervention of the sisters who have stayed at home. It is tempting to see this reconciliation as somehow symbolic of the Northern Ireland of the 1990s and 2000s but the more important point is that Madden switches focus from the male-dominated world of public politics to the female world of the family.

This switch from the political to the personal is a key component of Northern Irish women's writing more generally. For example, *No Mate for the Magpie* (1985), a novel by Frances Molloy (1947–91), creates a highly ironic portrayal of the disparity that existed between education as an ideal and education as a material practice in the 1950s and 1960s. Molloy's protagonist, Ann Elizabeth McGlone, is involved in repeated departures from one institution to another: school, factory, hospital, convent, asylum, supermarket, priest's house, and hospital again. At each step, her lived experience contrasts and conflicts with ideas she has developed in school and through reading. When Ann's Da is imprisoned during the Troubles, it is her

Protestant neighbours rather than her Catholic comrades who are kindest to her. This gives rise to a reciprocal arrangement with the Protestant girl, June, whereby each agrees to go on the other's sectarian march. Though this plan fails, it enables Molloy to portray Ann's transition from naïvety to critical scepticism. The loss of innocence is represented in Ann's beating by a brutal policeman during the 1968 peace marches to Derry, and her parents are even led to believe that she has been killed:

> The crowd caught a hoult of the polisman an' started te pull him limb from limb. Wheniver a tried te stap them a nearly got mesel' kilt be me own admirers of a minute before so a went away feelin' sorry for the polisman, because a knew that he was only tryin' te do hes duty be upholdin' the laws that were made for all of us be the acutely deranged, imbecilic, illegitmate, offspring of the mother of parliaments.
>
> They say that bad news travels fast an' a suppose they must be right, because word of my death reached home before a did.[19]

Molloy's protagonist rejects the impulse to sectarian thinking that has led to the violence. When the crowd rescues Ann from the policeman, she protects him from them. *No Mate for the Magpie* thus illustrates Longley's argument that Northern Irish writing is intertextual because it opens up a critical consciousness beyond the inherited narrow divisions and definitions within and between different sectarian communities. In Molloy's novel, this intertextual quality operates on two levels, both in the refusal to be tied to binary communities and in Molloy's commitment to the use of contemporary Northern Irish speech. In the passage quoted, this vernacular speech has the effect of enlarging political consciousness precisely because it comes from a domestic – as opposed to a political – space.[20] In the end, Ann is thrown out of her lodging for having been arrested during an anti-Vietnam march, and realizes that she will have to leave Ireland altogether if she is to escape the violence. This again signifies the movement from the political to the personal.

A similar fate befalls Kathleen Doherty in Jennifer Johnston's *Shadows on Our Skin* (1977), another novel concerned with the domestic effect of the Troubles. It portrays the relationship between Joe Logan, his older brother Brendan and the teacher Kathleen, whose fiancé is in the British army. When Joe suspects his brother of murdering two soldiers, Brendan cannot risk letting Kathleen pass his identity to this fiancé. She leaves Derry after being beaten up by his friends, but also gives Joe a present, *A Golden Treasury of Verse*, as a final gift of hope. Where Molloy uses Ann's reading ironically to reject institutional education in favour of developing a critical consciousness, Johnston uses the book as a metaphor for escape. Joe seeks refuge from the Troubles by writing poetry in his head – hence the refrain of the titular poem: 'Now we have time to kill / Kill the shadows on our skin' – as if to ask whether Joe is killing time or being killed by his time.[21]

The question of timeliness is perhaps even more prescient in Johnston's earlier novel *How Many Miles to Babylon?* (1974), which uses history to set two difficult topics at a safe distance. Material about Irish nationalism is associated with the past, as if it were too fraught to be discussed in contemporary fiction in 1974. Moreover, *How Many Miles to Babylon?* constantly hints at the homoeroticism of men in the trenches. This issue cuts across national, class, and sectarian divides and may also have been more difficult to set in the Irish present of 1974. Just as Longley argues that the association between Irish nationalism, Catholic doctrine, and national literature forecloses debates of interest to feminists, the same can be said of homosexuality, and Johnston's hints concerning homosexuality are always deflected. A similar response is evident in Sinéad Morrissey's collection of poetry *The State of the Prisons* (2005). Its title poem is a poetic biography of the eighteenth-century prison reformer John Howard, rather than a portrayal of political imprisonment in Northern Ireland more recently. Howard is first compared to Luther writing a 'list of grievances' and then visits 'the Roman fisherman' in order to learn more about the penal code in other countries.[22] One can read this as allegorical of Northern Irish society in the late twentieth century. Yet, as with Johnston's fiction, the poetry projects into the past a concern that may be too painful or controversial to address in the present.

How far Morrissey creates an intertextual relationship between past and present can be seen by reading *The State of the Prisons* alongside Colette Bryce's poem '1981' from her collection *The Full Indian Rope Trick* (2005). '1981' is about the hunger strike by prisoner Bobby Sands. It creates a sense of a disturbed temporality and of an achievable future that is rooted somehow in the past. The 'hunger' with which the striker speaks is his only way of expressing his otherwise muted voice. This hunger in turn is transformed into a crowd speaking with 'anger' in the second stanza, where 'We stall / in twos and threes in the town centre, / talk it over, say it with anger'.[23] With the introduction of the word 'we', the horizon separating reader from object is crossed so that the reader becomes an active participant. In the final stanza the muted voice belongs not only to the hunger striker but also to the crowd of people waiting to hear news of his fate:

> Over graves and funeral cars
> the vast bays of colour say it
> with flowers, flowers everywhere;
> heads are bowed as mute as theirs,
> that will find a voice in the darker hours,
> say it with stones, say it with fire. (p. 11)

In this stanza something new has entered the poem. The refrain 'say it with hunger' / 'say it with anger' has become transformed again into the much more tactile 'say it / with flowers', substituting questions of political anger to operate in a different kind of textual economy. Bryce's 'bays of colour' recall the lines 'How vainly men themselves amaze / to win the palm, the oak or bays' from Andrew Marvell's poem 'The Garden'.[24] In Ancient Greece, laurels of palm and oak were awarded respectively for military achievement or civic accomplishment. A bay laurel was the reward specifically for literary success. In the use of flowers, Bryce aligns herself with a poetic-literary tradition in direct contrast to a military or political one.[25] Longley has demonstrated that Medbh McGuckian's poems often use floral images to open up a dialogue between conventionally masculine symbols like hard wood, and softer, feminine materials such as flowering stalks and stems which are associated with a challenge to male cultural authority.[26] By contrasting 'say it with flowers' with the sterner 'say it with stones, say it with fire' at the conclusion of '1981', Bryce also poses symbols of femininity as a challenge to those of male authority.

As a final example of this challenge, Leontia Flynn's poem 'Snow' from the collection *These Days* (2004) explicitly opens up a dialogue with Louis MacNeice's earlier poem of the same title. Flynn's 'Snow' is followed by 'Nocturne', in which she explores the role of the contemporary female poet in Northern Ireland:

> Trying to figure that *je ne sais quoi* a poem takes to get published:
> a clerical temp, capitalising on the caesura
> in his working day – sweet little night enjambing
> from the blue scraps of his evening
> ...
> My tongue cleaves to my mouth O Lord, The Words not coming
> he writes, The Words not ... Wha?
>   Whaddya mean already written? What?
> Louis? Louis who?[27]

In this portrayal of a male typist awaiting instruction from the female poet, Flynn reverses conventional hierarchical work relations. By cultivating a persona unfamiliar with MacNeice's prior poem entitled 'Snow' and seemingly ignorant of the existence of MacNeice himself – 'Louis who?' – Flynn signals her subtle subversion of the cultural authority that has generally been reserved for male writers, especially within a nationalist canon. Like McGuckian or Bryce, she brings her work into a dialogue with those earlier male writers, laying down a challenge to them.

Fate, fortune, and elective affinity in Scotland

For Scottish women writers also, putting new literary texts into dialogue with those associated with male authority and national canons can be seen as an example of 'writing back'. Prominent writers who have used this technique include Ellen Galford, whose novel *Queendom Come* (1990) juxtaposes the Thatcherite onslaught against working-class communities in Scotland during the 1980s with a counter-factual history in which an ancient Brythonic warrior maiden rises from the sleep of centuries to retake Britain on behalf of the Scottish; hence, the novel 'writes back' to the legend of Queen Boadicea. Equally, 'writing back' is a technique used by the poet Carol Ann Duffy in her collection *The World's Wife* (2000), which gives a fictional voice to the female partners of male historical and cultural pioneers.

Janice Galloway takes a different approach to the challenge of creating space for the inclusion of female voices in a male canon. In *All Made Up* (2011), a fictionalized memoir of growing up in a working-class community in Ayrshire in the 1950s and 1960s, Galloway relates her vocation to be a writer to a wider series of challenges faced by working-class women at different stages of their lives. The adolescent Janice feels that the reading she is given at school says little to her as a young Scottish woman: 'nothing that induced lust'.[28] In other words, there is an imbrication of literary sensibility with gender and sexuality. She rejects her schoolbooks and starts reading illicit material, listening to alternative music, and having secret meetings with boys. Her pursuit of Latin and music throw up their own problems, most notably in Janice's rivalry with her mother and sister, whose main response to those subjects is to assert that they are 'not for the likes of you' (p. 125) and to ask, 'who do you think you are?' (p. 193). Galloway's memoir portrays, from a specifically feminist standpoint, the same cultural anxiety over class and education as Williams's *Border Country*. There is also a new element, one that can be categorized as Galloway's fictive exploration of the relationship between luck, fate, and chance.

Michael Gardiner argues that the portrayal of chance is highly significant in Scottish working-class writing as a symbol of political disempowerment that should be resisted.[29] Members of such communities are often portrayed in their inability or failure to participate in political processes, so the consequences of political decisions taken outside the community are ironically seen as the random effect of chance when really they are the result of contingently taken political decisions.[30] Thus, in *All Made Up* Janice's mother does not want her to take school subjects that she deems unsuitable because of a belief that 'reducing a child's odds to the inevitable' was better than 'allowing them to struggle in vain' (p. 58). The metaphor of the 'odds' reduces any sense of self-determination to either fate or the role of blind chance. By contrast, in Galloway's vocation to be a writer, rejecting dominant (male) cultural values is associated with a growing awareness of her own sexuality. Rather than waiting for the ideal sexual partner to claim her, Janice engages in sexual experimentation of her own, just as she experiments in her own reading and writing practices rather than following the prescribed syllabus. These actions can be seen as tantamount to a refusal of the roles of chance or fate, in favour of conscious decisions that are recoded as a different kind of luck: '*Lucky* wasn't in it' (p. 158, emphasis in original). *All Made Up* represents Janice's gradual ability to read the world critically and make her own luck by refusing conformity to other people's conventions even when these are presented as fate. Perhaps for this reason, Galloway's first novel, *The Trick is to Keep Breathing* (1989), ironically juxtaposes the magazine horoscopes read by its protagonist Joy with her conscious decision first to check into and, subsequently, out of psychiatric care. A.L. Kennedy performs a similar juxtaposition in her novel *The Blue Book* (2011), where the idea of a preordained fortune is again denied: the clairvoyant is shown to be a trickster.

The portrayal of chance and predetermined fate is important in Scottish women's writing more generally. Jackie Kay's *Red Dust Road* (2010) initially appears to endorse the concept of fate or predetermination but ultimately problematizes it. *Red Dust Road* is an autobiographical account of how Kay, who was adopted at birth, traced her birth parents during adulthood. Her Scottish birth mother Elizabeth and her Nigerian father Jonathan had met in Aberdeen where he was studying agriculture. They gave their baby up for adoption at once because the social mores of the time frowned both on 'mixed race' relationships and on unmarried mothers raising children. Helen and John, Kay's adoptive parents, were able to jump the waiting list for babies because they did not share the racial prejudice of many people at the time, who only wanted to adopt 'white' babies.

Before recounting how she finally traced her birth father, Jonathan, a Born-Again Christian in Nigeria, Kay writes of how she discussed the process with Helen and John. She reflects that if they had not lied about being regular churchgoers in the 1960s, they would never have been allowed to adopt her, and she would have ended up in another family. Or, if they had chosen to stay permanently in New Zealand where they had lived and worked when they were young, they might have adopted a Maori baby. But Helen brings this speculation to a swift end: '"Maybe," my mum says, not much interested in this game of *what ifs*. "It's all a lottery," she says. "It's all pure luck."'[31]

As in *All Made Up*, a reappraisal of luck opens into a broader investigation of fate and predetermination. Kay takes that interest in two new directions in *Red Dust Road* by linking fate with a biological sense of predetermination expressed by genetics and by interrogating a religious sense of predestination. Thus after meeting her birth mother for the first time, Kay reflects on the coincidence of each of them giving the other the same gift (an orchid): 'I wonder if that choice is anything to do with genetics' (p. 62). In other words, strongly related to the portrayal of her search for her birth parents is an implicit question about whether or not the kind of person she is in adult life, her personality, her interests, her choices at even the most minute level, might be genetically determined.

Similarly, during the course of that meeting with her birth mother, Kay reports '[s]he told me that the Mormons believed that adopted people ask to be adopted whilst still in the womb and that she believed the perfect parents had been found for me because she'd prayed for them' (p. 69). This initially seems illogical and nonsensical to Kay. However, she goes on to say 'on the other hand, I had always felt *fated* to be with my mum and dad. What was the difference between my sense of fate and her Mormon God?' (p. 70, emphasis in original). Starting with the notion of luck, and then working it up into the concept of fate, the role of fate is expressed first through the possibility of genetic inheritance and then through the metaphysical concept of a controlling deity in order to help Kay answer the initial question: what makes her the person she is?

However, during the course of the narrative Kay discovers that knowing her birth parents is not a way of knowing herself. This discovery is important because it brings her quest not so much to an end – she does not find herself by finding her natural parents – but to a disavowal of both genetic determinism and religious predestination: 'You cannot find yourself in two strangers who happen to share your genes ... Finding a strange, nervous Mormon mother and finding a crazed, ranting, Born-Again father does not explain me' (p. 47).

By disavowing the possibility of finding out something about herself by tracing her birth parents, Kay simultaneously disavows the notion that luck, genetics, or predestination have determined who she is. The notion of fortune is then replaced with a sense of conscious choice, prompting Kay to reflect on the cliché that none of us can choose our own family: 'the thing that used to strike me about that cliché was that in my mum's case it wasn't true: she had chosen her family' (p. 34).

Although *Red Dust Road* disavows chance in favour of choice, the narrative moves full circle, returning to the examination of luck with which it started. This time, however, it is recoded as a different kind of luck. At the end of the text, Kay's birth father Jonathan refuses to see her a second time, fearing it will scandalize his Christian church. Instead though, his son Sidney (her brother) is willing to embrace her as a sibling and sends her home from Nigeria with some seeds from a tree, *moringa olifera,* that he has cultivated. She does not know if these seeds will grow back home in Scotland, but decides, 'I will chance my luck. I will plant the tree to mark meeting my brother Sidney' (p. 289). This image of seeds being taken from Africa back to Europe symbolizes a sort of acceptance of Kay by her African relatives and hence her own ability to make peace both with them and with herself. Moreover, the luck she will chance in trying to grow the tree is very different from the kind of luck expressed at the start of the novel. It is an ironic form of anti-luck, replacing the idea of an uncontrollable destiny with her conscious decision to plant the tree and hence accept her sense of who she is.

In a slightly different context, the ironic thematization of luck, fate, and fortune is an important element in the fiction of Agnes Owens (1926–2014). For example, Betty in *A Working Mother* (1994) is married to a man who cannot work and so she finds casual employment through Mrs Rossi's recruitment agency. Mrs Rossi reads Betty's fortune, so that Owens juxtaposes Betty's conscious decision to look for work with the idea that her fate is inescapably laid down in advance. The act of fortune-telling is used to suggest a quasi-philosophic dialogue between the symbolism of the novel (which implies predestination) and the plot of the novel (which denies it). That dialogue has the effect of putting to the reader the question: to what extent is Betty's exposure to the sexual predator Mr Robson and her eventual internment in a hospital the effect of random uncontrollable fate and to what extent are those experiences the result of decisions and interventions taken by both her and others?

These questions are again raised by Owens's novel *For the Love of Willie* (1998), where retrospective narration is used to examine the relationship between choice and predestination. The novel moves between Peggy's tale of her affair with Mr Roper during the Second World War and the hospital ward in which she is narrating her story to her listener, the 'Duchess', in the present. The uncouth language with which the Duchess interrupts the narrative – 'Cunt! I'm going to kill you' – invites us to think that she is suffering from some kind of dementia.[32] In this way, Owens plays with dominant cultural assumptions that older 'feminine' women do not 'naturally' speak in this aggressive way. Peggy responds to the Duchess's outbursts by saying, 'I keep forgetting nothing is real with you. You could be Alice in Wonderland and me the White Rabbit for all you know' (p. 328). As with the fortune-telling in *A Single Mother,* the allusion to *Alice in Wonderland* is implicitly also a reference to the Knave of Hearts, creating a visual reference to a pack of cards, the deal of the hand, and, hence, to the roles of luck and fate. We might expect this symbol of fate to dictate her future. However, as in *A Single Mother,* it has the opposite effect. Due to her loss of memory, any sense of the Duchess's identity is destabilized rather than confirmed, inviting readers to ask questions about both her past and her future as if each is amenable to redefinition and alteration rather than following a predestined path. The symbols of predetermination are used in a plot that rejects the concept, allowing readers to wonder how much Peggy's fate is predetermined and how much it is the consequence of contingently taken actions and decisions, including her own.

Just as the denial of the role of chance in shaping personal and political destinies is a recurring theme in the work of Scotland's female novelists, so too is it an important component in the work of two of Scotland's contemporary female dramatists. Probably the best-known play by a Scottish woman is Liz Lochhead's *Mary Queen of Scots Got Her Head Chopped Off* (first performed in 1987), a play that uses the techniques of Brechtian theatre to make its historical content resonate in the present day. Set in a period when England and Scotland were separate nations, and written during a period when the politics of Thatcherite London appeared increasingly remote from the daily lives and experiences of the Scottish people, the play employs an everyday Scots vernacular language to emphasize Scottish distinctiveness. On the other hand, set at a time when both Scotland and England had powerful Scottish female monarchs (Elizabeth and Mary), and written during a period when Britain as a whole had both a female Prime Minister and a female monarch for the only time in its history, the play also raises profound questions about what independence means for Scottish women. That is, rather than articulating the concept of independence along state and nationalist lines, Lochhead uses her dramatization of historical women, whose private lives were treated as public property, to explore the possibility of women living independently from men. As Robert Crawford says, the play 'highlights how difficult it is for a woman to identify with ideals of independence in a world where the odds – in terms of national and gender politics alike – seem weighted against her'.[33] This metaphor of the odds is apt, because Lochhead is also interested in expounding a critique of the role played by chance and blind fortune. At the mid-point of the play, Mary has her fortune told by her lover, Riccio, using a pack of tarot cards.

The idea of a predetermined fate that can be expressed through the cards is given added impetus by the fact that, for the contemporary audience, Mary's fate *is* predetermined: they already know that Mary Queen of Scots got her head chopped off. On the other hand, even though the audience recognize it as a historical fact, Mary's execution is not presented as inevitable in the play. Thus when Queen Elizabeth declares 'Such is the wheel of fortune!' in the same scene that she orders Mary's execution, the words inevitably seem ironic, disavowing the operation of fortune that they affirm by revealing that Mary's fate was not predestined, but the result of a conscious decision.[34] Because it maintains a double perspective, looking at two periods at once, Crawford suggests that the play invites the audience to relate historical events to their own world. Denigrating the role of the fortune-teller denigrates also the idea that the characters have a predetermined future and emphasizes instead individual agency. In turn, Crawford argues, this invites members of the audience to decide for themselves the kind of country they wish to inhabit (p. 215). This commitment to political agency and choice was particularly important during the period when Crawford was writing: the run-up to the Scottish independence referendum of 2014.

Maya Chowdhry's very different play *The Crossing Path* (2003) also suggests an ethics of responsibility in the act of decision-making. Gregory, a capitalist, warns the idealistic student, Rhiannon, that she should not go on an anti-globalization protest just to please her peers because, if she is tired, she might fail her university interview later that day. Rhiannon admits she has been 'bumbling along letting destiny decide' but Gregory tells her that whether or not she goes to the protest or to the interview, each is a 'conscious decision'.[35] Chowdhry portrays Rhiannon and Gregory as learning to think through the potential consequences of their choices, without simply adhering to a predetermined fate, symbolized by the tarots Rhiannon uses to amuse her friends. The play suggests that what feels like the luck of the draw is really the result of one or more specific interventions, and this is true of how we experience global capitalism.

This idea of contingent choice is an important one in understanding the work of Imtiaz Dharker, a sometimes-Scottish poet who consciously transcends national, cultural, and generic boundaries and whose work presents nationality itself as an elective affinity. In her collection *I Speak for the Devil* (2001), Dharker portrays many of the commonalities of female experience in conflict with male authority in a number of different global locations. Poems such as 'The Djinn in Auntie', 'All of us', 'Power', 'Breeding Ground, Chicago', 'Learning to Speak in Birmingham', and 'Being Good in Glasgow' evince a commitment to transnational feminism so that her poetic persona bespeaks an identity politics at times Indian, American, English, Scottish, and so on.[36] Dharker's use of different relationships to symbolize different cultures is important in the complex sequence 'Remember Andalus' from her second collection *The Terrorist at my Table* (2006). Anadalusia is central to Dharker because it represents a place and a time when European and Moorish cultures met. In her poetic imagination, the meaning of that meeting is not fixed in time; it has constantly to be remade. Her poem 'The Last Sigh' alludes to Salman Rushdie's *The Moor's Last Sigh* (1995) and gives a voice to the imagined Moor whose portrait is at the heart of Rushdie's novel.[37] Like Rushdie, Dharker is interested in questioning the notion of racially 'pure' cultural origins and, therefore, throughout the sequence shows a shift from an ethnically pure view of cultures to one based on elective affinity. The whole of 'Remember Andalus' presents nationality as a question of consciously chosen affiliation, where this affiliation is often expressed in the different roles played by the women.

Dharker's work generates a very strong sense of her commitment to transnational feminism, on the one hand, and to national identity as elective affinity on the other. This idea of active choice contrasts sharply with the idea of fortune as always already laid down by destiny. Thus her recent collection, *Leaving Fingerprints* (2009), concludes with a long sequence of poems about fortune-tellers struggling to read the palm of a woman who has many different lives and fortunes to tell. In 'Either Way' she compares herself to an Indian potter who holds his fate in his hands and whose future could go one way or another. It is followed by a series of poems in which the palm reader fails to assert a predetermined fate so that the poems again refuse the concept of fortune or chance, portraying a world where we make our own destinies.

This chapter has presented three principal arguments: that Welsh women writers have recently started to express a greater level of cultural confidence both as women and as Welsh writers than was available to them in the past; that the work of Northern Ireland's women writers challenges nationalist literary and historical traditions and so can be considered intertextual because it exists in dialogue with those histories; and that Scottish women writers deny chance or fate, asserting instead their capacity to make their own decisions and shape their own lives. Many of the ideas that have been expressed about one particular writer or one particular nation have strong resonance with other contemporary women writers in the other nations of Britain. Thus ideas about cultural confidence in Wales, history and intertextuality in Northern Ireland, and the refusal of predestination in Scotland are relevant to each of the other nations discussed. In the last instance, this commitment to the making of deliberate choices reveals national identity itself to be based on elective affinity and this is as true of Wales and Northern Ireland as it is of Scotland.

Notes

1. Throughout this chapter the terms 'nationalism' and 'nationalist' will be used to refer to the specific nationalisms of Wales, Scotland, and to some extent Ireland (but see note 2 below), rather than British nationalism. The difference between a kind of nationalism that upholds the centrality of the British nation, and these counter-nationalisms that question the pan-British version, is discussed by Raymond Williams. See 'Are We Becoming More Divided?' in his *Who Speaks for Wales?*, ed. Daniel Williams (Cardiff: University of Wales Press, 2003), p. 188.
2. In the context of Northern Ireland, the term 'unionist' (or sometimes 'loyalist') is used to describe a cultural or political loyalty to the United Kingdom of Great Britain and Northern Ireland and hence refers to the pan-British version of nationalism mentioned above in note 1. By contrast, the word 'nationalist' in both Northern Ireland and the Republic of Ireland refers to the cultural and political aspiration towards a separate and united Ireland. Thus 'nationalist' in Northern Ireland very rarely refers solely to Northern Ireland, and the concept of a specifically Northern Irish nationalism has not been strongly articulated in the past. For further discussion, see Tom Nairn, 'Northern Ireland: Relic or Portent?', *The Break-Up of Britain: Crisis and Neo-Nationalism* (London: Verso, 1977), pp. 205–44.
3. Megan S. Lloyd traces the prevalence of this idea in the English imagination back at least as far as Shakespeare. See 'Rhymer, Minstrel Lady Mortimer and the Power of Welsh Words', *Shakespeare and Wales: From the Marches to the Assembly*, ed. Willy Maley (Farnham: Ashgate, 2010), pp. 59–74.
4. Claire Flay discusses the dominance of male writers in 'The Library of Wales', *Planet: The Welsh Internationalist*, 202 (May 2011), pp. 91–7.
5. Arthur Aughey, *Nationalism, Devolution, and the Challenge to the United Kingdom State* (London: Pluto, 2001), p. 56.
6. See Raymond Williams, 'Freedom and a Lack of Confidence', in Williams, pp. 169–72.
7. Gwyneth Roberts, 'The Cost of Community: Women in Raymond Williams's Fiction', *Our Sisters' Land: The Changing Identity of Women in Wales*, ed. Jane Aaron (Cardiff: University of Wales Press, 1994), pp. 214–27.

8. Morag Shiach, 'A Gendered History of Cultural Categories', *Cultural Materialism: On Raymond Williams,* ed. Christopher Prendergast (Minneapolis: University of Minnesota Press, 1995), pp. 51–70.
9. Katie Gramich, 'Both In and Out of the Game: Welsh Writers and the British Dimension', *Welsh Writing in English,* Vol. 7, ed. M. Wynn Thomas (Cardiff: University of Wales Press, 2003), p. 261.
10. See David Williams, *About Cardiff* (Cardiff: Graffeg, 2005).
11. Linden Peach, *Contemporary Irish and Welsh Women's Fiction* (Cardiff: University of Wales Press, 2007), p. 18.
12. Charlotte Williams, *Sugar and Slate* (Aberystwyth: Planet, 2002), p. 47.
13. See Homi K. Bhabha, *The Location of Culture* (London: Routledge, 1994).
14. Kym Lloyd, *The Book of Guilt* (London: Sceptre, 2004), jacket blurb.
15. Jane Aaron and M. Wynn Thomas, '"Pulling You Through Change": Welsh Writing in English Before, Between and After Two Referenda', in Thomas, pp. 278–309.
16. That literary prizes are indicators both of increased cultural confidence and political control since the referendum on home rule in 1997 is also an argument that can be made about Scottish culture. The inaugural Scottish Arts Council (now Creative Scotland) Book of the Year was awarded in 2002 to Ali Smith for *Hotel World* (2001) and in 2011 it was awarded to Jackie Kay for *Red Dust Road.*
17. Again, Maud Sulter makes a similar point about black women artists in the Scottish context. See Sulter, *Passion: Discourses on Blackwomen's Creativity* (Hebden Bridge: Urban Fox Press, 1990), p. 10.
18. Edna Longley, *The Living Stream: Literature and Revisionism in Ireland* (Newcastle upon Tyne: Bloodaxe, 1994), p. 191.
19. Frances Molloy, *No Mate for the Magpie* (London: Virago, 1985), p. 138.
20. See Eve Patten, 'Fiction in Conflict: Northern Ireland's Prodigal Novelists', *Peripheral Visions: Images of Nationhood in Contemporary British Fiction,* ed. Ian A. Bell (Cardiff: University of Wales Press, 1995), p. 133.
21. Jennifer Johnston, *Shadows on Our Skin* (London: Hamish Hamilton, 1977), p. 121, p. 185.
22. Sinéad Morrissey, *The State of the Prisons* (Manchester: Carcanet, 2005), pp. 55–6.
23. Colette Bryce, *The Full Indian Rope Trick* (London: Picador, 2005), p. 11.
24. Andrew Marvell, 'The Garden', *The Complete Poems,* ed. George deF. Lord (London: Everyman, 1984), p. 48.
25. For a comparative reading of Marvell alongside a number of poets of the Troubles, see Christopher Ricks, 'Its Own Resemblance', *Approaches to Marvell,* ed. C.A. Patrides (London: Routledge, 1978), pp. 108–20.
26. Longley, p. 54, pp. 245–8. Examples she gives of McGuckian's poems are 'Aviary', 'Mr McGregor's Garden', 'The Seed Picture', and 'The Flitting'.
27. Leontia Flynn, *These Days* (London: Cape Poetry, 2004), p. 22.
28. Janice Galloway, *All Made Up* (London: Granta, 2011), p. 237.
29. Michael Gardiner, *The Cultural Roots of British Devolution* (Edinburgh University Press, 2004), p. 141.
30. See also Julia Jordan, 'A Fine Thing: A History of Chance', in her *Chance and the Modern British Novel* (London: Continuum, 2010), pp. 1–35.
31. Jackie Kay, *Red Dust Road* (London: Picador, 2010), p. 21, emphasis in original.
32. Agnes Owens, *For the Love of Willie,* in *Complete Novellas* (Edinburgh: Polygon, 2009), p. 312.
33. Robert Crawford, *Bannockburns: Scottish Independence and Literary Imagination, 1314–2014* (Edinburgh University Press, 2014), p. 213.

34. Liz Lochhead, *Mary Queen of Scots Got Her Head Chopped Off* and *Dracula* (Harmondsworth: Penguin, 1989), p. 59.
35. Maya Chowdhry, *The Crossing Path*, in *Shell Connections: New Plays for Young People*, ed. Suzy Graham-Adriani (London: Faber and Faber, 2003), p. 133.
36. Imtiaz Dharker, *I Speak for the Devil* (Tarset: Bloodaxe, 2001), pp. 57–68.
37. Imtiaz Dharker, *The Terrorist at my Table* (Tarset: Bloodaxe, 2006), p. 80.

14
Unsettling the Centre: Black British Fiction

Suzanne Scafe

'Black British', as a category of ethnic, racial, or political identity, is leaky and imprecise, serving most usefully to describe how individuals and their work are positioned both in contemporary British society and in relation to their pasts. In the late 1970s and 1980s 'black British' was commonly used to designate 'an "imagined community" comprising Caribbean, African, and South Asian experience in Britain', whose presence reflected its historical entanglement and the continued movement of populations between colonial territories and the metropolitan centre.[1] 'Black' also defined a culturally 'united front against an increasingly explicit racialised white national community', and was/is used as an aesthetic signifier of difference (Procter, p. 5). While more recently 'black' has been used to refer to a specific cultural heritage, whose identity is marked on the body as 'blackness',[2] such a designation necessarily exists in the context of a view of culture that 'accentuates its plastic, syncretic qualities and which does not see culture flowing into neat ethnic parcels but as a radically unfinished social process of self-definition and transformation'.[3] It is a view of history as a process of '*re-collection*, a re-assemblage of the past' (Procter, p. 2). As Buchi Emecheta's character Francis implies in *Second-Class Citizen* (1974), 'black' was a learned and, for many migrants, a deficit identity: 'West Indian, the Pakistanis ... Indians [and] African students are usually grouped together ... We are all blacks ... and the only houses we can get are horrors like these.'[4] It is not until his wife Adah reads James Baldwin that for her 'black' is transformed from a 'second-class' identity to one of positive value. Emecheta's example helps us comprehend how 'black' has functioned simultaneously as a divisive as well as an empowering concept, at once marking a mode of discrimination and a means of resistance.

The writers I discuss in this chapter inhabit more than one national or cultural location and are variously defined as African, Caribbean, British and/or black British; the locations and subjects of their fiction are equally diverse and complexly patterned. Despite a continuing tendency to read black women's writing for its representative function and for its potential to engage with issues of black Britishness, the effect of such multiple positioning has been, increasingly, to expand the critical parameters within which their work is discussed and to allow for critical approaches that are open to the works' interrogation of national, cultural, and locational borders. Emecheta sets much of her fiction – *Second-Class Citizen, Destination Biafra* (1982), *Gwendolyn* (1989), *Kehinde (*1994), and *The New Tribe* (2000), among others – in England and West Africa and has achieved in these texts both the construction of a dialogue between what is habitually defined as two opposing cultures and the expression of conflict and difference within cultures that are assumed to be homogeneous.

The fiction of a younger generation of writers also reflects the impossibility of fixed, stable identities: novels such as Bernardine Evaristo's *Lara* (1997), Diana Evans's *The Wonder* (2009), and Nadifa Mohamed's *Black Mamba Boy* (2010) use water as a dominant motif, reflecting the narratives' multiple crossings between continents – Africa, the Americas, and Europe – and the resulting emergence of plural, interconnected identities.[5] Few of the countries' borders are today the same as on the 1935 map that describes the world in which much of *Black Mamba Boy* is set: many names reflecting colonial ownership have changed – Anglo-Egyptian Sudan, Belgian Congo, Aden Protectorate – and what was (British) Somaliland does not now officially exist, except as a footnote on maps. Mohamed's novel opens in Richmond Park and ends in a series of locations in London: Piccadilly Circus, Soho, and finally aboard a ship in the East India docks, but the protagonist, Jama, begins his life as a market boy, wandering Aden's bustling, cosmopolitan capital. His search for freedom and material betterment takes him into Italian-occupied East Africa, where he is recruited as a soldier in Mussolini's colonizing army: the scenes that describe his journey from K'eftya on the Ethiopean and Eritrean border, to Alexandria, where he has heard he can obtain a British passport, are at once harrowing and fantastical, and are used to interweave the novel's political, historical, and personal themes. Through their representations of place – North West London, 'Londinium', or Notting Hill – these writers reveal the imprint of Britain's multicultural past on its present. Their work contests a 'deeply essentialist and internalist way of thinking about a place and its character', demonstrating rather that places are constructed from routes of 'interconnectedness with elsewhere' through histories of colonialism and the borderless reach of capital.[6]

'Writing reality'[7]

Whereas the work of a younger generation of writers resists an obligation to narrate black Britain, or 'to "speak for" the whole of that imagined community', an earlier writer such as Emecheta uses her writing to present sociocultural issues: forced or abusive marriages, political corruption, racism, and welfare dependency (Procter, p. 7). In *Second-Class Citizen,* Adah angrily opposes the assumption on the part of her husband, his friends, and their community of Nigerians that she would, like most Nigerian parents, send her children to foster parents, explaining in detail its hazards and its basis in negative experiences. For her husband, however, '[o]nly first-class citizens lived with their children, not the blacks' (p. 46). It is not surprising then that in *The New Tribe* she focuses on the experiences of a Nigerian boy, Chester, the son of white adoptive parents, who grows up as the only black child in a small English coastal town. In this novel, Emecheta returns to Liverpool, the place of arrival of her first protagonist, Adah, and transforms what had seemed to have been its grey monochrome into a hybrid, transcultural space marked by a constant flow of arrivals, departures, and settlement. As with most of her fiction, Emecheta does not allow a potentially traumatic experience to destroy her protagonist. The novel ends with a moving, if slightly contrived, moment of syncreticism: having travelled to Nigeria to find his 'true' identity in the kingdom of childhood visions that were derived from his adoptive mother's paintings, Chester encounters instead repeated corruption and a culture that is predicated on false identities. The 'home' to which he returns is the site of the painting's origins, of his adopted family, and his 'new tribe' of British-based friends.

In contrast to Emecheta, the fiction of Guyanese-born Beryl Gilroy (1924–2001), the other significant black woman writer of the 1970s, has suffered critical neglect. This is in part because her work resists generic classification and in part because it seems not to reflect the concerns of the writing community in which it participates. Despite having lived in England for most of her adult life, she is usually identified as a Caribbean woman writer and, with the exception of *Frangipani House* (1986), scholars have treated her fiction ambivalently.[8] Like Emecheta's *The New Tribe*, Gilroy's *The Green Grass Tango* (2001), published posthumously, returns to and transforms the urban space depicted in her previous fiction. Whereas in her first novel, *In Praise of Love and Children* (1994), completed in 1959 but published more than 30 years later, the London of her protagonists is used to reinforce racial difference, the South London park that is the setting of this work is a space that enables cultural transformation through individual, personal encounters.

Several black women writers who were publishing fiction in the 1980s and early 1990s were concerned to document lives that were hitherto invisible. Vernella Fuller's limpid prose and the quiet, simple plot of her first novel *Going Back Home* (1992) are used to emphasize her characters' ordinariness. Her protagonists' strong family structures are the spaces within which conflicts can be resolved through the care and kindness among families, to which Joan Riley's *A Kindness to the Children* (1992) gestures. Although Leone Ross's recent short fiction is more experimental, the popular realism of her first novel, *All the Blood is Red* (1996), depicts her female characters' experiences of economic and professional success but also their sexual exploitation in public and domestic spaces. Its focus, however, is the refusal of victimhood by her four first-person narrators and their achievement of agency. Simi Bedford's autobiographical novel, *Yoruba Girl Dancing* (1991), is similarly concerned with its protagonist's resistance and optimism: it opens with a portrait of a vibrant and culturally diverse Lagos, where her father is its richest man. Like Mohamed's Aden, it is, in the early to mid-twentieth century, 'always already a product of wider contacts ... already in part a product of global forces' (Massey, p. 83). The influence of these global forces is evident in Remi's family history: her grandmother is white and English, and her great-great-grandfather was an African slave in America who, in exchange for fighting for the British in the American wars of independence, was transported to Sierra Leone and promised freedom. This past is the subject of her novel *Not With Silver* (2007). The life Bedford narrates in *Yoruba Girl Dancing* is characterized by multiple dislocations which her protagonist survives, in part because of the security and privilege afforded by her early years in Lagos and in part because of an 'ironic distance' which she maintains from her own experiences. This distance is the source of Remi's sharp humour and offers her a psychological freedom: by the end of the novel, her unbelonging has become 'a kind of valued commodity'.[9]

John McLeod argues that, 'in contrast to Emecheta's work, Riley offers few obvious resistant or transformative resources for her central characters and their mercilessly bleak experiences' (2004, p. 111). In Emecheta, alienation and experiences of oppression are obstacles that have to be negotiated and overcome whereas in Riley they become her protagonists' identity. The focus of her novels is women who, like Adella in *Waiting in the Twilight* (1987), were part of the 'Windrush generation' of migrants, and their children, also migrants who, like the author herself, arrived in Britain as adolescents.[10] The title of her first novel, *The Unbelonging* (1984), has become a metaphor for the dis/ease experienced by those for whom racism inhibited any feeling of 'home' either in Britain or the Caribbean. Her female characters are trapped in the grim documentary style of Riley's prose and in the small, domestic spaces to which they are confined in both Britain and Jamaica. In the case of the first two novels, their lives in Britain are characterized by the 'harsher forms of patriarchal oppression within the isolation of the nuclear family'.[11] Riley's fourth novel, *A Kindness to the Children*, is set entirely In Jamaica. In an interview that coincided with its publication, Riley identified Sylvia, a qualified social worker specializing in child protection and on holiday in rural Jamaica, as the novel's 'main character', though not its protagonist.[12] The voice of the narrator and, indeed, the implied author is also that of the social worker, whose documenting of Jean's life has the cause and effect logic of a case study. Riley describes her protagonist's predicament using the first person:

> So Jean represents that kind of very painful reality ... Being emotionally attached to the Caribbean, I cannot leave the Caribbean, I cannot go back

> and I cannot leave; it's too much a part of my reality. I carry with me that space and yet I've made connections in another space and so I feel torn all the time. It's a form of psychosis sometimes. (p. 96)

Jean's brutal death frees all the characters in the novel, but primarily her children, who are saved from the cycle of destruction wrought by her 'psychosis': aided by the kindness of Sylvia, and their father who lives in Britain, the children escape to their home, England. Riley has said that she writes 'reality' and because her work's 'rhetorical power ... appear[s] to offer ... direct access to authentic subjective experience', her fiction has been read by critics as a testimony of recent black migration to Britain (Weedon, p. 90). It is also possible to read all her work as being, above all, preoccupied with patriarchal violence and abuse and the impossibility of its articulation. It is this that results in the women's dispossession and what Fred D'Aguiar has described as an '[u]nbelonging ... to my body', a separation or distance of mind from body that in D'Aguiar's own work is creative but in Riley's fiction results in the breakdown of either body or mind.[13] Rather than representative of 'reality', Riley's fiction presents particular experiences of damage and dysfunction. Her characters' migration to Britain does not in itself result in their anguish and dispossession: it is rather that their experience of abuse reconfigures the locations in which they are situated. In *A Kindness to the Children*, England is a place of safety, once the characters' own connections with an abusive past, and its destructive potential in the present, is broken.

'Extra dimensions': Bernardine Evaristo, Helen Oyeyemi, and Diana Evans[14]

Having begun writing in the 1990s, Evaristo could be considered a contemporary of Ross, Bedford, and even Riley. She has been more prolific, however, and unlike other texts discussed in this chapter, her work consistently confronts and resists realistic conventions. Although the writing for which she is most well known is defined as fiction or novels, she has said that the form that most interests her is poetry. She is drawn to poetry's 'linguistic inventiveness, imagistic freedom and the craft of concision' as well as its rhythm and sound.[15] Her novels-in-verse, *Lara* (1997) and *The Emperor's Babe* (2001), and her novel-with-verse, *Soul Tourists* (2005), reflect her interest in blurring generic categories, in formal experimentation, and in subverting expectations of both form and content. The second edition of the semi-autobiographical novel *Lara* includes changes to the text's paratexts – its cover, the table of contents, the epigraphs and so on – as well as an amplification of the content. The form of the work is reconfigured and, whereas the first edition uses page-long unrhymed verse, the 2009 edition uses the unrhymed couplets of *The Emperor's Babe*. These formal and structural adjustments to the novel significantly reconfigure its meaning and are evidence of Evaristo's determination to disrupt literary conventions and to confound critical responses to her work. The closing scenes of the novel, which depict a return to West Africa and Brazil, have suggested to many critics of the first edition that, although the identity the novel claims is British and is culturally and racially mixed, it privileges and recovers the African past of Lara's father.[16] However, the detailed accounts of her mother's German and Irish Catholic ancestry that appear in the second edition counter this, as does the cover photograph of the author's white British mother and black African-born father.

Subsequent novels also explore the past and its significance to the present, evident in the epigraphs to *The Emperor's Babe* and *Blonde Roots* (2008), both of which point to the importance of power, ownership, and perspective in historical narratives. By casting the slaves as British and white and the slave owners as black Africans, *Blonde Roots* unsettles racial discourses embedded in fictional and historical accounts of the Atlantic slave trade. Racial roles are not simply inverted: the narrative also scrambles historical time and space. It includes witty revisions of Conrad's *Heart of Darkness* (1899), parodic uses of nineteenth-century slave narratives, and, more problematically, Toni Morrison's American novel *Beloved* (1987). Even where the use of parody does not function to ridicule but to 'distance and, at the same time, to involve both artist and audience in a participatory hermeneutic activity',[17] its use is, as Judie Newman suggests, a 'risky strategy'.[18] Yet, where the text succeeds is in exposing the power relations that make possible a racialized discourse of dominance.

Less controversially, *The Emperor's Babe* is set in 'Londinium' during the decade before AD 211, the year that a legion of Moors was posted at Hadrian's Wall. Evaristo has acknowledged, both in interviews and in the text itself, the influence of Peter Fryer's *Staying Power: The History of Black People in Britain* (1984) on her decision to locate events in the novel during this period and it is perhaps this acknowledgement that has led to the repeated claim by critics that the novel 'documents' and reimagines Roman Britain or that it performs a 'counter-historical project'.[19] The African-born Roman Emperor Septimius Severus, Zuleika's Nubian identity, and characters such as Lucan Africanus, the baker of Fenchurch, invite such readings, but expectations that the novel will deliver a historically accurate narrative that recasts Roman London with diverse characters representing the reach of the Roman Empire are quickly subverted. A torrent of anachronisms, such as 'Fenchurch', demonstrates that a recovery of the past by seemingly straightforward manoeuvres, such as the inclusion of black characters in this otherwise populist version of history, is highly problematic. Counter-narratives that recover hidden or 'lost' pasts do so inevitably through a contemporary lens. In a detailed and astute reading of the novel, Dave Gunning argues that while Evaristo's Londinium is able to 'present the cosmopolitan reality of the modern metropolis', it also presents the city as a site of 'alienating power relations' and inequalities.[20] Through its representations of Zuleika and her participation in the culture of pampered luxury that confines her and makes her vulnerable to the envy of others – notably her Caledonian slave girls – the narrative offers a witty but trenchant critique of contemporary consumer culture and, in particular, the popularity of the self-regarding 'babe' or 'it girl' whose world is reflected in the pages of the '*Daily Looking Glass*' or 'the news tablet *Ave!*'[21] The consequences of imperial dominance and male sexual violence are everywhere in the narrative but Zuleika's lack of compassion, accompanied by a capacity for self-pity, is repeated several times. This lack reveals a shallow narcissism that is reflected in her attempts at poetry. While she aspires to be a great poet, her lines' lack of seriousness is heightened by the many references to Juvenal and Horace and, by implication, their use of poetry for public satire: her own art misses the opportunity to critique the world that imprisons and finally destroys her.

Although her novels, so far, do not exhibit the formal daring of Evaristo's work, Helen Oyeyemi's fiction is also complex and experimental. Despite her works' preoccupation with its own textuality and the repeated references to American and European writers, it is impossible to access the complexity of Oyeyemi's first three novels, *The Icarus Girl* (2005), *The Opposite House* (2007), and *White is for Witching* (2009), without an understanding of the importance of the 'world of signs rooted in Yoruba cosmology'.[22] Several critics have pointed to the recurrence of the figure of the twin in West African literature and in particular among the Yoruba, for whom the *ibeji* are believed to share a single soul.[23] *The Icarus Girl* combines both the mythic attributes of the dead twin, believed to haunt the living until it is appeased, and mythic references to the *abiku*, a negative figure in Nigerian literature, sometimes depicted as a 'spirit child ... the child who appears and disappears' (Bryce, p. 6).

These myths provide the context within which the character of Jessamy Harrison emerges, a precocious eight year old, who intuits late in the novel that she is the surviving twin. It is her twin's death that provides the novel with its themes of haunting and possession. Jessamy is a 'half-and-half child'.[24] The figure of the twin allows for the development of ideas concerning both the incomplete half and doubling, in the representation of Jess's biracial heritage, the narrative's use of two languages, and its crossing of two cultures and two mythological systems.[25] Both the half identity and structures of doubling suggest 'a loss of the spiritual link to Nigeria through physical displacement' (Bryce, p. 63). By 'writing back' to a tradition of male Yoruba writers, Amos Tutuola and D.O. Fagunwa in particular, but placing the 'feminine' as central to the narrative, *The Icarus Girl* effects a recovery of this connection.[26] Citing Oyeyemi's use of the Yoruba concept of the 'eerie bush', Diana Adesola Mafe argues that like these earlier male writers, Jess has to negotiate the ghostly bush, identified as various testing locations in the novel and serving as a 'haunted proving ground for her selfhood as a hybrid postcolonial subject' (p. 22). In this reading, Oyeyemi's 'postcolonial Female Gothic novel', with its concerns with repressed sexuality, creativity, and childbirth, appropriates the symbols of male power that include her literary antecedents, as well as her father, grandfather, and even her London therapist, in order to achieve an identity reflecting a cultural amalgam, rather than one that is half and half, or split in two (p. 31). The end of the novel is ambiguous and it is not clear what kind of rebirth is envisaged for Jess. At its most optimistic, the identity with which Jess emerges in the closing scenes is one that reflects the narrative itself. It is border crossing, experimental, and hybrid.

London-born Diana Evans's first novel, *26a* (2006), also uses twins as its central protagonists and, although the narrative moves easily from the spiritual to the real, its exploration of a mythic dimension does not suggest an indebtedness to Yoruba mythology or Nigerian literary traditions. *26a* is also concerned with hybridity as a site from which plural, overlapping identities emerge and, though less allegorically than Oyeyemi, with the consequences of being both half and double. Having migrated from Nigeria to Neasden, North London, as the very young bride of an older Yorkshire husband, Ida, the twins' mother, carries within her an inviolable space that is her first home. Her acute feelings of displacement result in the kind of psychosis to which Riley refers:

> For her, home was not homeless; it was one place, one heat, one tree. She made herself a bubble and it was called Nigeria-without-Aubrey ... At dinner, Ida sometimes said 'pass the pepper' in Edo ... in the early mornings she said, 'At home now, they're singing'.[27]

The family house, 26 Waifer Avenue, is not simply a materially defined location, but full of 'affective spaces', an emotionally charged place of colliding geographies, cultures, and identities.[28] It reflects and is defined by the parents' seeming incomprehension at the family they have created and by the children's encounters with the culture of the everyday: hair products, Michael Jackson posters, fish-tail skirts. As Ida sews her dressing gown, made from African fabric bought in Harlesden, she is returned to her past in Eruwa. This repeated image of the gown reflects the historical processes of circulation within and between particular spaces that cast and recast the hybrid locations of Evans's texts. The twins inhabit a space, the loft 26a, that is both their centre and a liminal space at the edge of the house, with its own additional inscription 'G + B' (p. 5). As McLeod argues, this address signifies both 'the crosshairs of the plus sign that beckons the nation into the novel's sights' and the text's 'cumulative twinning as a significant structural and conceptual device' (2010, p. 48).

One aspect of this 'conceptual' twinning is found in the narrative's concern with home and homelessness. For Georgia, the fragile, sensitive twin, 'home' is also one place: it is England not Nigeria, where they spent three years as young children. Scarred by her experience there of sexual abuse, Nigeria becomes a place and time to be feared. In contrast, her twin Bessi and the narrative itself privilege 'homelessness' which, like D'Aguiar's 'unbelonging', is a creative space and a means by which time and space can be collapsed and borders transgressed. Evans uses but does not romanticize the mythic or the spiritual. The oldest sister's spiritual powers are both enabling and limited; she senses Georgia's abuse and allows her to articulate her experience. Yet, though she dreams of Georgia's suicide, she is unable to prevent it. Furthermore, while the dead twin of the grandfather's Nigerian folk tale foreshadows her death, Georgia's fragility, in fact, mirrors her mother's: both characters are out of place.

Dislocation is a trope to which Evans returns in her second novel, *The Wonder* (2010), a text also characterized by the unexpectedness of the real and the fantastic. As with *26a,* its spaces of homelessness are both enabling and unsettling and its characters too are haunted by loss and absence. The novel opens with the son, Lucas, articulating his own moment of crisis, one which then introduces the novel's many themes: 'He was becoming aware that something happened to you at twenty-five ... a kind of dismantling, a poltergeist in the mind.'[29] Although the novel is structured around Lucas's quest to discover the identity of his father, Antoney, it is a complex, intricately structured, and self-reflexive narrative that uses detailed reference to dance to meditate on its own art and what it means to be an artist. The text's evocation of place is dense and absorbing but, at the same time, the characters seem unmoored from their surroundings, with the male characters in particular privileging the places their imaginations construct rather than a space in which they might be rooted. The words of Antoney's own father – 'If you stay in one place for too long you start to dry out ... You need a little stretch of sea between the years or the months' (p. 26) – predicts his lack of rootedness. He seems to be always on a 'magic carpet' of dreams and ambition and is unable to engage with the world below the clouds: 'there was a quality of lightness in him that gave rise to illusion. If you were not looking down at his feet, it was possible to suspect that he was afloat, that he was suspended just above water' (p. 51). That lightness becomes a thinning, a loss of self, and eventual disappearance in the face of repeated loss. The narrative offers no definitive ending to Antoney's story since, by the end of the novel, his presence has become more mythical than real.

Migratory circuits and 'real' places

The success of Zadie Smith's first novel, *White Teeth* (2000), was in some measure due to the perception that the narrative both participates in and critiques the fabrication of a 'Cool Britannia' and the collapsing of racial and cultural barriers that this identity invoked.[30] Casting a shrewd eye over the work's early critical reception, Philip Tew argues that responses 'memorialized the meaning of both the first novel and its author in culturally symbolic terms', both to confirm the text's success in seeming to register the new millennial zeitgeist and to express a 'neo-liberal, multicultural positivism – the very perspective her novel parodies and subverts'.[31] Smith's writing demonstrates the author's awareness of its 'worldliness or circumstantiality', of being 'always enmeshed in circumstance, time, place, and society'.[32] *White Teeth* maps out the preoccupations reflected in Smith's later work – with form, with place (North West London in particular), with the politics of culture and 'diversity', and with her work's place 'in the world' (Said, p. 35). It reflects what Laura Moss defines as 'the quotidian state of hybridity', which is neither antithetical to racism, nor to the history of violence that determined and continues to shape the contexts within which hybrid identities are formed. Rather, in Moss's analysis, the narrative employs hybridity as a contested but historically inevitable and therefore ordinary British identity.[33]

On Beauty (2005) is also concerned with the politics of hybridity and, as in *White Teeth*, with the limits of multiculturalism. Much critical attention has focused on its stated and evident intertextual relations with E.M. Forster, particularly *Howards End* (1910), and with Elaine Scarry, from whose study, *On Beauty and Being Just* (2001), the novel's title derives.[34] One of its central figures is the Haitian Vodou goddess Erzulie, who signifies the hybrid nature of a religion that combined beliefs from Europe, Africa, and the Americas.[35] As Susan Alice Fischer argues, the novel also positions itself in relation to traditions of African American women writers, in particular Zora Neale Hurston (1891–1960), whose interest in the African origins of syncretic religious practices in America led her to the study of Caribbean religions.[36] Most importantly, *On Beauty* addresses the 'worldliness' of its own identity, in a so-called post-racial America, and the socio-political contexts of aesthetic production. References abound to the Iraq War, to the 1991 Gulf War, to Black Power politics, poverty, exclusion, and, of course, to migration, arguably one of the novel's central interests. These references reflect Smith's concern both with the ways in which class, race, and gender intersect and transform seemingly natural categories, and with the social and material exclusions on which the production of beauty, art, and intellectual endeavour depend.[37]

Whereas *On Beauty*'s vast array of characters, and its emplotment of their interconnected lives through what seems to be Smith's trademark emphasis on coincidence, are all carefully controlled within a tightly managed narrative structure, *NW* (2012) self-consciously displays the limits of her own stylistic excesses. Despite its stylistic playfulness and Smith's sharp, satirical humour, as with *On Beauty*, its concerns are also with the unevenness of the circumstances within which lives intersect and with the inequalities on which success is predicated. Although Carl's exit from *On Beauty* might seem 'the weakest turn' of its intricate plotting, his departure reinforces the narrative's critique of the class privilege that underpins liberal ideologies (Batra, p. 1090). His failure to escape his class origins, and Howard's successful but conflicted escape, suggest that routes to social mobility, involving the complexities of both class and race, are hazardous and unpredictable. This is also the preoccupation of *NW* which uses a black woman, Keisha/Natalie, to dramatize and racialize the kind of unease Howard feels. In *NW*, more attention is paid to socially marginalized characters like Carl, though their presence is fleeting or ephemeral and their disappearance from the narrative is abrupt. Their function seems to be to expose the inadequacies of linear realism, with its dependence on rounded characters and on cause, effect, and coherence: these figures are so marginalized and under-examined in contemporary socio-cultural narratives, they elude representation. Although the dramatic but perfectly poised ending of *On Beauty* does not resolve the narrative's many conflicts, the dream-like quality of the journey that precedes the ambiguous, inconclusive ending of *NW* effects a textual unravelling that suggests an abdication of authorial control. The questions *NW* asks cannot be answered within the conventional borders of its realist form.

A similar preoccupation with realistically imagined place, with socio-historical issues, and with novelistic form, characterizes Andrea Levy's fiction, though the themes of her first four novels are more conventionally autobiographical and their form more typically realist. Her third novel, *Fruit of the Lemon* (1999), returns to the autobiographical figures of her first two novels, *Every Light in the House Burnin'* (1994) and *Never Far from Nowhere* (1996), but its more complex narration, in particular its use of multiple perspectives and synchronic temporalities, reflect the preoccupation with voice and with history that characterizes her later novels, *Small Island* (2004) and *The Long Song* (2010). The second half of *Fruit of the Lemon*, entitled 'Jamaica', is framed by the mother's repeated injunction to her daughter that she should know her roots. Identity is thus constructed as a question of place, necessitating a return to an imagined origin, Jamaica, in order that its protagonist can be at 'home' in England, despite its racism and the exclusions she had experienced. The Jamaican family's tales of her Scottish and Irish grandparents and great-grandparents are used to demonstrate the shared past of Britain and its colonies but also serve as a reminder of the ways in which colonialism continues to mark the bodies of its ex-subjects. Faith's blue-eyed cousin, Constance, attaches herself to an African-centred culture, producing in her a splitting, masking, and a breakdown that mirrors Faith's own and which, for both, results from experiences of exclusion based on perceptions of their otherness. Such scenes have been read as evidence of the narrative's concern with the traumatic effects of colonialism.[38] They also reflect the preoccupation in Levy's later novels with overlapping histories and identities and attest to the fact, as H. Adlai Murdoch points out, not only that 'migration and displacement have long been critical factors in shaping Caribbean sites both home and overseas' but that British identities at 'home and overseas' are always already hybrid (p. 87).

Murdoch further argues that writers such as Levy 'draw on their sense of Caribbeanness as a way of reconstituting their cultural identities within a new framework of subaltern metropolitan resistance', and the use of the backward glance certainly determines the construction of the present in Levy's recent novels (p. 83). As with her previous work, the characters' experiences in *Small Island* are drawn from Levy's own: her father was a *Windrush* migrant, arriving in Britain in 1948, and her mother and mother-in-law are reflected in the characters Queenie and Hortense.[39] Levy uses her first-person narrators' voices, Queenie's elocution-inflected English, and Hortense's awkward reaching after Standard English to reflect their class, as well as cultural identity.[40] Her use of four intersecting first-person narrators allows her to engage sympathetically with her white English characters, to present Bernard's racism as a component of, perhaps even deriving from, his many inadequacies, and to allow Queenie to carry the emotional weight of the novel; the articulation of her anguish at having to give her son away creates one of the novel's most affecting scenes. The birth of Michael, Queenie's illegitimate son by Hortense's cousin and first love, allows all four characters an opportunity to connect for the first time in the novel but it also represents the culmination, evident throughout the novel, of Levy's interest in the plural, interconnecting identities that are the product of a history of slavery, colonialism, and empire. The narrative privileges the creolized identities of its Caribbean subjects; thus, Michael's 'mixed-race' identity reflects that of his adoptive as well as his biological parents. However, as Queenie eloquently argues, the racism that characterizes the novel's setting, late 1940s England, and that prevents the possibility of real interconnection, means that Michael has to be adopted. Nevertheless, Michael has not been abandoned and it is possible to read Gilbert and Queenie's acceptance of their adopted baby as a gesture that looks forward to a society that will benefit from the tolerance and generosity of its former colonial subjects.

The writers discussed in this chapter both use and contest the category 'British', predicting, through their privileging of circuits of identities, a post-national and increasingly globalized future. Aminatta Forna and Delia Jarrett-Macauley have both written novels that explore the civil conflict that destroyed Sierra Leone, during the 1990s: for both it involved an imaginative return to the country of their parents – the father in the case of Forna. The novels use the perspectives of outsiders: in Jarrett-Macauley's *Moses, Citizen and Me* (2005), her protagonist is a girl travelling from London to visit family in Sierra Leone, and in Forna's second novel, *The Memory of Love* (2010), one of the main characters is a white English clinical psychologist who goes to work with the war's casualties. Like much of the writing discussed in this chapter, their fiction intersects the personal and the political. The novels focus on the ways in which civil wars involve personal traumas and betrayals; individuals are murdered by their neighbours or a family member becomes the enemy. In Forna's text, sexual intimacies are used to dramatize the awareness of 'bodily disappearance – of missing limbs ... of the corpse'.[41]

Although black women's writing might be thought to express a minor key in contemporary literary production, their fiction has transformed and continues to test simple generic categories. Their work actively intervenes in contemporary novelistic traditions, extending and transforming the genre in bold or in more subtly challenging ways. By so doing, these novels enliven and renew a form whose death is routinely foretold. Several writers explored here have won or been shortlisted for international literary prizes: Emecheta, Oyeyemi, Mohamed, and Smith (on two occasions) have been included in the *Granta* Best of Young British Novelists, an influential list of 20 writers, drawn up every ten years. It can be argued that black British women's writing is in the vanguard of black British literary production: it interrogates and continues to redefine concepts of 'Britishness' but, more broadly, contests assumptions about individual, cultural, and national identities.

Notes

1. James Procter, ed., *Writing Black Britain, 1948–98: An Interdisciplinary Anthology* (Manchester University Press, 2000), p. 5.
2. Henry Louis Gates Jnr, 'A Reporter at Large: Black London', *Black British Culture and Society*, ed. Kwesi Owusu (London: Routledge, 2000), p. 178.
3. Paul Gilroy, *Small Acts: Thoughts on the Politics of Black Cultures* (London: Serpent's Tail, 1993), p. 61.
4. Buchi Emecheta, *Second-Class Citizen* (Oxford: Heinemann, 1994), p. 35.
5. For a detailed discussion of water imagery in *Lara*, see John McLeod, *Postcolonial London: Rewriting the Metropolis* (London: Routledge, 2004), pp. 177–88.
6. Doreen Massey, 'Places and Their Pasts', *History Workshop*, 39 (1995), pp. 182–92.
7. Joan Riley, 'Writing Reality in a Hostile Environment', *Kunapipi*, 16:1 (1994), pp. 547–52.
8. Sandra Courtman, 'Women Writers and the Windrush Generation: A Contextual Reading of Beryl Gilroy's *In Praise of Love and Children* and Andrea Levy's *Small Island*', *EnterText*, 9 (2012), pp. 84–104; Abigail Ward, 'Postcolonial Interventions into the Archive of Slavery: Transforming Documents into Monuments in Beryl Gilroy's *Stedman and Joanna*', *The Journal of Commonwealth Literature*, 45:2 (2010), pp. 245–58.
9. Martin Japtok, 'Two Postcolonial Childhoods: Merle Hodge's *Crick Crack Monkey* and Simi Bedford's *Yorbua Girl Dancing*', *Jouvert: A Journal of Postcolonial Studies*, 6:1–2 (Fall 2001). Para. 16, http://english.chass.ncsu.ed/jouvert/v6i1-2/con61.htm, accessed 20 November 2013.
10. In May 1948 the *Empire Windrush* arrived in Tilbury Docks, Essex carrying, among its other passengers, 492 migrants from the Caribbean. This is often depicted as a founding moment in the history of Caribbean migration to the United Kingdom. Those arriving from the Caribbean during this period are referred to as the 'Windrush generation'.

11. Chris Weedon, 'Identity and Belonging in Contemporary Black British Writing', *Black British Writing*, ed. R. Victoria Arana and Lauri Ramey (Basingstoke: Palgrave Macmillan, 2004), p. 81.
12. 'Joan Riley, with Aamer Hussein', *Writing Across Worlds: Contemporary Writers Talk*, ed. Susheila Nasta (London: Routledge, 2004), p. 95.
13. Fred D'Aguiar, 'Home is Always Elsewhere: Individual and Communal Regenerative Capacities of Loss', in Owusu, p. 197.
14. John McLeod, 'Extra Dimensions, New Routines', *Wasafiri*, 25:4 (2010), p. 45.
15. Michael Collins, '"My Preoccupations are in My DNA": An Interview with Bernardine Evaristo', *Callaloo*, 31:4 (2008), p. 1199.
16. Kadija Sesay, 'Transformations Within the Black British Novel', in Arana and Ramey, p. 102; Pilar Cuder-Domínguez, 'Evaristo's *Lara* and *The Emperor's Babe*', *Imagined Londons*, ed. Pamela K. Gilbert (Albany: State University of New York Press, 2000), p. 178; Şebnem Toplu, *Fiction Unbound: Bernardine Evaristo* (Newcastle upon Tyne: Cambridge Scholars Press, 2011), p. 45.
17. Linda Hutcheon, *A Poetics of Postmodernism: History, Theory, Fiction* (London: Routledge, 1988), p. 35.
18. Judie Newman, 'The Black Atlantic as Dystopia: Bernardine Evaristo's *Blonde Roots*', *Comparative Literature Studies*, 49:2 (2012), p. 286.
19. See Maria Helena Lima, 'The Politics of Teaching Black *and* British', in Arana and Ramey, p. 61; Cuder-Domínguez in Gilbert, p. 182; Toplu, p. 26.
20. Dave Gunning, 'Cosmopolitanism and Marginalisation in Bernardine Evaristo's *The Emperor's Babe*', *Write Black, Write British: From Post Colonial to Black British Literature*, ed. Kadija Sesay (Hertford: Hansib Publications, 2005), p. 167, p. 170.
21. Bernardine Evaristo, *The Emperor's Babe* (Harmondsworth: Penguin, 2001), p. 99, p. 174, p. 175.
22. Jane Bryce, '"Half and Half Children": Third Generation Women Writers and the African Novel', *Research in African Literatures*, 39:2 (2008), p. 53.
23. Diana Adesola Mafe, 'Ghostly Girls in the "Eerie Bush": Helen Oyeyemi's *The Icarus Girl* as Postcolonial Female Gothic Fiction', *Research in African Literatures*, 43:3 (2012), p. 24; Pilar Cuder-Domínguez, 'Double Consciousness in the Work of Helen Oyeyemi and Diana Evans', *Women: A Cultural Review*, 20:3 (2009), p. 279.
24. Helen Oyeyemi, *The Icarus Girl* (London: Bloomsbury, 2006), p. 15.
25. Madelaine Hron, '*Ora Na-azu nwa*: The Figure of the Child in Third Generation Nigerian Novels', *Research in African Literatures*, 39:2 (2008), p. 37.
26. See Mafe, p. 30 and Bryce, p. 63.
27. Diana Evans, *26a* (London: Vintage, 2006), p. 97.
28. Nigel Thrift, 'Space', *Theory, Culture and Society*, 23:2–3 (2006), p. 143.
29. Diana Evans, *The Wonder* (London: Vintage, 2010), p. 12.
30. 'Cool Britannia' is a term coined and perpetuated by the British media to describe the optimism and reinvigorated and culturally inclusive patriotism that defined the late 1990s. This supposed redefinition of Britishness saw the return of a Labour government after an absence of almost 20 years. In *Creolizing the Metropole: Migrant Identities in Literature and Film* (Bloomington: Indiana University Press, 2012), H. Adlai Murdoch uses this term to describe the Britain to which *White Teeth* refers (p. 173).
31. Philp Tew, *Zadie Smith* (Basingstoke: Palgrave Macmillan, 2010), p. 118, p. 125.
32. Edward W. Said, *The World, the Text, and the Critic* (London: Faber and Faber, 1984), pp. 34–5.
33. Laura Moss, 'The Politics of Everyday Hybridity', *Wasafiri*, 38:3 (2003), pp. 11–17.

34. See, for example, Alice Ridout, *Contemporary Writers Look Back: From Irony to Nostalgia* (London: Continuum, 2010), pp. 103–22; Ann Marie Adams, 'A Passage to Forster: Zadie Smith's Attempt to "Only Connect" to *Howards End*', *Critique*, 52:4 (2011), pp. 277–399. Lourdes Lopez-Ropero also notes intertextual links to campus novels of writers such as David Lodge and Malcolm Bradbury in 'Homage and Revision: Zadie Smith's Use of E.M. Forster in *On Beauty*', *Commonwealth Essays and Studies*, 32:2 (2010), pp. 7–20. See also Dorothy J. Hale, '*On Beauty* as Beautiful? The Problem of Novelistic Aesthetics By Way of Zadie Smith', *Contemporary Literature*, 53:4 (2012), p. 815.
35. Nicole King, 'Creolisation and *On Beauty*: Form, Character and the Goddess Erzulie', *Women: A Cultural Review*, 20:3 (2009), p. 267.
36. Susan Alice Fischer, 'A Glance from God': Zadie Smith's *On Beauty* and Zora Neale Hurston', *Changing English*, 14:3 (2007), pp. 285–97.
37. For a political reading of *On Beauty*, see Regine Jackson, 'Imagining Boston: Haitian Immigrants and Place in Zadie Smith's *On Beauty*', *Journal of American Studies*, 46:4 (2012), pp. 855–73, and Kanika Batra, 'Kipps, Belsey and Jegede: Cosmopolitanism, Transnationalism, and Black Studies in Zadie Smith's *On Beauty*', *Callaloo*, 33:4 (2010), pp. 1079–92.
38. See Maria Helena Lima, 'Pivoting the Centre', in Sesay, p. 71; Ole Birk Laursen, '"Telling Her a Story": Remembering Trauma in Andrea Levy's Writing', *EnterText*, 9 (2012), pp. 53–68; Claudia Marquis, 'Crossing Over: Postmemory and the Postcolonial Imaginary in Andrea Levy's *Small Island* and *Fruit of the Lemon*', *EnterText*, 9 (2012), pp. 31–52.
39. Blake Morrison, 'Andrea Levy Interviewed by Blake Morrison', *Women: A Cultural Review*, 20:3 (2009), p. 331.
40. Cynthia James, '"You'll Soon Get Used to Our Language": Language, Parody and West Indian Identity in Andrea Levy's *Small Island*', *Anthurium: A Caribbean Studies Journal*, 5:1 (2007), 29 paras, http://scholarlyrepository.miami.edu/anthurium/vol5/iss1/3, accessed 20 November 2013.
41. Zoe Norridge, 'Sex as Synecdoche: Intimate Languages of Violence in Chimamanda Ngozi Adiche's *Half of a Yellow Sun* and Aminatta Forna's *The Memory of Love*', *Research in African Literatures*, 43:2 (2012), p. 35.

15

Redefining Britishness: British Asian Fiction

Ruvani Ranasinha

This chapter argues that British Asian women's fiction does not stem from a solely ghettoized presence, nor from a separate, segregated history as is sometimes assumed. Rather, this body of writing tends to redefine notions of 'Britishness' as well as what constitutes feminism. The reworking of Euro-American feminism by some British Asian female authors points to their impact on contemporary women's writing. Many of the concerns of these writers about the legacies of colonialism for women, the burden and appeal of home and family in British Asian contexts, and the patriarchal underpinnings of nations and religious or caste-based communities overlap with key debates in postcolonial feminism. This work constitutes an intervention that is redefining two of the most prominent disciplinary formations, postcolonialism and feminist studies, each in its double role as institutional discourse and political movement. In recent years, a new globalized generation of female-authored texts have probed the relationship between postcolonial feminism and globalization. Situated within a postcolonial feminist paradigm, these fictions resonate with the ampler spatial, political, and conceptual reaches of globalization.

There is a long history in Britain of Asian women writers – Cornelia Sorabji (1866–1954), Atiya Fyzee (1877–1967), Attia Hosain (1913–98) – and of Asian feminism.[1] The Indian princesses Sophia Duleep Singh (1876–1948) and Catherine Duleep Singh (1871–1942) were involved in the suffragette movement, and the Indian poet-politician Sarojini Naidu (1879–1949) emphasized the role of women in sustaining cultural nationalism in Ireland and India in late Victorian London. Asian feminists in Britain have long been motivated by an international feminism of equals, rather than the idea that the British were responsible for the emancipation of Asian women.

South Asian migration to Britain dates back to the seventeenth century and has a much longer and more complex history than is usually acknowledged in the customary emphasis on postwar migration. However, unprecedented waves of South Asian migrants to Britain arrived as a direct result of the aftermath of colonialism. In the wake of Indian independence in

1947 and Sri Lankan in 1948, the Nationality Act (1948) gave citizens of the former colonies rights of residence in Britain. Perceived links to the 'mother country' made Britain with its open door policy, fuelled by its need for labour, a natural choice for migrants. This was the case not just for the 492 'West Indian' arrivals on the *Empire Windrush* but also for many South Asians fleeing from the turmoil of partition. Riots in London, Liverpool, and Birmingham against the newly arrived 'coloured' immigrants followed. This period marked the establishment of black and Asian populations and an important shift in British identity. During the late 1950s and early 1960s, large numbers of economic migrants arrived from India and Pakistan, settling in the northern industrial cities of Manchester and Leeds as well as London. The regional loyalties these areas invite are crucial in the formation of British Asian identities. Kenyan and Ugandan Asians, expelled from Kenya in 1969 and Uganda in 1971, fuelled the widespread use of the term 'Asian' as a collective category for all subcontinentals in Britain. Bangladeshi communities followed, leaving floods and civil war in the early 1970s. Smaller numbers of Sri Lankans arrived in Britain in the context of a Marxist insurrection and its brutal suppression in 1971. The waves of immigration resulted in new laws to restrict Asian and black migration. The Immigration Act of 1971 removed the *automatic* right of dependents to join families. Received ideas on race, citizenship, and nationality were dismantled and documented anew by the next wave of South Asian, African, and Caribbean writers to arrive in Britain.

Historical contexts and literary genealogies

Indian writers such as Kamala Markandaya (1924–2004) and Anita Desai first launched their literary careers in Britain in the mid-1950s and 1960s respectively when, in sharp contrast to today, South Asian material was considered a commercial liability in metropolitan publishing houses. Although somewhat supported by the development of liberal university interest in Commonwealth Literature in the 1960s, Markandaya stopped writing in 1982 when literary conditions in Britain were no longer auspicious for her rarefied, leisurely novels about the Indo-British encounter and feminized, exotic versions of India. In contrast, the fictions of Desai and Hosain, which placed women at the centre of their chronicles of newly independent India and Pakistan, increased in popularity over time. However, the occasional migrant writer does not constitute a category. Minority literature is a matter of mass and becomes a phenomenon when substantial numbers of writers constitute a literary scene. Thus postwar migration radically changed the context for the appreciation and consumption of South Asian minority culture in Britain.[2]

Since the 1970s, Asian women have established an increasingly strong presence on the British cultural scene and their work has become increasingly marketable. During the 1970s, black and Asian feminist activity was largely expressed through grassroots political action and an involvement in labour struggles. The strike at the Grunwick Film Processing Laboratories exploded stereotypes of passive Asian women and marked their public assertion of rights as workers and British citizens. Similarly, the surge of British Asian women fiction writers (Meera Syal, Ravinder Randhawa, Rukhsana Ahmad, and Farhana Sheikh) during the 1980s and 1990s was provoked by the politics of Thatcherism in this period, particularly the cuts to public spending and the racialization of immigration. This flowering was supported at first by the Greater London Council (GLC), media institutions such as Channel 4 (created in 1982), and by the then newly established feminist publishing houses. The GLC funded the Asian Women Writers Collective (AWWC 1984–97) founded by writer-activist Randhawa, which provided a platform for several women who became established writers, notably Ahmad and Syal. It produced two landmark anthologies of British Asian women's writing, *Right of Way: Prose and Poetry* (1988) and *A Flaming Spirit* (1994), both published by The Women's Press. The Women's Press also published several foundational British Asian novels by female authors: Leena Dhingra's *Amritvela* (1986), which addresses the question of living between two cultures through the story of a woman's return to India after years of being in England; Randhawa's *A Wicked Old Woman* (1987), which traces Kulwant Singh's escapades as she challenges the Orientalist fantasies of ex-boyfriends and Labour Party comrades; and Sheikh's *The Red Box* (1991), discussed below. In this climate, Virago republished Hosain's *Sunlight on a Broken Column* (first published in 1961 but out of print for many years) in its Modern Classics series. Set on the brink of independence, Hosain's exploration of the emerging gendered national identities of India and Pakistan has influenced younger writers such as Kamila Shamsie and Tahmima Anam.

During this period, diverse black and Asian feminists formed anti-racist, anti-sexist, and socialist collectives such as the Southall Black Sisters (1979) and Women Against Fundamentalism (1990), publishing co-operatives (Sheba) that shared a common membership with the AWWC, and theatre and film collectives such as the British Asian Theatre Company, Asian Theatre Co-operative, Tamasha, Tara Arts, and the Kali Theatre Company. These groups were formed, in part, to protest against the racial attacks on Asian communities and to draw more Asian women into the theatre. However, the explosive 'black' urban uprisings in Southall (1979), Bristol (1980), and Toxteth and Brixton (1981) overtook these responses. This heady mix of political activism and diverse generic and cultural influences stimulated writers such as Ahmad, co-founder of Kali Theatre Company, and the actress, screenwriter, and novelist Syal, whose fictions are imbued with references to popular culture and Bollywood films. Ahmad recalls how 'the AWWC was an exciting discovery – a group of women from the subcontinent all interested in writing, in feminist politics and in each other's work'.[3]

Syal's semi-autobiographical first novel, *Anita and Me* (1996), set in a declining West Midlands mining village, and Ahmad's debut novel, *The Hope Chest* (1996), about three women linked though service and friendship, offer perspectives from different generations of British Asian females and insights into the complexities of mother–daughter relationships. Both counter the elision of female diasporic identity in patrilineal, normative accounts of diaspora. They question what Gayatri Gopinath identifies as the centrality of the male–male or father–son trope in imagining diaspora, in addition to destabilizing what Stuart Hall terms as 'the essential black subject' with their flawed, complex minority characters.[4]

By the late 1980s, the solidarity that prompted diverse Africans, Caribbeans, and Asians to form co-operatives and to categorize themselves as 'black' began to founder politically. Some Asians felt they were subsumed within the 'black anti-racist' model: in 1987 the AWWC decided not to include the term 'black' in the name of their organization. The term 'Asian' was retained because it was felt that a forum for specifically Asian women writers in Britain was necessary. In 1988, the Commission for Racial Equality recommended that people of South Asian origin should no longer be classified as 'black'. This indicated the emergence of the term 'British Asian' and the geographical and political category 'South Asian' which originated in the US. One could argue that 'British Asian' is now an outdated construct given how mainstream is the fiction of these writers. Yet 'British Asian' and 'South Asian' continue to be powerful marketing categories.

Anti-racist, 'black' British, and postcolonial feminist aesthetics

From the 1980s, the emergent field of postcolonial feminist scholarship marked a rising discontent with Eurocentric, white, middle-class models of feminism where questions of race, class, caste, language, religion, and location remained relatively unaddressed. The ground-breaking, historically specific scholarship of black and Asian feminists including bell hooks, Gayatri Chakravorty Spivak, Chandra Talpade Mohanty, and Trinh T. Minh-ha presented a significant challenge to mainstream Western feminism.[5] Similarly, Hazel Carby's influential article 'White Woman Listen! Black Feminism and the Boundaries of Sisterhood' (first published in 1982) represents the debates among black and Asian feminists in Britain that influenced British Asian women novelists.

Collectively, albeit in diverse ways, authors such as Randhawa and Syal engage with the argument of Mohanty et al. that Western feminist theory enacts discursive colonization: the assumptions about Third World oppression mean 'Western feminists alone become the true "subjects" of this counter-history. Third-world women, on the other hand, never rise above the debilitating generality of their "object" status.'[6] For instance, Kulwant, the protagonist of Randhawa's *A Wicked Old Woman* (1987), finally finds community in a group of women who overcome their differences as they fight against the popular misrepresentation of British Asian female identities. Other novelists, such as Ahmad and Syal, highlight ethnocentric feminism's blindness to white, patriarchal structures by delineating the gendered constraints that affect women of British as well as subcontinental backgrounds. Ahmad's *The Hope Chest* features a white protagonist, Ruth, whose fraught relationships with her foster mother and her husband undermine the exclusive focus on the control of women in the Third World and the polarity of 'modern' relationships versus problematic arranged marriages. These writers also assert the importance of subcontinental feminisms. Syal cites the Indian feminist journal, *Manushi*, as a key influence on her writing: 'each issue I tracked down was treasured. It made me realise that feminism was not a Western invention'.[7] Challenging assumptions within Euro-American feminism that framed Third World women as victims, her novels emphasize how women can claim agency, an affirmative energy, and dignity in the most difficult of circumstances. Drawing on the insights of postcolonial feminists, the representation of agency, subjectivity, and the formulation of a politics of resistance to different forms of patriarchal oppression emerge in all the fiction of these women writers.

While none of her feisty British Asian women characters are victims, Syal does not overlook culturally specific gendered and patriarchal expectations. These roles are not merely rearticulated but heightened in the process of migration by both the majority and minority community. British Asian women are positioned at an especially painful intersection between the West and their ethnic background. In a very different kind of story to *Anita and Me*, Syal's second novel *Life Isn't All Ha Ha Hee Hee* (1999) explores in the style of chick lit the particular experiences of three middle-class 30-something women from East London's British Asian community who have been friends since childhood. The novel is divided into two halves that correspond to different seasons, winter and spring. The two halves are each divided into three sections that shift the narrative point of view between the three central female characters, Chila, Sunita, and Tania. Their portrayals reveal the distinct ways in which the socialization and subordination of some British Asian women can reproduce relations of domination and subordination. The novel charts Chila's growth to feminist realization as her marriage falls apart. Sunita's promising career as a lawyer seemed certain; now a dissatisfied mother, she contemplates her vanished career, veering between guilt and the fear that she will become like so many of her mother's friends, reeking of the 'sour, damp smell of unfulfilled potential'.[8] Tania, a chic TV producer with a white British boyfriend, makes an analogous recognition of the way some British Asian women excel in the workplace: where they 'meet the world head on, we meet our men and we bow down gratefully ... we hear our mothers' voices and heed them' (p. 145). Syal counters her own emphasis on the performative nature of cultural identity with the insight that certain gendered expectations humorously named 'the Sita Complex' (the internalization of the idea that marriage and partnership are equated with trial and suffering) are harder to evade than others. Tania concludes: 'Everything else I can pick up or discard when I choose: my culture is a moveable feast. Except for this rogue gene which I would cauterise away if I could' (p. 146).

Syal's second novel explores the challenge of culturally specific forms of oppression and the dilemma of the black/Asian feminist writer who is required to say nothing about gender oppression within minority communities and to keep hidden what could be pathologized within a context of racism. The novel thematizes this very problem when Sunita plans to expose hospitals that refuse to tell pregnant Asian women the sex of their babies only to be 'caught out by the enemy within' when she hears about an Asian clinic 'where they guarantee you will have a boy: there wasn't any point in pursuing it after that' (p. 213). The burden of representation on British Asian women writers is doubly determined: feminist critiques of patriarchal practices within South Asia or amongst ethnic minority communities are interpreted as not only pathologizing communities but also as colluding with Eurocentric Western feminism.

Syal places considerably more emphasis on male–female relationships amongst the South Asian diaspora in Britain than Ahmad or Randhawa, allowing for a wider representation of South Asian diasporic and white British masculinities; this is, perhaps, an influence of the rise of Men's Studies and the new critical reflection on men and masculinity in the 1990s. She balances her negative portrayal of traditional South Asian men with an awareness of how seemingly progressive versions of white male identity often mask strategies for reinforcing traditional gender hierarchies. For example, in contrast to patriarchal South Asian men like Chila's husband, Deepak, who attempts to control women by denying them access to paid labour, Tania's boss, Jonathan, welcomes women into the workforce. Nevertheless, Jonathan's support of women entering the labour market is dependent on them occupying subordinate positions that do not challenge his membership in an elite 'panel of forty-something white men' (p. 188). Consequently, Tania observes that beneath his 'smiling exterior' and superficially egalitarian conception of gender, Jonathan remains ruthlessly determined to retain his privileged position in the world system (p. 61). Jonathan's ostensibly non-confrontational approach to business leadership within his company and the absence of masculinist attributes exemplify the new feminized versions of elite white male identity that have emerged in response to multinational business practices. But, as Jonathan demonstrates, this shift in identity does not come with a commensurate shift in power. A similar recentring of white male identity is evident in Martin, who has 'a developed feminine side'. Yet, Tania remarks of Martin, 'scratch a New Man and a prehistoric snake always slithers out' (p. 144). Consequently, Tania's increasing success and greater earning power lay bare that Martin's embrace of his feminine side is primarily a strategy for attracting women, which, as with Jonathan, does not extend to a legitimate desire to share power in his relationship with Tania, or with women more broadly.

However, the most distinctive and significant feature of Syal's aesthetic is her portrayal of feminist British Asian characters who subvert patriarchal structures whilst remaining *within* their community. Both *Anita and Me* and *Life Isn't All Ha Ha Hee Hee* are peopled with British Asian female characters 'always proud to be who they were, but not scared to push back the boundaries' (*Life*, p. 84). When Syal's work first came to the fore her intervention in this regard stood in marked contrast to options outlined for Asian feminists in existing cultural representations. Notably, Hanif Kureishi's British Asian feminist characters from Muslim backgrounds – Yasmin in *Borderline* (1981), Tania in *My Beautiful Laundrette* (1986), and outspoken, self-educated feminist Jamila in *The Buddha of Surburbia* (1990) – can only achieve autonomy and self-liberation by withdrawal and rejection of community, culture, and religion. In this way, his work repeats hegemonic constructions of British Muslim women by continuing to represent assimilation into a *secular* British culture/Western global modernity as a progressive narrative for South Asian Muslim women.

From British Asian to British Muslim

Syal's characters subvert patriarchal structures within notably *non*-Muslim British Asian communities and this marks the emerging split between British Asian female subjectivity and British Muslim female subjectivity. This is not to say that agency and resistance to assimilation are not depicted in relation to British Muslim female subjectivities. In Farhana Sheikh's neglected novel *The Red Box* (1991), the British Muslim female protagonist Raisa embodies an even-handed approach to cultural exchange and, hence, her ideas of gender are not only shaped by Western culture, but also by an Islamic world-view, as well as the expectations and values of her Pakistani family. *The Red Box* investigates the complexity of gender identities within a British Asian community in London by representing the lives of three women from very different backgrounds: Raisa, Tahira, and Nasreen. The narrative is organized around the meetings of these three women as part of Raisa's academic research project, enabling Sheikh to explore the memories, expectations, and identities of the women and their families. The looseness of the structure allows for a variety of narrative modes to be employed: sections are written in both the first and third person, while the transcription of the interviews between the three women constructs a dramatic dialogue that creates the impression of each woman being given an unmediated voice in the text. The novel ends with a long letter written by Raisa to Tahira and Nasreen that attempts to explain her own complex family background and make sense of the lives that her research has uncovered. This lack of narrative unity reflects Sheikh's refusal to collapse the three women's subjectivities into a monolithic female identity, or even a more nuanced division between British Asian or Muslim female identity. Rather, the novel illustrates that gender is negotiated within a complex series of relationships and interconnected narratives that reveal globalization to have uneven and, at times, conflicting effects on the gender identities and lives of the women.

Like Syal's protagonists, Raisa refuses to reject her South Asian background. So, in her work with Tahira and Nasreen, she explicitly frames issues of gender quality within the context of the Quran. Consider the following exchange between the three women:

> Allah regards all men and women as equal, Nasreen read from her notes and then expanded on them.
> —You know, even though they have different roles to play, He still regards both as being equal and does not see one superior to the other, and He will give both His full protection, and give both equal unmatchable rewards, you know, as no other can.
> —God! Tahira breathed out loudly. —She does sound like a book and she ain't even reading.
> Raisa said, —When you say they are equal but they have different roles, what do you mean?
> —Like in the eyes of Allah, He sees both men and women as equal. I mean, if man does good, He won't think it's better than if the woman did good. He rewards equal rewards to both.
> —What about these different roles? Does this text tell you what the roles of a woman are?
> —No, but it's sort of, Nasreen was struggling for clarity, —you know the woman, she brings up the children, and she looks after the house, she cooks the dinner, and she washes her husband's clothes. Everything like that, and the man's sort of the breadwinner. He earns for them.
> —Is that written here? Where does it tell you that?
> —It implies it. Nasreen looked at the table top.
> —Perhaps you bring the idea from somewhere else. Perhaps you read it somewhere else. Maybe in your particular translation of the Qu'ran.[9]

Raisa's reading of the Quran here is grounded in what she refers to as its radical teaching on sexual equality. From this perspective, the gender roles that Nasreen identifies in Islam are not supported textually by the Quran but are rather ideas that she brought 'from somewhere else' (pp. 128–9). According to Raisa, therefore, problematic gender roles and identities for women evident in certain Muslim societies are not inherent to the Quran but rather reflect how it has been used to justify patriarchal practices. The distinction is important because it means that a conception of gender equality can be worked out within Islamic culture, thereby contesting oversimplified representations of Islam as inherently oppressive to women.

Novelists Monica Ali and Kamila Shamsie similarly deconstruct hegemonic ideas of Islam as inherently patriarchal. Their later fiction needs to be seen in relation to the increasing number of fictional and non-fictional representations of Islam and Muslims by both Muslim and non-Muslim authors and commentators. Their work connects to a number of public and political discourses: realignments since the Cold War; the Rushdie affair (1989); the ongoing effect of international suspicion and demonization of Muslim identities since the 9/11 attacks; the inception of the so-called 'War on Terror'; the London bombings of 2005; and the negative effects of contemporary discourses of Islamophobia.[10] These responses include increasingly reductive views of Islam and Islamic fundamentalism and a more pronounced dichotomy between Islam and 'the West', alongside hegemonic representations of Islam as inherently oppressive to women. Like Sheikh, Shamsie's early fictions about Pakistan – *In a City by the Sea* (1998), *Salt and Saffron* (2000), *Kartography* (2002), and *Broken Verses* (2005) – emphasize that it is patriarchal interpretations of the Quran that oppress women, rather than the teachings of the Quran itself. This is particularly so in *Broken Verses*, a family mystery concerning a 30-year-old female protagonist, Aasmaani, a researcher for a Karachi TV station, who is still coming to terms with the disappearance of her activist mother, the inspirational feminist icon Samina Akram. Samina is presumed drowned, unable to cope with the imprisonment and murder of her dissident lover, 'The Poet' – a character modelled on the lionized poets Faiz Ahmed Faiz and Habib Jalib – whose work was critical of the excesses of Pakistan's military regime. This familial narrative is embedded within a larger story of the resistance to the rise of the Islamic Right: Zia ul-Haq's military dictatorship, notably the Hudood ordinances and the rigorous campaign to infuse in the ideological consciousness of the public the infamous slogan, 'the veil and the four walls'.

Shamsie's novel, peopled by Pakistani secular feminists, only touches on what constitutes the main focus and particular achievement of Ali's *Brick Lane* (2003). In the story of Nazneen, the young Muslim female protagonist who moves from a village in Bangladesh and adapts to life in London's East End, there is a representation of a feminist agency that does not require a rejection of Islamic faith. Nazneen's feminist self-realization and trajectory towards a more empowered subject position requires her 'to make [her future] for herself', rather than wait for the future to be 'revealed' as her mother had advised.[11] The text presents the conviction of Nazneen's mother that 'fighting against one's Fate can weaken the blood' and that 'Fate cannot be changed' as internalized patriarchal oppression (pp. 10 and 16). 'If God wanted us to ask questions he would have made us men' is challenged by Nazneen's subsequent decisions to act rather than endure (p. 64). At the close of the novel, Nazneen refers to her recent past as a time 'before I knew what I could do' (p. 407). Thus, in different ways, all these British Asian female novelists challenge what Inderpal Grewal identifies as a widespread motif in the subgenre of Asian American fiction: the valorization of assimilation from South Asian traditions to Americanized modernity. According to Grewal, this motif reinforces hegemonic ideas about the progressiveness of American-led globalization and perpetuates a backward and culturally static image of South Asia.[12]

The issue of class also distinguishes Sheikh and Ali from Syal, who focuses on middle-class Hindu cultural identities that are more readily absorbed and accepted within Britain's shifting racialized boundaries. Both Sheikh and Ali share a consciousness of the relations between the workings of global capital and the new subalterns in their depiction of lives, identities, and localities reconfigured by the intensified global circulations of peoples, ideas, texts, images, and goods. *The Red Box* and *Brick Lane* show that exploited labour conditions and the re-inscription of a submissive female identity are central to the experience of globalization for many working-class women in Britain and Dhaka. Sheikh's detailing of Nargis's life at the factory brings the disjuncture between Nargis's experience of globalization and that of Raisa into sharp relief:

> Raisa had asked her of details of her present job, and Raisa would speak and write still more words. She was educated and she might write about all this, but what did she know? Nargis pulled out an unchecked dress. Chic and expensive; she could imagine Raisa wearing it. Bulquis Ehsan had spread the word that her grandfather was rich in Pakistan and owned carpet factories. Nargis passed the dress. The girl could not be blamed for her grandfather's factories. You could see she was trying to do the right things. Nargis snipped at loose threads and fixed on the designer tags. (p. 162)

By shifting the narrative to Nargis's point of view in this passage, the novel avoids trivializing the class differences that Raisa identifies earlier.

Class, in this context, is not simply something that makes Raisa feel excluded from East London's British Asian community; nor is it a barrier that can be overcome by the considerable empathy that Raisa shows towards Nargis. Rather, class defines what choices are available in life to Nargis compared to Raisa. The disparity in agency between the two women is succinctly captured in the image of Nargis sewing designer tags onto dresses. This connects the new gender identities that global consumer culture represents for women like Raisa to the labour of women like Nargis who produce such goods. Indeed, insofar as traditional female identities are integral to keeping labour costs low at Mr Khan's factory, then the positive effects that global consumer culture represents for some women appear to come at the expense of women like Nargis or Nazneen in *Brick Lane*. In this respect, both novels strongly corroborate Marxist discussion of how gender is integral to the division of labour and the ability of capitalists like Mr Khan to maximize profits.

New ways of being British?

In marked contrast to other British Asian women writers of her generation writing in the 1990s, the fiction of the novelist and scientist Sunetra Gupta (Professor of Theoretical Epidemiology at the University of Oxford) does not focus on identity politics, the politics of place, or defining new ways of being British Asian. Gupta is the author of intensely lyrical, evocative, and fluid novels about displacement, interiority, and infidelity – *Memories of Rain* (1992), *The Glassblower's Breath* (1993), *Moonlight into Marzipan* (1995), and *A Sin of Colour* (1999). In both the content and in her eclectic, intertextual references and influences, she defies categorization concerning what constitutes or defines British Asian female-authored fiction. The references to Rabindranath Tagore reflect her Bengali family and culture while the dense allusions to Greek myths, Virginia Woolf (1882–1941), Rilke, and Nabokov illustrate that influences cannot be contained by nationality, region, canon, or genre, and that her intellectual formation is moulded by many cross-cultural, transnational factors.

Yet for others, such as Randhawa, imagining a new vision of British identity remains central and is achieved by recounting colonial history. The protagonist of Randhawa's third novel, *The Coral Strand* (2001), is named Sita/Ferret because, as she comments, 'ferret is often followed by *out*, to find by persistent investigation, for example, *to ferret out, to search around*'.[13] The importance of history and memory to the construction of British identity is implicit in the structure of *The Coral Strand* and its dialectical organization around two narratives: one that centres upon colonial Bombay 1935–47 and the other upon London 1947–97. This organization renders contemporary Britain historically bound to India and provides the structural foundation for the motif of doubling that occurs throughout the novel, most notably in Sita/Ferret's name. In the last five chapters, Sita/Ferret's quest to utilize the past synthesizes the two narratives, unifying the Indian and British dimensions of her background that had been bifurcated throughout the novel. In this respect, the text corroborates Steven Connor's contention that the British novel since the 1950s should be read 'not just as passively marked with the imprint of history, but also as one of the ways in which history is made and remade'.[14]

The Coral Strand re-envisions British history and Britishness by collapsing numerous boundaries of identity between India and Britain; it thus destabilizes the ethno-nationalist formulation of Britishness conceptualized by Emily in the text. The process of destabilizing Emily's colonial conception of British identity is achieved through narrating the lives of three generations of South Asian women and depicting the varying degrees of subordination that they face. More central to the concerns of the novel, however, is the way in which Britishness is evoked in Sita/Ferret through a strong sense of belonging. In contrast to her mother's erasure of national identification, Sita/Ferret shows how second-generation British Asians are able to re-territorialize their identities by reimagining what Britishness means. Sita/Ferret is very much at home in London – a sentiment that is emphasized towards the end of the novel by the image of her 'melt[ing] into the London crowd' (pp. 200–1).

Post-national identity

Since the 1980s, the impact of British Asian women's fiction has increased considerably, particularly in the wake of the extraordinary critical and commercial success of Arundhati Roy's Booker Prize-winning debut *The God of Small Things* (1997). Roy's novel sold four million copies by the end of 1997 and has been translated into over 25 languages. Another notable example of success is Ali, who received a £30,000 advance on the basis of a few chapters of her debut novel, *Brick Lane,* which dominated the bestseller charts when published in 2003. In the same year, Ali featured in *Granta*'s selection of 20 'Best of Young British Novelists', a once-in-a-decade list regarded as an unofficial census of Britain's shifting cultural landscape. In 2013, Shamsie and Anam were selected. However, although Shamsie and Anam currently write and are based in Britain, they differ from British-born or 'post-migrant' writers such as Ali and Syal in significant ways.[15] Born in Dhaka to an English mother and Bengali father, Ali has lived in Britain since her family moved to England to escape the war of independence of 1971. She and British-born Syal grew up in Britain and engage with, and have been formed by, British multiculturalism.

Shamsie and Anam straddle and move between several countries and reflect a changing sense of Britishness. Born and educated in Karachi, Shamsie has an MFA from the University of Massachusetts and now lives in both London and Karachi, writing fiction and working as a columnist and reviewer for British and Pakistani newspapers. She has won the Pakistani Award for Literature three times, received international acclaim in Britain and the US, and her novels have been translated into many languages. Anam was born in Bangladesh, and studied in France and the US before moving to Britain to pursue an MA in creative writing. Her debut novel about the creation of Bangladesh, *A Golden Age* (2007), won the Commonwealth Writers Best First Book Prize (2008), and was followed by the critically acclaimed *The Good Muslim* (2011). Like Shamsie, she spends time in her country of origin and writes both fictional and non-fiction articles on Bangladesh. Thus Shamsie and Anam are part of a new globalized generation that inhabit the term 'British' or 'British Asian' differently to their precursors. Shamsie and Anam define themselves globally rather than postcolonially. They transcend the binary logic and teleologies of origin and destination entrenched in perceptions of diasporic writing. Such critical tools become less useful in reading fiction as the history of British colonialism recedes and a new phase of global integration intensifies. Their fiction needs to be seen in the context of the move away from national paradigms and borders towards a focus on interrelated nation-states and part of the current debate on whether there is a role for national canons in a globalized transnational era.

Shamsie's novels bestride Karachi and London and develop a feminist aesthetic that influences conceptions of dual or multiple forms of nationality as enabling. Unlike Ali, Shamsie is less concerned to explore why Islam appeals to some second- and third-generation British-born Muslims, a demographic with whom she has stated she remains unfamiliar. Instead she explores epic transnational articulations of Islam and geographical imaginaries on a global scale in her Orange Prize nominee *Burnt Shadows* (2009) with its depiction of intercultural bonds between two families across three generations of world conflict within the sweep of a violent century. *Burnt Shadows* traverses Japan, Pakistan, the US, and Afghanistan. Like Shamsie, Anam interleaves issues of nationalism, Islam, and female emancipation in feminist fictions that trace the growth of Islam in the subcontinent and explore the varied challenges to the Islamization of the region. Anam's *A Golden Age* is refracted through the story of Rehana Haque, a housewife, widow, and mother, as war intrudes on the normal rhythms of her domestic life. Rehana is drawn into the fight for Bangladesh's independence largely through her poet-turned-fighter son, Sohail, and activist daughter, Maya. It is a war that killed over two million and 'has taken so many sons' and 'burned so many daughters'.[16] The darker, more disquieting sequel to *A Golden Age* is the second of a projected trilogy about Bangladesh. *The Good Muslim* explores the appeal of Islam in the aftermath of the 1971 war of liberation and the failure of postwar idealism, alongside the gendered parameters of Islam, piety, and secularism.

Drawing on their Pakistani, Bangladeshi, and Sri Lankan backgrounds, the other significant change this new generation of British Asian women fiction writers has produced since the 1990s is their challenge to the literary dominance of India and Indian writers in British Asian (and South Asian categories). India, as the overarching political and economic signifier of the region, has tended to subsume smaller cultures and nations under a common rubric of the Indian subcontinent. In such narratives, South Asia typically becomes a shorthand description for India. This challenge to Indian dominance is in part a result of geopolitical shifts that have changed the world's awareness of these smaller nations. The surge of interest in Anglophone fictions from Pakistan corresponds to the increased NATO presence there and its uneven and unequal relationship with North America. Seen as under grave threat from Islamic extremists, Pakistan is often headlined as the most dangerous place in the world. Shamsie tries to bring the predicament of her country of origin to an international audience fixated on its turbulent political situation.

Similarly, the controversial ending of Sri Lanka's 30 years of armed conflict in 2009 reshaped the country's international standing. But it has also fuelled interest in Sri Lanka-born British author Roma Tearne's love story, *Mosquito* (2007), set during Sri Lanka's civil war, and in her multi-generational narrative of a family tracing its origins, *Bone China* (2008). In British-born Roshi Fernando's *Homesick* (2012), the lives of diasporic, exiled Sri Lankans are explored. Her finely structured debut collection of linked short stories gives voice to four generations of a Sri Lankan family in South London and unravels their lives from their arrival over the next 30 years.

A new generation of British Asian writers expresses impatience with the expectation that their fiction must revisit dominant tropes of culture clash, generational conflict, and doomed arranged marriages. As Kavita Bhanot, editor of an anthology of 21 British Asian short stories, *Too Asian, Not Asian Enough* (2011), explains: 'Every time another British Asian novel, film or memoir appears we can't help feeling a sense of deja-vu. Some of us feel that these stories have nothing to do with our lives, some of us don't want to write about our lives at all.'[17] The collection combines established writers Gautam Malkani and Bidisha with new voices. Sarfraz Manzoor wonders in his review of this uneven collection if 'freedom from the familiar anchors has left the authors flailing'.[18] This is not to suggest that there is no longer a market for these dominant ways of perceiving British Asian culture, as the commercial success of British-born Nisha Minhas attests. Her fictions are as commercially opportunistic, stifling, and formulaic as their titles suggest: *Chapatti or Chips?* (2002), *Sari and Sins* (2003), *Passion and Poppadoms* (2004), *Bindis and Brides* (2005), and *Tall, Dark and Handsome* (2007).

However, there is a distinct geographic shift beyond Britain in the work of British-born writers such as Nikita Lalwani. She transcends the British Asian scene of her first, Booker long-listed novel, *Gifted* (2007), a charming tale of a maths prodigy struggling to cope with her family's expectations. Inspired by her visit to India, Lalwani's second novel, *The Village* (2012), is a disturbing morality tale set in a self-sustaining village modelled on a real-life open prison in Rajasthan in India. The village is visited by a BBC crew making a series on prison life and the novel poses questions on the difficulty of documenting reality. Similarly, Roopa Farooki of Pakistani/Bangladeshi descent has moved away from her multi-generational familial novels based in London: *Bitter Sweets* (2007), *Corner Shop* (2008), and *The Way Things Look To Me* (2009). Her most recent novel, *Half Life* (2012), is set in London, Singapore, and Malaysia. Farooki resists being compared to Ali and Zadie Smith, and to being courted only to represent and popularize British Asian experiences of culture clash.[19] Like others of her generation, her literary production is not necessarily 'Asian'. Not unlike their precursors, this new generation wishes to transcend ethnicity, religion, nationality, and culture and tell 'universal' stories. This is an aspiration that is no longer synonymous with 'white' and that depends, in great measure, on their literary forerunners.

Notes

1. See Siobhan Lambert-Hurley and Sunil Sharma, *Atiya's Journeys: A Muslim Woman from Colonial Bombay to Edwardian Britain* (Oxford University Press, 2012).
2. While the contested category of 'Black British writing' has produced much fruitful literary criticism and anthologizing, the establishment of the category 'British Asian' and research into the varied and complex literary historiography of Asians in Britain is relatively new. See C.L. Innes, *A History of Black and Asian Writing in Britain, 1700–2000* (Cambridge University Press, 2000); Susheila Nasta, *Home Truths: Fictions of the South Asian Diaspora in Britain* (Basingstoke: Palgrave Macmillan, 2002); Sukhdev Sandhu, *London Calling: How Black and Asian Writers Imagined a City* (London: HarperPerennial, 2004); and Ruvani Ranasinha, *South Asian Writers in Twentieth-Century Britain: Culture in Translation* (Oxford University Press, 2007).
3. Rukhsana Ahmad, 'In Search of a Talisman', *Voices of the Crossing*, ed. Ferdinand Dennis and Naseem Khan (London: Serpent's Tail, 2000), p. 110.
4. See Gayatri Gopinath, *Impossible Desires: Queer Diaspora and South Asian Public Cultures* (Durham, NC: Duke University Press, 2005), p. 5. Stuart Hall describes the representation which is able to constitute minority subjects as 'new kinds of subjects' in 'Cultural Identity and Diaspora', *Identity: Community, Culture, Difference*, ed. Jonathan Rutherford (London: Lawrence and Wishart, 1992), p. 222.
5. See bell hooks, *Yearning: Race, Gender, and Cultural Politics* (Boston: South End Press, 1990); Chandra Talpade Mohanty, *Feminism without Borders: Decolonizing Theory, Practicing Solidarity* (Durham, NC: Duke University Press 2003); Gayatri Chakravorty Spivak, 'Can the Subaltern Speak?', *Marxism and the Interpretation of Culture*, ed. Cary Nelson and Lawrence Grossberg (Urbana: University of Illinois Press, 1998), pp. 271–313; Trinh T. Minh-ha, *Woman, Native, Other* (Bloomington: Indiana University Press, 1989).
6. Chandra Talpade Mohanty, 'Under Western Eyes: Feminist Scholarship and Colonial Discourses', *Third World Woman and the Politics of Feminism*, ed. Mohanty, Ann Russo, and Lourdes Torres (Bloomington: Indiana University Press, 1991), p. 71.
7. Meera Syal, 'Influences', *New Statesman*, 19 April 1996, p. 21.
8. Meera Syal, *Life Isn't All Ha Ha Hee Hee* (London: Transworld Publishers, 1999), p. 242.
9. Farhana Sheikh, *The Red Box* (London: The Women's Press, 1991), pp. 128–9.
10. A death threat, sanctioned by Iran's Ayatollah, was issued against Rushdie for his portrayal, in *The Satanic Verses* (1989), of the Prophet Mohammed and his wives. The portrayal was perceived by some Muslims as blasphemous and insulting. See note 2 in Chapter 16 for further details about the Rushdie affair.
11. Monica Ali, *Brick Lane* (London: Doubleday Transworld Publications, 2003), p. 11.
12. Inderpal Grewal, *Transnational America: Feminisms, Diasporas, Neoliberalisms* (Durham, NC: Duke University Press, 2005), p. 4.
13. Ravinder Randhava, *The Coral Strand* (London: House of Strauss, 2001), p. 259.
14. Steven Connor, *The English Novel in History, 1950–1995* (London: Routledge, 1996), p. 1.
15. The term 'post-migrant' is intended to capture both the importance of histories and the distance that separates these people from the direct migration experience of their parents and grandparents.

16. Tahmima Anam, *A Golden Age* (London: John Murray, 2007), p. 274.
17. Kavita Bhanot, *Too Asian, Not Asian Enough: Fiction from the New Generation* (Birmingham: Tindall Street Press, 2011), p. ii.
18. Sarfraz Manzoor, *Guardian Review*, 4 November 2011, www.theguardian.com/books/2011/nov/04/too-asian-kavita-bhanot-review, accessed 11 July 2013.
19. Roopa Farooki, interview, 'Nationality Does Not Matter', *Metro*, 22 January 2010, http://metro.co.uk/2012/01/22/roopa-farooki-my-father-went-to-harrods-and-never-came-back-298815/, accessed 11 July 2013.

Part V
Writing Now

16
Writing Now

Claire Chambers and Susan Watkins

This chapter considers the preoccupations and forms that characterize British women's writing in the new millennium. We argue that these are, firstly, multiculturalism with its questioning of race, religion, and culture, and its relationship, if any, to terrorism. Secondly, this chapter will address the treatment in fiction of the issue of an ageing population, and the resultant concerns with women's changing roles in relation to employment, fertility, and childcare. Thirdly, an anxiety about climate change and environmental catastrophe manifests itself in a renewed interest in dystopian, post-apocalyptic writing. Finally, we consider the impact of technological change. The fact that publishing faces its greatest upheaval since Johannes Gutenberg's fifteenth-century invention of the printing press is leading to contemporary women's diverse interest in new technologies, including the internet, ebook and digital publishing, and other interactive online formats.

Multiculturalism

This millennium opened with Bhikhu Parekh's ground-breaking multiculturalism report, *The Future of Multi-Ethnic Britain* (2000), and with the northern riots of 2001, followed by the 7/7 London bombings of 2005. Internationally, the events of 9/11 and subsequent assaults on the Middle East, and Central and South Asia provoked a response from women writers. These authors engage with matters of multiculturalism, race, religion, and terror, and with rising concerns about refugees and asylum seekers. We interpret multiculturalism as at once encompassing the everyday lived experiences of mixed cultures, races, and religions, and as an aspect of Britain's changing policy since the late 1960s towards its immigrant population. Whereas only unashamed racists could object to the first definition, multiculturalism as policy has come under attack, in recent years, from both the political Right and the Left. Multicultural policy in the UK is usually traced back to the 1966 speech of Roy Jenkins, then Labour Home

Secretary. In this speech, Jenkins argues against an assimilatory 'melting pot' model, stating that Britain instead needs immigration to pivot on 'equal opportunity, accompanied by cultural diversity, in an atmosphere of mutual tolerance'.[1] However, since the Rushdie affair, and accelerating as 9/11, 7/7, and the rise of Daesh or so-called Islamic State prompt difficult questions about 'home-grown terrorists', multicultural policy is judged by many to have failed.[2] For example, speaking soon after 7/7, the chairman of the Commission of Racial Equality, Trevor Phillips, averred that the policy creates ghettoization, or what he described as the phenomenon of 'sleepwalking to segregation'.[3]

From a feminist perspective, Susan Moller Okin controversially argued, in her important article 'Is Multiculturalism Bad for Women?' (1997), that the radical notion of 'group rights' for minorities within multicultural societies can obfuscate the conservative politics of those who claim to speak on behalf of these minorities. Okin asserts that this often has severe fallout on non-Western women as a minority within a minority whose rights tend to be overlooked: 'group rights are potentially, and in many cases actually, antifeminist'.[4] A dozen years later, Marie Macey reframes Okin's titular question as 'Doing Harm By Doing Good?', in the subtitle of her 2009 monograph *Multiculturalism, Religion and Women.*[5] With a focus on religion, forced marriage, and notions of democracy amongst predominantly Kashmiri populations in Bradford, Macey's conclusions about multiculturalism are similarly pessimistic to Okin's. By contrast, the turn towards postsecularism, particularly in debates surrounding Muslim women and the mainstream's 'rhetoric of salvation' towards them, counters Okin's and Macey's assumption that 'minority ethnic women are generally more vulnerable to oppression and violence than are their Western counterparts' (Macey, p. ix).[6]

Some feminists with heritage in the global south such as Lila Abu-Lughod suggest that Western feminists see themselves as 'saving' their benighted Muslim sisters (pp. 788–9). Abu-Lughod wrote her essay 'Do Muslim Women Really Need Saving?' in 2002 against the backdrop of the war in Afghanistan's initial phase. She takes as her point of departure the toxic but hilarious George W. Bushism 'women of cover', which conflates the politically sensitive American term 'woman of colour' with the issue of modest Muslim dress (p. 783). By contrast, Abu-Lughod provides a textured reading of the veiling debate. Rather than the universal symbol of oppression that many Americans assume it to be, the burqa is a Pashtun garment and there can be empowerment in it; she quotes the anthropologist Hanna Papanek who describes it as 'portable seclusion' (p. 785). Abu-Lughod disagrees with any enforcement of the wearing of burqas, but observes that many women wear these outfits voluntarily and do not wish to discard them. Abu-Lughod next challenges the speech of George W. Bush's wife,

Laura, in which she implicitly assumes that Afghan women will automatically be delighted to be rescued by American troops:

> It is deeply problematic to construct the Afghan woman as someone in need of saving. When you save someone, you imply that you are saving her from something. You are also saving her to something. What violences are entailed in this transformation, and what presumptions are being made about the superiority of that to which you are saving her? (pp. 788–9)

Without endorsing cultural relativism, Abu-Lughod encourages us to think about women who may or may not want rescue, but more importantly need justice.

Rather than focusing on the secular, 'Western', or majoritarian white British responses to the 'problem' of Muslim women, this chapter concentrates on literature produced by contemporary women writers, both Muslim and non-Muslim. Much of this work demonstrates that everyday experiences of mixed culture are being reshaped by those most affected by multiculturalism as political policy: ethnic minority women. Nonetheless, as we have seen, one charge that is frequently levelled against multiculturalism is that it is inimical to women, especially women from the very minority groups that the policy claims to help. This accusation is often reinforced by reference to minority women's restricted employment, sartorial, and sexual choices.

Many contemporary women writers reflect on or challenge arguments about multiculturalism's imagined and quotidian aspects, and its impact on women. In *Brick Lane* (2003), for example, Monica Ali makes clothing an important motif around which discussion of identity, religion, and culture coalesces. The novel's protagonist, Nazneen, a housewife who becomes a seamstress, has an arranged marriage with an older man, Chanu. Yet Ali does not let Nazneen remain in the apparently automatically oppressive space of her arranged marriage. She moves the character out of her religio-cultural milieu once Nazneen starts to take in sewing and has an affair with the younger British Muslim overseer, Karim. *Brick Lane* met with commercial success and critical plaudits, as well as criticisms that Ali did not have the right to represent the British-Bangladeshi community. Germaine Greer, for example, took Ali to task for her choice of language and ventriloquism of the voice of Nazneen's Bangladeshi sister, Hasina: '[Ali] writes in English and her point of view is, whether she allows herself to impersonate a village Bangladeshi woman or not, British.'[7] However, when Ali wrote about a topic not associated with 'her' group, in the follow-up novel *Alentejo Blue* (2006), set in Portugal, negative reviews ensued.[8] There has also been something of a backlash against her 'girly' novel about Princess Diana, *Untold Story*

(2011).[9] This may partly be due to the uneven quality of the writing, but it is also because her later novels do not operate 'in an expected way', which, as Ana María Sánchez-Arce argues, is demanded by established notions of ethnic minority 'authenticity'.[10] This seems a curious double bind, whereby a mixed-heritage writer like Ali is damned if she does write about Muslims in Britain and damned if she does not.

Towards the end of 2013, reports emerged that three women aged between 30 and 69 had been held in slavery in South London for approximately three decades.[11] Given the higher profile that human trafficking has had in recent years, it is perhaps unsurprising that a concern with refugees, asylum seekers, and modern forms of slavery is increasingly prominent in contemporary women's fiction. In her somewhat more enthusiastically received third novel, *In the Kitchen* (2009), Ali brings together a large and discrepant cast of characters from the Caribbean, Africa, South Asia, Eastern Europe, the former Soviet bloc, and beyond, who all work in the suggestively named Imperial Hotel in London. From the perspective of her protagonist Gabe Lightfoot, who is one of the novel's few Englishmen and an executive chef, Ali writes:

> Every corner of the earth was here: Hispanic, Asian, African, Baltic and most places in between ... It was touching, really, to watch them all, every race, every colour, every creed.[12]

This passage clearly dramatizes Paul Gilroy's vision of Britain's twenty-first-century 'unkempt, unruly, and unplanned multiculture'.[13] Gabe celebrates the mostly 'convivial' coexistence of very different people within exponentially internationalizing London (p. 105). However, it emerges that the Slavic grill man, Ivan, is in cahoots with the restaurant manager, Gleeson, and housekeeper, Branka, to traffic women. These girls of all nationalities work on menial wages at the hotel, and the gang benefits from the high value of 'human capital' to 'sell ... them like meat ... two dollars a kilo' (p. 364).

The interest in displaced, exploited, and imprisoned peoples continues in the theatre, with plays including Kay Adshead's *The Bogus Woman* (2000), Victoria Brittain and Gillian Slovo's *Guantanamo: 'Honor Bound to Defend Freedom'* (2004), Sonja Linden's *Crocodile Seeking Refuge* (2005), Christine Bacon's *Rendition Monologues* (2008), Rukhsana Ahmad's *Letting Go* (2008), Natasha Walter's *Motherland* (2008), and Gbemisola Ikumelo's *Next Door* (2010). *Letting Go*, for example, written by British-Pakistani author Rukhsana Ahmad, was part of a Pursued by a Bear Theatre double bill entitled *Footprints in the Sand*, and dealt with the issue of refugees. The play is set in and around Dover beach and its nearby shared housing, detention, and advice centres, 'touchstone' spaces for multiculturalism. All of these impoverished and punitive locations loom large for the African and South Asian asylum seekers who live (and die) in the play. Starkly illustrated is the refugees' lack of human rights, liberty, and housing of a standard 'adequate for ... health'.[14]

Brittain and Slovo's *Guantanamo* also explores human rights and focuses on what Gilroy describes as 'the critical figure of the person who [can] be killed with impunity', in this case, the Guantanamo Bay detainee (Gilroy, p. 53). The play is based on testimony from so-called enemy combatants including Moazzam Begg and Jamal Al-Harith, their relatives and legal defenders, politicians, and other involved parties, including the brother of one of the almost 3000 people killed in the World Trade Center attacks. Brittain and Slovo unsettle the widespread Western assumption that Afghanistan is backward and lacking in human rights while the West is the model for progress and civil liberties. This is also a point made by the solicitor, Gareth Peirce, in the play:

> The [boys] are three young British lads who are like all our children – they're people who are very familiar, very easy to feel immediately comfortable with. And yet the story they tell is one of terrible stark medieval horror ... [of] being tortured in a prison in Afghanistan, being interrogated with a gun to your head, being transported like animals to a country you don't know where you are, and being treated like animals from start to finish for two years.[15]

Peirce's emphasis here on the 'knowability' and ordinariness of 'the Three' is contrasted with the extraordinary, almost inhuman, treatment they received from the Americans and their allies in Afghanistan and Cuba.

Multicultural women writers often attract controversy. In 2006, the filming of Ali's *Brick Lane* on the 'real' Brick Lane was famously challenged by protesters who disliked the novel's depiction of the Bangladeshi community. The storm surrounding American Sherry Jones's *The Jewel of Medina* (2008), a romantic novel about the Prophet Mohammed's favourite wife Aisha, led to her UK publisher being firebombed.[16] Finally, from outside the issue of Muslim 'offence', a production of Gurpreet Kaur Bhatti's play *Behzti* ('Dishonour') was cancelled in 2004 by the Birmingham Rep, because Sikh activists were angered by its use of religious iconography.[17] Violence against women was one of its key themes and, in her introduction to the printed version of the play, Bhatti writes of her interest in 'those who are not beacons of multiculturalism, who live with fear and without hope and who thrive through their own versions of anti-social behaviour'.[18] Yet the protests centred on the play's use of sacred texts such as the Guru Granth Sahib and on its sacred setting in a gurdwara, rather than its social criticisms as in the *Brick Lane* dispute.

The *Behzti* furore indicates that artistic–religious controversies in the period following the Rushdie affair have involved not only Muslims. The *Behzti* protests were largely initiated by working-class, British-Punjabi Sikh men, a group often seen as 'pioneers of British multiculturalism'. Perhaps because of perceptions of their model minority status, these angry Sikh responses 'failed to evince the usual derision reserved for minority ethnic communities', according to Gurharpal Singh.[19] Shortly after the *Behzti* affair, English PEN members, including Monica Ali, Zadie Smith, Gillian Slovo, and Maggie Gee, lobbied the government against the proposed incitement to religious hatred legislation, arguing that it would dangerously curtail freedom of expression and criticism, and that it would only encourage disputes such as those surrounding the play.[20] Yet Rehana Ahmed and Claire Chambers have argued elsewhere that protests against the cultural products of Ali, Jones, and Bhatti (as well as better-known controversies surrounding male-authored texts such as Rushdie's *The Satanic Verses* or the Danish *Jyllands-Posten* cartoons) should not be understood in conventional terms such as the limiting of 'free speech' versus 'censorious religion'.[21] Instead, thinking about the unequal access to cultural and economic capital that frequently marks such disputes, and about who has access to and who feels excluded from the texts that are so vigorously debated, opens up more illuminating perspectives.

Official multicultural policy has always coped inadequately with deeply felt religious difference and, in the 1980s and 1990s, was widely derided for its apparent reliance on 'saris, samosas and steel bands', cultural markers particularly associated with women. After 7/7, however, 'soft' multiculturalism got tough as Tony Blair, then Prime Minister, announced that 'the rules of the game are changing' and suspended civil liberties for terror suspects.[22] In a 2011 speech, David Cameron, having been appointed Prime Minister in 2010, outlined his idea of 'muscular liberalism' in preference to the so-called 'passive tolerance of recent years'. Cameron declared that even non-violent extremists who are opposed to 'British values' (the benchmarks of which are, apparently, the equality of the sexes, liberalism, democracy, and freedom of sexuality) cannot be tolerated: the 'Other', it seems, must be 'civilized' or expelled. Cameron also emphasized 'free speech and intellectual enquiry'.[23] As our discussion of *Brick Lane* and *Behzti* indicates, it is not so easy to reconcile the ethics of representation with the 'right' of art to offend. Ultimately, women's writing post-millennium suggests that more rather than less multiculturalism is needed, if Britain is to inculcate a genuine (if multifarious) sense of citizenship in its diverse populace. As women's apocalyptic writing also suggests, the rise of fundamentalism needs to be countered and challenged by an emphasis on plural narratives (faith-based and otherwise) that avoid judgement.

Ageing

The literary preoccupation with ageing can be seen as a creative response to statistical realities such as an ageing population in the UK, the tendency (amongst middle-class women in particular) to delay the decision to have children, and cuts in welfare and other provision for older people in poverty.

Resentment of the 'baby-boom' generation for their supposed property wealth, final-salary pension entitlements, free bus passes, and winter fuel payments hides a prosaic reality: older people tend to be poor, and it is often women who do the work of caring for elders, sometimes alongside bringing up baby and working outside the home. British women writers publishing since the millennium suggest a significant generational shift. Whereas women once wrote from the point of view of daughters challenging their mothers – for example Doris Lessing in the *Children of Violence* novels (1952–69) – those daughters have now become the older generation. Recent novels by writers in their fifties, sixties, and beyond, such as Liz Jensen, Michèle Roberts, Alison Fell, and Penelope Lively, demonstrate a transition in perspective: the older woman can now be the subject of the narrative rather than its object, or in some cases she can be both subject *and* object.

The age of 50 is a crux point for the protagonists in Fell's *Tricks of the Light* (2004) and Roberts's *Reader, I Married Him* (2005). Broom, the heroine of Fell's novel, comments that 'her body, which she still intermittently loved, was wise; it seemed to know a lot'.[24] The sense that Broom implicitly trusts her body, if not her culture's valuation of it, is important. Kathleen Woodward argues that women who are actually in midlife feel old before men of the same age. The cult of youth, the negativity surrounding the menopause, and the prominence of conventional narratives of ageing, which tend to embrace what Margaret Morganroth Gullette calls 'decline ideology', all contribute to this.[25] Woodward demands that we 'attend to the articulations of women's experience of the shadow of aging cast by our culture at midlife'.[26] The idea of being 'aged by culture', as Gullette's title claims, is challenged in these two novels, along with the assumption that the age of 50 marks the beginning of decline for women. In both novels, the heroines experience pleasurable sex with new partners, are creatively productive, and come to terms with the loss of previous partners, even if, as Sarah Falcus notes in relation to Roberts's novel, celebrating 'sexual fulfillment and the pleasures of the physical' leads to 'its own version of age denial or effacement'.[27] Lessing's *Love, Again* (1996) and the title novella of *The Grandmothers* (2003), and Jenny Diski's *Happily Ever After* (1991) provide further examples of the sexually adventurous or desiring older woman.

What Barbara Frey Waxman refers to as the 'dialogic qualities' of women's writing about ageing – its attempt to provide a multiplicity of voices on the topic – suggests an explicit desire to complicate the binary thinking apparent in the two most popular narratives of ageing: progress/maturation (what she elsewhere terms the 'novel of ripening', or *reifungsroman*), versus decline/downfall.[28] Lively's novel *Family Album* (2010), for instance, ends with Alison and Ingrid, wife and au pair/mistress respectively of Charles, writer and patriarch, setting up home together after his death and starting a business running cookery courses and growing vegetables. Their relationship's alteration from rivalry to partnership suggests not so much decline or ripening as a major reassessment of their previous connection with each other, their entire family, and the narrative of ageing itself.

Rather than focusing solely on images of older women in contemporary women's writing, it might be more fruitful to rework Edward Said's idea of 'late style' to refer not merely to the author's own experience of ageing and how that affects late work but to the creative representations of ageing in British women's post-millennial writing.[29] For Said, late style is about 'irresolution and unsynthesized fragmentariness'.[30] However, Gordon McMullan argues that the 'most obvious immediate critical blind spot in studies of late style [is] systematic exclusion of women'.[31] He demonstrates that the absence of discussion of *women's* late style corresponds to an unwillingness to see them as geniuses. In other words, to embody the qualities of late style you have to be, or once have been, a genius. This is, of course, an apparently universal quality that is actually more likely to be ascribed to men than women.

Contrary to the claim that late style is the preserve of male writers, we argue that in the literature of British women writing after the millennium a gendered 'late writing' makes clear the importance in women's lives of connections between the work of caring (whether for elders or children) and the work of writing. This literature also attempts to complicate and challenge conventional narratives of growing old and makes use of multiple perspectives and subject positions on the ageing process. In addition, ageing affects the *form* of many of these narratives. In Jensen's novel *War Crimes for the Home* (2002), the ageing protagonist Gloria gradually confronts her traumatic experiences on the 'home front' in the Second World War. Through doing so, she starts to understand that time and memory function in non-sequential, simultaneous, sometimes awkward, ways. As she puts it: 'you got in a time muddle. Like forgetting the bloody punchline'.[32] This understanding affects the reader's experience of the novel and generates formal experimentation with ways of presenting time.

In relation to formal experimentation, it is necessary to comment on the recent phenomenon of ageing memoirs. These include Penelope Lively's *Ammonites and Leaping Fish: A Life in Time* (2013) and Diana Athill's *Somewhere Towards the End* (2008). In addition, Jane Miller's *Crazy Age: Thoughts on Being Old* (2010) and Lynne Segal's *Out of Time: The Perils and Pleasures of Ageing* (2014) have interesting hybrid forms, incorporating elements of auto/biography, essay, and political tract. For a novelist like Lively, who has addressed this topic in her fiction, the hybrid form is a product of a new understanding of time generated by ageing. She argues that ageing brings a 'new and disturbing relationship with time ... time has looped back, regressed, it no longer lies ahead, but behind'.[33] In a section on memory, she argues that 'the most effective method of memoir writing seems to be ... to try to reflect the processes of memory itself rather than the artificial plod through time of routine autobiography' (p. 127). The book achieves this by using six well-loved objects from Lively's house, as well as the books she has read, to prompt her recollections, and a selection of events (for example the Suez Crisis) which pinpoint key historical moments and significant personal memories. She concludes that her method acknowledges that identity is palimpsestic: '[w]e are all of us palimpsests; we carry the past around, it comes surging up whether or not we want it' (p. 174).

Lynne Segal's understanding of identity in old age resembles Lively's. As she puts it, 'the older we are the more we encounter the world through complex layerings of identity'.[34] She also comments on the increasing numbers of memoirs being published, where the connections between the younger and older self are clear and where mourning and loss can be creative rather than solely negative experiences. Segal's magisterial book is partly a polemic calling for the acknowledgement of dependency as key to all forms of identity (rather than solely the aged self). She challenges the privileging of 'independence' in narratives about the self and the body (especially the ageing self and body), arguing that 'differing modes of dependence are essential to the human condition' (p. 35). She also champions the older woman's right to be a desiring subject and questions the prevalence of narratives by older women that confidently protest celibacy as a release from the perils of desire.

In *Somewhere Towards the End*, publisher and writer Athill explores the impact of ageing on her sexuality, mobility, hobbies, attitude to religion, and relationships with others. Written when she was 89, Athill is disarmingly frank about the facts that she still drives a car but no longer has sex. She has gone off reading novels, an activity which provided her living as senior editor at André Deutsch, but now enjoys perusing and reviewing works of non-fiction. Her atheism has gained in stridency rather than becoming weaker as she faces her 'end'. However, whereas she remembers her Christian upbringing with affection for the ethics and stories it taught her, she has no time for Islam. Discussing the 'deep and tangled roots' that attach to the notion that a wife must be faithful to her husband, she observes that these are:

> based not only on a man's need to know himself to be the father of his wife's child, but also on the even deeper, darker feeling that man *owns* woman, God having made her for his convenience. It's hard to imagine the extirpation of that: think of its power in Islam! And woman's anxious clamour for her husband's fidelity springs from the same primitive root: she feels it to be necessary proof of her value.[35]

In the light of Abu-Lughod's comments about saviour discourse, discussed earlier, this throwaway remark about Islam in an otherwise thoughtful and lively memoir reveals Athill's simplistic assumption that Islam has a markedly regressive approach to gender relations.

Catastrophe and apocalypse

In Miller's *Crazy Age* she admits that she is still drawn, 40 years after her first reading, to Frank Kermode's *The Sense of an Ending* (1967), where he calls *tick-tock* the ubiquitous attempt to organize both the typical plot and the typical life. Kermode's *The Sense of an Ending* is also attracted to what Edward Said referred to as 'late style', arguing that the history of fiction suggests a move from visions of the 'end of days' or apocalypse to an understanding of the course and conclusion of the individual lifespan. Kermode suggests that 'literary fictions changed in the same way – perpetually recurring crises of the person, and the death of that person, took over from myths which purport to relate one's experience to grand beginnings and ends'.[36] In the post-millennial moment, it is perhaps hardly surprising that British women's writing is attracted as much to 'grand beginnings and ends' – maybe even what has been called 'the end of history' – as to more focused narratives of ageing and the end of the individual human life experience.[37]

A large number of millennial British women writers have imagined the end (and sometimes limping survival) of days. These novels often use the science fiction device of extrapolation to create future societies in which some kind of systemic collapse leading to an apocalypse has either taken or is taking place. The causes and symptoms of such destruction are manifold, though all are related to late twentieth- and early twenty-first-century phenomena: the excesses of techno-science, globalization, corporatization, consumerism, and climate change are all implicated. Impending catastrophe can undermine human rights. For instance, Ali Smith in *Girl Meets Boy* (2008) explores the threat that consumerism and branding represent to freedom of speech and the right to love. A character working for the Pure Corporation on a new brand of bottled water remarks that 'water is not a human right. Water is a human need. And that means we can market it. We can sell a need. It's our *human right* to.'[38] Imogen, who by the end of the text transforms from an anorexic, homophobic corporate drone to a more resisting character, refutes this, saying, 'Those words you just used are all in the wrong places' (p. 124).

Some texts focus on changes in accepted ideologies of female embodiment, gender, and sexuality that arise as a consequence of falling birth rates. In a number of recent 'demodystopias', population decline is of particular concern although, in others, fear of population excess leads to repressive measures.[39] For example, in Sarah Hall's *The Carhullan Army* (2008), as a result of the collapse of civil society and the scarcities attendant upon the consequences of climate change, a repressive 'Authority' runs the UK and insists that all fertile women are fitted with a contraceptive coil. In Jane Rogers's *The Testament of Jessie Lamb* (2011), a catastrophic worldwide population decline and anxieties about climate change lead to a disturbing change in conventional gender roles and a return to patriarchal attitudes linking 'nature' with the female body.

Rogers imagines a world where women are either idolized or hated after MDS (Maternal Death Syndrome), a genetically engineered virus supposedly created by terrorists, makes all pregnancies generate a fatal auto-immune Prion disease (akin to CJD) in the pregnant woman. A number of changes in sexual and family conventions occur in response. Jessie Lamb speculates that 'now sexual reproduction was over, all those old commandments against homosexuality were melting away and millions more men were coming out'.[40] Jessie notices that the sexes begin to cluster together in a terrified reaction to MDS and its consequences. This sexual segregation results in the 'Othering' of the 'opposite' sex and an increasing reliance on binary thinking that sees 'boys' and 'girls' as irremediably different; such difference is no longer attractive but to be feared.

Homosociality and homosexuality also increase in Maggie Gee's *The Ice People* (1998), where, as the previously temperate northern climes cool, men and women start to live in all-female and all-male communities (known as 'segging'). As in Rogers's novel, this is a source of anxiety and concern for the male narrator, although his response is satirized. UK politics are affected when the women-only 'Wicca' Party beats the male 'Scientists' in the general election. Both Gee's and Rogers's novels also adumbrate the increase of children-only communities who refuse to live with adults. Lisa, one of the characters in Rogers's novel, argues that adults are sick, usually dependent on alcohol, drugs, or just routine, like 'those horses in the olden days that used to walk round in a circle to turn a mill wheel' (p. 48).

Some texts point to post-human technology – the robot or cyborg – as having the capacity to break down distinctions such as those between nature and science, animal and human, and organic and inorganic matter, in order to transform the body, identity, and sexuality in positive ways.[41] Jeanette Winterson's *The Stone Gods* (2007) imagines these kinds of changes in attitudes to human and machine bodies. In the first part of the novel, the heroine, Billie, falls in love with a *robo-sapiens* called Spike. Spike refuses to distinguish between the human and the robot. Such a distinction is no longer meaningful in the world of the novel, where the human *and* the *robo-sapiens* body is subject to continual genetic modification and 'enhancement', as a way of avoiding the 'decline narrative' associated with ageing. Despite the ban on inter-species sex, the homo- and *robo-sapiens* desire each other and begin a relationship. The novel strongly suggests that it is the *robo-sapiens* that stands a chance of surviving the apocalypse and that this is not necessarily tragic. Margaret Toye argues that contemporary feminist theory should revisit Donna Haraway's figure of the cyborg, particularly in relation to how women SF writers use the cyborg to 'help us to rethink embodiment'.[42] Much of British women's post-millennial apocalyptic writing does this via what Stacey Alaimo refers to as 'transcorporeality', her term for the interconnections, interchanges, and transits between human bodies and non-human natures.[43]

A return to the maternal body, or *mater*, as a source of imagery and narrative structure is also important. Aaron Rosenfeld asserts that conventional post-apocalyptic narratives 'work towards the recovery of patriarchal norms'.[44] Understandably, therefore, they are often preoccupied with father–son relationships. Gee's *The Ice People* is ironic about the father's obsessive focus on his relationship with his son. By contrast, Rogers's novel is concerned in interesting ways with the father–daughter relationship. Jessie's father imprisons her rather than allowing her to become a 'Sleeping Beauty', a young woman who fatally volunteers to incubate embryos vaccinated against MDS. Other writers make use of maternal metaphors that are implicitly associated with the idea of return home. Winterson's *The Stone Gods* positions mother–daughter love and the post-human same-sex desire between Billie and Spike against the discovery that humanity's self-destructive, greedy behaviour in relation to the environment is repeated across time, space, and place. This is also the case in *The Carhullan Army*, in which the protagonist–narrator 'Sister' finds refuge from the Authority in Carhullan, an all-women community in the rural north.

At the end of these novels, the reader senses that humanity's self-destruction is inevitable while, at the same time, bonds between women can still suggest resistance. *The Carhullan Army* implies the failure of the women's uprising against the Authority by using a frame for the text which indicates that Sister's record is that of a prisoner. Nevertheless, the final words of the novel are Sister's: 'I do not recognize the jurisdiction of this government.'[45] Equally, Rogers's *Testament* concludes with Jessie leaving a final message for the child she hopes she is carrying, an ending that could be viewed as either tragic, utopian, or both.

The choices these women make take place in a context where they are uncertain about the validity or effectiveness of their own interventions in the drift towards apocalypse, or the recovery afterwards. Jessie, for instance, comments, in the face of parental opposition to her decision to volunteer for the Sleeping Beauty programme, that 'deciding what I'm going to do, and setting that in motion, is giving me power ... for the first time in my life I feel safe, and in control' (p. 204). Whether to agree with her position, or with her parents' attempts to stop her, is one of the questions the reader has to try to answer. Greg Garrard claims that 'the drama of apocalypse is shaped by a "frame of acceptance" that may be either "comic" or "tragic". The choice of frame will determine the way in which issues of time, agency, authority and crisis are dramatized.'[46] Hence, the individual in the tragic narrative cannot affect its outcome or progress, whereas the comic narrative is open-ended and permits agency and change. Writers like Rogers make judicious use of this distinction, often making it the fulcrum of their texts.

Both individual life narratives of ageing and 'end-of-world' narratives can be related to Steven Connor's description of the 'contortions introduced by the very notion of representing the end of representation'.[47] It is arguably this idea of creative narrative 'contortion' that interests post-millennium British women writers. At the conclusion of Jensen's *Rapture* (2009), a tsunami destroys the world, but the protagonist reveals that she is expecting a child and looks forward, imagining the hand-to-mouth existence that child will have, as well as looking back to the world as it was before the disaster. In a similar way, Gee's *The Flood* (2005) begins and ends with sections titled 'Before' and 'After' the deluge, which describe human existence in a paradisiacal city. While, in the main body of the text, she imagines the Flood's complete destruction of humanity, the novel paradoxically allows all its characters to survive the Flood and exist in a space/time outside the conventional narrative chronotope.

New technologies

If the end of representation and the rise of extremism generate difficulties that are creatively productive for many women writers, then the same can also be said of the increasing dominance of new technologies. New technologies and online or virtual publication can constitute a positive challenge to supposedly static national boundaries and fixed subject positions in terms of gender, sexuality, class, and age. Narrative structures, which had initially been based on the codex, longhand writing, and sequential reading, were challenged, before 1970, by writers including Christine Brooke-Rose and Eva Figes. Since the millennium, conventional models of authorship and publication have been altered by the collaborative writing of fan fiction and by virtual online communities of writers, as well as by the blog. Suniti Namjoshi's *Building Babel* (1996) was pioneering in its invitation to readers to collaborate by concluding the novel online.[48] Canadian-born Kate Pullinger's 'networked' novel, *Flight Paths* (2005), tells the story of Yacub, an immigrant worker in Dubai whose attempt to stow away on a plane fails when he crashes into a supermarket car park. It includes visuals and music and encourages contributions from readers/viewers.[49] Pullinger's *Inanimate Alice* is a transmedia story designed to unfold over time and on multiple platforms. It uses text, images, music, sound effects, puzzles, and games, inviting the reader to drive the action forward at her own pace and encouraging her to co-create her own version(s) of the story.[50] It is striking that these narratives share a concern in their subject matter with displacement and transnationalism, which suggests that this subject is one that lends itself to an innovative transmedia form.

This connection is also made in Kamila Shamsie's *Kartography* (2002), which addresses the legacy of the 1971 war in Pakistan but also evinces a concern with remapping the city of Karachi from various perspectives in order to challenge the patriarchal–colonial history of conventional mapping. Shamsie juxtaposes the insider's view of the city with the tourist's Lonely Planet perspective. Furthermore, she imagines an interactive internet map where people can click on links to pictures and sound-files, anticipating the creation of Google Earth in 2005. In effect, her attitude to these new technologies and their possibilities for storytelling constructs, as Caroline Herbert argues, 'a dialogue between narrative and non-narrative modes that opens a space for difference and non-identification'.[51] While Shamsie's novel was authored, published, and read in the conventional way, her attempt to create what Herbert refers to as 'lyric maps' suggests connections between new narrative forms, new technologies, and new approaches to nation.

In October 2012, the collaboratively written zombie novel of Naomi Alderman and Margaret Atwood began to appear on Wattpad, a website that allows readers and writers to publish and read stories for free. While the Jewish author Alderman notes an interesting correspondence between the appearance of George A. Romero's *Night of the Living Dead* (1968) and the Holocaust trial of Adolf Eichmann of 1961, she also argues that '[p]erhaps the zombie represents our society's increasing yearning for immortality, and the increasing necessity therefore to imagine it as horrifying'.[52] Engagement with the non-human, the 'Other', and the inanimate is another appropriate topic (along with transnationalism and displacement) to explore in non-traditional, virtual form, and vice versa.

The question of the extent to which this networked society affects the life of the subaltern, and the subaltern woman in particular, is a theme that preoccupies many of the women writers we discuss here. George P. Landow argues that the predilection of French poststructuralist and deconstructivist theorists for images of webs and networks is indicative of an epistemological shift that results from a widespread recognition of the need to abandon 'conceptual systems founded upon ideas of center, margin, hierarchy, and linearity'.[53] What Landow does not explore, but is implicit in his choice of words, is that the replacement of hierarchical structures with networks may have an impact on the relationships between hegemonic and subaltern groups.

The assumption that hypertext will automatically lead to experimental, decentred writing is not always borne out by developments in cyberspace. Wattpad illustrates the online writers' unashamed preference for pulpy, plot-driven genre forms including science fiction, fantasy, horror, historical fiction, and chick lit (Wattpad's only categories that might include literary fiction are the mysteriously titled 'Non-Teen Fiction' and 'Spiritual'). Similarly, the most successful novel by a British woman writer in the last five years, E.L. James's 'erotic' *Fifty Shades of Grey* (2011), which has spawned a whole industry including a branded collection of wine, famously started its life as online fan fiction. It was written in response to Stephenie Meyer's *Twilight* series, and was posted on fanfiction.net and later on James's own website, fiftyshades.com, where it developed a word-of-mouth following.

Mercilessly satirized as 'S-and-M Cinderella', 'mommy porn', and even '50 Heaves of Puke', no one could accuse this once hypertext-based novel of being experimental or challenging.[54]

Perhaps more interesting are those examples of literary production which use digital and other technologies to make us question the relation between technological and other forms of production and consumption. In an environment increasingly threatened, as we have already discussed in relation to post-apocalyptic writing, by the negative impacts of climate change and a systemic waste of natural resources, the poet and 'inTer-active artist' Maya Chowdhry 'explores the juxtaposition and conflicts of new media with the "natural world", utilising text, film, animation, photography and the Web'.[55] Chowdhry is Scottish-born, of Indian heritage and resident in Manchester. Her work includes installations, community collaborations, films, poetry disseminated on and through the internet, and a Tumblr blog. She is notably concerned with the importance of water and impending water scarcity. Her work 'Haiku', a collaboration between herself and another poet, Sarah Hymas, used words from their poetry to produce a haiku grown in cress seeds. Her *Water is Priceless* installation consists of a hydroponic herb garden, 'made from upcycled water bottles, which triggers animations that tell the stories of water, whilst a barcode scanner triggers a webcam that captures the audience's image and refracts it into a mosaic of images of water'.[56] Here we can see Chowdhry manipulating new technologies to challenge us to rethink what technology means, and question where our reliance on it has brought us. In combination with the politics of water consumption and production, the question of who has access to new technologies has new resonance.

Other writers who have begun to make use of the creative potential of social networking sites such as Tumblr and Twitter include Caitlin Moran, whose Twitter feed has become an A-level set text on the OCR exam board syllabus alongside Samuel Pepys's diary. The controversy caused by this decision focused on whether those who chose to use this exam board would get into good universities, but in her response Moran argued that English is a living language and that change can only be positive:

> It's an insanity to say that 'English' only happens in 'proper' books and coursework. English is made by the people who use it every day. One report suggested that more than 1.8 billion new words are invented every year – think of 'twerking', 'Bitcoin', 'tbh', 'selfie', 'shamazing', 'trolling' – all made up by people, normal people, just typing and chatting away.[57]

The examples of new word coinages that she mentions were in several instances ('Bitcoin', 'tbh', 'selfie', and 'trolling') created in the digital environment. In some cases, writing in the digital environment encourages new attitudes to authorship: Nigerian writer Chimamanda Ngozi Adichie, for example, has begun blogging as the character Ifemelu from her most recent novel, *Americanah* (2013).[58]

In conclusion, many forms of women's literary production – including those taking place in cyberspace, written in hypertext and collaboratively authored – contest boundaries between nations and between fixed identities. Authorial identities and the identities of different ethnic groups, as well as the boundary between the human/non-human, and that between technological and other forms of production and consumption are questioned. However, such contestation is not an inevitable response within new media writing environments. Just as some 'multicultural' women's writing can enunciate a conservative agenda, so too online interactive fiction expresses a range of political positions. As we inch closer to the third decade of this millennium, we believe that women's interest in the themes of multiculturalism, ageing, and the environment will accelerate still more, fuelled by ever more innovative and digitized forms.

Notes

1. Quoted in Michael Banton, *Ethnic and Racial Consciousness* (Abingdon: Routledge, 2014), p. 61.
2. Salman Rushdie's depiction, in his 1988 novel *The Satanic Verses*, of a character called Mahound (an archaic, derogatory name for the Prophet Mohammed) led to widespread protest in 'the Muslim world' for its apparently blasphemous content. Iran's Ayatollah Khomeini issued a *fatwa*, or Islamic jurisdictional opinion, on Valentine's Day 1989, calling for capital punishment against Rushdie and his publishers. Rushdie went into hiding that spring and only emerged from concealment in the late 1990s. Several people died in connection with the *fatwa* and it had a tremendous impact on British Muslims' self-perceptions as a distinct community to be defended.
3. Trevor Phillips quoted in 'Britain "Sleepwalking to Segregation"', *Guardian*, 19 September 2005, www.theguardian.com/world/2005/sep/19/race.socialexclusion, accessed 22 October 2014.
4. Susan Moller Okin, 'Is Multiculturalism Bad for Women?', Susan Moller Okin et al., *Is Multiculturalism Bad for Women?* (Princeton University Press, 1999), p. 12.
5. Marie Macey, *Multiculturalism, Religion and Women: Doing Harm By Doing Good?* (Basingstoke: Palgrave Macmillan, 2009).
6. For examples of postsecular approaches, see Rosi Braidotti, 'In Spite of the Times: The Postsecular Turn in Feminism', *Theory, Culture and Society*, 25:6 (2008), pp. 1–24, and Lila Abu-Lughod, 'Do Muslim Women Really Need Saving?: Anthropological Reflections on Cultural Relativism and Its Others', *American Anthropologist*, 104:3 (2002), p. 788.
7. Germaine Greer, 'Reality Bites', *Guardian G2*, 24 July 2006, p. 24.
8. For an exemplary negative review, see Natasha Walter, 'Continental Drift', *Guardian Review*, 20 May 2006, p. 16. Her conclusion is that 'you can't help wishing that Monica Ali had chosen to write about somewhere she knew better, or wanted to know better', and that 'somewhere' is taken to be the Bangladeshi milieu of *Brick Lane*.

9. Tibor Fischer, 'Untold Story by Monica Ali – Review', *Observer*, 3 April 2011, 'The New Review' section, p. 39, www.theguardian.com/books/2011/apr/03/monica-ali-princess-diana-untold, accessed 17 November 2014. The byline for this review states, '*Monica Ali's* what-if *novel* based on *Princess Di* is classy commercial *fiction* – but a bit too girly for Tibor Fischer'.
10. Ana María Sánchez-Arce, '"Authenticism", or the Authority of Authenticity', *Mosaic*, 40:3 (2007), pp. 139–55, p. 139.
11. Patrick Butler and Owen Borcourt, 'How Tiny Charity Uncovered Britain's Most Extreme Case of Domestic Slavery', *Guardian*, 22 November 2013, p. 3.
12. Monica Ali, *In the Kitchen* (London: Black Swan, 2009), p. 129.
13. Paul Gilroy, *After Empire: Melancholia or Convivial Culture* (London: Routledge, 2004), p. x.
14. UN General Assembly, *Universal Declaration of Human Rights*, 10 December 1948, 217 A (III), www.refworld.org/docid/3ae6b3712c.html, accessed 22 November 2013.
15. Victoria Brittain and Gillian Slovo, *Guantanamo: 'Honor Bound to Defend Freedom'* (London: Oberon, 2004), pp. 51–2. The solicitor Gareth Peirce is renowned for her defence of human rights and campaigns against miscarriages of justice.
16. Suzanne Goldenberg, 'Novel on Prophet's Wife Pulled for Fear of Backlash', *Guardian*, 9 August 2008, p. 18; Jamie Doward and Mark Townsend, 'Terrorism: Firebomb Attack on London Book Publisher', *Observer*, 28 September 2008, p. 9.
17. For a useful survey of *Guardian* reporting of this Sikh cultural flashpoint, see http://arts.guardian.co.uk/behzti. For an academic article which pays close attention to the Sikh context and perspective, see Gurharpal Singh, 'British Multiculturalism and Sikhs', *Sikh Formations*, 1:2 (2005), pp. 157–73.
18. Gurpreet Kaur Bhatti, *Behzti* (London: Oberon, 2012), n.p.
19. Singh, p. 169.
20. Alastair Niven, Lisa Appignanesi, and signatories, 'Full Text of the Authors' Letter', *Guardian*, 13 January 2005, www.guardian.co.uk/politics/2005/jan/13/immigration policy.politicsandthearts, accessed 22 November 2013.
21. Rehana Ahmed and Claire Chambers, 'Literary Controversies Since the Rushdie Affair', *Huffington Post*, 20 September 2012, www.huffingtonpost.co.uk/dr-claire-chambers/rushdie-muslims-books-controversy_b_1895954.html, accessed 3 April 2015.
22. Tony Blair, 'The Prime Minister's Statement on Anti-Terror Measures', *Guardian*, 5 August 2005, www.theguardian.com/politics/2005/aug/05/uksecurity.terrorism1, accessed 22 November 2013.
23. David Cameron, 'Full Transcript: Speech on Radicalisation and Islamic Extremism (Munich)', *New Statesman*, 5 February 2011, www.newstatesman.com/blogs/the-staggers/2011/02/terrorism-islam-ideology, accessed 22 November 2013.
24. Alison Fell, *Tricks of the Light* (London: Black Swan, 2004), p. 52.
25. Margaret Morganroth Gullette, *Aged by Culture* (University of Chicago Press, 2004), p. 19.
26. Kathleen Woodward, ed., *Figuring Age: Women, Bodies, Generations* (Bloomington: Indiana University Press, 1999), p. xiii.
27. Sarah Falcus, 'Addressing Age in Michèle Roberts's *Reader, I Married Him*', *Contemporary Women's Writing*, 7:1 (2013), p. 32.
28. Barbara Frey Waxman, *To Live in the Center of the Moment: Literary Autobiographies of Aging* (Charlottesville: University Press of Virginia, 1997), p. 13; *From the Hearth to the Open Road: A Feminist Study of Ageing in Contemporary Literature* (New York: Greenwood Press, 1990), pp. 1–22.

29. See Susan Watkins, '"Summoning your youth at will": Memory, Time and Aging in the Work of Penelope Lively, Margaret Atwood and Doris Lessing', *Frontiers: A Journal of Women's Studies,* 34:2 (2013), pp. 222–44.
30. Edward W. Said, *On Late Style: Music and Literature Against the Grain* (London: Bloomsbury, 2006), p. 12.
31. Gordon McMullan, *Shakespeare and the Idea of Late Writing* (Cambridge University Press, 2007), p. 17.
32. Liz Jensen, *War Crimes for the Home* (London: Bloomsbury, 2002), p. 29.
33. Penelope Lively, *Ammonites and Leaping Fish: A Life in Time* (London: Penguin, 2013), p. 43.
34. Lynne Segal, *Out of Time: The Pleasures and Perils of Ageing* (London: Verso, 2014), p. 4.
35. Diana Athill, *Somewhere Towards the End* (London: Granta, 2008), pp. 21–2.
36. Frank Kermode, *The Sense of an Ending: Studies in the Theory of Fiction* (Oxford University Press, 1967), p. 35.
37. See Francis Fukuyama, *The End of History and the Last Man* (New York: Free Press, 1992).
38. Ali Smith, *Girl Meets Boy* (Edinburgh: Canongate, 2007), p. 124.
39. Andreu Domingo coins this term to describe dystopias relating to demographic change and population concerns. See 'Demodystopias: Prospects of Demographic Hell', *Population and Development Review,* 34:4 (2008), p. 725. Thanks to Sarah King for this reference.
40. Jane Rogers, *The Testament of Jessie Lamb* (Dingwall: Sandstone Press, 2011), p. 62.
41. See Susan Watkins, 'Future Shock: Rewriting the Apocalypse in Contemporary Women's Fiction', *LIT: Literature, Interpretation, Theory,* 23:2 (2012), pp. 119–37.
42. Margaret Toye, 'Donna Haraway's Cyborg Touching (Up/On) Luce Irigaray's Ethics and the Interval Between: Poethics as Embodied Writing', *Hypatia,* 27:1 (2012), p. 191.
43. Stacey Alaimo, *Bodily Natures: Science, Environment and the Material Self* (Bloomington: Indiana University Press, 2010), p. 2.
44. Aaron S. Rosenfeld, 'Re-membering the Future: Doris Lessing's "Experiment in Autobiography"', *Critical Survey,* 17:1 (2005), p. 40.
45. Sarah Hall, *The Carhullan Army* (London: Faber and Faber, 2007), p. 207.
46. Greg Garrard, *Ecocriticism* (London: Routledge, 2004), p. 87.
47. Steven Connor, *The English Novel in History, 1950–1995* (London: Routledge, 2001), p. 205.
48. See Suniti Namjoshi, *The Reader's Text of Building Babel: A Novel with Interactive Hypertext Links* (Melbourne: Spinifex Press), www.spinifexpress.com.au/BabelBuildingSite/, accessed 22 November 2013.
49. Kate Pullinger with Chris Joseph and participants, *Flight Paths: A Networked Novel,* http://flightpaths.net/, accessed 17 November 2013.
50. Kate Pullinger and Chris Joseph, *Inanimate Alice,* www.inanimatealice.com/index.html, accessed 22 November 2013.
51. Caroline Herbert, 'Lyric Maps and the Legacies of 1971 in Kamila Shamsie's *Kartography*', *Journal of Postcolonial Writing,* 47:2 (2011), pp. 159–72, p. 171.
52. Naomi Alderman, 'The Meaning of Zombies', *Granta,* 20 November 2011, www.granta.com/New-Writing/The-Meaning-of-Zombies, accessed 17 November 2013.
53. George P. Landow, *Hypertext: The Convergence of Contemporary Critical Theory and Technology* (Baltimore: Johns Hopkins University Press, 1992), p. 2.
54. Alessandra Stanley, 'Glass Slipper as Fetish', *New York Times,* 2 April 2012, www.nytimes.com/2012/04/03/books/fifty-shades-of-grey-s-and-m-cinderella.html,

accessed 22 November 2013; Ben Quinn, 'British Author's "Mommy Porn" Becomes US Bestseller', *Guardian*, 12 March 2012, p. 14; Amberance, 'The *Fifty Shades* Reviews', http://bizzybiz.blogspot.co.uk, accessed 22 November 2013.

55. See Chowdhry's website, www.interactiveartist.org/, accessed 2 November 2014.
56. See the documentation of this installation at http://vimeo.com/16482997, accessed 2 November 2014.
57. Caitlin Moran, 'Should My Tweets be on the A-Level Syllabus?', *Times*, 8 May 2014, www.thetimes.co.uk/tto/life/article4083402.ece, accessed 11 November 2014.
58. See 'The Small Redemptions of Lagos', http://americanahblog.com/, accessed 11 November 2014.

Electronic Resources

A-Gender: http://a-gender.org/poets/
Introductions to living, published women poets in the UK.

The BBC Writers' Archive: www.bbc.co.uk/archive/writers/
The BBC's archive of interviews with modern writers, including women writers from 1965 to 2009.

Black British Women Writers: www.vub.ac.be/TALK/BBWW/
Features helpful bibliographies, details of events and links, and information about researchers in the field.

The British Council: www.literature.britishcouncil.org/writers/
Biographical and critical introductions to contemporary writers, among whom women writers feature prominently.

The British Library: www.bl.uk/nls/authors/
A developing project of interviews with contemporary authors, including a good number of women authors. Two further, important links on this site are: www.bl.uk/spare-rib, which contains the full run of *Spare Rib*, and www.bl.uk/sisterhood, which provides an oral history of the Women's Liberation Movement.

The Contemporary Women Writers Association: www.the-cwwa.org/
An association dedicated to developing academic interest in contemporary women's writing. Some bibliographies.

Contemporary Women's Writing:
www.oxfordjournals.org/our_journals/cww/interviews.html/
Offers free access to interviews that have appeared in the journal *Contemporary Women's Writing* (Oxford University Press).

English PEN: www.englishpen.org/
An international network of writers campaigning on issues of freedom of expression.

The Feminist Library: http://feministlibrary.co.uk/
Holds an extensive collection of Women's Liberation Movement literature.

The International Gothic Association: www.iga.stir.ac.uk/
An interest through conferences and the journal *Gothic Studies* (Manchester University Press) in contemporary women's Gothic.

The Literary Encyclopedia: www.litencyc.com/
A rapidly expanding site offering critical introductions to authors, individual texts, thematic groupings, etc.

The Modern Novel – Women Writers: www.themodernnovel.com/women/women.htm/
Useful links to women fiction writers, polemical articles, publishers, genre websites, etc.

Modern Writers Collection: www.bbc.co.uk/archive/writers/
The BBC's archive of interviews with twentieth-century writers including contemporary women writers.

Mslexia: www.mslexia.co.uk/
Website linked to *Mslexia* magazine. Contains supportive advice for new writers, details of prizes, events, etc., information about the publishing industry.

National Life Stories: www.bl.uk/nls/authors
Interviews with authors including Hilary Mantel, Penelope Lively, P.D. James, Eva Figes, and Beryl Bainbridge.

The Orlando Project: www.arts.ualberta.ca/orlando/
Focuses on the literary history of British women's writing.

The Royal Society of Literature: www.rsliterature.org/1/Home/
The online library contains audio recordings, images, and selected articles from the *RSL Review*.

The Scottish Theatre Archive: www.gla.ac.uk/services/specialcollections/collectionsa-z/scottishtheatrearchive/
Includes women's contribution to Scottish theatrical history and links to other useful sites.

The University of Bristol Theatre Collection: www.bristol.ac.uk/theatrecollection/
Contains a significant number of collections including the Women's Theatre Collection and links to other relevant sites.

The Wiley-Blackwell Encyclopedia of Literature: www.literatureencyclopedia.com/public/
Extensive coverage of authors, texts, genres, literary theory, etc.

The Women's Library @ LSE: www.lse.ac.uk/library/collections/featuredCollections/womensLibraryLSE.aspx/
A major resource of books, pamphlets, periodicals, archives, and museum objects.

Women's Life-Writing Network: www.womenslifewriting.net/
Fosters interest in both the writing and critical study of women's life-writing.

Writers at Warwick Archive: www2.warwick.ac.uk/fac/arts/english/writingprog/archive/
Recordings of contemporary writers giving readings, in interview, and responding to audience questions. Searchable by author, date, and theme.

Select Bibliography

Acheson, James and Romana Huk (eds), *Contemporary British Poetry* (Albany: State University of New York Press, 1996).

Acheson, James and Sarah C.E. Ross (eds), *The Contemporary British Novel Since 1980* (Edinburgh University Press, 2005).

Adiseshiah, Siân, *Churchill's Socialism: Political Resistance in the Plays of Caryl Churchill* (Newcastle upon Tyne: Cambridge Scholars, 2009).

Adiseshiah, Siân and Rupert Hildyard (eds), *Twenty-First Century Fiction: What Happens Now?* (Basingstoke: Palgrave Macmillan, 2013).

Alcobia-Murphy, Shane and Richard Kirkland (eds), *The Poetry of Medbh McGuckian: The Interior of Words* (Cork University Press, 2010).

Alfer, Alexa, *A.S. Byatt: Critical Storytelling* (Manchester University Press, 2010).

Alfer, Alexa and Michael J. Noble (eds), *Essays on the Fiction of A.S. Byatt: Imagining the Real* (Westport, Conn.: Greenwood Press, 2001).

Andermahr, Sonya (ed.), *Jeanette Winterson: A Contemporary Critical Guide* (London: Continuum, 2007).

—— *Jeanette Winterson* (Basingstoke: Palgrave Macmillan, 2008).

Andermahr, Sonya and Lawrence Phillips (eds), *Angela Carter: New Critical Readings* (London: Bloomsbury, 2014).

Angier, Carole, *Jean Rhys* (1985; Harmondsworth: Penguin, 1992).

Arana, R. Victoria, *'Black' British Aesthetics Today* (Newcastle upon Tyne: Cambridge Scholars, 2007).

Armitt, Lucie, *Contemporary Women's Fiction and the Fantastic* (Basingstoke: Palgrave Macmillan, 2000).

Aston, Elaine, *Feminist Views on the English Stage: Women Playwrights, 1990–2000* (Cambridge University Press, 2003).

—— *Caryl Churchill* (1997; Plymouth: Northcote House, 2010).

Aston, Elaine and Janelle Reinett (eds), *The Cambridge Companion to Modern British Women Playwrights* (Cambridge University Press, 2000).

Aston, Elaine and Elin Diamond (eds), *The Cambridge Companion to Caryl Churchill* (Cambridge University Press, 2009).

Aston, Elaine and Geraldine Harris (eds), *A Good Night Out for the Girls: Popular Feminisms in Contemporary Theatre and Performance* (Basingstoke: Palgrave Macmillan, 2012).

Barreca, Regina, *Fay Weldon's Wicked Fictions* (Lebanon, NH: University Press of New England, 1994).

Baxter, Jeannette and David James (eds), *Andrea Levy* (London: Bloomsbury, 2014).

Benson, Stephen (ed.), *Contemporary Fiction and the Fairy Tale* (Detroit: Wayne State University Press, 2008).

Bentley, Nick (ed.), *British Fiction of the 1990s* (London: Routledge, 2005).

—— *Contemporary British Fiction* (Edinburgh University Press, 2008).

Bertram, Vicki (ed.), *Kicking Daffodils: Twentieth-Century Women Poets* (Edinburgh University Press, 1997).

—— *Gendering Poetry: Contemporary Women and Men Poets* (London: Rivers Oram Pandora Press, 2004).

Boccardi, Mariadele, *A.S. Byatt* (Basingstoke: Palgrave Macmillan, 2013).

Brabon, Benjamin A. and Stéphanie Genz (eds), *Postfeminist Gothic* (Basingstoke: Palgrave Macmillan, 2007).
Bradford, Richard, *The Novel Now: Contemporary British Fiction* (Oxford: Blackwell, 2007).
Brannigan, John, *Pat Barker* (Manchester University Press, 2005).
Brennan, Zoe, *The Older Woman in Recent Fiction* (Jefferson, NC: McFarland, 2005).
Bristow, Joseph and Trev Lynn Broughton (eds), *The Infernal Desires of Angela Carter: Fiction, Femininity, Feminism* (London: Longman, 1997).
Broackes, Justin (ed.), *Iris Murdoch, Philosopher* (Oxford University Press, 2011).
Burgass, Catherine, *A.S. Byatt's* Possession: *A Reader's Guide* (London: Continuum, 2002).
Burkhart, Charles, *The Pleasure of Miss Pym* (Austin: University of Texas Press, 1987).
Bush, Sophie, *The Theatre of Timberlake Wertenbaker* (London: Methuen Drama, 2013).
Cadman, Eileen, Gail Chester, and Agnes Pivot, *Rolling Our Own: Women as Printers, Publishers and Distributors* (London: Minority Press Group, 1981).
Campbell, Jane, *A.S. Byatt and the Heliotropic Imagination* (Waterloo, Ont.: Wilfred Laurier University Press, 2004).
Carr, Helen (ed.), *From My Guy to Sci-Fi: Genre and Women's Writing in the Postmodern World* (London: Pandora, 1989).
—— *Jean Rhys* (1990; Plymouth: Northcote House, 2011).
Castagna, Valentina, *Shape-Shifting Tales: Michèle Roberts's Monstrous Women* (Bern: Peter Lang, 2010).
Chambers, Claire, *British Muslim Fictions: Interviews with Contemporary Writers* (Basingstoke: Palgrave Macmillan, 2011).
Chester, Gail and Sigrid Nielsen (eds), *In Other Words: Writing as a Feminist* (1987; London: Routledge, 2013).
Cheyette, Bryan, *Muriel Spark* (Plymouth: Northcote House, 2000).
Childs, Peter, *Contemporary Novelists: British Fiction 1970–2003* (Basingstoke: Palgrave Macmillan, 2004).
Christianson, Aileen and Alison Lumsden (eds), *Contemporary Scottish Women Writers* (Edinburgh University Press, 2000).
Conradi, Peter J., *The Saint and Artist: A Study of Iris Murdoch's Works* (1986; London: HarperCollins, 2001).
—— *Iris Murdoch: A Life* (2001; London: HarperCollins, 2010).
Cooper, Katherine and Emma Short (eds), *The Female Figure in Contemporary Historical Fiction* (Basingstoke: Palgrave Macmillan, 2012).
Cotsell, Michael, *Barbara Pym* (Basingstoke: Palgrave Macmillan, 1989).
Crawford, Robert and Anne Varty (eds), *Liz Lochhead's Voices* (Edinburgh University Press, 1993).
Day, Aidan, *Angela Carter: The Rational Glass* (Manchester University Press, 1998).
Donato, Deborah, *Reading Barbara Pym* (Madison, NJ: Fairleigh Dickinson University Press, 2006).
Dowling, Finuala, *Fay Weldon's Fiction* (Madison, NJ: Fairleigh Dickinson University Press, 1998).
Dowson, Jane (ed.), *The Cambridge Companion to Twentieth-Century British and Irish Women's Poetry* (Cambridge University Press, 2011).
Dowson, Jane and Alice Entwistle, *A History of Twentieth-Century British Women's Poetry* (Cambridge University Press, 2005).
Duncker, Patricia, *Sisters and Strangers: An Introduction to Contemporary Feminist Fiction* (Oxford: Blackwell, 1992).
Eagleton, Mary, *Figuring the Woman Author in Contemporary Fiction* (Basingstoke: Palgrave Macmillan, 2005).

Easton, Alison (ed.), *Angela Carter* (Basingstoke: Palgrave Macmillan, 2000).
Ellam, Julie, *Love in Jeanette Winterson's Novels* (Amsterdam: Rodopi, 2010).
English, James F. (ed.), *A Concise Companion to Contemporary British Fiction* (Oxford: Blackwell, 2006).
Entwistle, Alice, *Poetry, Geography, Gender: Women Rewriting Contemporary Wales* (Cardiff: University of Wales Press, 2013).
Falcus, Sarah, *Michèle Roberts: Myths, Mothers and Memories* (Bern: Peter Lang, 2007).
Faragó, Borbála, *Medbh McGuckian* (Cork University Press, 2014).
Faulks, Lana, *Fay Weldon* (Boston: Twayne, 1998).
Ferriss, Suzanne and Mallory Young (eds), *Chick Lit: The New Woman's Fiction* (New York: Routledge, 2006).
Fiander, Lisa M., *Fairy Tales and the Fiction of Iris Murdoch, Margaret Drabble, and A.S. Byatt* (New York: Peter Lang, 2004).
Finney, Brian, *English Fiction Since 1984: Narrating a Nation* (Basingstoke: Palgrave Macmillan, 2006).
Flynn, Leontia, *Reading Medbh McGuckian* (Sallins: Irish Academic Press, 2014).
Franken, Christien, *A.S. Byatt: Art, Authorship, Creativity* (Basingstoke: Palgrave Macmillan, 2001).
Gamble, Sarah, *Angela Carter: Writing From the Front Line* (Edinburgh University Press, 1997).
—— (ed.), *The Fiction of Angela Carter: A Reader's Guide to Essential Criticism* (Basingstoke: Palgrave Macmillan, 2001).
—— *Angela Carter: A Literary Life* (Basingstoke: Palgrave Macmillan, 2001).
Ganteau, Jean-Michel and Susana Onega (eds), *Trauma and Romance in Contemporary British Literature* (London: Routledge, 2013).
García-Sánchez, M. Soraya, *Travelling in Women's History with Michèle Roberts's Novels: Literature, Language and Culture* (Bern: Peter Lang, 2011).
Gardiner, Michael and Willy Maley (eds), *The Edinburgh Companion to Muriel Spark* (Edinburgh University Press, 2010).
Gauthier, Timothy, *Narrative Desire and Historical Reparation: A.S. Byatt, Ian McEwan, and Salman Rushdie* (London: Routledge, 2007).
Germanà, Monica, *Scottish Women's Gothic and Fantastic Writing* (Edinburgh University Press, 2012).
Germanà, Monica and Emily Horton (eds), *Ali Smith* (London: Bloomsbury, 2013).
Gerrard, Nicci, *Into the Mainstream: How Feminism Has Changed Women's Writing* (London: Pandora, 1989).
Gifford, Douglas and Dorothy MacMillan (eds), *A History of Scottish Women's Writing* (Edinburgh University Press, 1997).
Goddard, Lynette, *Staging Black Feminisms: Identity, Politics, Performance* (Basingstoke: Palgrave Macmillan, 2007).
Gömceli, Nursen, *Timberlake Wertenbaker and Contemporary British Feminist Drama* (Palo Alto, Calif.: Academica Press, 2010).
Goodman, Lizbeth, *Contemporary Feminist Theatres: To Each Her Own* (London: Routledge, 1993).
Gramich, Katie, *Twentieth-Century Women's Writing in Wales: Land, Gender and Belonging* (Cardiff: University of Wales Press, 2007).
Greene, Gayle, *Changing the Story: Feminist Fiction and the Tradition* (Bloomington: Indiana University Press, 1991).
—— *Doris Lessing: The Poetics of Change* (Ann Arbor: University of Michigan Press, 1995).
Grice, Helena and Tim Woods (eds), *'I'm telling you stories': Jeanette Winterson and the Politics of Reading* (Amsterdam: Rodopi, 1998).

Griffin, Gabriele, *Contemporary Black and Asian Women Playwrights in Britain* (Cambridge University Press, 2003).

Gruss, Susanne, *The Pleasure of the Feminist Text: Reading Michèle Roberts and Angela Carter* (Amsterdam: Rodopi, 2009).

Gunning, Dave, *Race and Antiracism in Black British and British Asian Literature* (Liverpool University Press, 2010).

Hadley, Louisa, *The Fiction of A.S. Byatt: A Reader's Guide to Essential Criticism* (Basingstoke: Palgrave Macmillan, 2008).

—— *Neo-Victorian Fiction and Historical Narrative: The Victorians and Us* (Basingstoke: Palgrave Macmillan, 2010).

Hanson, Clare, *Hysterical Fictions: The 'Woman's Novel' in the Twentieth Century* (Basingstoke: Palgrave Macmillan, 2000).

Harrison, Nancy Rebecca, *Jean Rhys and the Novel as Women's Text* (Raleigh: University of North Carolina Press, 1989).

Harzewski, Stephanie, *Chick Lit and Postfeminism* (Charlottesville and London: University of Virginia Press, 2011).

Head, Dominic, *The Cambridge Introduction to Modern British Fiction, 1950–2000* (Cambridge University Press, 2002).

Heilmann, Ann and Mark Llewellyn (eds), *Metafiction and Metahistory in Contemporary Women's Writing* (Basingstoke: Palgrave Macmillan, 2007).

Herman, David (ed.), *Muriel Spark: Twenty-First-Century Perspectives* (Baltimore: Johns Hopkins University Press, 2012).

Hosmer Jr, Robert E. (ed.), *Contemporary British Women Writers: Texts and Strategies* (Basingstoke: Palgrave Macmillan, 1993).

Howells, Coral Ann, *Jean Rhys* (London: Prentice Hall, 1991).

Janik, Vicki K., Del Ivan Janik, and Emmanuel Sampath Nelson (eds), *Modern British Women Writers: An A-to-Z Guide* (Westport: Greenwood Publishing Group, 2002).

Jarvis, Matthew, *Ruth Bidgood* (Cardiff: University of Wales Press, 2012).

Joannou, Maroula, *Contemporary Women's Writing: From* The Golden Notebook *to* The Color Purple (Manchester University Press, 2000).

Keen, Suzanne, *Romance of the Archive in Contemporary British Fiction* (University of Toronto Press, 2003).

Kennedy, David and Christine Kennedy, *Women's Experimental Poetry in Britain 1970–2010: Body, Time and Locale* (Liverpool University Press, 2013).

Kenyon, Olga, *Women Novelists Today: A Survey of English Writing in the Seventies and Eighties* (Brighton: Harvester Wheatsheaf, 1988).

Kiliç, Mine Özyurt, *Maggie Gee: Writing the Condition-of-England Novel* (London: Bloomsbury, 2013).

Kim, Julie H. (ed.), *Murdering Miss Marple: Essays on Gender and Sexuality in the New Golden Age of Women's Crime Fiction* (Jefferson, NC: McFarland, 2012).

King, Bruce, *The Oxford English Literary History, 1948–2000: The Internationalization of English Literature* (Oxford University Press, 2004).

King, Jeannette, *Doris Lessing: Modern Fiction* (London: Edward Arnold, 1989).

—— *Women and the Word: Contemporary Women Novelists and the Bible* (Basingstoke: Palgrave Macmillan, 2001).

—— *The Victorian Woman Question in Contemporary Feminist Fiction* (Basingstoke: Palgrave Macmillan, 2005).

Komporaly, Jozefina, *Staging Motherhood: British Women Playwrights, 1956 to the Present* (Basingstoke: Palgrave Macmillan, 2006).

Kostkowska, Justyna, *Ecocriticism and Women Writers: Virginia Woolf, Jeanette Winterson, and Ali Smith* (Basingstoke: Palgrave Macmillan, 2013).

Lane, Richard J., Rod Mengham, and Philip Tew (eds), *Contemporary British Fiction* (Cambridge: Polity Press, 2003).
Leader, Zachary (ed.), *On Modern British Fiction* (Oxford University Press, 2002).
Lee, Hermione, *Penelope Fitzgerald: A Life* (London: Chatto & Windus, 2013).
Leeming, Glenda, *Margaret Drabble* (Plymouth: Northcote House, 2005).
Leeson, Miles, *Iris Murdoch: Philosophical Novelist* (London: Continuum, 2011).
Liddell, Robert, *A Mind at Ease: Barbara Pym and Her Novels* (London: Peter Owen, 1989).
Luckhurst, Mary (ed.), *Companion to Modern British and Irish Drama: 1880 to the Present* (Oxford: Blackwell, 2006).
Makinen, Merja (ed.), *The Novels of Jeanette Winterson: A Reader's Guide to Essential Criticism* (Basingstoke: Palgrave Macmillan, 2005).
Marsh, Huw, *Beryl Bainbridge* (Plymouth: Northcote House, 2014).
Maslen, Elizabeth, *Doris Lessing* (1994; Plymouth: Northcote House, 2014).
Maurel, Sylvie, *Jean Rhys* (Basingstoke: Palgrave Macmillan, 1998).
McLeod, John, *Postcolonial London: Rewriting the Metropolis* (London: Routledge, 2004).
McQuillan, Martin (ed.), *Theorising Muriel Spark: Gender, Race, Deconstruction* (Basingstoke: Palgrave Macmillan, 2002).
Meaney, Gerardine, *(Un)Like Subjects: Women, Theory, Fiction* (London: Routledge, 1993).
Meyers, Helene, *Femicidal Fears: Narratives of the Female Gothic Experience* (Albany: SUNY Press, 2001).
Miles, Rosalind, *The Female Form: Women Writers and the Conquest of the Novel* (London: Routledge, 1987).
Mills, Sara and Lynne Pearce (eds), *Feminist Readings/Feminists Reading* (1989; London: Harvester Wheatsheaf, 1996).
Mitchell, Kaye, *A.L. Kennedy* (Basingstoke: Palgrave Macmillan, 2007).
—— (ed.), *Sarah Waters* (London: Bloomsbury, 2013).
Monteith, Sharon, *Pat Barker* (Plymouth: Northcote House, 2002).
Monteith, Sharon, Jenny Newman, and Pat Wheeler, *Contemporary British and Irish Fiction: An Introduction Through Interviews* (London: Hodder Arnold, 2004).
Monteith, Sharon, Margaretta Jolly, Nahem Yousaf, and Ronald Paul (eds), *Critical Perspectives on Pat Barker* (Columbia: University of South Carolina Press, 2005).
Morrison, Jago, *Contemporary Fiction* (London: Routledge, 2003).
Moseley, Merritt, *The Fiction of Pat Barker: A Reader's Guide to Essential Criticism* (Basingstoke: Palgrave Macmillan, 2014).
Munford, Rebecca (ed.), *Re-Visiting Angela Carter: Texts, Contexts, Intertexts* (Basingstoke: Palgrave Macmillan, 2006).
—— *Decadent Daughters and Monstrous Mothers: Angela Carter and the European Gothic* (Manchester University Press, 2013).
Munt, Sally R., *Murder by the Book? Feminism and the Crime Novel* (London: Routledge, 1994).
Murphy, Neil and Wai-chew Sim (eds), *British Asian Fiction: Framing the Contemporary* (Amhurst: Cabria Press, 2008).
Murray, Simone, *Mixed Media: Feminist Presses and Publishing Politics* (London: Pluto Press, 2004).
Nasta, Susheila (ed.), *Writing Across Worlds: Contemporary Writers Talk* (London: Routledge, 1994).
Neumeier, Beate (ed.), *Engendering Realism and Postmodernism: Contemporary Women Writers in Britain* (Amsterdam and New York: Rodopi, 2001).

Norquay, Glenda (ed.), *The Edinburgh Companion to Scottish Women's Writing* (Edinburgh University Press, 2012).
Onega, Susana, *Jeanette Winterson* (Manchester University Press, 2006).
Oró-Piqueras, Maricel, *Ageing Corporialities in Contemporary English Fiction: Redefining Stereotypes* (Saarbrücken: Lap Lambert Academic Publishing, 2011).
Palmer, Paulina, *Contemporary Women's Fiction: Narrative Practice and Feminist Theory* (Hemel Hempstead: Harvester Wheatsheaf, 1989).
—— *Contemporary Lesbian Writing: Dreams, Desire, Difference* (Buckingham: Open University Press, 1993).
Parker, Emma, *Kate Atkinson's* Behind the Scenes at the Museum: *A Reader's Guide* (London: Continuum, 2002).
—— (ed.), *Contemporary British Women Writers* (Woodbridge: D.S. Brewer, 2004).
Peach, Linden, *Contemporary Irish and Welsh Women's Fiction: Gender, Desire and Power* (Cardiff: University of Wales Press, 2007).
—— *Angela Carter* (1998; Basingstoke: Palgrave Macmillan, 2009).
Philips, Deborah, *Women's Fiction: From 1945 to Today* (London: Continuum, 2014).
Plain, Gill, *Twentieth-Century Crime Fiction: Gender, Sexuality and the Body* (Edinburgh University Press, 2001).
Pyrhönen, Heta, *Bluebeard Gothic:* Jane Eyre *and Its Progeny* (University of Toronto Press, 2010).
Raschke, Debrah, Phyllis Sternberg Perrakis, and Sandra Singer (eds), *Doris Lessing: Interrogating the Times* (Columbus: Ohio State University Press, 2010).
Rawlinson, Mark, *Pat Barker* (Basingstoke: Palgrave Macmillan, 2009).
Rees-Jones, Deryn, *Consorting with Angels: Essays on Modern Women Poets* (Tarset: Bloodaxe, 2005).
—— *Carol Ann Duffy* (1999; Plymouth: Northcote House, 2010).
Rennison, Nick, *Contemporary British Novelists* (London: Routledge, 2004).
Reynolds, Margaret and Jonathan Noakes, *Jeanette Winterson: The Essential Guide* (London: Vintage, 2003).
—— *A.S. Byatt: The Essential Guide* (London: Vintage, 2004).
—— *Iris Murdoch: The Essential Guide* (London: Vintage, 2004).
Ridout, Alice, *Contemporary Women Writers Look Back: From Irony to Nostalgia* (London: Continuum, 2011).
Ridout, Alice and Susan Watkins (eds), *Doris Lessing: Border Crossings* (London: Continuum, 2009).
Rine, Abigail, *Irigaray, Incarnation and Contemporary Women's Fiction* (London: Bloomsbury, 2013).
Rossen, Janice, *The World of Barbara Pym* (London: Macmillan, 1987).
—— (ed.), *Independent Women: The Function of Gender in the Novels of Barbara Pym* (Brighton: Harvester Press, 1988).
Rowe, Anne and Avril Horner (eds), *Iris Murdoch: Texts and Contexts* (Basingstoke: Palgrave Macmillan, 2012).
Rowe, Margaret Moan, *Doris Lessing* (Basingstoke: Macmillan, 1994).
Rowland, Susan, *From Agatha Christie to Ruth Rendell: British Women Writers in Detective and Crime Fiction* (Basingstoke: Palgrave, 2001).
Sadler, Lynn Veach, *Anita Brookner* (Boston: Twayne, 1990).
Sage, Lorna (ed.), *Flesh and the Mirror: Essays on the Art of Angela Carter* (London: Virago Press, 1994).
—— *Angela Carter* (1994; Plymouth: Northcote House, 2007).

Sánchez-Arce, Ana Mariá (ed.), *Identity and Form in Contemporary Literature* (London: Routledge, 2013).

Saunders, Graham, *'Love me or kill me': Sarah Kane and the Theatre of Extremes* (Manchester University Press, 2002).

Schoene, Berthold (ed.), *The Edinburgh Companion to Contemporary Scottish Literature* (Edinburgh University Press, 2007).

Sellers, Susan, *Myth and Fairy Tale in Contemporary Women's Fiction* (Basingstoke: Palgrave, 2001).

Sesay, Kadija (ed.), *Write Black, Write British: From Post Colonial to Black British Literature* (Hertford: Hansib Publications, 2005).

Severin, Laura, *Poetry Off the Page: Twentieth-Century British Women Poets in Performance* (Aldershot: Ashgate, 2004).

Simons, Judy and Kate Fullbrook (eds), *Writing: A Woman's Business* (Manchester University Press, 1998).

Simpson, Anne B., *Territories of the Psyche: The Fiction of Jean Rhys* (Basingstoke: Palgrave Macmillan, 2005).

Smith, Patricia Juliana, *Lesbian Panic: Homoeroticism in Modern British Women's Fiction* (New York: Columbia University Press, 1997).

Spear, Hilda D., *Iris Murdoch* (1995; London: Palgrave Macmillan, 2007).

Sprague, Claire (ed.), *In Pursuit of Doris Lessing: Nine Nations Reading* (New York: St. Martin's Press, 1990).

Stannard, Martin, *Muriel Spark: The Biography* (London: Weidenfeld & Nicholson, 2009).

Steveker, Lena, *Identity and Cultural Memory in the Fiction of A.S. Byatt: Knitting the Net of Culture* (Basingstoke: Palgrave Macmillan, 2009).

Stevenson, Randall, *The Oxford English Literary History, 1960–2000: The Last of England?* (Oxford University Press, 2006).

Tew, Philip, *Zadie Smith* (Basingstoke: Palgrave Macmillan, 2009).

—— *Reading Zadie Smith: The First Decade and Beyond* (London: Bloomsbury, 2013).

Todd, Richard, *A.S. Byatt* (Plymouth: Northcote House, 1996).

Tonkin, Maggie, *Angela Carter and Decadence: Critical Fictions/Fictional Critiques* (Basingstoke: Palgrave Macmillan, 2012).

Toplu, Şebnem, *Fiction Unbound: Bernardine Evaristo* (Newcastle upon Tyne: Cambridge Scholars Press, 2011).

Tucker, Lindsey, *Critical Essays on Angela Carter* (Boston: Twayne, 1999).

Turner, Nick, *Post-War British Women Novelists and the Canon* (London: Continuum, 2010).

Tylee, Claire M. (ed.), *In the Open: Jewish Women Writers and British Culture* (Newark: University of Delaware Press, 2006).

Varty, Anne (ed.), *The Edinburgh Companion to Liz Lochhead* (Edinburgh University Press, 2013).

Vijayasree, C., *Suniti Namjoshi: The Artful Transgressor* (Jaipur: Rawat, 2002).

Walker, Dorothea, *Muriel Spark* (Boston: Twayne, 1988).

Wallace, Diana, *The Woman's Historical Novel: British Women Writers, 1900–2000* (Basingstoke: Palgrave Macmillan, 2004).

Wallhead, Celia, *A.S. Byatt: Essays on the Short Fiction* (Bern: Peter Lang, 2007).

Walters, Tracey L. (ed.), *Zadie Smith: Critical Essays* (Bern: Peter Lang, 2008).

Wandor, Michelene (ed.), *On Gender and Writing* (London: Pandora Press, 1993).

Watkins, Susan, *Twentieth-Century Women Novelists: Feminist Theory into Practice* (Basingstoke: Palgrave, 2001).

—— *Doris Lessing* (Manchester University Press, 2011).
Waugh, Patricia, *Feminine Fictions: Revisiting the Postmodern* (London: Routledge, 1989).
Waxman, Barbara Frey, *From the Hearth to the Open Road: A Feminist Study of Aging in Contemporary Literature* (New York: Greenwood Press, 1990).
Weld, Annette, *Barbara Pym and the Novel of Manners* (Basingstoke: Macmillan, 1991).
Werlock, Abby H.P. (ed.), *British Women Writing Fiction* (Tuscaloosa and London: University of Alabama Press, 2000).
Westman, Karin, *Pat Barker's* Regeneration: *A Reader's Guide* (London: Continuum, 2001).
Wheeler, Pat (ed.), *Re-reading Pat Barker* (Newcastle upon Tyne: Cambridge Scholars, 2011).
Whelehan, Imelda, *The Feminist Bestseller: From* Sex and the Single Girl *to* Sex and the City (Basingstoke: Palgrave Macmillan, 2005).
Whyte, Christopher (ed.), *Gendering the Nation: Studies in Modern Scottish Literature* (Edinburgh University Press, 1995).
Williams-Wanquet, Eileen, *Art and Life in the Novels of Anita Brookner: Reading for Life, Subversive Re-writing to Live* (Bern: Peter Lang, 2004).
Wilson, Janet, *Fleur Adcock* (Plymouth: Northcote House, 2007).
Wilson, Rebecca E. and Gillian Somerville-Arjat (eds), *Sleeping with Monsters: Conversations with Scottish and Irish Women Poets* (Edinburgh: Polygon, 1990).
Wisker, Gina, *Angela Carter: A Beginner's Guide* (London: Hodder & Stoughton, 2003).
Yorke, Liz, *Impertinent Voices: Subversive Strategies in Contemporary Women's Poetry* (London: Routledge, 1991).
Young, Emma and James Bailey (eds), *British Women Short Story Writers: The New Women to Now* (Edinburgh University Press, 2015).

Index

Printed and bound by CPI Group (UK) Ltd, Croydon, CR0 4YY